UNLEASHED DESIRE

"You may think me mad, my lord, but at least I'm no fool. It is not I who forgot we are married." Chelsea swiveled on her heel and stalked toward the stairs. "Though it would be easy enough to forget—and I may choose to do just that."

Brandon was across the room in a flash. He caught her midway up the stairs. His hand on her arm swirled her around. "You'll not forget," he growled, then pulled her to him as his mouth crushed against hers in a fierce kiss.

Chelsea struggled in his arms, her hands pressing against his chest, her mouth trying to break free. Brandon paid her struggles no heed. He knew only that he must make her unable to ever forget that she was his wife and he was her husband.

Other Leisure Books by Robin Lee Hatcher:

ROBIN LEE HATCHER

DREAM TIDE

LEISURE BOOKS   NEW YORK CITY

To Ted and Eunice Neu, for welcoming me into your wonderful family. (Thanks for raising Jerry to be the man I fell in love with!)

To Stan and Lucille Blair, for being such special grandparents.

To my "Neu" brothers and sisters-in-law—David & Claudia, Ron & Terri, and Mike & Teresa—I couldn't have hand-picked a better bunch than you.

And finally, to Jerry—husband, hero, lover, best friend—for all the laughter and joy you've brought into my life. You've made my world a beautiful place to be.

I love you all.

A LEISURE BOOK®

January 1990

Published by

Dorchester Publishing Co., Inc.
276 Fifth Avenue
New York, NY 10001

Printed in the United States of America.

DREAMTIDE

by

Robin Lee Hatcher

In dreams I found you.
We strolled in fields of clover;
We laughed amid the wildflowers;
We danced beneath the moonlight;
We loved until the dawn.

Too soon, the dawn.

Now I'm awake and wonder,
Were you real, my love,
Or an illusion of my heart?

PROLOGUE

England, 1828

"He's dead, Larry. You've killed him."

Lawrence Fitzgerald, the young Duke of Foxworth, stepped toward the still, twisted body lying on the ground beside his cousin. He perused the scene through drink-bleary eyes. "But I . . . I didn't even touch him. I swear I didn't. He must . . . he must have fallen on his own."

"There's no time to lose, Larry." His cousin Alastair jumped up and grabbed Lawrence's shoulders, turning him away from Theodore Pickering's body. "You've got to get away from here. The Pickerings will see you hang for certain this time."

"But . . . but it was an accident."

"And who's going to believe that? After the

1

row you two had at the inn last night, no one will. By heavens, Larry, you swore in front of a dozen people that you were going to kill him."

"But I was drunk. We were only joking with each other."

"You drink too much. You're always drunk," Alastair ground out in disgust, then added, "When will you learn that you can't hold your liquor? Damnation, Larry, everyone heard you telling Teddy to keep an eye out because you'd get him when he least expected it." Alastair's tirade ended on an ominous note. "Even *I* wonder if it was an accident."

Lawrence raked his fingers through his thick brown hair, then rubbed his forehead. This was crazy. It didn't make sense. He and Teddy had just been racing their horses. One minute Teddy had been beside him, the next he was on the ground.

"But I swear . . ." He let his words die away.

Alastair was right. No one would believe him. The trouble over his duel with Teddy was just beginning to die down; there'd been the devil to pay over that fiasco. He hadn't meant to actually shoot him. The pistol had misfired. After all, he and Teddy had known each other since they were just boys in the school room. They were always fighting in one form or another, but it was all in fun. He wouldn't ever want to really hurt Teddy.

Gad, if he just hadn't had so much to drink, he knew he could make sense of it all.

"What am I going to do, Alastair?"

His cousin frowned thoughtfully. "There's

an American ship in the Channel. We'll see if they'll take on a passenger. We'll give them another name. You can't travel as the duke. Yes, that's what we'll do. We'll get you to America." He glanced behind him, then urged Lawrence toward his horse. "Mount up, Larry. There's no time to lose."

Lawrence swayed drunkenly and grabbed for the cantle of the saddle to steady himself. "But I can't just disappear. They'll keep on looking for me." He couldn't think straight. His palms were sweating. "And what about Reggie? I'll have to tell Reggie."

Gad, he hadn't meant to hurt Teddy.

"You can't tell anyone, you fool. Especially not that child. Don't worry. I'll handle everything here, and I'll write to you when the matter's cleared up. When things have settled down, you can come home." He glanced back at the body lying in the grass beside the trail. "Now, get on that damn horse while I hide Teddy in the brush. I'll come back for him later."

Lawrence tried to think of a different solution, but his thought processes were dulled. His head ached while his world crumbled. Teddy was dead and it was his fault. Alastair's plan seemed the only answer.

"You're a sport for helping me, Alastair, old man," Lawrence mumbled as he dragged himself up into the saddle. "A real sport."

CHAPTER ONE

America, 1887

Brandon Fitzgerald laid the letter down on the mahogany desk top and rose from his chair. Hands clasped behind his back, he stepped toward the window and let his thoughtful gaze sweep across the green lawn and flowering gardens of Foxworth Place until he located his grandfather.

The old man was seated in his wheelchair, a brown and tan plaid blanket tucked carefully beneath his knees and a brown shawl around his bent shoulders to ward off the early spring chill. His hair was pure white now, and his hands shook with palsy. As Brandon watched, his grandfather was besieged with a fit of coughing. A nurse instantly materialized to fuss and care for him.

Brandon turned his back to the window. He couldn't bear to see his grandfather so frail. His memories of Lawrence Fitzgerald were of a strong, virile, adventuresome man with no regard for his advancing years. This sickly, white-haired old man was a stranger to him, a painful reminder of how little time was left for them to share.

Brandon had been only five years old when his father, Peter Fitzgerald, went off to fight the Rebels while his grandfather continued to run Foxworth Iron Works, building an even greater fortune for the Fitzgerald family. Brandon's father never returned from his sojourn in the South, and so Lawrence had become Brandon's father as well as his grandfather. He loved the old man fiercely.

His dark brown eyes swept back to the white paper lying on his desk. If there was anything that might keep his grandfather alive, this was it. If they waited for solicitors and investigators and courts, Lawrence Fitzgerald would never live to see it happen.

He returned to his desk and sat once again in the leather chair. He picked up the letter and scanned it quickly.

Have been contacted by your solicitor . . . want only what's right . . . family, after all . . . avoid scandal to the honorable name of Fitzgerald . . . protect our daughter . . . marriage by proxy . . .

And then he stared for a long time at the signature.

Hayden Fitzgerald, Duke of Foxworth

It was a lie! The real Duke of Foxworth was sitting right outside Brandon's window. Lawrence Fitzgerald had been cheated out of his title nearly fifty-nine years before by this imposter's father, Alastair Fitzgerald. But now Brandon had the chance to win the title back for him before he died. He didn't care for himself. He had no interest in inheriting the title. He would be just as satisfied to stay in New York and run the iron works, but if he could do this for his grandfather. . . .

He swore as he tossed the letter aside. Hayden was a shrewd one, all right. He knew he would lose once the truth was told, but he also knew Lawrence Fitzgerald was old and ailing. He had that bargaining chip on his side, and he was playing it for all it was worth.

Brandon got up from his chair once again and paced to the window. The nurse was pushing his grandfather's wheelchair toward the house, returning the old man to his room.

If I don't do something soon, he's going to die without seeing Hawklin Hall again.

He wondered then about this daughter who was to be bartered to him in exchange for a quick resolution. She must be fat or ugly or something, or else she would have been married off long ago to some wealthy nobleman. But no one said he had to live with her for long. Lawrence Fitzgerald was seventy-nine years old, after all. Brandon could bear to live with the girl for the short time left to the old man, no matter what she was like. He would do anything to make his grandfather's last days happy ones.

Lawrence's faded brown eyes stared at the fire on the hearth, but his mind was seeing into the past, replaying as it so often did the day he'd learned of Alastair's deception.

Justin had burst into the library in his usual enthusiastic manner. "Grandfather, I'm home and I've brought a surprise with me. A fellow Englishman. He's in school with me, and I've brought him home for the holiday."

Lawrence smiled tolerantly at his youngest grandson, then rose from his chair to stretch out a hand to their guest.

"Grandfather, meet Rodney Pickering. Roddy to all his friends. Roddy, this is my grandfather, Lawrence Fitzgerald."

"Pleasure to meet you, sir," Roddy said as he shook the older man's hand.

"Pickering? I knew some Pickerings when I was a boy in England."

Roddy peered up at him, then said, "I wonder if I don't know some of your family, sir. You remind me a bit of the old Duke of Foxworth. And, you know, sir, your home here even looks a bit like the old hall. Smaller but similar."

Lawrence stiffened.

"Course, I was wondering if there might be some relation, what with you calling this Foxworth Place and your name being Fitzgerald. Justin's talked about you and your home so often, I feel like I've been here before. Are you related to the duke?"

"Yes," he answered abruptly. Lawrence turned his back on the young man, motioning to some chairs. "Sit down, boys."

It couldn't be, of course. Roddy Pickering couldn't be any relation to Teddy. Teddy was an only child when he died and his parents had been aging even then. But the boy apparently knew the Fitzgerald family at Hawklin Hall, or at least knew of them. He wondered if the boy was playing some sort of ruse. Perhaps he was merely using Justin to get to Lawrence's money.

Lawrence settled once again into his comfortable chair. "Tell me about your family, Roddy. I'd like to know if I remember any of them."

"There's a lot of us to remember, Mr. Fitzgerald. My grandfather had thirteen children, every one of them living. I've got seven brothers and sisters myself."

"What was your grandfather's name?"

"Theodore Pickering, sixth Earl of Linden."

Lawrence felt a sharp stab of pain in his forehead. "Theodore?" It couldn't be. It was impossible. "Teddy Pickering?"

"That's him. Everyone calls him Teddy." Roddy grinned. "You do know him, then? What ho! That does make me feel at home."

"Your grandfather's still alive?"

"Pardon me for saying so, sir, but I don't imagine the old war-horse will ever die. He's eighty years old and as hale and hearty as they come. Won't even quit riding his horse. My uncle Charles wonders if he'll ever be earl or if Teddy means to outlive us all."

The pain increased behind his eyes. It had to be a mistake. Teddy couldn't possibly be alive. . . .

Brandon found his younger brother riding in the paddock near the stables. He watched Justin as he schooled the young stallion, waiting until Justin noticed him before he called, "I need to talk to you. Can you spare a minute?"

"Sure, Brand," his brother answered with a wave of his hand. He drew back on the reins, stopping the sleek black. "That's all for today, Sam," he said to the groom who waited by the gate. "Give him a good rubdown for me."

"Yes, sir, Mr. Justin."

The younger Fitzgerald brother hopped down from the saddle with fluid grace and sauntered across the paddock. His brows drew together in a frown as he noted Brandon's somber expression. "What is it, Brand? Nothing wrong with Grandfather, is there?"

"No."

Justin stepped onto the bottom rail, then vaulted over the fence.

"I've heard from England."

"What's Crossing got to say this time?"

"It wasn't from Crossing," Brandon answered, referring to their solicitor. "It was from Hayden Fitzgerald."

Justin raised a black eyebrow.

"He's proposed a way to settle this out of court and as quietly as possible."

"Which is?"

Brandon began walking away from the paddock, and Justin fell into step at his side. He glanced at his younger brother surreptitiously. The boy was still young, just twenty-three this year, but he was intelligent and eager. He reminded Brandon a lot of himself when he was that age. In fact, except for their coloring —Justin with his black hair and eyes, Brandon taking after his father and grandfather with chocolate brown eyes and dark chestnut hair— they were much alike. They were both tall and lean, broad shouldered and strong. They were both fond of good food, fine horses, and pretty women.

"He wants me to marry his daughter."

"He *what*?" Justin exclaimed. "He must be joking."

"No, he's not."

Justin stopped abruptly and grabbed Brandon by the arm, spinning him around. "Good heavens, man! You're actually considering it."

Brandon nodded.

"But they haven't a leg to stand on. We've got enough evidence now to prove Grandfather was tricked into leaving England. We can probably see old Pickering thrown into prison and Hayden Fitzgerald and his family out on their ears. They can't possibly keep the title from Grandfather once the truth is out."

"I know." Brandon began walking again. His gaze wandered over the estate he knew as

11

home, the estate his grandfather had built in memory of Hawklin Hall and his Fitzgerald heritage.

Two hundred acres of woods and parklands, protected by high brick fences and black iron gates, surrounded the Fitzgerald manor on Long Island. The house itself was a three-story brick and glass structure with spacious, high-ceilinged rooms and all the modern conveniences, yet maintaining the old-world elegance. The intricate gardens surrounding the manor were fastidiously groomed, flowers blooming in all but the cruelest winter months.

Brandon spoke again as his gaze returned to his brother. "But that could take months, even years. Grandfather will never live that long. If I marry the girl, we can leave for England right away. We can live at Hawklin while the title business gets straightened out."

"Does Grandfather know about this?"

"Not yet."

"He won't like it, Brand."

"Perhaps not." Brandon shrugged away his grandfather's disapproval. "But he'll agree when he sees how determined I am. You know, Justin, you'll be in charge of the business once we're gone."

A grin broke across Justin's face. "So I shall. That might be an interesting challenge. Can I help you pack, Brand?"

Chuckling, Brandon threw his arm over his brother's shoulders. "Then you don't mind taking it on while we're away? I know we always planned we'd run it together once you were out of school, but . . ."

"Don't worry," Justin assured him, his smile fading into seriousness. "I won't let you down. I'll keep the place going strong until you get back. Just don't forget to come back, Brand."

Lawrence was dozing fitfully. His half-wakeful dreams flitted through time, recalling bits and pieces of his life.

At twenty, the tormented voyage to America. The months that followed, not knowing what had happened in England, his money quickly spent. Alastair's letter, explaining that the only way he could save Lawrence was to let it be known he had drowned and his body was lost at sea. Lawrence Fitzgerald, the eleventh Duke of Foxworth, was dead. Only Lawrence Fitzgerald, the man, remained.

At twenty-two, working in the iron works, half-starved but determined. His loveless marriage to Elizabeth Brackett—sour, colorless Elizabeth, the boss's daughter.

At twenty-four, the birth of his only child, Peter. Peter, the son he barely knew, for they had so little time together. The long hours at the factory, building the renamed iron works —Foxworth Iron Works—into a major concern. Determined to never be poor again.

At thirty-three, the death of Elizabeth and the building of Foxworth Place on Long Island. The emptiness of his life. The wondering what might have been if Teddy Pickering had never fallen from his horse. The futile search for happiness through the making of more money.

At forty-six, Peter's wedding to the beautiful and warm-hearted Diana. Diana, who brought life into Foxworth Place and thawed an old man's heart. Diana, who began to teach him to live in the present and not to resent the past.

At fifty-one, the birth of his first grandchild, Brandon, and the beginning of real happiness.

At fifty-seven, the birth of his second grandchild, Justin, and the death of Diana from childbirth fever. And the same year, Peter's death at the siege of Atlanta.

The good years that followed, raising his grandsons, teaching them to ride and shoot, training them to be gentlemen—*English* gentlemen. And finally, when they were old enough, sharing with them how he had come to lose his title and warning them against the dangers of drunkenness.

But there was no bitterness in the telling. The bitterness was gone at last.

Gone . . . until Roddy Pickering shattered the peace he had found.

"I can't let you do this."

Brandon sat on a chair facing his grandfather. His elbows rested on his knees and his clasped hands nearly touched the floor as he leaned forward for emphasis. "It isn't a question of letting me do it. I'm *going* to do it."

Lawrence shook his head slowly from side to side. He raised a palsied hand toward Brandon, pointing his finger. "You don't know the girl.

You don't love her. Don't marry for any reason but love, boy. You'll regret it every day of your life if you do."

"Listen, Grandfather. I'm twenty-eight years old. I know what I'm doing."

"Then wait until you get to England. Meet her first."

Brandon stubbornly shook his head. "Hayden knows what he's doing too, Grandfather. Marriage by proxy is the agreement. So there's no backing out once I get over there and see the girl." He leaned over even farther and placed a hand on Lawrence's knee. "Listen, we'll take care of the legal arrangements and perform the ceremony. Then, as soon as we can get things in order here, you and I will sail for England. I'm taking you home, Grandfather. Back to Gloucester and Hawklin Hall. The real hall. Not just our American miniature. You'll be home, Grandfather."

Brandon knew he'd won his argument when he heard Lawrence's whispered, "Home."

"Her grace is waiting for you in the drawing room," Bowman said as he took the duke's hat and riding crop.

Hayden Fitzgerald nodded mutely at the butler, then walked across the great hall, the heels of his riding boots clicking sharply against the marble floor. "Glorious day for a ride, Sara," he announced as he entered the room.

Sara Fitzgerald was quickly on her feet. A handsome woman at forty-one, she had admirably maintained her figure. She was still desirable, and not just to her husband. They were two of a kind, he and his wife. Lovers of pleasure, anywhere and everywhere they could find it. That's probably why they'd got on so well all these years.

"Hayden, where have you been?" she asked in a sharp tone.

His eyebrow arched in surprise. "Why, riding, of course. Just where I told you I'd be. Is something wrong?"

"Is something wrong? *Everything* is wrong!" She waved a hand in the air. "What if this . . . this *cousin* of yours won't marry Alanna? What if they've already learned the truth about her? What then? You're about to lose your title. We're nearly penniless. Our daughter is insane. And you're out riding your infernal horse as if the sun will never set on the Empire."

"Sara, Sara," Hayden crooned as he approached her to lay a comforting arm around her. "You mustn't fret so. It makes you frown and gives you tiny lines about your eyes." He kissed her forehead.

She jerked away from him. "Really, Hayden. You can be such a boor."

He laughed as he moved to pour himself a glass of brandy from a crystal container on a nearby table. "If you're worried about Brandon Fitzgerald accepting our proposal, don't. He'll accept. From what I've learned, old cousin Lawrence hasn't much longer to live. If he wants to see Hawklin again and reclaim his title in time, the young man will have to accept. Parting with a little of his money and giving his name to our daughter isn't too much to ask in return for a quick solution to the family dilemma, is it?"

"And what about when he sees Alanna? What then?" Sara demanded.

Hayden turned and leaned against the table as he sipped his drink. "What's this, Sara? Maternal concern? Forget it. They'll already be married. What can he do except what we've done? Just keep her shut away with that nanny of hers. She'll never know the difference."

"You make us sound so cold, Hayden."

"We are cold, Sara, my dear. Bloody cold. Haven't you noticed that about us before?"

CHAPTER TWO

She was surrounded by flames. Everywhere, the hot fingers of death reached out to consume her. Strong arms reached for her, held her. Someone was dying. She screamed.

"There, my Alanna, my luv. There. Molly's here. Your Molly's here."

She was spiraling, spiraling.

"Come now. Wake up, luv, wake up."

A hand touched her cheek, drawing her back from a frightening black abyss. Slowly, she opened her eyes.

"There now. That's right. It's time for your medicine, luv."

The room was dimly lit and seemed to be turning slowly. The room appeared empty. A sense of panic gripped her. She reached out, groping, trying to find the woman who kept speaking to her.

"Be still, Alanna. You've been terrible sick."

Quickly, she turned her head on the pillow and was overcome by the urge to retch. She rolled onto her stomach, her head hanging over the side of the bed, and violently emptied herself into a waiting pot.

Soothing hands caressed the back of her neck. "Poor girl," a voice crooned. "My poor girl. My poor Alanna."

She tried to think clearly. Who was the woman speaking to her? Where was she? But nothing made sense. Everything was dim, fuzzy, unreachable.

"Lady Alanna?"

A damp cloth touched her lips. She took hold of it with weak fingers and washed away the traces of her sickness, then rolled slowly onto her back once more. This time, her eyes found the woman.

She was dressed in a black and gray striped gown with a bibbed white apron. Her curly red hair, generously sprinkled with gray, was mostly hidden beneath a white cap. Dark green eyes peered from a wrinkled but kindly face. "There. Is that better, m'lady?"

She opened her mouth to speak, then realized her throat was raw and painfully sore. She closed her mouth without a sound.

"That's right, luv. You mustn't speak. The doctor says you must save your voice. You've been terrible ill, Lady Alanna."

Who was Lady Alanna? Was it she? And who

was this woman? Molly. Isn't that what she'd heard her say? *Molly's here*. Was Molly her nurse? Her head hurt. She felt so dizzy. Would she be sick again?

"Come now. Take your medicine, m'lady. The duchess'll be terrible displeased if she comes an' you've not taken it." Molly held out a spoon toward her patient.

The fire. It wasn't a dream then. There had been a fire. That's why she was sick. That's why her throat hurt.

"The fire . . ." she whispered hoarsely. "There was . . . someone . . . in the . . . fire."

Molly pulled the untouched spoon away. She shook her head. "What fire, m'lady?"

She touched her throat. "The fire . . ."

Molly's weathered hand touched her cheek once again. Her voice was gentle with concern. "You were just dreamin' the fire. Please, luv. You must forget it. You must get well."

Just dreaming? But . . . ? She closed her eyes against the swirling confusion.

"Please now, Lady Alanna. Take your medicine."

She forced her eyelids open. Molly was once again holding the spoon close to her lips. Obediently, she opened her mouth and swallowed the bitter liquid.

"There now. It's done," Molly said softly.

She lifted her gaze to the woman's face. "Am I . . . Alanna?" she asked.

Molly's eyes brimmed with tears, then spilled over. A tiny sob escaped her as she lifted the corner of her apron to dry her cheeks. "Yes, m'lady. You're my Alanna. You'll always be my Alanna."

"I don't . . ." Her eyes drifted shut. She felt as if she were floating away. ". . . don't feel . . . like . . . Alanna."

The drive leading to Hawklin Hall wound its way for nearly a mile through a forest of tall trees. Sunlight and shadow flashed rapidly as they passed beneath the verdant canopy, nearly blinding Brandon. He turned his head from the carriage window and looked at his grandfather. He could feel the old man's tension and anxiety as he awaited the first sight of his ancestral home in nearly six decades.

The long ocean voyage had been a difficult one for the elderly Fitzgerald. Brandon had often wondered if his grandfather would even live to reach England, let alone recapture his title. But, even with his nervousness making deep creases in his forehead, Lawrence looked more alive at this moment than he had for over a year. The palsied quiver of his hands had all but disappeared. His shoulders were no longer noticeably stooped. There was a renewed gleam in his light brown eyes. It seemed their arrival in England had given Lawrence Fitzgerald back years he had long since lost.

"Look, Brandon. You'll see it any moment now."

Obediently, he turned his gaze out the carriage window once again. The forest ended with startling abruptness, throwing them suddenly into the full light of a glorious August day, the blue sky miraculously free of clouds. In that same instant, Brandon's eyes fell upon Hawklin Hall.

Three-storied and many-gabled, the gray stone manse stood with quiet authority amidst a blanket of green lawn. With well over one hundred rooms, Hawklin Hall was more than five times the size of the Fitzgerald home in America, yet the similarities were so strong, so evident, that Brandon could almost believe he had never left Long Island.

"It's remarkable, Grandfather. It looks just like Foxworth Place. Even the gardens."

Lawrence's brown eyes sparkled. "Yes. Yes, it does," he answered, a note of wonder in his voice. "Sometimes I wasn't sure. It's been so long, and I thought perhaps I'd forgotten. But I didn't, did I?" The wonder had changed to pride.

Brandon smiled as he settled back against the seat to wait out their final approach to Hawklin Hall. No matter what transpired in the next hour or even weeks, the look on his grandfather's face had already made it worthwhile. Even the matter of his "wife" couldn't dim his pleasure over Lawrence's happiness. Actually, Brandon had thrust any thought of the Lady Alanna from his mind the moment the proxy ceremony had concluded back in New York. But the time was quickly approaching when he would be forced to think of her.

The carriage drew to a halt before the elaborately columned front entrance.

"I won't be needing my wheelchair," Lawrence said firmly. "I mean to face them on my own two feet."

Immediately there were two footmen beside the carriage to open the door and help Lawrence to the ground. Brandon followed, his eyes sweeping once again over the magnificent building. He couldn't help but wonder what one family could possibly want or do with so many rooms.

A stern-faced gentleman, his lofty demeanor proclaiming him the head butler, awaited them at the door. "The duke and duchess are in the great drawing room, Lord Lawrence." He nodded his head. "Please follow me."

"What's your name, fellow?" Lawrence asked sharply, stopping the butler in his tracks.

"Bowman, my lord."

"Well, Bowman, you needn't show me the way. This is my home. I know where the great drawing room is."

"As you wish, my lord." Bowman nodded once again, his face expressionless.

Lawrence flashed a smile toward his grandson. "This way, Brandon."

There was almost a spring in the old man's step as Brandon followed him across the marble floor of the entry hall, around the sweeping, curved staircase and through an enclosed courtyard.

Lawrence stopped before the doors of the great drawing room and looked over his shoulder at his grandson. "Are you ready, my boy?"

"I'm ready, your grace," he answered with a grin.

"There!" Molly exclaimed, stepping back from her handiwork. "I've not seen you look so pretty in weeks, m'lady."

"I . . . I think I feel stronger today. Not nearly so dizzy. Thank you for washing my hair."

Molly plumped the pillows behind the girl's back. "Do you remember about today, Lady Alanna? I told you we had a special surprise for you."

"Molly, won't you please call me Chelsea? It's such a pretty name. I . . . I would like to be Chelsea."

"Oh, m'lady," the red-haired woman said with a sigh, "you know how displeased it makes the duke when you pretend to be someone else. And today of all days, m'lady."

As usual, her thoughts were in confusion. It seemed as if she had been floating in and out of consciousness for weeks. When she was awake, she would try to separate reality from dreams, but it was all so difficult. She couldn't seem to remember anything beyond the walls of her room. Even her parents, the Duke and Duchess of Foxworth, seemed to be strangers to her.

"But, Molly, I've told you I don't *feel* like Lady Alanna. I feel like Chelsea," she persisted. "When you call me Alanna, I . . . I think you're speaking to someone else."

Molly sighed again as she sat on the edge of the bed and took the girl's hand in her own. "M'lady, I've been carin' for the Lady Alanna

24

since she was just a babe. I've loved her like she was my own." Tears appeared in her eyes. She dashed them away as she cleared her throat. "Now, that girl is you, whether you feel like her or not, and you mustn't make the duke an' duchess unhappy with this pretendin' of yours. They'll have the doctor in again an' you'll be forced to take more of that medicine. You know how sick it makes you when you have to take so much, m'lady. You've felt ever so much better since you're only takin' it twice a day."

"All right, Molly." She squeezed her nanny's hand. "I won't say anything. I promise." She smiled then. "But is it all right if I still *think* of myself as Chelsea? It's such a pretty name, and it makes me feel so much better."

Tears welled up once again in Molly's green eyes as she bent forward to kiss the girl's forehead. "Yes, luv. If it makes you feel better, it's all right with Molly. You can call yourself anything you like. You can think you're Queen Victoria her royal self if it makes you feel better. I just want you to get well, luv."

Lawrence pushed the drawing room door open and walked boldly inside. Brandon stepped up beside his grandfather as the older man paused in the middle of the room.

Hayden and Sara Fitzgerald were seated in matching chairs at the far end. They looked up in unison, then rose together. The room remained silent as the four occupants studied each other.

Brandon's gaze went first to Hayden. He had

the Fitzgerald height and the long, straight nose, but his chin was weak and his sandy brown hair was receding at his forehead. His paunchy figure was clad in a frock-coat of excellent broadcloth with a silk facing on the lapel. His waistcoat was cut low to show a silk cravat with a high, starched collar above it. A heavy gold watch chain disappeared into a waistcoat pocket.

Sara was likewise elegantly clad in a Parisian walking dress of red *toile de Jouy*. The gown accentuated her generous curves and threw color into her ivory cheeks. Her golden hair was swept high in a cluster of curls and held there with ruby and pearl combs. She was undoubtedly a handsome woman whose beauty was undimmed by the passing years.

Brandon was certain it was Foxworth Iron Works which would be paying for the clothing they already wore. He knew, despite the grandeur of Hawklin Hall and the elegance of Hayden's and his wife's attire, that the coffers of the Duke of Foxworth were close to empty. It was no wonder they were so ready to welcome into the family their wealthy exiled cousin and his grandson from America.

Hayden was the first to break the pregnant silence. "Cousin Lawrence. I would know you anywhere." He came forward, his hand outstretched in welcome. "We're glad you've made it to England safely. We've been awaiting your arrival with great anticipation."

"No doubt," Lawrence answered dryly as he shook his cousin's hand.

"And you must be Brandon. By gad, you're the image of the ninth Duke. Wait until you see old Jonathan Fitzgerald's portrait in the gallery. It could be *your* portrait. Look at him, Sara. There's no mistaking you for other than a Fitzgerald, young man. Welcome to Hawklin Hall."

"Thank you, sir." He refused to call Hayden "your grace." He would save that style of address for his grandfather. "I trust you received my letter and everything is in order here."

Hayden appeared a little taken aback by Brandon's forthrightness. He cleared his throat. "Yes. Yes, everything is in order. We are to meet with the solicitors in London as quickly as is convenient. As we agreed, there will be no blame publicly ascribed to my father and we'll keep old Pickering's name out of it altogether. The newspapers will only be told that Lawrence, the Duke of Foxworth, who was believed lost at sea, has returned to England and that the title, wrongfully passed to his cousin upon the untimely announcement of his death, has been restored to its rightful owner."

Hayden ran his hand nervously over his receding hair and cleared his throat again. His gaze never quite met Lawrence's or Brandon's eyes. "Sara and I, of course, will move into our London house as we agreed. Most of our things have already been removed there, along with our personal staff. We shall be comfortable, I think."

They'll be more than comfortable with the sum

27

we settled on them, Brandon thought, a frown creasing his forehead. Hayden must think him either an idiot or a soft touch.

"I'm certain you will be *very* comfortable, cousin," Brandon said, his tone clearly disdainful.

"Yes . . . well . . ." Hayden stammered. "As I said before, all is in order here."

"And the matter of my bride?"

"Your wedding was duly recorded, Brandon." Sara walked gracefully across the room toward the three men.

Brandon allowed his gaze to move around the great drawing room before returning once again to the former duchess. "Then why isn't she waiting here with you?"

Sara and Hayden exchanged worried glances before Hayden answered Brandon's question. "Our daughter is unable to join us here. She has been ill for some time."

So that was it. His bride was sickly. He wasn't surprised. He'd known there had to be something wrong with the girl or, as he'd reasoned more than once, they would have found her a wealthy husband long before this. After all, she was already twenty-one.

"May I see her?"

Again they exchanged glances. Again it was Hayden who replied, "Shall we sit down first? We would like to tell you about Alanna before we take you to her."

There was a light scratching at her bedroom door. Molly rose from a nearby stool and went to answer it. She drew a key from the pocket of her apron and unlocked it, then opened the door a crack.

"They're here," a feminine voice whispered. "They're with the duke an' duchess right now."

"Thank you, Elsbeth," Molly replied softly. She closed the door again but didn't relock it as she usually did. She turned around, leaning her back against the door. "He's here, m'lady."

Chelsea wondered if she were expected to know to whom Molly was referring. Molly had told her something this morning, right after she'd washed her hair. If only her mind weren't so foggy, she could remember. She always felt this way after awakening from one of her afternoon naps. After lunch, Molly would fill a spoon with the bitter medicine and Chelsea would obediently, if reluctantly, swallow it. Then Molly would sit by Chelsea's bedside and chatter endlessly until Chelsea drifted into a confused sleep, her dreams strange and disjointed. When she awakened, she always felt lost and afraid.

"*Who* is here, Molly?" she asked, forcing herself to fasten onto one single thought.

"Lord Brandon, m'lady. Your husband. That's our special surprise. He's come at last."

"My husband?" She was alarmed. "I have a *husband*?"

"Oh, yes, Lady Alanna. He's a fine man who's been livin' in America. But he's truly an English nobleman. He's in line to inherit the dukedom. You'll be a duchess one day, luv. Imagine that. A duchess at Hawklin Hall."

29

Chelsea felt a wave of panic sweep over her. "But . . . but Molly, I don't remember him!" It was terrible not remembering. There had been many times when she wanted to scream her frustration, to cry with fear over a past she couldn't recall or make sense of. But this was the worst it had ever been. To have a husband and not remember him. To have a husband and not be able to envision his face or recall his name.

Molly was instantly at her bedside. "It's all right, m'lady," she clucked soothingly. "Of course you can't remember him. You've never met him."

"Not met . . ." She pressed her fingers to her temples and closed her eyes. A husband she'd never met? Why, oh why, did nothing make sense? "How can he be my husband if we've never met?"

"The duke arranged the marriage, luv. You were married by proxy more than two months ago."

"I don't remember," she moaned softly. And finally, she spoke aloud what she'd been suspecting for weeks. "Molly? My illness? It's . . . it's in my mind, isn't it?"

Molly paled but was silent.

"It isn't only that I'm weak and sick. It's . . . it's that my mind isn't right. That's why I can't remember the things you talk about. That's why I feel like someone else. That's why I don't even seem to know my own parents."

"The duke and duchess have never spent much time in your apartments, m'lady," Molly replied, the tone of her voice clearly revealing her opinion of the neglectful parents. "My girl's had little enough chance to know them."

"They're ashamed of me because I've always been ill. I *have* always been ill, haven't I, Molly? All of my life."

The nanny sat beside her as she did so often, taking hold of Chelsea's hand. "But you *can* get well. I know it's true, luv. You can get well if you try."

"Can I?" Chelsea wondered aloud.

"Yes, luv. Yes, you can," Molly replied, then cheerfully added, "Now, let me brush your hair. And wouldn't you like to put on one of these pretty new gowns the duchess sent up? It isn't every day a young bride greets her husband for the first time."

Sara Fitzgerald lifted her chin to a regal pose. "The truth is, Brandon, our daughter has suffered a . . . a malady of the mind since she was a young girl. She has never had a season nor been introduced to society. She has lived here at Hawklin Hall, with her nanny seeing to her care, all these years. Often, sometimes for months at a time, she seems to be normal and we have dared to think . . . But then . . ." Sara stopped speaking and stared at her clenched hands in her lap.

"What kind of *malady* of the mind?" Brandon asked, a deep frown furrowing his brow.

Hayden patted his wife's hands, then looked toward his new son-in-law. "Usually it's simple things like nightmares. She lives in a constant state of confusion. Sometimes she thinks she is someone else. Or perhaps she merely pretends to be someone else; we've never been certain. But . . ." He glanced at Sara again, his voice dropping to a lower key. "But things are much worse now. A few weeks ago—long after the marriage was arranged, mind you—Alanna set fire to the old nursery. The entire northeast wing, perhaps the whole house, might have been destroyed. We were lucky, however. Only the nursery rooms were ruined. Unfortunately, one of our servants was killed trying to rescue Alanna."

"Our daughter was struck by a falling beam," Sara interjected. "It nearly killed her. She has no memory of the fire or the accident or of the girl who died. In fact, she has no memory at all. She has been bedridden since the accident." Sara drew a dainty handkerchief from the bodice of her gown and dabbed at her eyes.

Hayden silently watched his wife for a moment before continuing. "Alanna has what the doctors call amnesia. Her physician says there is no way to treat the disease. It is most likely due to the blow on her head . . . but it could also be just another symptom of her . . . of her insanity. If she were . . . normal, she would most likely awaken one day and remember everything. But, of course, she is not normal. She probably will never remember again. We . . . we keep her locked in her rooms now, and she is never left alone. Not even for a moment. It's safer for everyone that way. If we'd had any idea Alanna was dangerous, that poor servant girl might still be alive. That is a tragedy we will have to live with forever.''

Brandon felt his grandfather's eyes upon him and knew what he was thinking. Lawrence had warned Brandon not to marry the girl until he'd seen her himself, but this was worse than he'd expected. Still, he had sworn anything would be worth it to give his grandfather back his rightful title. He would allow himself no regrets.

''Brandon, my boy,'' Hayden continued, ''let's be frank with one another. Perhaps this arrangement isn't fair to you, but you must remember, we were about to lose everything. We had to protect our daughter. We love her, and she is quite helpless. We couldn't bear to think of her being locked away in some . . . in some asylum.''

Brandon had a hard time believing his cousin's portrayal of himself and his wife as the doting parents. Still, he couldn't deny the logic of his explanation. Brandon rose from his chair, stating in a solemn voice, ''I understand, Lord Hayden. Now, I would like to meet my wife.''

CHAPTER
THREE

The door opened and Hayden stepped inside.
Chelsea felt his careful perusal of her appearance before his eyes slipped to Molly. "Brandon Fitzgerald is waiting outside."

Molly nodded. "We're ready, your lordship,"
she said, then moved away from the bed, retiring to a dim corner of the room.

Her father's gaze returned to Chelsea. "Molly
has told you who is waiting to see you?"

Chelsea nodded.

"Then I'll bring him in."

She felt her stomach tighten with fear. She
thought she might be sick. She prayed she
wouldn't. What would he be like? What would
he expect from her, his insane wife? Would he

beat her, misuse her? Why had he married her, being as she was?

Hayden opened the door again. There was a moment's hesitation before a tall, dark figure filled the doorway. Her gaze dropped to his shiny black boots, the only safe place to look at the moment.

"Alanna, my dear," her father said, "may I present Brandon Fitzgerald, your husband. Brandon, the Lady Alanna, your wife."

Slowly, her eyes traveled up the long legs of his black trousers, moving from his well-muscled thighs to his slim hips, past the gray waistcoat and black frock-coat worn over his broad chest and shoulders, and finally reaching his face.

She hadn't known what to expect, but surely it hadn't been this handsome gentleman who stood before her, his chocolate brown eyes studying her with frightening intensity. His face was patrician, filled with sharp angles, boldly appealing. His skin had been bronzed by the sun. His chin was strong and smooth shaven. His mouth, though at the moment grim, seemed destined to smile often.

She tried to think of something to say to break the interminable silence. Her hand moved to the hollow of her throat and lingered there in a purely feminine gesture.

Brandon felt equally speechless. As Hayden led him from the great drawing room up a flight of stairs and down a long hallway to a far wing of the manse, he'd formed a picture in his mind of a wild-haired, wild-eyed harridan. Instead, his eyes had fallen upon a creature of incredibly delicate beauty.

Her hair was the color of wheat in the moonlight, almost yellow, almost silver. It fell in abundant waves over the pillow at her back and the pink shoulders of her morning gown, surrounding her like a cloud. Her ivory skin had a musk-rose flush over her cheekbones. Her face was oval, her nose exquisitely dainty, her eyes round with wonder and perhaps a little fear. Her eyes were blue, the color of a summer sky. Her beauty was marred only by the gray shadows that filled the hollows beneath those blue eyes. Yet, instead of lessening her beauty, the shadows seemed to add a gentle, helpless quality that tugged at his heart.

He saw her swallow, watched her mouth open as if to speak, saw the hand flutter to her throat and linger there, witnessed the fear and uncertainty.

"Leave us," he said, his voice firm and commanding.

There was a pause before Hayden, standing behind him, replied, "As you wish, my boy."

Brandon's glance darted to the corner of the room, settling on the white-capped servant woman. This must be the nanny who had cared for Alanna all these years. "I would like to be alone with her."

The woman rose stiffly. Her gaze fastened on her charge, and he thought for a moment she would refuse to leave the room. He saw the battle of emotions in her face and knew without a doubt that here was someone who wanted to protect Alanna, even from her own husband.

"Please. I wish to speak to Lady Alanna alone." His voice was gentler when he spoke this time.

The nanny looked at him again, nodded, and slipped silently out of the room, closing the door behind her.

Brandon's gaze returned to his bride. He was surprised by the tenderness he felt toward the girl, this stranger, his wife. He suddenly wanted everything to go well between them. He took two steps toward the bed.

"May I sit down?" he asked.

"Please do, my lord," she whispered.

He couldn't stop looking at her, couldn't stop the feeling that he would like to hold her in his arms and protect her. She looked so frail.

"Since we are man and wife, I wish you would call me Brandon. This nobility business is new to me." He offered her a smile.

She hesitated only a second before returning his smile tenfold. It was like the sun breaking out suddenly from behind a cloud after a dreary black rainstorm. If he had thought her delicately beautiful before, she was devastatingly so now.

"And may I call you Alanna?"

Her smile vanished. A thoughtful frown creased two tiny lines between her dusky-gold eyebrows. Her gaze dropped from his to stare at her fingers as she traced the lace down the front of her gown. A fan of golden-brown lashes, long and softly curled, hid her eyes from his view.

"Have I said something amiss, Lady Alanna?"

"I . . ." She still didn't look at him. "The duchess would be terribly angry."

His voice hardened a little. "Angry if I call my own wife by her name?"

Her eyes flew to his. "No, my lord. She just wouldn't . . ." He could see she was struggling for words. "You see, I don't want to be Alanna."

Brandon wrestled with his own confusion. He hadn't given much consideration to the girl's feelings in the matter of their marriage. Before he'd met her, he'd assumed she was as eager as her parents to be married off to a wealthy man who would soon enough make her a duchess. When he was told she was insane, he'd thought she would be unaware of the arrangement and so it would matter little to her one way or the other. Instead, he was faced with a fragile, frightened young woman who very much understood that she was legally his wife, and it was equally apparent that she wanted no part of him. But now that he'd seen her, he didn't want to think she might abhor being his wife enough to wish she were someone else.

Softly, he put his thoughts into words. "Is it because of me you don't want to be Alanna?"

"Oh, no, my lord," she answered, shaking her head. "You seem . . . you seem quite nice, after all."

"Then what is it? Who is it you want to be?"

38

Her blue eyes suddenly swam with tears. "I . . . I want to be Chelsea," she whispered over a restrained sob.

She was like a wounded bird, helpless and frightened. He again felt the urge to enfold her in his arms, but believing it would only frighten her further, he resisted it.

"Chelsea? Who is Chelsea?"

She was still trying to blink back the tears as she met his gaze. "She's me, I think. The real me."

"The *real* you? I don't understand."

"The *real* me. You see, Alanna . . . Alanna is a lady. She's supposed to be bright and pretty and witty. But I . . . I don't . . . I'm afraid . . ." She swallowed hard. "I should just rather be Chelsea, my lord."

"Then you shall be Chelsea. Chelsea Fitzgerald."

A tremulous smile curved her lovely mouth. "Thank you . . . Brandon."

It was some time later before Molly returned to Chelsea's room. As soon as she poked her red hair in the door, Chelsea was smiling.

"He wasn't awful, Molly. He was very kind and understanding. It isn't going to be so terrible being married to a stranger."

"I'm glad, m'lady." Relief flooded the nanny's face as she carried a supper tray into the room and set it on the table beside the bed. "I've been terrible worried about you, luv. I wouldn't want anythin' to happen that would hurt you an' make you unhappy."

"Do you suppose he'll visit me often? Do you suppose he'll stay longer next time?" Her eyes sparkled with fresh enthusiasm, and her cheeks were flushed with color.

Molly looked down at her with a fond gaze. "I hope so, m'lady, since it seems to make you happy."

"And I feel stronger, too, Molly. I truly do. Maybe you're right. Maybe I can get well, if I really and truly want to."

Molly patted Chelsea's cheek and nodded.

"And tomorrow, I want to get out of bed, just for a little while. I could sit in that chair by the window and see the sunshine, couldn't I?"

"Of course you could, m'lady." Molly sat down and held out a bowl of thick, hot stew. "Now, I want you to eat this. Every bite. And then we'll get you ready for bed so you'll be all rested in the mornin', just in case his lordship comes to see you."

"Well, Brandon?"

"She's not at all what I expected, Grandfather."

The two men were alone in Lawrence's apartments on the first floor of Hawklin Hall. Lawrence hadn't had an opportunity to be alone with his grandson since the young man went upstairs to meet his bride. Upon Brandon's return to the drawing room, the butler had announced supper was ready to be served, and the four cousins had retired to the dining room for a long meal. Lawrence had found

Hayden's ceaseless stories about the gentlemen at his club unspeakably boring. After years of hard work to survive and then to build a business, he'd realized how different he was from the young man who fled England nearly sixty years before. Then he had been a man much like those Hayden talked about, men who spent their time in idleness, in sport, and simply in the pursuit of pleasure.

Well, no more. He would spend his remaining years—or months, or whatever time was left to him—acquainting his grandson with the Fitzgerald estates and all that went into properly managing them. He would rebuild them to their former greatness. He would restore honor to the family name. He would . . .

Lawrence brought his wandering thoughts back to the moment at hand. "What is she like, Brandon?"

"She's ill and frail, but she's lovely. She . . . she seems different, but she doesn't seem . . ," He searched for the right word.

"Crazy?" Lawrence suggested.

"No, she doesn't seem crazy. A little confused, perhaps."

"I see." But he didn't. He would have to meet her himself. It still seemed to him a crime that Brandon had married the girl and promised to support Hayden and Sara in a generous manner in exchange for a quick solution to the matter of his title. He should have refused to allow the marriage ever to take place. He should have waited the matter out in the courts. He knew firsthand what a marriage without love could do to a man. It was far too costly.

Lawrence sighed inwardly. Perhaps, he admitted to himself, his own loveless marriage hadn't been all bad. If it weren't for Elizabeth, Peter would never have been born, and if not for Peter, he wouldn't be here this moment with Brandon. His grandson was everything Lawrence could have wanted him to be— handsome, bright, good-hearted, honest, brave. He had been a great favorite with the ladies back in New York, but there had never been any one special girl in his life, no one he ever loved. If he had fallen in love, perhaps he wouldn't now be married to some half-wit girl who had to be locked up in her apartments with only her old nanny for company. If he had fallen in love, he wouldn't now be facing an empty marriage such as his grandfather had known.

Suddenly, he thought of Reggie. Dear Reggie. Could she still be alive? It was the first time in perhaps thirty years or more that he had thought of her, yet for so many years in America, he had dreamed of finding her again one day. Oh, how he had loved his little Reggie. She'd been only fourteen when he fled England. Still just a child, so he'd never had a chance to tell her he loved her, never had a chance to see her grow into a young woman, never had a chance to make her his bride.

Well, there was no point in belaboring the past. Besides, he was weary, and he still had a difficult week ahead of him.

"Hayden said he and Sara are leaving for London tomorrow. I think I shall go with them. I see no point in delaying these proceedings with the solicitors and the magistrates and whoever else is involved."

"Sounds sensible," Brandon replied as he rose from his chair and stretched his arms high above his head. Yawning, he added, "Although I can't say I'm eager for another long carriage ride quite so soon."

"You needn't go, Brandon, if you'd rather remain at Hawklin."

"Not go?" His grandson looked at him as if he'd lost all touch with reality. "And leave you alone with those two barracudas? Not a chance, Grandfather."

Lawrence chuckled. "All right then. Let's go to bed."

Hayden found Molly in her own stark room next to Chelsea's. As she rose from her chair near the fire, the nanny had difficulty disguising her dislike for her former employer.

"How is she?" he asked without preamble.

"She's better now that you've not got her so drugged, m'lord. The medicine makes her quite ill."

"Has she remembered anything about the fire?"

"Only the nightmares."

Hayden nodded. "My wife and I leave tomorrow for London. See that you look after the girl.

43

If I hear . . ." His mouth hardened. "See that nothing goes amiss, my good woman, or you'll regret it."

He caught the fear in her eyes and was satisfied Molly would keep a close watch on the girl. His future seemed secure.

"Good night, Molly," he said as he let himself out of her room.

Brandon Fitzgerald was not unfamiliar with the habits and customs of the privileged class. Although he took great enjoyment in the management of Foxworth Iron Works, his grandfather's financial success had earned him the right to move in the higher echelon of New York society. He had attended Harvard and courted many a debutante at her coming out. Already he'd found English society to be not so terribly different, except that there was great emphasis placed on official titles and rank rather than mere social position and wealth.

In his first week in London, he found himself a curiosity when the story of Lawrence Fitzgerald first broke. Then he discovered that he was highly sought after because he was next in line to inherit the title of Duke of Foxworth. Although the financial aspects of the title had been severely diminished in years past, it was also known that Lawrence, Duke of Foxworth, and his grandson, Brandon Fitzgerald, the new Viscount Coleford, were extremely wealthy men in their own right.

They were awaiting supper at his grandfather's old club on their last night in London when they were approached by a black-haired fellow, about thirty years of age, with swarthy good looks and a friendly grin. He introduced himself as Wellington Randolph-Smythe, Earl of Roxley, and the closest neighbor to Hawklin Hall.

"Won't you join us, Lord Roxley?" Lawrence invited. "We're about to have our supper."

"Thank you, your grace. I believe I will." He pulled out a chair and sat down. "Do call me Roxley. All my friends do." With a grin, he turned his dark eyes on Brandon. "You two have certainly given all of London plenty to gossip and speculate about this past week. And you had best beware, my friend. The ladies are quick to spot a handsome bachelor."

"I'm afraid my grandson is not a bachelor."

"Really?" Roxley cocked a black eyebrow. "Why, I'd heard . . ."

"My wife is Hayden Fitzgerald's daughter."

"Good lord! Alanna Fitzgerald? But she's . . ." Roxley had the good sense to clamp his mouth closed in time.

Brandon exposed him to a harsh glare, daring him to speak unkindly of his bride.

Roxley lowered his voice and leaned close to the table. "How is she?"

"She's been ill," Brandon replied in a reserved tone, obviously reluctant to answer any questions.

"Don't misunderstand me. You see, I saw her once or twice when she was a little girl. When I was at Rosemont during holiday from school, I saw her out with her nanny, riding in her pony cart. Pretty little thing with gold curls and a strange smile. She never said much, but I remember thinking her a sweet child. Then, the next time I was home, I heard my parents say she . . ." He stopped and looked around to make sure no one was eavesdropping. "They said she'd lost her mind and been locked up. No one has seen her since. The duke and duch . . . I mean, Lord and Lady Fitzgerald, never spoke of her. I thought perhaps she'd died. Most people have probably forgotten Hayden ever had a daughter."

"Perhaps it's better that way," Lawrence said. "It might be kinder for the girl."

"Well, since you have thought well enough of her to marry her, my parents must have been mistaken. I hope to get to see her again, once she's feeling better. I'd like us to be friends, Lord Fitzgerald. And I'll help in any way I can."

Brandon sensed the earnestness of Wellington Randolph-Smythe. He believed Roxley would, indeed, be a good friend. He smiled for the first time since the man sat down. "I'd like that, too, Roxley." He held out his hand across the table. "My friends call me Brand."

Lawrence leaned back in his chair, watching the two young men shake hands. He was glad Brandon seemed to have found a friend. Lawrence had had a few doubts about how Brandon would view the British aristocracy. His grandson had more than a dash of stubborn American independence about him.

"Good lord!" Roxley exclaimed in a hushed

voice. "I haven't seen old Pickering in this club in years. I wonder what's brought him to London."

Lawrence turned quickly in his chair, his eyes falling upon a stout gentleman with a shiny bald head and drooping white mustache. Teddy Pickering. He never would have known him if it weren't for Roxley. But then, why should he? It had been nearly sixty years since he'd seen Pickering. His old friend was past eighty years old now; a man had a right to change after so many years.

"Excuse me," the duke said as he rose from the table.

"Grandfather . . ."

"It's all right, Brandon. I just want to say hello to an old friend."

He didn't look back to see what Brandon's reaction was. He weaved his way through the chairs and tables in the club, his gaze never wavering from Teddy Pickering as the old man settled into a high-backed leather chair, a newspaper in his lap and a pipe in his hand.

"Good day, Teddy," Lawrence said softly as he stopped in front of Pickering's chair. "It's been a long time."

Pickering looked up. There was a moment's hesitation, then his mouth dropped open slightly.

"I guess you didn't expect to see me." Lawrence sat down across from Pickering.

"Larry, I . . ."

The duke raised a hand to silence him. "Don't worry. I have no intention of causing a scene. What's done is done."

Pickering's jowls quivered.

"But I would like to know *why*, Teddy." Lawrence leaned back in his chair and waited.

Pickering glanced around the room one more time. Finally, his eyes returned to Lawrence. "It was a lark, Larry. It was Alastair's idea, to get even with you for the duel. I didn't know what he intended. It was just supposed to give you a scare."

"A lark . . ." Lawrence shook his head sadly. To think of the years he'd lost because of a lark.

"Alastair didn't tell me the truth until later. I thought you were dead. I thought you'd been lost at sea. I blamed myself for your death for years. I knew if it weren't for my prank, you would have still been alive." Pickering scratched his head, then continued. "It wasn't until Alastair was dying that he told me the truth. I suppose it was bothering his conscience. About to die and all. But by then it seemed too late to do anything about it. You'd been in America all those years. If Alastair had known where you were, perhaps he would have told me, but . . . well, Hayden was all set to step into his father's shoes. It seemed best to leave sleeping dogs lie."

"Yes," Lawrence said as he stood once again, "I guess you would have seen it that way."

Pickering stood too. "Larry, I am dreadfully sorry."

Lawrence stared at his old friend. Yes, he supposed the things Pickering had said were true. He supposed he was sorry for the things that had happened. Sorry didn't change things, but at least now he knew Pickering hadn't done it maliciously. No, maliciousness was more Alastair's style.

"I don't suppose we'll be seeing each other again, Teddy." He held out his hand. "But I'm glad we had this talk. Good-bye."

"Good-bye, Larry. I truly am glad you're back."

Lawrence walked away.

Chelsea was disappointed when he didn't come the next day, and even more disappointed when she learned he had left for London. But each day, in anticipation of his possible return, she asked Molly to brush her hair, and she put on one of the pretty morning gowns hanging in her wardrobe.

And each afternoon, because it was Chelsea's wish, Molly brought a footman to her room and had him carry her to the chair by the window, for she was still too weak to walk. Each day she was able to sit there a little longer before the dizziness forced her to return to her bed. She spent long periods in silence, trying to recall moments from her past, but it seemed as if she hadn't any past. She had only these recent weeks, her bleak room with its locked door, Molly and her medicine.

It was a particularly pretty day, this day in August. The sky was a powder blue, dotted with fluffy clouds that skittered before a light summer breeze. Chelsea's window overlooked the sculptured gardens behind the mansion. Her eyes fell to the hedge maze. If she could walk and run, she would want to play hide-and-seek within its green walls.

"Molly," she asked, not turning her gaze from the window, "did I ever play in the gardens when I was a child?"

"What, m'lady?"

"I was just thinking I'd like to hide in the maze. Did I ever do that when I was a girl?"

"Yes, indeed. More than once I had a terrible time findin' my Alanna in that confusin' thing. I would hear her laughin' at me, but I couldn't find her."

Chelsea turned from the gardens below to look up at Molly, now standing at her side. "Why do you do that?"

"Do what, m'lady?"

"Why do you sometimes speak of me as if I were someone else?"

Molly's face flushed. "Do I? I . . . I guess it's just my way of talkin', Lady Alanna."

"Or is it because I *was* someone else before . . . before I lost my mind?"

"Don't speak of it that way, luv!" her nanny protested vehemently.

"How old was I when they knew I wasn't right? How long have I been locked up here, Molly? I can't remember. I can't remember anything." Chelsea's voice, tinged with panic, rose to a high pitch. "Please won't you tell me? I want to know. I must know."

"Stop, luv. You mustn't upset yourself."

Chelsea grabbed for her hand. "Molly, I need

your help. I want to get well, but I can't if I don't remember." Tears welled in her eyes. "Don't you see? I *must* remember."

"You don't need to remember the way things was, luv. You just think of now and you'll be fine. You hear me, Lady Alanna? You stop tryin' to remember. It'll do you no good." She straightened, pulling her hand from Chelsea's grasp, and her face became stern. "Now, you've tired yourself with your fussin'. I'll send for Gerald and get you back into bed. It's time for your medicine and a nap."

"But I don't want a nap," she sobbed. "And I don't want my medicine. I just want to remember. Dear God in heaven, why can't I remember?"

Molly, her face lined with anxiety, hurried to the door and unlocked it. "I'll get Gerald." She pulled the door open, intent on leaving, but she stepped suddenly back as Brandon Fitzgerald strode into view. "Oh my," she breathed.

Brandon's speculative gaze slid from Molly to the bed and then swept the room until he found Chelsea beside the window. She was weeping. Her hands clutched at her skirt with white-knuckled fingers. Her chin was dropped forward, her shoulders hunched in despair.

"What's wrong here?" he demanded.

Chelsea's head came up. Her eyes flew open. Her gaze held a mixture of emotions which he couldn't begin to understand.

"Nothing's amiss, my lord," Molly replied quickly. "The lady is just tired and needs to be carried back to her bed. She's upset and needs her medicine. I was about to get the footman to help us."

Ignoring the nanny, Brandon walked across the room and knelt beside Chelsea's chair. He gazed upon her lovely face, then surprised even himself as he reached up to lift a tear from her cheek with a fingertip. The teardrop jiggled and shimmered on his rough, brown skin. They both stared at it a moment, then raised their eyes to meet the other's gaze.

Her eyes were so round, so very blue, but he saw no fear of him hidden in their depths.

"Is that true, Chelsea? Are you tired and ready to go back to your bed?"

She shook her head slowly, causing her cascading tresses to sweep gently about her shoulders.

"And what would you like to do, if you had your choice?"

Her voice was sweet and musical. "I should like to go sit in the garden, my lord. If I were well enough to do so."

He had been away from Hawklin more than a week, and during that time, except for the brief visit with Roxley, he hadn't given his bride more than a passing thought. His time had been filled with business and meeting new people and becoming familiar with London. Yet, when they left the city and began their journey home, he'd discovered he was eager to see Chelsea once again, to see if she was as lovely as he pictured her in his mind.

In truth, she was even more so. And he wanted nothing so much as to give her what would make her happy.

"If a visit to the gardens is what you want, then you shall have it."

With that, he rose and lifted her from her chair. She was as light as a feather. Her arms wrapped quickly around his neck, and he could see her rapid pulse in the hollow of her throat.

"My lord, what is it you're doing?" Molly demanded as he swept past her and into the hallway.

Chelsea ducked her head against his chest, as if hiding from her nanny's disapproval.

"I'm taking my wife to the gardens."

"But . . . but Lord Coleford, she should be in bed."

"Nonsense."

With quick strides, he carried her through the hallway, down the stairs, and out into the gardens behind Hawklin Hall. The mid-afternoon sun threw a golden coverlet over the verdant lawns, as if in invitation to come and enjoy. A gentle breeze cooled the August heat and fluttered stray wisps of silver-blond hair against her ivory cheeks.

Brandon took her into the midst of the maze, understanding somehow that here was where she wished to be, lost in a cool, green world. Kneeling, he set her on the ground. His hands lingered on her arms, as if to keep her from toppling over.

"Is there anything more you wish, Chelsea?"

he asked, hoping he would be able to provide it if she should voice a desire for something more.

Her trusting, innocent eyes, lovely and haunting, turned up to him as a hesitant smile stole across her heart-shaped mouth. "Only that you sit with me, my lord. If you would be so kind."

CHAPTER FOUR

Lawrence was already in the dining room when Brandon joined him that evening for supper. The old gentleman was strolling around the room, his eyes moving slowly over the paintings and the carved designs over the doorways and across the ceiling, his hands sliding over the sideboards and tables, the fireplace mantel, the vases and bric-a-brac.

Brandon stopped just inside the doorway and observed him, understanding his grandfather's mood. Although he'd eaten supper in this room their first night at Hawklin Hall, Lawrence Fitzgerald was now viewing it through the eyes of a duke once more.

Lawrence turned another corner and became aware of his grandson. A sheepish grin curled his mouth. He shrugged wordlessly.

Brandon laughed as he walked toward his grandfather. "You have a right to feel this way. It's yours again, your grace." He clasped Lawrence's hand, repeating, "your grace," as he met the older man's gaze.

They held their pose a moment, their expressions solemn.

Lawrence was the first to break the silence. "Shall we dine? I confess to a great hunger."

As soon as they sat at the table, servants appeared out of nowhere, filling the crystal goblets with wine, carrying in platters of food, then disappearing once again.

Lawrence separated a slice of juicy beef with his knife, but before he carried it to his mouth, he asked, "And where have you hidden yourself all afternoon, my boy?"

"I've been with Chelsea in the maze."

"Chelsea?"

"My wife." He answered Lawrence's next question before he could ask it. "She prefers that name to Alanna."

"I see. And how is she?"

Brandon pictured her as she'd looked, sitting on the grass. They'd spoken not at all the entire time they remained within the maze, not once from the moment she asked him to join her until the moment she asked to return to her room. He had spent the time looking at her while she had spent the time staring at the sky, her face turned upward. Brandon had been filled with a strange protectiveness, wishing he could shield her from anything unpleasant. She was like a lost child. At that moment, he didn't think of her as his wife, or even as a woman. She was Chelsea—fragile, delicate Chelsea— and she needed his strength to protect her from a world she couldn't face on her own.

"She seemed stronger today," he answered at last. "She was sitting up in a chair when I arrived. That nanny of hers didn't like the idea of my taking her outside." He frowned. "I wonder how long it's been since anyone has let her outside that room."

"From what they say, it isn't safe to let her out."

"I can hardly believe that, Grandfather."

"Mmm. I think I'd like to meet the girl."

Brandon nodded. "I'll bring her down tomorrow and introduce you. I'm not sure she even knows about her parents being gone or that you're the duke now. I didn't take the time to talk to Molly to see what Chelsea's been told."

"Wouldn't it be better if I went to visit her in her room?"

"No. She needs to get out. Her room is dismal. I'll bring her to you."

"As you wish, my boy."

Chelsea awoke before dawn. She couldn't remember a day when she'd awakened with such a feeling of well-being. This morning it didn't seem to matter that she couldn't remember anything from her past. It was enough that she could remember the gentleness of her husband.

Her husband. How strange. How strange to have a husband and know nothing about him except his name and that he treated her with kindness.

Chelsea tossed aside the blankets and slid her legs over the side of the bed. She drew a deep breath, determined not to allow the familiar dizziness to return. And, to her surprise, it didn't. She allowed her feet to touch the floor, then pushed herself up from the bed. Her legs wobbled beneath her, unaccustomed as they were to being used.

She set her jaw at a stubborn angle, drew another deep breath, then took her first step, hanging onto the nearby furniture as she did so. Her destination was the window. She wanted to look at the garden as the sun came up. Her eyes were focused on the window. It couldn't be more than ten steps away. Surely she could walk ten steps.

She was frustrated by her slow progress, but finally she reached the window. And it was none too soon. She sank onto the window seat and closed her eyes for a moment, exhaustion sweeping over her.

Molly would scold her when she saw what she'd done. But at the moment, Chelsea didn't care. She was up, and she'd done it by herself. If she could do this, perhaps . . .

She opened her eyes and fixed her blue gaze on the gardens below. The morning sun was obscured behind steel-gray clouds. She felt the sting of disappointment. It had been such a beautiful day yesterday. She had reveled in the feeling of warm sun upon her face. Secretly, she'd hoped Brandon would come to her room again and carry her down to the garden. But if it rained . . .

Just then she saw Brandon walking across the lawn, headed toward the stable. He was clad in riding attire and was idly striking his leg with the riding crop he held in his hand. She wished she could go with him.

Could she even ride? Had she ever been allowed out of this room long enough to learn?

She had a sudden sense of the wind blowing in her hair and thundering hooves beneath her. She caught the breath in her throat, waiting for the feeling to materialize in her mind, waiting for it to become a memory rather than a fleeting thought.

Just then Brandon stopped and looked up toward her window. She could see a flash of white teeth as he smiled. He raised an arm and waved at her. All else was forgotten in that moment as she returned the wave.

"Lady Alanna! What're you doing out of your bed?"

Chelsea turned toward Molly's disapproving voice. "I wanted to look at the garden."

Molly's expression was a study in consternation. "You shouldn't be doin' such things on your own, m'lady. What if you'd fallen and hurt yourself and I wasn't here to help you? I couldn't bear it if I was to lose you." She appeared to swallow back sudden tears, then added, "Come now. Let's get you back into bed."

"But I don't want to be in bed, Molly." She glanced back down at the lawn, but Brandon was no longer to be seen. A sigh escaped her. She'd hoped . . .

Just what was it she'd hoped?

"Well, it's into bed you need to be. Come now. Let me help you." Molly reached for Chelsea's arm.

Chelsea pulled away from the nanny and was just rising from the window seat when Brandon came through the open doorway. Their eyes met as she took an uncertain step.

Brandon's dark eyes widened in surprise, then a smile brightened his face. "Chelsea, you're standing up alone!"

"Yes, my lord." Strange. Her knees felt even weaker now than they had before.

"She's up, all right," Molly grumbled. "But she shouldn't be. She needs to be in bed. I need to give her her medicine. She didn't take it yesterday, and you see what she's about now."

"Maybe not taking it is why she's feeling so much better," Brandon interrupted. "Look at her. There's new color in her face."

Under his scrutiny, she felt heat rising in her cheeks as pleasure at his approval washed over her. Her gaze faltered, dropping to the floor.

"But, my lord, she *must* take her medicine," Molly responded in a horrified tone. "His lordship will have my . . ." She stopped abruptly.

"What's the medicine for, Molly?"

"Why, to keep her calm, m'lord. So she doesn't harm herself or . . ."

"She seems calm enough to me." Brandon

crossed the room in several long strides.

Chelsea saw his boots first, then felt his finger beneath her chin as he raised her head.

"What do you think, Chelsea?" His eyes searched her face. "Do you need it now?"

"I . . . I don't know, sir. I . . . I don't *like* to take it. It tastes vile and makes me feel so strange and sleepy, like . . ." Her voice faded away as she met his eyes. Her throat tightened. It wasn't that she was frightened of him. He just seemed so . . . so overwhelming.

"Molly, I don't think Chelsea needs any of your medicine today. Perhaps not tomorrow either. Do you understand me?"

Reluctantly, the nanny answered, "Aye, m'lord."

"Good." A smile returned to lift the corners of his mouth. "Now, how would you like to put on one of those pretty dresses of yours and join me and my grandfather for supper tonight?"

"Downstairs?" she echoed.

"Downstairs," he answered firmly. He turned a commanding gaze upon Molly. "You send for me when she's ready, and I'll come to take her down."

Molly nodded.

As the door closed behind him, Chelsea asked, "Have I ever been downstairs, Molly?"

"Not in a very long time, my dear. Not since you first . . . not in a very long time."

Lawrence rose from his chair as Brandon entered the room, carrying the girl in his arms. Even after his grandson's assurances about

61

her, he'd still been prepared to confront someone—or something—much different from what he found.

Her hands were clasped trustingly behind Brandon's neck. Her blue eyes were eagerly surveying the room. Lawrence was enchanted by her delicate beauty and fair coloring. She had certainly not taken after the Fitzgeralds in looks. There was nothing dark or bold about her. And when her eyes met his, despite the uncertainty lingering there, he thought he perceived . . . It couldn't be intelligence, for the girl was known to be mad. Still . . . Well, whatever it was, it wasn't what he'd expected.

Brandon gently lowered her feet to the floor. Unsteadily, she faced Lawrence, Brandon's hand beneath her elbow.

"Grandfather, may I present my wife, Lady Chelsea Fitzgerald."

Lawrence glanced at Brandon. He wasn't sure it was wise to humor her with this charade. But when he looked back at her, even he found it impossible to deny her such a simple thing. So what if the girl didn't like her name?

"My dear girl," he said, reaching out to take her hand. "I am delighted to meet you."

She curtsied. "Your grace," she whispered with lowered eyes.

"Now, we'll have none of that when we're alone. I'm merely Grandfather."

Chelsea glanced up at him as a smile played across her mouth. "Grandfather," she whispered. "I've never had a grandfather." Then, as suddenly as it had come, the smile vanished.

The sparkle left her blue eyes. "At least, I don't remember knowing my grandfathers. Do you suppose I ever met them?"

It was easy to see why his grandson was so captivated by his wife. Lawrence wanted nothing more than to see her smile return. "Come now," he said, a bit gruffly. "We won't give another thought to what you can't remember. This is an evening for gaiety. I have much to celebrate. I've come home to England, and I have a beautiful new granddaughter."

His ploy worked. The smile returned, first to her lips and then to her eyes.

"Thank you . . . Grandfather."

Chelsea was exhausted, but she didn't want the evening to end. She hadn't felt so alive in . . . in as long as she could remember. Lawrence and Brandon had both delighted her with outrageous tales of their ocean voyage and their first days in England, making her laugh until her sides ached and her eyes watered. Brandon talked of his brother, Justin, and their home on Long Island. Lawrence related some of the mischief he'd gotten into as a boy, roaming the grounds of Hawklin Hall.

But, finally, she couldn't control the fatigue any longer. While Lawrence talked, her eyelids drifted closed.

"Chelsea?"

She felt his hand on her arm and slowly opened her eyes. Brandon was kneeling beside her chair, his face close to her own.

"We'd better see you back to your room."

She wanted to tell him not yet, but she hadn't the strength to argue. She nodded.

Brandon pulled her chair back from the table and lifted her into his arms. His dark brown eyes gently caressed her as she clasped her hands behind his neck. She felt her face growing warm beneath his gaze.

"Well, my dear . . ."

Reluctantly, she broke free of Brandon's perusal and turned her head toward the old man's voice. Lawrence had come from his place at the end of the table to stand at her shoulder.

"I hope we shall share many a meal."

"I hope so, too, Grandfather."

"Good night then." He bent forward and placed a kiss on her cheek.

"Good night," she whispered in return.

With long strides, Brandon carried her from the dining room. Chelsea let her eyes close once again, enjoying the feel of his arms around her. She wondered what it would be like if he should kiss her cheek. She thought she might like it immensely.

As his feet reached the top of the stairway to the second floor, Chelsea opened her eyes, gazing over Brandon's shoulder toward a darkened hallway. Suddenly, she was afraid. There was something down that hallway. . . .

"Brandon?" Her hands tightened around his neck.

He stopped and looked at her. "Yes?"

"What's down there?" she asked.

He turned, following her gaze. "I have no idea. Just another wing full of rooms. Why do you ask?"

"I don't know . . ." She lifted her eyes toward his. His face was marked by concern. She didn't want that. She wanted the smiles and laughter they'd enjoyed all evening long. She didn't want his concern—or his pity. "It's nothing," she said, forcing the fear from her voice. "I was just curious."

His expression relaxed and he began walking again. Unable to stop herself, Chelsea looked once more behind him. The darkened wing seemed to be waiting for her.

She hid her face against his shoulder.

Hot flames surrounded her, licking at her skirts. Dense smoke was choking her. Behind her lay escape, but she could still hear the screams. She had to find the woman who was screaming. Whoever it was needed her help.

Suddenly, an enormous flame flared before her. It wore a face. The face of death.

It was then she realized that it was she who was screaming, she who was trapped and dying in the fire.

Chelsea sat up in bed as her eyes flew open. She choked on the silent scream still tearing at her throat. Her blood pounded in her ears. She gasped for air and waited for the terror to pass.

As her pulse slowed, she slipped from her bed and padded on bare feet to the window, then moved aside the draperies. The glow of a full moon bathed the maze in a soft white light.

The nightmare had seemed so real. It always seemed real. Always the same dream, except lately the dream seemed to last longer. Sometimes she would swear she was about to find the other woman before death separated them. And sometimes she would swear it wasn't a dream at all. That it had happened, just as she dreamed. But Molly swore there'd never been a fire, and she saw no reason for Molly to lie to her. Molly loved her.

"I *am* mad," she whispered.

Wanting to think of things more pleasant, she turned her thoughts to Brandon. Her pulse immediately quickened. She thought of how he always looked at her with such tenderness, such concern. She felt wonderful when she was with him. She felt free . . . free of everything that kept her locked in this room. But she wanted more. She wanted Brandon to feel wonderful, too. She wanted him to look at her as a woman. She wanted him to look at her as his wife.

Her fingers tightened around the edge of the draperies. "I don't want to be the mad Alanna any longer. Chelsea wouldn't be mad."

She watched as a falcon, wings stretched wide, soared above the night-blackened forest, rising gracefully until it too was silhouetted against the moon. As she watched, her heart lifted, soaring with the regal bird. It was an omen, a promise. Like the falcon rising above the dark forest, it seemed to promise she could rise above her madness. She could be Chelsea. She could be the girl she wanted to be. She could be Brandon's wife.

Wearing a hopeful smile, she let the draperies fall back into place and returned to her bed. Tomorrow she would truly be Chelsea.

CHAPTER FIVE

Chelsea was already dressed when she heard Molly's key in the lock. She rose from her chair as the door opened.

Molly's green eyes widened. "M'lady, what is it you're doing?"

"I want to join my husband for breakfast."

"But, my dear, he ate his breakfast long ago and took himself off somewheres. I saw him leavin' myself."

Chelsea felt a stab of disappointment. She'd been so eager to show him what she could do when she set her mind to it.

"Besides," Molly continued, "you're far too weak to be takin' such things upon yourself, even if I was allowed . . ."

Chelsea shook her head. "No, I'm not, Molly.

I'm much better. But I won't be getting any stronger if all I do is lie in bed all day long." She crossed the room and took Molly's hand. "Please, Molly. Is it any wonder I'm mad, kept prisoner here in this room? I *am* better. I'm not going to hurt anyone." Her voice rose as she pleaded, "Please believe me."

Molly stared at her for a long time, her gaze flicking across Chelsea's face, meeting one eye, then the other. A glimmer of tears gathered at the rims of her green eyes, and she sniffed noisily. "I believe you, lamb," the nanny finally said as she touched Chelsea's cheek with cool fingertips. "It's a cruel trick of fate that put you in this room, and I've grown to love you enough to be the one to open the door for you."

Tears swam in eyes of blue. "Thank you, Molly. Thank you."

"Hear now." Molly cleared her throat and brushed away tears of her own. "You dry those eyes. It won't do for Lord Brandon to be seein' you cryin'. You put on that pretty smile of yours. I've never seen a soul prettier than you when you're smilin'." She stepped back from Chelsea. "When his lordship gets back, I'll send Gerald to let him know you want to come downstairs."

"Wait. I . . . I'd rather surprise him."

"But you haven't the strength. . . ."

"I think I can do it, Molly. At least let me try."

Roxley's spirited gray cantered smoothly behind Brandon's lanky bay stallion. Riding alongside the new viscount was Roxley's sister, Maitland Conover, Lady Bellfort. Roxley and his sister had chanced upon Brandon while out for an early morning ride. There was nothing shy or retiring about the beautiful widow of the Marquess of Bellfort. Once introduced to Roxley's handsome new neighbor, Maitland had simply invited herself back to Hawklin Hall, and Roxley had had little choice but to tag along. Not that he minded the viscount's company. He truly liked the fellow, American or no. He was certain they were going to get on swimmingly.

Roxley shook his head as he watched his sister in action. Maitland was flirting openly with Brandon, although she knew good and well he was married to Alanna Fitzgerald. But he wasn't surprised. Maitland was not always discreet in her dalliances. She'd been lucky the marquess had never caught wind of her indiscretions before his death. Of course, that was how she had nabbed the old fool for a husband, flaunting her generous bosom and fluttering her pretty brown eyes his way.

Roxley just hoped Maitland's behavior wouldn't mar things for her son, Edgar, the new Marquess of Bellfort. He was still just a child, but things like this had a way of getting back to children. The boy could be hurt by the stinging gossip of his schoolmates. Roxley just wished he knew how to control Maitland. But, then, there never had been anyone who *could* control her.

As the road left the woods, Maitland raised

her riding crop. "I'll race you there!" she cried, then dropped the crop against her horse's rump.

The dappled mare shot forward. There was only a moment's hesitation before the two men took up the challenge and spurred their mounts after her. The three of them arrived at the front of Hawklin Hall almost side by side.

Maitland's laughter filled the air. "I won!" she declared.

"I believe, Lady Bellfort, that it was a tie." Brandon dismounted and stepped over to her horse.

"My dear viscount, I'm sure you are wrong." She reached forward, placing her hands on his shoulders, then slid from the saddle, leaning into Brandon as he lowered her to the ground.

Brandon's voice was low as he answered, "I'm certain I'm not."

"Then perhaps we shall have to have another contest some time, my lord." Maitland's eyes smoldered with unspoken promises.

Roxley frowned as he watched.

Maitland caught his look. She returned it with a defiant shake of her head before meeting Brandon's gaze once more. "Now, you must show me your house. Do you know, I've never once been inside. The duke and duchess did all their entertaining in London, and I've simply *longed* to see it. It's so much grander than Bellfort. And Rosemont pales in comparison." She slipped her hand into his arm.

"I'd be pleased to show you around, Lady Bellfort, but my grandfather would be much better at it than I. He grew up here and knows its history.''

''Is it true there's been a fire?'' Maitland's eyes swept over the front of the mansion. ''I'd heard your wife was . . .''

She was going too far this time. ''Brand, my friend,'' Roxley interrupted quickly, ''I'm about to die of thirst. Any chance we could go inside and have something to drink?''

Maitland knew what he was doing. She laughed aloud, letting her head fall back just a fraction to reveal a stretch of white throat above the collar of her umber riding habit. ''Yes, my lord. Do take us inside. I'm rather thirsty myself.''

It was true, Brandon reflected. Maitland Conover was a beauty. She had a creamy, flawless complexion. Her almond-shaped brown eyes were flecked with gold; her mouth was rose-hued and generous. She was petite but with ample curves to please the taste of most men.

Brandon had met more than one woman like Maitland. Those others weren't titled, but they were wealthy and bored and sought their excitement in the beds of men other than their husbands. Of course, the marchioness was a widow, but Brandon's wife was living. That made the game more exciting in her eyes, but it was a game he preferred not to play. Still, he liked her brother and so he could put up with the woman—on occasion.

Brandon led the way into the house, taking them across the great hall and back to the drawing room. "Please, make yourselves comfortable. I'll have Bowman order a tea tray for us. I confess that ride worked up a bit of an appetite."

"You needn't go to any trouble for us," Maitland said, still holding onto his arm. She turned, rubbing her breast against him. "I'm sure—"

But Brandon wasn't looking at her any longer. At the sound of the opening door, he'd turned his head, expecting to see Bowman standing there. Instead, his gaze fell upon Chelsea. She was watching him with wide blue eyes. Her willowy frame seemed to waver, as if she might soon crumple to the floor.

"Chelsea." He extracted himself from Maitland's grip and hurried across the room. "What are you doing here?" he asked in a whisper as he put a bracing arm around her back.

"I . . ." Her gaze flicked nervously toward the couple at the far end of the drawing room. "I wanted to see you," she finished weakly. "If you're busy, perhaps I can come back later."

Brandon saw the uncertainty in her face and cursed himself for his stupidity. "Don't be silly," he said gently. "Come and meet our company." He drew her with him across the room. "Roxley, Lady Maitland, I would like to introduce you to my wife, Lady Alanna Fitzgerald."

Roxley was struck dumb. He never would have dreamed the child he remembered would blossom into such a glorious flower as the one who stood before him. She was tall but ever so slender, a mere slip of a girl, yet utterly feminine. Her hair, once so gold, was now a silvery blond, and it swirled softly around the shoulders of her pink dressing gown. Her round blue eyes, the color of a summer sky, looked at him and stole his heart in that moment. He wanted to protect her, to be her champion, to be her most trusted friend.

"My dear, this is the Marchioness of Bellfort."

Maitland eyed the girl with a cool stare. "How very interesting to meet you at last, Lady Alanna. You have been quite a mystery." She glanced at Brandon. "But you have done quite well despite keeping yourself locked away, haven't you?"

Brandon's wife paled. If possible, her round eyes grew even rounder, and she seemed to lean more heavily upon her husband's arm. Roxley wanted to slap his sister's pretty face—and he might do just that once they were alone. He took a quick step forward.

"And this," Brandon continued in a controlled voice, "is Wellington Randolph-Smythe, the Earl of Roxley. His estate borders Hawklin Hall."

Roxley bowed slightly at the waist as he reached forward to take her hand. "Lady Alanna, this is a great pleasure." He kissed her knuckles. As he straightened, their eyes met again. "My friends call me Roxley. And I hope we shall be friends."

Hesitantly at first, she smiled. "And I prefer

that my . . . friends . . . call me Chelsea."

As soon as the words were spoken, she looked uncertain and glanced up at Brandon. Roxley saw him give a slight nod of his head. He wondered what the exchange was about, but soon forgot it as Brandon led the way to a grouping of chairs and bade them all sit down.

Maitland leaned forward and placed a familiar hand on Chelsea's arm. "Well, *Chelsea*." She put great emphasis on the name, a smirk in her sultry eyes. "You must tell us what you've been doing with yourself all this time. All of London will be just dying to hear." Her smile was sugary sweet, chokingly so.

Roxley wanted to box her ears.

Chelsea's first reaction to Maitland Conover had been to bolt from the room and hide in her upstairs apartment, locking the door behind her. But suddenly she was angry. This was *her* home. It was *her* husband she had seen the woman leaning against, throwing herself at in her obvious manner. Chelsea was not the one who should have to run and hide. She'd done nothing to be ashamed of.

She pasted an innocent smile on her lips. "Most recently, Lady Bellfort, I have been hiding away with my husband." Her hand rested familiarly on Brandon's knee. "Wouldn't you do the same if he were *your* husband?"

She heard Roxley's muffled laughter as she watched Maitland's face grow pink. She turned to look at the earl, then dared to glance at Brandon. In Roxley's eyes she had read amusement and approval. She wasn't sure what she could see in Brandon's. Surprise, mostly.

Still chuckling, Roxley rose from his chair. "I say, Brandon, I've enjoyed meeting your charming wife and would love to stay and have tea with you, but I think it's time my sister and I were on our way back to Rosemont. Come along, Maitland. I think these two would rather be alone."

Maitland obeyed stiffly. Her brown eyes shot covert daggers at Chelsea before she turned a more genial gaze on Brandon. "I hope to see you again soon, dear viscount. I plan to extend my visit at Rosemont. Do come see us."

Brandon's hand on Chelsea's shoulder told her to remain seated, then he walked with his guests to the entrance hall. Alone in the drawing room, she felt her insides begin to quake. What had come over her to behave so abominably to Brandon's friends? A marchioness and an earl, and she had acted like . . . like an idiot.

He would hate her now. It wasn't enough that his wife was mad and had to be kept locked away. Now she was insulting his peers. She had to get out of there before he returned. She couldn't face him. Not now.

Chelsea rose quickly and hurried across the drawing room. She opened the door and peeked out. Brandon was nowhere to be seen. On light feet, she darted for the stairs and fairly flew up them. She paused on the second floor, gasping for air and feeling the weakness swirling in her head.

He would look for her in her rooms. She

didn't want him to find her. She couldn't bear to see him yet. Eventually she would have to face his disappointment in her, but not yet.

She turned away from her bedroom and hurried down the hallway into the northeast wing. All was quiet around her. No servants bustled in and out of the rooms. The entire wing seemed to be deserted.

Chelsea turned a corner, stopped, and stared down another long hallway. Toward the end was a narrow staircase.

Servants' quarters, she thought.

Then her heartbeat quickened, and her skin grew cold. There was something about those stairs.

She began walking once again.

I'm too old to live in the nursery. I'm too old for a nanny.

She gasped and whirled around, certain whoever was speaking had to be nearby. No one was there. Not even a curtain stirred.

Once more she faced the stairs. Stairs that led to the nursery.

The nursery.

I don't want her here, Nanny. Take her away!

Chelsea's hand shook as it touched the railing. She glanced up the darkened staircase. Her blood pounded in her ears.

Chelsea, come look. Come look.

She wanted to run away, but she couldn't. There was something—or someone—up there. She had to see. She had to know.

"No, m'lady!" Molly's alarmed voice carried down the hall.

She turned and watched with wide eyes as Molly came rushing toward her.

"What do you think you're doing?" her nanny asked in a breathless voice.

"That's the nursery, isn't it, Molly?"

Molly's fingers closed around her arm and tugged her away from the step. "Yes, m'lady. It was the nursery all right."

"I . . . I want to see it. Molly, there's something . . ."

"There's nothin' to see up there. It's been closed for ages. The stairs are likely all rickety. Come away, Chelsea."

Her head felt light. "You called me Chelsea."

"I . . . well, of course. It's what you've wanted."

"Thank you, Molly," she whispered, and then the floor rose toward her face.

"Haven't I warned you somethin' like this would happen? Haven't I told you she shouldn't be wanderin' about by herself? She'll be gettin' herself hurt, she will, and then who'll be to blame for it?"

Brandon stared down at Chelsea's white face. "That's enough, Molly."

In truth, he was more than a little disturbed. Finding Chelsea gone from the drawing room, Brandon had hurried up the stairs to her chambers only to find them empty as well. He'd only begun his search when he'd heard Molly's distraught cry for help. He'd found the nanny bending over Chelsea in the deserted northeast wing and had carried his wife quickly back to her room.

"Lord Coleford, you must listen to me. I've been takin' care of the Lady Alanna since she was just a babe, and I know her well. You mustn't encourage her to leave her rooms, m'lord."

Chelsea's eyelids fluttered.

"Be quiet," he ordered Molly once again.

Her eyes opened.

"You frightened us," Brandon said gently.

"What . . . ?" Confusion played across her face.

"You fainted." He placed a hand behind her shoulder. "Do you think you could sit up and sip some tea?"

She nodded and allowed him to pull her upright.

"You're trying to do too much," he scolded as he handed her a cup of the steaming brew. "You mustn't tackle those stairs alone. Next time, you wait for me."

"The stairs." Her hand began to shake, and she sloshed tea onto the bedspread.

Quickly, Brandon grabbed the cup from her quivering fingers. "What is it, Chelsea?"

She looked at him, her blue eyes round and frightened. "The stairs," she repeated. "They go to the nursery."

Brandon glanced across the bed toward Molly, silently asking for help. He found her face stubbornly closed to him.

"Brandon . . ."

"Yes?" He returned his gaze to his wife.

"There's . . . *something* . . . in the nursery."

Her words, spoken in a low voice, sent shivers down his arms. Her eyes seemed—what was it? They seemed haunted. Was there madness there after all?

"Brandon, I . . . I'm frightened."

No, he thought as he gathered her to him, holding her head against his chest. It wasn't madness. It was fear. And fear he could deal with.

He laid her gently back against her pillows. "There's nothing to be afraid of, Chelsea. Molly's here, and I'm here. There's nothing going to hurt you. I promise. Do you trust me?"

She stared at him for what seemed the longest time. Finally, she nodded, and he saw the haunted look in her eyes recede.

"Now, I want you to close your eyes and go to sleep."

"Will you stay?"

"I'll stay."

CHAPTER SIX

Brandon paused at the bottom of the stairs and glared at the closed door at the top. He didn't know what Chelsea feared beyond that door, but he meant to find out. He took the steps two at a time. His hand closed round the doorknob. He took a deep breath, and his nostrils were filled with an acrid odor.

Of course. The fire.

He tried the knob. The door was locked. He paused a moment and considered finding the housekeeper with the key. Then, discarding the notion, he gave the door a shove with his shoulder, once, then twice. On the third try, it gave way to him.

The blackened remains of the nursery apartments spread before him. The windows were boarded over, the roof patched where the fire had burned through. Hayden had told him about Chelsea setting fire to the nursery, but he'd forgotten it. And for some reason, he'd never wandered into this area of the house—perhaps because no one else ever seemed to come this way either.

He stepped inside, squinting into the gloom. It seemed little had been done to clean up after the fire. Charred remains of furniture cluttered the room like black skeletons.

He moved through what appeared to have been a sitting room, perhaps where the nanny had spent her evenings reading to Chelsea or knitting after the girl had gone to sleep. In past years, it might even have been the schoolroom for the younger children before they were sent off to boarding school.

The next room must have been the nanny's bedroom, he guessed. It was small and bare. Only the frame of the narrow bed remained.

The last room had, before the fire, been spacious and airy. There'd been many windows, all boarded up now, and a large fireplace at the far end of the room. He saw the remains of two narrow beds in one corner. A charred beam, broken midway across the ceiling, divided the room in two.

"That's where we found her."

Brandon jerked around at the sound of Molly's voice.

"She was under that beam. Patrick found her just before the fire reached her, thank the good

Lord, but she was near enough dead anyway. When she awoke, she'd lost all memory. Amnesia, the doctor calls it. Poor lamb. As if she didn't have enough trouble. . . ."

Brandon looked at the beam once again. She might have been dead before he ever reached England. He might never have seen her beautiful face nor gazed into those mysterious blue eyes. What a loss, and he would never have known what fate had kept from him. He, too, was thankful for God's sparing of Chelsea's life.

He walked farther into the room, feeling the horror surrounding him, sensing what it must have been like for her, surrounded by flames. As he neared the beam, his boot kicked something. He bent over and picked it up. What now was little more than burned fabric had at one time been a doll.

"M'lord," Molly whispered. "May I . . . may I please have that?"

He glanced over his shoulder. Molly was walking toward him with an outstretched hand, her eyes filled with tears. He nodded.

The woman took the doll and clutched it to her breast. "My Alanna. My poor, poor Alanna," she mumbled.

"Was that very special to her?"

"Since she was a babe. But it's ruined now."

"Perhaps I should get her another one just like it."

Molly's tears flowed over and spilled down her cheeks. "Wouldn't do no good, m'lord." She turned slowly and walked back through the charred rooms to the door. With her back still toward him, her hand on the latch, she spoke again. "Mark my words, your lordship. She doesn't remember the fire or what came of it, and it's best she doesn't. You seal off these rooms. Don't let her come back and see this. Only bad can come of it. She's been through enough."

"Chelsea, come look. Come look."
The stairs were steep and narrow. She climbed, one step after another, but she never seemed to come any closer to the door at the top of the staircase. The girl's voice called to her over and over.
"Chelsea, come look. Come look."
"I'm coming."
It was difficult to breathe. Why was the air so thick?
Suddenly, she was in the nursery. The crackle of the fire filled her ears while the smoke assaulted her lungs and stung her eyes.
"Where are you?" she cried.
Laughter. It was laughter she heard above the din.
Turn . . . Run . . .
Death waited for her beyond the next room. But she couldn't leave without her, the girl who called to her, the one who laughed as the nursery burned. She couldn't leave her to die. She had to find her.
All about her was ablaze, orange fingers reaching out to lick at her skirts. Was it smoke that choked the air from her lungs? Or was it simply her own fear?

And then she saw her.

She was dancing on the ledge outside the window, her golden hair flying out from her head as she whirled in wild abandon. Her nightgown was on fire. "Chelsea, come look. Come look."

She opened her mouth to scream, just as the ceiling came tumbling down upon her.

The piercing wail cut through Brandon's sleep like a sharp-edged blade. It lodged in his heart, leaving him feeling torn and bleeding.

"Chelsea!"

He bounded out of bed and hurled himself down the hall toward his wife's apartments. He found Molly there before him, holding onto Chelsea as she struggled to reach the door.

"Let me go! Let me go!"

Her silver-blond hair flew wildly about her shoulders. Her eyes were aglow with a strange light; she stared right through him without seeing. She swung her fists at the nanny, striking Molly about the shoulders.

"Chelsea!" Brandon said sternly, drawing her gaze.

"She's up there! She's on fire! Let me go to her! Let me go!"

Brandon slowly approached the two women. He forced his voice to sound calm as he responded, "There's no fire, Chelsea. Everything is all right."

Her face was so pale in the flickering candlelight. "You don't understand. She was calling for me. I heard her. I saw her." She spoke in a raspy whisper now.

"Whom did you see, Chelsea?" he asked gently.

There was no disguising the horror of discovery that suddenly filled her. She shrank away from Molly. She pressed the back of her hand against her lips. Her eyes flicked back and forth from Brandon to Molly, then to Brandon again.

"Chelsea?"

"I saw . . . I saw Alanna. Alanna set the fire."

It was Molly's turn to gasp.

"Dear Father in heaven," Chelsea pleaded as tears welled in frightened eyes of blue. "Help me."

Brandon felt as if someone were squeezing the life from him, as if a mighty band was tightening around his chest. He would give his right arm to take that fear from her eyes, to remove the nightmare from her memory, to set her world right for her.

Instinctively, he moved forward and gathered her against him, stroking her hair with a gentle hand. "It's all right, Chelsea. It was only a bad dream. We all see"—he sought for the right word—*"unusual* things in our dreams."

"But . . . but you don't understand. She . . . I . . ." Her fingernails dug into his upper arm as her head dropped back so she could look at him. "Brandon, I'm so afraid. It was as if I were two people. Alanna and Chelsea. I could see her so clearly. She was laughing and . . . It was more than a dream. It . . . Oh, I don't want to be Alanna ever again." She swallowed hard as two tears slipped from watery eyes to trail down her cheeks. "Please help

me, Brandon. I don't want to be mad anymore."

A fierce protectiveness filled his chest. "Then
you won't be." His large hand cradled her chin.
"I promise."

He watched as the terror slowly receded
from her beautiful eyes, leaving only a weariness of the soul in its wake. And then he saw
something else. A spark of trust. She believed
him.

But did *he* believe what he told her himself?
He wasn't sure.

"Brandon?"

"Yes?"

"Will you take me away from here?"

At that moment, he would have tried to give
her the moon and stars if they were what she
wanted. "Where would you like to go, Chelsea?"

"Anywhere. Anywhere away from here."

The carriage rocked on its hinges as the
matched set of blacks trotted briskly along the
country road through the pouring rain. The sky
was as dark as night, despite its being nearly
noon, and the wind blew with the promise of
an early winter in its breath.

Chelsea sat with hands clenched in the folds
of her skirts, her fingers twisting and worrying
the fabric. She gnawed on her lower lip as she
stared down at her lap and contemplated her
new circumstances. She couldn't remember
ever being outside of Hawklin Hall before, and
here she was, only a few hours since she'd

asked Brandon to take her away, heading toward an undisclosed destination.

Brandon had told her only that they were going to visit some of the duke's other properties, and though she was filled with curiosity, she couldn't bring herself to ask him any questions. He was doing this for her, to help her escape the nightmares and the madness. What if she failed him? What if the nightmares followed her wherever she went? What if there were no escaping the madness?

"The day is gray enough without your frowns, my Lady Chelsea."

She cocked her head to the side and glanced over at him. He was watching her, a teasing glint in his chocolate brown eyes. Then he grinned, his look encouraging her to do the same.

"Ah, I believe I see a hint of sunshine."

She offered an uncertain smile.

"I was right. It is the sun."

"Perhaps a poor imitation, my lord."

"Do you question my wisdom, madam?" He raised an eyebrow and drew back in mock surprise. "Are you, perhaps, Molly in disguise?"

Chelsea couldn't resist his humor. This time her smile was genuine. She covered her mouth to stifle the laugh that rose in her throat. She could still see Molly's thunderous look as Brandon escorted her from her room, Gerald not far behind with a trunk filled with her clothing. She could only imagine what the old nanny had said to Brandon about the wisdom of taking her from the safety of Hawklin Hall.

But it didn't matter now. She was suddenly awash with a sense of freedom. It felt wonderful. She was almost giddy with happiness. She pushed aside the curtain and stared out at the rolling green countryside. The downpour had subsided to a gentle rain. The air was sweet, though cool.

"Brandon . . ." Her hand fell on his arm. "Stop the carriage."

She didn't meet his gaze when he looked at her. She knew he must be frowning, wondering what might be about to go wrong. But she didn't know how to tell him that nothing was going wrong because everything was going right. She didn't know how to explain what it was she felt or why she needed to stop. Then she heard his command to the driver. The carriage slowed, then rolled to a halt.

Before Brandon could ask any questions, Chelsea was opening the carriage door and hopping to the ground. Mud splattered over her shoes and onto her ankles. She didn't care. She turned her face up toward the clouds and let the cool rain pelt her skin. She lifted her arms and opened her mouth and twirled like a schoolgirl.

Suddenly, she stopped and looked toward the carriage. Brandon was watching her from the doorway.

"Isn't it wonderful?" she called to him. "Come on."

She began to run across the field, holding up her cloak and skirts, her laughter trailing behind her. She didn't know if Brandon followed. She only knew she wanted to glory in this wonderful taste of freedom. It might be gone tomorrow. It might even be gone before nightfall. She wanted to feel it—really feel it—while she could.

Finally, gasping for breath, she was forced to stop. How she hated the persistent weakness that slowed her down so!

Sensing his gaze upon her, she turned. Brandon had followed after all and watched with a worried expression.

"Don't you be the one who frowns now, my lord. Didn't you ever frolic in the rain as a child? Don't you love the way it feels against your skin? It's better when it's not so cold, but still . . ." She held out her hand toward him. "Come. Join me."

Brandon stepped forward and took her hand, but still he didn't smile.

"Please not so grim, my dear viscount." Unconsciously, Chelsea mimicked Maitland Conover's superior tone and stance. "We simply *must* have a smile from you or I shall be unable to bear another moment."

He bowed smartly and kissed her knuckles. "A thousand pardons, Lady Fitzgerald. I don't know what came over me." When he raised his head, he was smiling at last.

She slipped her hand from his and began to turn slowly, once again raising her arms toward the sky. "I used to do this all the time when I was a girl. We would stand in the rain and spin around until we were too dizzy to—"

Brandon was standing beside her again. She stopped turning, her eyes inextricably drawn to his. The rain had matted his chestnut hair against his scalp. She saw the beads of water clinging to his nose and upper lip. Suddenly, it was no longer cold. Of its own volition, her right hand moved to brush a raindrop from his mouth. Her fingers lingered there as a strange heat spread through her veins.

"Chelsea," he whispered, his mouth moving beneath her hand.

Her breathlessness returned, leaving her unable to speak.

"You're so very beautiful."

Her hands slipped to brace against his chest as he leaned forward and she rose on tiptoe. His fingers held her shoulders and drew her even closer to him. The kiss was light, tender, and wonderfully frightening. It was everything she thought a kiss should be, except it was far too short.

Brandon's mouth released her as he stepped backward. He studied her for several seconds, his dark eyes roving over her face, searching for answers to unspoken questions.

She felt almost stripped bare before him. Uncertain. Confused. She wanted to run, but not away from him. She wanted to run back into his arms and stay there forever.

"I think it's time we were on our way," he

said, his voice a husky whisper. "It will be dark before we reach Teakwood."

Teakwood Manor was located near the mouth of the River Severn. The house was built entirely of teak shipped from the Foxworth plantation in India. Where Hawklin Hall was enormous and imposing, Teakwood was small and friendly, and Chelsea felt immediately at home within its walls.

The front door opened to the parlor, where a fire burned warmly on the hearth. The room was filled with chairs and sofas and even a pianoforte. Through the open doorway to the right of the parlor, Chelsea could see a small library, its walls lined with books. To the left was a dining room with a large oak table surrounded by eight chairs, and beyond it, the kitchen.

A white-capped woman—middle-aged and slightly plump, with chestnut curls peeking from beneath the cap—hurried out from the kitchen to greet them, dark blue eyes snapping. "Saints be! I thought you'd ne'er be gettin' here. Come in. Come in. You're lettin' in a terrible draft, and that's for certain."

Brandon removed Chelsea's cloak and handed it to the maid.

"Heavens. And have you been standin' in the rain for hours 'fore you come in? Look at you. You're soaked clean through to the bones."

"You must be Mrs. O'Grady," Brandon said as he shrugged out of his own wet coat.

"That I am. And you must be Viscount

Coleford, or I've let the wrong man in." Mrs.
O'Grady glanced at Chelsea, her sharp eyes
taking in the wet, tangled hair and the damp
bodice clinging to her breasts. "Lady Coleford,
it's pleased I am you've come to Teakwood at
last. But it's not standin' here chattin' we
should be. A hot bath and a shot o' whiskey will
have you feelin' spry in no time at all."

Chelsea had no time to respond. Mrs.
O'Grady's hand grasped her elbow and she was
pushed up the stairs. Before she had time to
more than catch her breath, she was sinking
into a tub filled with hot, rose-scented water
and relaxing as the cloud of steam floated close
to her face. The house was totally silent, and as
her body warmed and relaxed, she let her eyes
drift closed.

Her thoughts flitted back to that same afternoon and the kiss she had shared with Brandon
in the meadow. What a wonderful sensation!
Their first kiss.

Was it *her* first kiss, as well? The question
caused a tiny frown to draw her eyebrows
closer together.

But how could she have ever been kissed
before? She'd always been locked away in her
rooms at Hawklin Hall. What chance had she
ever to have been kissed? What chance had she
ever to fall in love?

Fall in love.

She thought of Brandon, his face so handsome, so appealing with its sharp angles and
dark complexion. His eyes fascinated her. Such
a rich brown, filled with humor one moment,

searching, probing the next. And his mouth. His lips had brushed hers with tender care, yet she had sensed a deeper, harsher demand lying just beneath the surface.

Have I ever been in love?

No. She thought not. Surely she would remember if ever she had loved someone. And who could it have been? A groom? The butler? Certainly not one of her peers. No one outside her family seemed to know for certain she even existed.

Brandon knew . . . and he married me.

But why had he married her? They'd never met. What had made him agree to marry a girl driven by madness?

Chelsea straightened in the tub, then splashed water on her face. The water had turned tepid. The room was clearing of steam.

Brandon.

She imagined his arms around her once again. She imagined their lips touching as the rain moistened their skin. She felt that same strange warmth flowing through her veins. The nipples of her breasts hardened and tingled.

I love him. The thought was accepted with a sense of amazement.

Brandon paced back and forth across the parlor, stopping each time for a moment to stare into the blazing fire. It didn't help that he kept imagining Chelsea in her tub, moisture gathering just above her mouth, her blue eyes round with wonder, her rose-tipped breasts just above the surface of the water.

He raked his fingers through his tousled brown hair, trying to rid himself of Chelsea's image, but it was useless. His mind darted to the moment when he'd kissed her. That was even worse. He wanted to kiss her again. He wanted to do much more than simply kiss her.

But what could he do? She was hardly more than a child. She'd never been outside of Hawklin Hall before. She'd never had a season, never danced with another man, never flirted with anyone. She was an innocent. Worse yet, they said she was mad, insane, crazy. And yet, all he wanted to do was take her to his bed.

Well, she is my wife.

But did that give him the right to use her lightly when he had no intention of remaining in England for long? And what happened if this outing proved more harmful than helpful? What if he had to lock her back up in those dreadful rooms again? What then?

"By gad, I may go insane myself," he muttered beneath his breath.

"Brandon?"

He turned and discovered her standing on the bottom step. She was wearing something ice-blue and flowing. Her pale hair floated around her shoulders like a soft cloud. There was just a hint of pink on each cheek. Her mouth was parted slightly, and uncertainty reigned in her blue eyes.

Desire returned to Brandon like a jolt of lightning. Only sheer will held him in his place, kept him from carrying her back up the stairs to his room right then.

"I . . . I'm sorry I took so long."

He shrugged, still not trusting himself to speak.

"Mrs. O'Grady said supper would be ready when we are. Are you hungry?" There was a slight quiver in her voice.

"Starved," he answered. *But not for food.*

She stepped down from the stairs and came toward him. The firelight danced in the silver and gold of her hair and warmed her cool blue eyes. She held her hands clasped in front of her, and he saw her nibble her lower lip.

Watching her, Brandon's desire increased tenfold. She was the most delicately, hauntingly beautiful woman he'd ever seen. There was no artifice about Chelsea Fitzgerald, except for her use of names. She was exactly as she appeared—fragile yet somehow very strong, uncertain yet undeniably brave, beautiful but delightfully unaware of it.

"Brandon, I . . ." She reached forward and hesitantly touched the back of his hand. "I want to thank you for bringing me here. I . . . I feel as if I've come home."

He would have to be patient. She was like a captured bird. If he moved too quickly, she might become frightened and injure herself trying to escape. She might never learn to fly.

"Then I'm glad, too, Chelsea. Now, let's dine. I'm famished."

Brandon sat alone in the parlor, staring numbly into the dying embers. He brought the tankard of ale to his lips and drained the last drop of the warm brew. It was hours since Chelsea had retired for the night, but Brandon had avoided his room, preferring instead to sit alone and drink himself into a stupor.

Supper had been a frightful experience. He'd had no appetite for food; he'd dined instead on his bride's beauty and wished for things he could, by rights, demand, but knew he never would. Chelsea had been understandably confused by his tense silence and had retreated to her room early, claiming she was exhausted by their journey.

Suddenly, Brandon thought of Justin. He could just imagine his brother's assessment of the situation. Justin would have burst into gales of laughter. Besotted fool! That's what Justin would have called Brandon if he were there.

And his brother would be right. He and Justin had squired the most elegant and elite of New York society to suppers and balls. They'd both had numerous opportunities to give up their bachelorhood, and to women with more money and more experience than Chelsea had. Brandon could honestly say he'd never even been tempted to make himself any woman's husband. He'd only become one to give his grandfather back what was rightfully his.

But that was before he'd seen Chelsea. What was it about her? Perhaps he would have wanted to marry her anyway. Marry her or not, he would have wanted her.

Hell's bells! He had to quit thinking about her.

Brandon dropped the empty tankard onto

the floor. It clanked near his foot and rolled across the room toward the fireplace. As he rose from the sofa, he ran his fingers through his hair in a frustrated gesture. Then he walked slowly toward the stairs, determined to fall into a mindless sleep.

But it was not to be. His dreams were of Chelsea.

CHAPTER
SEVEN

By morning, the clouds had entirely disappeared. In its wake, the storm had left a crystal-blue sky and a rain-freshened scent. Birds chirped in the branches of the sycamore outside Chelsea's window, happily announcing the coming of a new day.

Chelsea awakened slowly. There was a moment of wonder over her surroundings, then she remembered and a smile drifted onto her lips. She and Brandon were at Teakwood Manor. She was free of the oppressing presence of Molly and the other servants. She was free of the locks on her bedroom door. She was even free of her dreams. Last night, she had slept as soundly as a lamb.

She tossed aside the covers and dropped her feet to the floor. She crossed the room, unlatched the window, and opened it to the brisk morning air. She drew a deep breath, then let it out with a satisfied sigh.

She glanced to the left. Brandon's window was closed against the glorious new day. She wondered when he had finally retired. He'd been in such a strange mood the night before. She'd felt very confused by his silence and the way he'd watched her from behind hooded eyes. If she didn't know better, she would have thought him angry with her for some reason. Unable to bear his glaring countenance any longer, Chelsea had excused herself shortly after supper and retired to her room. She'd feared she would lie awake and toss and turn, wondering what she had done to make him so silent and surly, but instead she had fallen into a deep, dreamless slumber.

A movement out of the corner of her eye caught her attention. She turned her head and leaned forward as far as she dared. Her sleep-tousled hair fell forward to obscure her vision, and she impatiently tossed the tangled locks over her shoulder.

The lawn behind the house sloped gently away, ending in a thick grove of trees. Her attention had been drawn off to the right, toward the stable and paddocks. The movement had been caused by a flaxen sorrel horse exercising in one of the paddocks on the end of a lunge line. The horse trotted in a circle around the groom, occasionally shaking its head with impatience, its tail raised high in a flowing plume.

Chelsea tingled with the desire to escape with the spirited animal in a mad gallop across a meadow.

"Why shouldn't I?" she asked herself aloud.

She drew back inside, not stopping to close the window.

Yes, why shouldn't she go for a ride? Brandon had said she could do whatever she wanted, and she wanted to go riding. She didn't bother, as she had in the past, to wonder if she even knew how to ride. She suddenly was filled with confidence. If she didn't know how, this was a good time to learn.

She hastily discarded her nightgown and performed her morning toilet, washing away the traces of sleep from her face. She dressed in the simple blouse and sand-colored skirt she pulled from the wardrobe, then ran a brush through her hair before tying it at the nape with a brown satin ribbon. She started to draw on a pair of soft leather shoes, then tossed them aside, suddenly wanting nothing more than to feel the earth beneath her feet, the grass between her toes. Feeling almost giddy, she opened the door and left her room.

Mrs. O'Grady was tidying the parlor when Chelsea came down the stairs. She glanced up, then straightened, putting a hand in the small of her back as she bent slightly backward. "Ach. It's a miserable back I've got," she mumbled, more to herself than to Chelsea. Then a broad grin split her round face. "What is it you're up to so bright and early, miss? You've a bright twinkle in your eye, you have. If you were my boy Willy, I'd be thinkin' you were up to mischief. Will you be havin' some breakfast before you're out the door?"

"Thank you, Mrs. O'Grady, but I couldn't. I'm still full from last night."

"Nonsense. It's the excitement that's taken your appetite. I can see it in your eyes."

"I—I thought I'd like to see the horses."

"Ah, I should have known you'd have a love for the wild creatures. There's a look of that about you." Mrs. O'Grady waved her hand. "Well, be off with you then. Stewart will see that you're taken care of." With a shake of her head, she went back to her cleaning. "Four-footed devils," she mumbled. "You'd not find me atop such a beast."

Chelsea couldn't help laughing at the house-keeper's comments. She spoke with such famil-iarity, her only notable submission to propriety her occasional use of m'lady and m'lord. And even that sounded friendly coming from Mrs. O'Grady.

She wondered if the woman knew of Chel-sea's past. Perhaps not. Perhaps she'd never even known the duke and duchess had a daugh-ter until just before their arrival yesterday. Why should she? Her parents had probably not come to Teakwood very often, if at all. It didn't exactly seem their style. The house was neither large nor grand.

But Chelsea loved it. She loved its quaint gables and its many shutter-framed windows.

She loved the gnarled sycamores scattered throughout the yard. She loved the chimneys and the thatched roof and the soft color of the teakwood walls and the flowers in the window boxes and . . .

Her thoughts fled as the paddock came into view. The mare had stopped dead still, her neck arched, her nostrils flared. The animal was watching Chelsea with alert black eyes. Suddenly, she neighed shrilly and pranced a few steps to one side, then back the other direction before freezing once again in her regal pose.

Chelsea felt a thrill of excitement and quickened her steps.

The groom, a short, slight fellow in his fifties, had also watched her approach, and as she neared, he walked across the paddock, leading the horse behind him.

"Good morning," she greeted him.

"Mornin', mum."

"Are you Stewart, by any chance?"

He pushed his hat back on his head. "I am." He squinted at her from a wrinkled, weathered face.

"Mrs. O'Grady said I should ask you to show me around the stables. I—I'd like to go for a ride."

He nodded and began to turn away.

"I'd like to ride this one," she said softly.

Stewart looked back at her. "This one, mum? I don't think that'd be wise. She's young and has a mind of her own. The duke keeps a nice, gentle—"

"This one, Stewart," Chelsea interrupted firmly, looking once again at the mare.

She was tall, nearly sixteen hands. Her light brown coat glistened with golden highlights, brushed to a high sheen. Her flaxen mane and tail were long, thick and wavy. Wide intelligent eyes watched Chelsea from beneath a heavy forelock. Deep-barreled with a long back and longer underbelly, her well-muscled shoulders and thighs promised speed and endurance.

"What's her name?" Chelsea asked, suddenly realizing how long she'd been standing there in silence, staring at the magnificent horse.

"Don't know, mum."

Chelsea reached out and stroked the mare's downy muzzle. "A fine lady like this should have a name."

Stewart cleared his throat. "Well, bein's she belongs to a duke, I've been callin' her Duchess myself."

"Duchess." Her fingers moved up to scratch the horse behind her ear. "Yes, I like that," she whispered, then added, "Saddle Duchess for me, please, Stewart."

"Yes, mum," the groom answered, shaking his head, his tone expressing clearly his disapproval as he led the mare toward the barn.

Chelsea waited impatiently while Stewart slipped a bit into Duchess's mouth and slid the headstall up behind her ears. When he turned his back and reached for the sidesaddle, Chelsea had a sudden, overwhelming inspiration. She stepped up to the skittish mare, murmured a few gentling noises, then gathered a clump of mane near the withers and swung up onto the mare's bare back. As soon as her legs gripped the sleek sorrel sides, she knew she was born to ride. She must have ridden before. It felt so wonderfully familiar.

How long ago? she wondered, then shook off the thought. This was not a moment to spend struggling with her past.

Stewart turned around. His mouth dropped open and he stared at the skirt pushed up above her knee, her bare calves and feet dangling at the horse's sides. "Mum, you can't—"

"Don't worry, Stewart. We'll get on famously."

Brandon's head pounded to the beat of a thousand tiny drummers, all of them marching inside his skull. He groaned as he rolled over and covered his face with a pillow against the daylight streaming in his window. He tried to go back to sleep, but he kept wondering what time it was and what Chelsea was doing.

Finally, admitting defeat, he pushed the pillow onto the floor and sat up, cringing beneath the objecting clamor in his head. His tongue felt as if it were swathed in cotton—dirty cotton. His eyes felt hot and bloodshot. His sleep had been fitful, plagued by dreams of Chelsea. He felt ill-tempered and irritable. This was not going to be one of his better days.

It was a good thing his grandfather hadn't accompanied them to Teakwood. If Lawrence had seen Brandon in his cups, there would have been no end to the upbraiding he would have received. And, he admitted to himself, it wouldn't be undeserved.

By the time he'd washed and dressed, Brandon was feeling some improvement. Perhaps, after a hearty breakfast, his good humor would return.

In the hall, he paused outside Chelsea's bedroom, wondering if she might be waiting there until he sent for her. As the hour was quickly approaching noon, he hoped she wasn't. He raised his hand and rapped on the door.

"You needn't bother knockin', m'lord," Mrs. O'Grady called from the bottom of the stairs. "The lady's long since been up and about."

He turned and looked down at her. "Where is she now?"

"She went for a ride, I believe, sir. Though why a pretty thing as she would want to risk life an' limb aboard such a beast . . ." Her voice trailed off as she retreated toward the kitchen.

"A ride? Mrs. O'Grady, wait!" Brandon hurried down the stairs, ignoring the increased throbbing in his temples.

The housekeeper turned and quirked her dark eyebrows in question.

"You say Chelsea went for a ride? But she doesn't know how to ride."

"Well, if she doesn't, your lordship, she was pretendin' mighty good when she went by here some time ago. Never in my life have I seen . . . Not even a proper saddle. But *such* a smile. In all my years, I've never seen one the likes of it. Puts the sun to shame, it does."

Riding? Without a saddle? Mrs. O'Grady

must be mistaken. Besides, Chelsea couldn't possibly know how to ride. When could she have learned? Hayden had made it clear they'd kept her shut away from the time she was very young. Perhaps, in her more lucid times, she'd taken some riding lessons at Hawklin. He hoped so. He'd feel much better when he found her and made certain she was all right. But what if he couldn't find her?

"M'lord." Mrs. O'Grady's voice stopped him as he headed for the door. "Might I be so bold t'say somethin' more to you?" She didn't wait for his agreement. "I'm not acquainted with how you Americans do things, and that I'll be admittin'. But you're a young man and the viscountess is wee more than a girl. The two o' you are just startin' out as man an' wife, and you should be sharin' a room. Two rooms are fine for the older gentry, but not for you." The woman actually winked at him. "I think my Mr. O'Grady would tell you 'tis true."

By gad! As if he had time to think of such things now.

Brandon ran toward the stables, hoping against hope he would find Chelsea already returned. But all he found was the groom and two young stablehands mucking out the stalls.

"Which of you helped Lady Chelsea with her horse?" he demanded as the three looked up at him.

"I did, m'lord. I'm Stewart, the groom."

"Saddle a horse for me, Stewart. And tell me which way she went when she left here."

CHAPTER EIGHT

Chelsea kept Duchess reined in for as long as either of them could stand it. When they were out of sight of the manor, she turned the mare off the road and eased up on the bit. Duchess broke immediately into a rhythmic canter. Chelsea reached back and pulled off the ribbon, allowing her hair to flap against her back. The cool air stung her cheeks. She laughed aloud and gave the mare her head.

Galloping hooves carried them quickly through the tall field grasses. Chelsea could feel the power of muscles and sinew against her thighs. Her pulse raced in time with the hoofbeats. She felt alive, exhilarated. She wished they could go on forever, she and Duchess.

She saw the low fence approaching and

started to draw in the reins. Then she felt
Duchess gathering herself. Instinctively, she
leaned forward as the mare left the ground.
Her knees tightened against the sorrel coat.
They soared in perfect unison over the fence.

They had cleared three more fences, half a
dozen hedges, one stone wall, and two broad
but shallow streams before Chelsea reluctantly
slowed the mare from her madcap gallop to a
more sedate walk. Common sense told her it
was time she turned back before she became
hopelessly lost—if it weren't too late already.
But she didn't want to obey common sense.
She wanted to keep going, to keep riding, to
keep feeling the wind in her hair.

Finally, however, she was forced to admit
defeat. She had been gone a long time, and
Stewart had been concerned about her welfare
even before she left. If she didn't return soon,
he might very well come looking for her. She
didn't want to be the cause of extra trouble for
him.

She turned Duchess around and headed for
home.

Perhaps, she thought, it would be Brandon
who came looking for her. She wasn't sure she
wanted him to. He'd been in such a strange
mood last night. Every action had been so
controlled, so polite, yet she had felt some great
energy emanating from him, as if any moment
he might explode. The smoldering look in his
dark eyes had seemed almost dangerous and
left her feeling nervous and unsettled.

She wondered what it was Brandon saw in

109

her. Was she merely a girl to be pitied and cared for? Was it only compassion that had caused him to bring her here? Why had he married her? Had he been tricked into it? Or was it a Fitzgerald practice for distant cousins to wed? It certainly hadn't been because he needed money; she had figured that out for herself. She wished she felt confident enough to ask Brandon, but she didn't. If only she felt she had something to offer him, something to give him in return for all he was doing for her. . . .

She had her love, of course, but it was too soon to offer that to him. Not while the shadow of her illness still lingered between them. What if this feeling of well-being were to end tomorrow? What if she were to slip back into her madness, never to join him again? No, it was too soon yet to tell him she loved him.

Duchess reached the first of the two streams they had jumped. The mare paused and lowered her head, plunging her muzzle into the water for a long drink. While she waited, Chelsea realized the need to stretch her legs. She tossed her right leg in front of her over the horse's neck and slipped to the ground, then waited patiently for Duchess to finish drinking before leading her across the stream.

She was walking slowly, lost deep in thought, when she heard the thunder of hoofbeats. She stopped, somehow knowing what was about to happen. She lifted her gaze and waited for him to come into view.

He crested a gentle hill on his sleek black hunter. Seeing her, he reined his mount to a halt, causing it to rise up on its hind legs. Expertly, he quieted the animal, then turned toward her again.

She could feel Brandon's intense gaze upon her even though she couldn't see his face clearly. Her heart seemed to skip a beat. Nervously, she reached up to smooth her wind-ravaged hair. Her mouth felt dry.

Brandon's blood pounded in his ears. He'd found her!

She was standing beside a stream. Her wheat-colored hair fell around her shoulders in alluring tangles. Her face was turned expectantly toward him. She was like a wild, fey creature. He could almost feel the excitement of her racing heart.

What made you do this? he asked silently, wishing he understood this wood-nymph wife of his. Yet he was afraid at times of what he might discover.

He was wearing buckskin breeches and a dark brown coat. Even from this distance, Chelsea could see the broad cut of his shoulders. She could only imagine the snug fit of the breeches against his muscled thighs.

She felt her face turning red and turned away, as if afraid he would see her blushing. With clumsy hands, she grasped for the mane and swung onto Duchess's sweaty back, quickly pulling her skirts down over her legs, but there was no concealing her bare feet. When she looked up again, Brandon was riding down the hill. There was little she could do but wait for him to reach her.

He stopped his mount a few yards away. His expression was grim as his eyes perused her carefully. "You're a long way from home, Lady Chelsea," he said at last. She saw his eyes widen a fraction when his gaze reached her feet.

"It was a lovely day for a ride." She fidgeted with the buttons of her blouse and tried to pull her feet up under her skirt.

Brandon's gaze shifted to Duchess. "Why did you insist on this horse?"

"Stewart told you?"

"I asked what horse you were riding."

"It wasn't his fault. I really did insist. He wanted to put me on a gentler mare, but I wouldn't have it. Please don't be angry with Stewart."

The tension around his mouth eased. It seemed he might almost smile. "Stewart told me you insisted."

"When I looked out the window this morning, I saw him exercising her. I just wanted so badly to ride her."

"Sheherazade is not known to be an ideal saddle-horse for a lady."

Chelsea's hand stroked the mare's neck. "You mean Duchess? But we've had a lovely time. She hasn't given me any trouble."

Now he grinned. "So you've managed to change her name as well as calm her temperament."

Chelsea relaxed. She returned his smile.

"Come on. It's time we were getting back."
He turned the black and they began walking.

"Tell me," Chelsea said after several minutes
of comfortable silence. "How did you know her
name when we only just came here yesterday?"

"Easy. The horses at Teakwood came with us
from America. Grandfather heard that Stewart
is an excellent horseman, and so he sent them
to be stabled and schooled here. Sheherazade
comes from a long line of champions." Brandon's eyes moved from the horse to Chelsea.
"She's always been one of my favorites, ever
since she was a filly." His voice was low and
intimate. It was almost as if he weren't talking
about a horse.

Chelsea felt the warmth returning to her
cheeks and glanced away.

"Chelsea?" His voice was still warm and
intimate.

"Yes?" she responded without looking at
him.

"Sheherazade—I mean Duchess. . . . She's
yours."

Maitland Conover swept into the entrance
hall at Bellfort, growling at the butler as she
passed him, "Sanders, send Paul to me at once.
I'll be in the drawing room."

She didn't wait to hear his reply. She knew
the footman would be rushing in very shortly.
If the servants at Bellfort knew anything, it was
to hasten to do Maitland's bidding or they
would find themselves out on their ears without
reference.

She tossed her gloves onto a satin brocade sofa, threw her cloak across a matching chair, then walked over to the window and glared outside. Her foul temper hadn't improved since the moment she learned Brandon Fitzgerald had left Hawklin with that half-wit bride of his. He must have known she extended her stay at Rosemont just so they could become better acquainted. Well, he wasn't going to slight her so easily. She *would* see him paying court to her before she was through. As for Alanna Fitzgerald, it would be interesting to find out more about the chit before teaching her a lesson or two.

"Lady Bellfort?"

She turned from the window, pushing aside her rosewood and white wool skirt. "Paul, there you are. I want you to take a message over to Teakwood Manor at once."

"Yes, my lady."

"You're to deliver it personally to Lord Coleford and wait for his reply. Do you understand me? Personally to the viscount."

"Yes, my lady."

Maitland crossed the room to the secretary, drew out a piece of paper, and dipped the pen in the inkwell.

Dear Viscount Coleford, she wrote. *I was pleased to learn you are visiting Teakwood and are now my nearest neighbor. I am planning a party at Bellfort in your and your wife's honor on Friday next. Please advise my servant Paul if you will be available on that day or if a different day would be better.* She thought a moment more, then smiled and signed it, *Your devoted friend, Maitland Conover, Marchioness of Bellfort.*

She rose from the secretary and turned with the note outstretched in her hand, then suddenly drew it back and wrinkled it in her fingers. "No, Paul. I've changed my mind. That will be all."

The footman bowed and left the room.

Maitland crossed the room to a large, gilt-framed mirror. Her hand patted her auburn hair, then flicked at an imagined object on the collar of her gown.

"No," she said to her reflection. "This is an invitation that should be given personally. You won't turn me down again, my dear colonial viscount. Maitland Conover always gets what she wants. Always."

Brandon didn't know how it was that Chelsea had swept away his anxiety and displeasure at her disappearance so easily. He'd been frantic when he'd learned she'd taken Sheherazade, certain that he would find her lying beside the road somewhere, her delicate bones broken. Or worse, that she had taken flight, never to be found. Instead he had discovered her with healthy color in her cheeks and a new brightness in her eyes that intrigued and delighted him.

Her concern for Stewart had erased his anger. He had seen too many people of wealth and position who thought of their servants as merely that—servants, not people. It pleased him that she had jumped to the groom's defense. Come to think of it, she'd even defended Sheherazade to him.

It hadn't been his intention to give the flaxen mare to anyone. She was sired by Lawrence's best Arabian stallion, and her dam had been given to Brandon when he was still a boy. Sheherazade had always held a special place in Brandon's heart. But Chelsea's sharp eye for good horseflesh had surprised him and won his prompt approval. Giving her the mare had just seemed right. The two were much alike— spirited, beautiful, elusive. No wonder Chelsea had tamed the horse so easily.

Brandon and Chelsea were riding toward the stable, still chatting amiably, when an open carriage rolled up the drive. Brandon dismounted, then walked behind his gelding to help Chelsea down. When he turned around, Maitland Conover had descended from her carriage and was strolling toward them.

"My dear viscount, what a pleasure." Her eyes flicked over to Chelsea. "Good heavens! Is that you, Lady Alanna? You look dreadful. Has there been an accident?"

Chelsea's hand tried fruitlessly to smooth her wind-tangled, silvery blond hair.

Maitland didn't wait for a reply. She stopped in front of Brandon and closed her gloved fingers over his forearm in a familiar gesture. "I was so delighted to learn you had come to Teakwood at just the time I returned to Bellfort. What a marvelous coincidence! Or was it a coincidence, my lord? Perhaps you followed me to the country?" She glanced at Chelsea, as if punctuating her last question to give it credence.

Brandon followed the gaze and noted Chelsea's look of surprise. Her eyes met his, revealing hurt in their blue depths.

Maitland, however, seemed triumphant. "And it is such a *perfect* time," she continued. "I have been meaning to have a ball at Bellfort. Now we can do it in your honor. Everyone is just dying to meet you. Oh, and your wife too, naturally. You simply can't say no. It would hurt everyone's feelings. Especially mine."

Irritated, Brandon extricated himself from her grasp and took hold of Chelsea's arm. "I'm not sure my wife is up to such a thing at the moment. She's been ill."

"Oh! How thoughtless of me." Maitland's face fell and she offered a look of pity toward Chelsea. "I should have known you wouldn't want to be subjected to so many people. After all, you've had no experience with this sort of social function and you—"

"Brandon and I would be delighted to come to your ball, Lady Bellfort. I'm feeling ever so much better, and I can't think of anything I would rather do."

Brandon glanced in surprise toward Chelsea. The icy spark in her blue eyes, matching the confident tone of her voice, had replaced her wounded expression of moments before.

"Are you sure?" he asked softly.

She never hesitated. "I'm sure."

He turned toward Maitland once again. "Then we'll be there."

Maitland's smile was barely civil. There was an angry flush on her cheeks. "Good. It's settled. Shall we say, in two weeks? On Friday. A masquerade, I think. Yes, a masquerade would be fun." She tilted her head to one side, offering Brandon a coquettish glance with her almondy eyes, trying hard to establish at least the possibility of intimacy with him. "Well, I must be off. Do come see me at Bellfort before the ball. Any time you're out riding."

"Perhaps," he replied, bored with her obvious flirtation and wishing she would leave.

"Good day, Lady Bellfort," Chelsea said in gentle dismissal.

"Good day . . . Chelsea, is it? Quaint little name. You must tell me sometime why you took such a nickname." To Brandon, she said, "Would you mind terribly walking me to my carriage?"

"Not at all, Lady Bellfort." He couldn't resist, however, goading her just a little more, if only for Chelsea's sake. He bent forward and kissed Chelsea's cheek. "I'll only be a moment, dear," he said in a low voice.

Her eyes widened, wonderment filling their cool blue depths. Then she smiled and whispered, "I'll be waiting."

Chelsea watched as Brandon escorted Maitland around the side of the house to her carriage. She was filled with a dozen or more conflicting emotions. She'd felt overwhelmed and unsure of herself when she saw the woman descending from her carriage. That feeling had intensified with the marchioness's comment about her appearance.

But when Maitland had taken hold so possessively of Brandon's arm, anger had flared. It was obvious she was flirting with Brandon, trying to steal Chelsea's husband right from under her nose—and too damned confident that she could do just that. Indignation had prompted Chelsea to accept the invitation to the ball.

Later, when she had more time to think about it, she would give in to the insecurities that were plaguing her over the idea of meeting so many people, but for now, she would rather bask in the warm glow that lingered from Brandon's kiss and his sweet words.

She knew he had done it to irritate Maitland. She was glad he didn't seem inclined to take the woman up on her obvious invitation for a more personal arrangement.

But even if it had been only for Maitland's benefit, she couldn't help wishing it meant more.

And maybe, just maybe, it did.

CHAPTER NINE

The next few days were too blissful for Chelsea to find time to worry about Maitland and her masquerade ball. A dressmaker arrived from London to provide Chelsea with the necessary wardrobe—morning gowns and traveling dresses and riding habits and ball gowns. She ordered costumes for the masquerade ball, including one for the duke should he decide to attend. She walked in the cool morning mist through dew-covered grass, and evenings she lolled by the warm fire.

But best of all, Brandon and Chelsea spent hours on horseback—Chelsea properly seated sidesaddle—familiarizing themselves with the rolling English countryside. Sometimes they would dismount and stroll side by side through the fields of clover. Once, Brandon plucked some wildflowers from beside a stream and slipped them into her hair just above her ear.

Since she had no memory of her own past, she plied him with a thousand questions about his boyhood, about his brother, about Foxworth Iron Works, about America. Only one question did she avoid purposefully.

Why did you marry me, Brandon?

It came to mind often enough, but she was afraid to ask it. She wasn't ready to hear him admit it was for less than love. And, of course, it couldn't have been for love. He hadn't even known her then. But he knew her now. If he could but learn to love her. . . .

Lawrence was surprised at how quickly the memories returned, how familiar it all looked to him. It was as if he'd only been gone for a fortnight rather than nearly three-score years.

He gazed out the carriage window. Gad, it was good to be back in England. It was good to have his title back—Lawrence Fitzgerald, the Duke of Foxworth. It was good to walk on his own lands and to stroll through the rooms of Hawklin Hall. It was good to travel to his other estates—Teakwood, Ravencrest, Sunningford, Terrington, Selsey—in one of his fine carriages.

Sometimes he tried not to be so pleased about it, especially when he thought of the sacrifice Brandon had made to make it all possible, marrying a girl held to reality by such a thin thread. It was all the more difficult for Lawrence because he truly liked the girl. From the moment he'd met her, Chelsea had taken a place in his old man's heart, a place he knew she would never relinquish.

It had saddened him to have Brandon leave with her so abruptly, but he'd agreed it must be done. After her last nightmare, how could he refuse to let Brandon take her away? She'd been so lost and frightened, so confused.

He shook his head. Now it was he who was confused. He'd thought Chelsea's illness must be growing worse, that soon she would have to be locked up again, that she would forget what little she remembered until finally she was entirely lost in some private world of terror. Instead, he'd received a note from Brandon, asking him to come to Teakwood and join them for the Marchioness of Bellfort's masquerade ball. That certainly didn't sound like a man whose wife was teetering on the brink of insanity.

The driver turned the ducal coach off the main road, and Lawrence knew they were little more than a half an hour from Teakwood. Soon he would see the stone pillar that marked the southwest corner of the Teakwood estate.

He was leaning forward for a better look when he felt the carriage slowing to a halt. "Russell, what . . . ?" he began. Then he saw the two riders racing across the field.

The man couldn't be anyone but Brandon.

Lawrence's eyesight wasn't what it used to be, but he could still spot a good horseman when he saw one, even from a distance. And there was no better horseman than Brandon Fitzgerald. His grandson was riding a shiny black steed; it had to be Warrior, one of the thoroughbred stallions they'd brought with them from Foxworth Place.

And, of course, the girl was Chelsea. Her bonnet had slipped from her head and was bouncing against her back. If her hair had ever been captured in a proper bun, it had long since escaped into disarray. She was wearing a sunshine-yellow riding habit, a cheerful color that brought a smile to Lawrence's mouth— but which was nothing to his pleasure with the way she sat her horse.

That horse!

Lawrence opened the carriage door and stepped down. He couldn't believe it. Was Brandon actually letting that girl ride Sheherazade? That mare was a handful for a grown man. He'd despaired more than once that she would ever be a decent saddle horse. Sheherazade loved to take the bit in her mouth and test a rider's skill.

Brandon and Chelsea reached the low stone wall. Their mounts soared gracefully over it, their forelegs touching the ground in unison. Then the riders pulled in on the reins and slowed the horses to a gentle canter as they approached Lawrence and his carriage.

"Grandfather!" Brandon called in greeting.

"I was beginning to think you weren't coming."

"And miss a masquerade at Bellfort? Not hardly." His gaze shifted to Chelsea.

Was this the girl who'd shivered in fear from her dreams? The girl who had begged Brandon to take her away from Hawklin Hall? If so, Brandon had been wise to give in to her request. She was positively exquisite. Her bright blue eyes sparkled with pleasure. She was smiling a smile that would win the hearts of kings and paupers around the world. She sat with confidence aboard the saucy Sheherazade.

"Chelsea, my dear, you're looking wonderful. Teakwood agrees with you then?"

"I like it here very much, Grandfather." She leaned over and took the hand he raised to her, squeezing his wrinkled fingers within her yellow gloves. "I'm glad you've come."

"Who taught you to ride like that?" Lawrence asked without thinking.

A shadow passed across Chelsea's face. "I don't know that anyone did."

"Terribly thoughtless of me, my girl. I'm sorry. But it doesn't matter who taught you or that you can't remember. You sit a horse with great style. You and Brandon look good together."

Lawrence glanced back at his grandson. It warmed his heart to see the look in the boy's eyes. Brandon was falling in love with Chelsea. How perfectly delightful!

* * *

124

Sara rose from the settee, the invitation in her hand. She wore a strained expression on her attractive face. "Hayden, look at this."

Hayden took the elegant notepaper from her and scanned the scrawled handwriting, then went back and read it much more deliberately. "Good lord, Sara. He's taken the girl out into society," he said in a horrified whisper. "What's that fool nanny of hers doing, letting this happen?"

"Whatever shall we do? If our friends find out about her. . . ."

"Well, they won't. We'll go up there at once. I'll have a long talk with Brandon Fitzgerald. I'll convince him everyone's much better off if she's kept safely in her rooms."

"Hayden, what if . . . ?"

"Don't say it," he snapped. "Don't even think it."

Chelsea was alone in the parlor, struggling with a piece of embroidery. Her fingers felt useless as she tried to keep her stitches straight and tiny. Frustrated, she set the handiwork aside and rose from the sofa, walking slowly to the window at the back of the house.

A fine, mist-like rain was falling, turning the afternoon a dismal gray. The rain had cancelled her daily ride with Brandon, but it had offered an opportunity for Brandon and Lawrence to accomplish some estate business. The two men had left in the closed carriage over two hours ago.

When the knock came at the door, Chelsea

didn't wait for Mrs. O'Grady to poke her head out of the kitchen. She crossed the parlor and opened the door.

The Earl of Roxley was standing just under the eaves. Clad in a black coat and a hat dripping with rain, he grinned when he saw who was standing there. "Lady Coleford?"

She nodded.

"Do you remember me?"

"I remember you. Roxley to your friends, correct?" She smiled back at him.

"Correct." He cleared his throat. "Excuse me for being so bold, but you look positively wonderful. I scarcely recognized you. I mean, your health has improved."

A giggle rose in her throat. "Why, thank you for noticing, my lord." She opened the door wider. "Please come in."

The earl stepped through the doorway. "My sister told me you and Brandon had come to Teakwood to stay, and I couldn't resist dropping in for a visit."

Chelsea glanced outside, almost afraid she would see Maitland coming up the walk. Relieved to find no one behind Roxley, she closed the door. "Brandon and the duke are away on business at the moment. But I'd love some company. Won't you sit down and join me for tea?"

"I'd be delighted."

"I'll tell Mrs. O'Grady." She motioned with her hands. "Why don't you put your wet things on the chair by the door? I'll be right back."

When she returned, she found Roxley standing with his back to the fireplace. He raked his fingers through his unruly black hair, a gesture that neither improved nor worsened its condition. Still, despite his dampened appearance, he was indisputably handsome with his black hair and eyes and his swarthy complexion. He was shorter by half a head than Brandon and had a much slighter build, but his smaller stature didn't make him look any less strong. Most attractive about him, however, was his contagious smile. Chelsea liked it best.

Suddenly she realized she was staring at him—and that he was staring right back. She blushed with embarrassment.

"Mrs. O'Grady will bring the tea in a moment. Please sit down, my lord."

"I thought we'd settled that title business. I'm Roxley and you're Chelsea."

She nodded, then slipped into a waiting chair.

"Are you ready for Maitland's *little* party?"

Chelsea caught his exaggeration of the word and guessed at what he was telling her. Nothing Maitland Conover did was probably ever small in any meaning of the word. "I think so," she answered, her uncertainty only thinly disguised.

"Don't let my sister frighten you, Chelsea. She'll try to bully you, but I have the feeling you can stand up to her." He sat down in a chair across from hers. Leaning forward, his forearms on his knees, he added, "And if you ever need any help, I hope you'll remember I'm your friend." There was no jesting in his expression now. His dark eyes bespoke frank admiration and warmth.

"Thank you, Roxley." There was a slight quiver in her voice. "You know, I don't think I've ever had a friend before."

He waved off her thanks, and his grin returned. "Well, even if there are others, I'd surely be your oldest. I took a fancy to you the first time I saw you, years and years ago."

"We met when I was a girl?" Chelsea's hands were clasped in her lap. She worried her lower lip before speaking again. "Roxley, do you know about my illness?" Her blue gaze didn't waver. She wanted an honest answer, not something to pacify her.

"I heard . . . rumors. A very long time ago."

"And do others know?"

Roxley met her gaze, his black eyes tender and concerned. "Only suspicions."

"I don't remember anything before the past few weeks. It's as if I'd been sleeping all my life and just awakened before Brandon came. But sometimes I have nightmares. They seem so real." She glanced down at her hands. "There was a fire, Roxley. I've only seen it in my dreams and they told me it never happened, but I know it did."

Roxley leaned forward and put his hand over hers, but he didn't speak.

"Tell me about when I was a girl," Chelsea asked at last, her voice soft and pleading.

"There's not much to tell. You were riding in a pony cart pulled by a dappled Shetland. Your nanny was with you. A short woman with lots of red hair. I was riding a new hunter and had jumped the fence between our properties when I came upon you. Your hair was a yellow-gold then, all tied up in tight curls, and your eyes were such a deep blue. You must have been about seven or eight years old. You didn't speak to me, but I remember thinking you had a very . . . a very strange smile."

She heard his hesitation and knew he was being careful, trying not to hurt her. She smiled at him, offering silent thanks.

"You've a much prettier smile now," he said.

"Funny you should like my smile so much. I was thinking earlier that it's what I like best about you, too. Your smile, I mean."

"I say, I hope there's more to me to like than just my crooked teeth."

"Your teeth aren't the least bit crooked, my lord. I would have noticed."

"You're quite mistaken, my lady." He rose from his chair and leaned forward. "Look here." And he opened his mouth wide, pointing at his bottom row of teeth.

It was at that moment the front door opened and admitted Brandon and Lawrence.

Brandon's eyes widened. A man was standing before Chelsea, leaning down toward her, their heads close together. Chelsea was wearing a mirthful expression; she looked as if she'd been laughing a lot. When they heard the door close, they both turned their heads. It was then that he recognized Roxley, but the fellow's identity didn't make him feel any better about the intimate nature of the scene that had greeted him.

Roxley straightened abruptly. "Here they are, Chelsea." He crossed the parlor and shook the duke's hand. "Your grace, you're looking well." Then he turned toward Brandon. "It's good to see you again, Brand. When Maitland invited me down for a masquerade ball, I thought I'd beg off until I saw it was for you and Chelsea. Then I knew I couldn't stay away."

"I tried to beg off myself," Brandon returned, "but Chelsea insisted she was feeling well enough."

"She looks wonderful."

Brandon frowned as he turned away from the earl. "Yes, doesn't she." He dropped his coat across the bannister at the base of the stairs, then walked over to Chelsea. He bent forward and lightly kissed her cheek. "I'm glad you've had such an enjoyable afternoon, my dear."

But he wasn't glad. He felt more than a little irritated at having found her in such obviously good spirits without him. The feeling surprised him. Never having been jealous of anyone before, he didn't recognize the emotion for what it was at first.

"I've invited the earl to stay for tea, Brandon."

"I hope you don't mind," Roxley said. "If you've got other plans . . ." He looked at Brandon with a puzzled expression.

Brandon realized how coolly he had received

Roxley. He mentally shook himself and offered a smile. "Mind? But of course, you must stay for tea. And look. Here's Mrs. O'Grady with the tray now."

Rain spattered against the window glass and wind rattled the shutters. Inside, the parlor was pleasant with a roaring fire on the hearth. Roxley had left several hours before, and Lawrence had already bade the young couple good night. Now they sat alone, the room silent except for the crackle of burning wood.

Chelsea felt nervous and kept fidgeting with the lace on her coral-colored blouse. Brandon had been acting so strangely this afternoon, not at all like the easygoing man she'd been riding with daily. It seemed there'd rarely been a moment all afternoon and on through supper when he hadn't been observing her with probing eyes. She knew if she looked across at him, she would discover him staring at her even now.

He was seated in a deep leather chair, smoking his pipe. The tobacco had a pleasant scent, and when she glanced surreptitiously up through her lashes, she could see the smoke forming a halo above his head. Yet he looked anything but angelic. The fire cast harsh light and conflicting shadows across his face. There was nothing soft nor gentle about him tonight. He was like some medieval warrior, she thought, just home from doing battle. His dark eyes looked as black as night, and they were, indeed, looking at her.

As she watched, Brandon leaned toward the table at his side and set his pipe down, then rose slowly from the chair. With measured steps, he came toward her. She held her breath and waited for him to reach her.

"Chelsea."

He held out his hand. When she took it, he drew her to her feet. His fingers cupped her chin and forced her head back. She shivered and closed her eyes.

His mouth touched hers with surprising gentleness, sending a shock wave down the length of her. His hands slid to the sides of her head, as if holding her there, forcing her to stay. In truth, she couldn't have moved. She felt rooted to the spot, helpless against the emotional and physical sensations raging within her.

The kiss deepened, lengthened, demanded. His probing tongue danced across her lips until she gave in to its insistence, allowing their tongues to meet. A hot spear seemed to set her vitals ablaze. She whimpered and placed her palms against his chest to steady herself.

When he lifted his head, she felt bereft, cheated. Reluctantly, she opened her eyes once more, meeting his hard gaze.

"It's time we went to bed." His voice was husky with emotion.

Gooseflesh rose on her arms. She nodded.

His hand beneath her elbow, they climbed the stairs. Chelsea could scarcely breathe, afraid yet . . .

Brandon stopped before the door to her bedchamber. He bent low and placed a gentle kiss on her forehead. "Good night, Chelsea," he whispered. Then he turned and left her standing there while he walked to his own bedroom and entered it alone.

Leaving Chelsea was the most difficult thing he'd ever done. But Brandon had done a lot of thinking that evening and he'd come to some hard decisions.

He had watched Chelsea with Roxley, and suddenly he'd realized that she'd never had a beau. Chelsea had never ridden in the park with anyone, never gone to a soirée, never flirted on the dance floor. She'd never had the chance to fall in love. Chelsea was an innocent.

It had been one thing to marry a girl by proxy when he thought she was, at the very least, aware of the arrangement, if not exactly enthusiastic about it. It was an entirely different thing to marry a girl who'd been locked up for most of her life. If he weren't so damned fond of her, it might be different. If she weren't so engaging and bright and pretty . . . She was all these things and more, and he wanted her to be happy as well.

He could have seduced her tonight. He could have seduced her many times before tonight. She was fond enough of him, of that he was certain. But he was the only man she'd ever been truly acquainted with. What if she cared for him only because she had no one else to compare him to? What if she were given the chance to fall in love with someone else, someone like Roxley? Would she?

And so Brandon had made his decision. He would win his wife's affections, but she would have plenty of opportunities to know him—and others—before they consummated this marriage of theirs. And if, by some wild chance, he did not win her love . . . Well, he would face that if he was forced to, but he didn't give the idea much credence. Brandon was no amateur when it came to the fairer sex.

Brandon cast aside his shirt and walked bare-chested to the window. The storm was still blowing, the night as black as ink. He rested his hot forehead against the cool glass and prayed for the night to pass quickly. Wanting her as he did, he knew there would be little sleep for him.

CHAPTER
TEN
___

Chelsea didn't sleep well either.

She felt grumpy when she arose late the next morning. Throughout the night, she had searched her mind time and again for a reason for Brandon's behavior but couldn't think of any. She was his wife. Why didn't he treat her that way? Didn't he care for her at least a little?

Well, Chelsea Fitzgerald wasn't about to give up so easily. She *was* his wife, and she meant to make him care for her *more* than a little. Maybe what he needed was a good shaking up. Perhaps, since she belonged to him in the eyes of the law and man, he was too confident of her affections. Perhaps the ball might be just the place to show him Chelsea wasn't entirely without the ability to attract the opposite sex.

She grinned, her good humor returning as a plan formed in her mind. She would make Brandon jealous. She would make him see her as attractive. She would make him want her if it was the last thing she ever did. She might be a novice, but she was a quick learner. Look at how quickly she'd mastered the horse. Impishly she wondered if a husband was so different.

She was seated at her dressing table, vigorously brushing her pale tresses, when she heard a commotion downstairs. Curious, she rose and hurried across her bedchamber on bare feet. She opened the door a fraction and peered out.

"Faith! But this *is* a surprise," she heard Mrs. O'Grady saying.

"Is Lawrence about?" a male voice asked.

"I'll call him at once, Lord Fitzgerald. If you and m'lady would care to wait . . ."

"Just hurry, O'Grady," Sara snapped irritably.

Chelsea closed the door and leaned her back against it. Her parents had arrived.

She felt little kinship with the former duke and duchess. The few times she remembered their visiting her had been strained. She sensed they were nervous around her. They always seemed to be waiting for her to do or say something wild.

But perhaps they had reason to think that way.

Chelsea returned to her bed and sat on the white coverlet. She closed her eyes and tried to summon Hayden and Sara to mind, tried to see their faces, tried to imagine them as caring, loving parents. She couldn't do it.

The door opened without an announcing knock.

"Mornin', luv."

Her eyes flew open. "Molly!"

The older woman entered the room and hurried forward, her arms outstretched. Chelsea slipped into them.

"Oh, my girl, my sweet girl. How I've missed you."

"I haven't been gone so terribly long."

Molly stepped back and studied her with a searching gaze. "There's no sense in askin' how you've been. You've a glow of happiness about you."

"Do I?"

"That you do." There was a wistful note in her words. "You won't be needin' your old nanny much longer, I'm afraid."

Chelsea gave the woman another quick hug. "Of course, I'll need you. Haven't you always taken care of me?"

Molly dabbed at a sudden tear, but made no reply.

"Did you come with . . . with my parents?"

"I did. Lord Fitzgerald came to Hawklin to see your husband, and when he found you weren't there, he was right upset, and that's a fact. He said at the very least I should be here to tend to you, and so he packed me up and brought me to you." Molly sniffed away the last of the tears, then stiffened her chin. "Well, now. We'd best see you dressed and downstairs.

They'll be wantin' to see you."

Chelsea nodded, but she wasn't eager to face them, especially knowing her father disapproved of her being away from Hawklin Hall. What if he convinced Brandon to take her back there and lock her in her rooms once again?

Molly shrugged out of her coat and draped it across the foot of the bed. "What dress is it you wish to wear, luv?" she asked as she moved toward the wardrobe. "My! You've so many to choose from."

"What?"

"Which one, dear? There's so many . . ."

"Oh, it doesn't matter, Molly. Anything."

Hayden paced back and forth across the small library at the back of the house. Lawrence was seated in a high-backed chair at the end of the long ebony table. Brandon was standing to the side, his hand on one of the carved spindles that rose above the padded leather back of the chair. Both men were observing Hayden with less than friendly eyes.

"You don't understand the delicacy of the situation. I know this girl. I've seen what can happen, just when you think everything is going fine and she's going to be normal."

"That may be true, Hayden," Brandon said in a carefully controlled voice, "but I will make the decisions about what is best for my wife."

"And you're going to take her to that blasted ball of Maitland Conover's? Have you considered everything that could go wrong?" Hayden's hands smacked down on the table.

"Good heavens, man, she's never been out in society before. She'll make a fool of us all. Don't you understand that we'll be ruined if the truth leaks out about her? Sara and I won't be able to hold our heads up in polite society."

"Balderdash!" Lawrence grumbled. "Hayden, you're a fool."

Hayden straightened as if he'd been struck. "You may think me a fool now, but you'll regret it when she proves me right. What if she starts telling people she thinks she's someone else? This . . . this Catherine or Charlotte or . . ."

"Chelsea," Brandon finished for him. "She likes to be called Chelsea."

"Do you see? She doesn't know who she is!"

"It's hardly criminal or insane to have a nickname." Brandon was disgusted with the man. If it were up to him, he would toss the pompous ass out on his ear.

Hayden's face was taut, his mouth grim. "*Alanna* is my daughter. I agreed to this marriage arrangement so that Lawrence could return to England without our family being involved in a scandal. And I certainly thought you would have sense enough to take care of her as we have through the years." He glared at Brandon with accusing eyes. "Do you think I don't know what can happen? And of all places, you're planning to take her to Maitland's ball. That woman is a shark. She's just waiting to tear Alanna to pieces."

Brandon had to admit that Hayden was right about the marchioness. He was certain that tearing Chelsea to pieces was exactly what

Maitland planned to do. But he wouldn't allow it. "Chelsea wants to go to this ball, Hayden, and I mean to take her. Don't worry about the marchioness. I'll take care of my wife."

"We'll live to regret this," Hayden said ominously. "Mark my words."

Chelsea's hand slipped from the knob as she backed silently away from the library door. Tears stung her pale blue eyes. Her accidental eavesdropping had gleaned the answer to a question she'd been too afraid to ask. Brandon had married her to silence a scandal— something to do with his grandfather returning to England. Her father had bartered her, and Brandon had purchased her. She'd known it had to be something like that, whether she'd admitted it to herself or not. So why did hearing it hurt so very much?

But even worse, they all expected her to fall to pieces at the ball. Even Brandon planned to watch over her, ready to whisk her away if she should act like a fool. Or worse yet, if anyone should guess she was a lunatic. And she'd thought he'd seen how much better she was. She'd thought he might be growing to care for her, but apparently he only felt sorry for her.

"Chelsea?"

She turned, surprised to hear her name whispered near her ear. Especially since Molly was always reluctant to call her Chelsea.

"Don't let them frighten you, luv. Don't you quit. You forget the sickness that kept my Alanna locked up before." Molly squeezed

Chelsea's shoulders. "There's naught wrong with you save a little forgetfulness. You're going t'be a duchess one day. You go to that ball and you show them what you're made of. Do you hear me, Chelsea girl? You show them all."

Chelsea threw her arms around the woman's neck and hugged her quickly as she swallowed back the tears.

Molly patted her back with mute assurance, then said gruffly, "Now. Enough of that. You march in there and let that so-called father of yours have a glimpse of the woman you've become." She gave Chelsea a little push. "Go on."

Chelsea nodded and sniffed, then lifted her chin, tossed back her shoulders, and headed into the lion's den.

Brandon turned as the door opened, admitting Chelsea. His heart immediately swelled with pride. Her silvery-yellow hair was gathered high on her head, exposing to advantage her long white throat. Wispy tendrils curled at her nape and near her temples. Her morning gown was a cherry-colored silk striped concoction of wool chamois. It had a full bustle at the back and was trimmed with bright blue ribbons. She moved gracefully across the room to his side.

"Good morning, Brandon," she said, as if she greeted him that way every day.

He caught the nervous quiver in her voice. He took hold of her hand and squeezed her fingers as he whispered in her ear, "The morning pales beside your beauty."

She thanked him with her eyes, then turned toward Lawrence, leaned forward, and kissed his cheek. "Good morning, Grandfather."

"By gad, Chelsea, my girl. You make an old man wish he were a far sight younger."

Her cheeks blushed the same attractive shade of cherry pink as her dress.

Hayden cleared his throat. "Don't you have a good morning for me, Alanna?"

Chelsea turned slowly toward him. "We didn't expect you . . . Father."

Brandon noticed how she stumbled over the word. He noticed the way the tiny crease formed between her brows as she contemplated it on her tongue. He wondered if there had ever been a time when father and daughter were close. He doubted it.

"We're on our way to Bellfort for the ball tomorrow night. Lady Bellfort invited us to stay there as her guests. It's too far to return to London after the masquerade, and Teakwood is already bursting at the seams." His gaze flicked over the room before he added, "This place never was a favorite of mine. Far too small for my taste."

Chelsea skirted the long table on her way to place a dutiful kiss on her father's brow. "Then you're fortunate you're no longer the duke. Grandfather Lawrence loves Teakwood Manor." Chelsea's words were spoken with a sweet smile.

Brandon muffled a laugh.

Hayden's face reddened and his neck seemed to bulge, but Chelsea didn't even notice. She

142

had already turned toward Lawrence and Brandon. "Mrs. O'Grady tells me our costumes have arrived for tomorrow's ball."

"Smashing!" Lawrence said as he rose from his chair. "I can't wait to see what you've chosen for me, my dear."

"Well . . ." Uncertainty clouded her pretty face once again. "I hope you'll like them. They might be a little . . . unusual." She glanced at Brandon.

He wondered if he could keep his promise to himself to move slowly, to allow her time to judge him against others and choose him of her own accord. When he was with her, when she looked at him that way, he wanted nothing more than to spirit her away to some remote and lonely place where they could spend every moment together.

"I'm sure we'll all think them smashing, Chelsea," he said, and meant it.

"I hope so. I do very much hope so."

Sara set the fine china cup back on its saucer and inclined her head to one side. "You really have been naughty, Brandon. All of London's been dying to meet you. You are somewhat of a mystery, you know. Coming here with Lawrence and marrying someone no one has ever seen." She clucked her tongue and leaned forward, providing him with a generous glimpse of cleavage. "And turning down so many invitations. It will never do if you're to be accepted."

Chelsea watched her mother with astonishment. Sara was actually *flirting* with Brandon.

"The word has already spread that you will be at Lady Bellfort's ball. I hope you will find time to dance with your mother-in-law." She batted her eyes. "Oh my! How I do hate that term. It makes me feel ever so much older than I am."

Brandon's returned look was bland and non-committal.

"There will be hundreds of less fortunate women who will be hoping you'll dance with them and shall not have the pleasure. I expect you to make them jealous of me."

Brandon grinned affably. "I shall try to dance with you, Lady Fitzgerald, but I shall most probably be too busy dancing with my own wife and fighting off her growing number of admirers."

Chelsea hadn't even a moment to bask in the tenderness of the gaze he turned her way.

"Chel—Alanna?" Sara's head jerked around. Her dark blue eyes stared, unbelieving, at Chelsea. "You're going?"

She was just ready to answer, "Of course, we're going. The ball is in our honor." But Sara hadn't really expected an answer.

She had turned a cold blue glare on her husband. "Hayden? Hayden, did you know Chelsea still intends to go tomorrow night?"

He sighed. "Yes, I know. There was no talking Brandon out of it. He doesn't believe we know what is best for . . ."

Hayden's voice continued, but Chelsea didn't hear what he was saying. She closed her eyes, fighting the anger that swelled in her, making the pounding in her head worse. What had begun as a small headache at her temples had spread up her forehead and down the back of her neck. Why did they talk about her like that, as if she weren't even present in the room? Didn't she have ears? Didn't she have feelings?

She rose suddenly from her chair, dropping her napkin onto the table next to her plate. "Excuse me." Her voice was soft and unruffled, belying the heat of anger that still surged through her veins. "It is my decision whether or not I attend this ball. Why does everyone persist in trying to decide what is best for me? I want to go, and I'm going to go. And if you fear I will embarrass you, then . . . then . . ."

Her resolve suddenly vanished. Unable to finish her sentence, she turned and fled. Once in her room, she shed her bustled gown and petticoats and crawled beneath the covers on her bed wearing her chemise and drawers.

Like an ostrich burying its head in the sand, she thought as she drew the comforter up high. Her chin quivered and tears stung the back of her eyes.

She hated to cry. But it hurt to be so unwanted by those who should love her. It hurt to be treated as if she didn't matter or as if she weren't even in the same room. It mattered not that her parents were selfish, shallow people. She wanted them to love her. She wanted *someone* to love her. *Someone* to believe in her.

The door opened. Brandon's tall frame filled the doorway. She looked at him a moment, then turned her face toward the wall and hoped he would go away. He was a part of her confusion. One moment it seemed that he might care for her, that he liked to be in her company. The next, he could be glowering at her with one of his dark stares, a look that left her quavering in her slippers. Right now she didn't think she could deal with him and the conflicting emotions that came with him.

"Chelsea?" He was standing beside the bed.

"Not now. Please, Brandon," she said in a hoarse whisper.

"I'm not afraid you'll embarrass me tomorrow night. I'm going to be the proudest man there."

CHAPTER ELEVEN

Mrs. O'Grady stood off to her left, Molly to her right.

"You're like nothin' I've ever seen, m'lady," Mrs. O'Grady sighed. "Fit for a king, or my name's not Kathleen O'Grady."

Chelsea stared at her reflection in the mirror and wondered if she had the audacity to wear something so outlandish. When she'd thought up the costumes, they'd merely seemed unusual. Looking at herself now, she thought perhaps she'd gone too far.

The soft white doeskin dress emphasized the swell of her breasts and curve of her hips. A brightly beaded belt called attention to her small waist. The sleeves had long fringe all along the seam that swayed with every move she made. The skirt stopped at mid-calf, then continued in leather fringe almost to the floor. When she walked, a surprising amount of leg was visible. Her feet were clad in leather moccasins, ablaze with brightly-colored beads. Her pale hair hung in two braids down her back. Several colorful feathers were woven into the braids behind each ear, and tiny leather thongs knotted the ends just below her waist.

"Don't forget this, my lady," Molly said, holding out the matching white mask.

"I believe his grace and his lordship are awaiting you downstairs." Mrs. O'Grady held up a doeskin cape and waited for Chelsea to turn her back to it.

Chelsea's stomach was tied in knots, yet it wasn't all fear and trepidation. Excitement was mingled in, too. For each thought she had of bolting her bedroom door and refusing to go, she had two others filled with eagerness to be there.

The cape tied at her throat with leather thongs, her mask dangling in her left hand, Chelsea glanced at the two women. "Wish me luck?" she asked in a soft voice.

"You'll need no luck, luv," Molly said brusquely. "You're a fine girl, and a beauty too. You've nothin' t'be afraid of."

"Thank you, Molly." She left her room and moved silently down the stairs.

The duke was seated in a chair near the fireplace. He was wearing the uniform of a U.S.

Cavalry colonel, his rank marking his shoulders, brass buttons in two rows down the front of the dark blue uniform. A sheathed sword rested across his knees; and his wide-brimmed hat lay on the arm of the chair.

For the first time all day, Chelsea smiled. The duke might be striking in his costume, but he didn't instill fear in her Indian maiden's heart. He looked kind and gentle, and she loved him especially at that moment.

Still unnoticed by the two men, she shifted her gaze to Brandon. She paused on the step, her breath caught momentarily in her throat.

Wearing an Indian chieftain's war bonnet, he stood next to the fireplace, an arm resting on the mantel, his painted face turned a golden brown by the firelight. The buckskin breeches clung to his muscular thighs; colorful beading and fringe covered the outside seams. His dark moccasins came nearly to his knees; leather thongs wound around his calves, their sides decorated with fringe and gold buttons. His buckskin jerkin was also heavily fringed and was open at the neck, revealing the dark hairs on his chest. The spectacular war bonnet covering his chestnut brown hair was covered with long white and black feathers, at least fifty of them. It was lined with bright red fabric. The train fell nearly to the floor.

He looked even better than she'd imagined he would. He was magnificent.

As if he suddenly sensed her presence, Brandon turned from the fireplace and gazed up at her. His eyes held her there as he memorized how she looked, then he pushed away from the mantel and came to stand at the bottom of the stairs.

"Indian princess too beautiful to go out among the white man," he said, his tone serious.

Her heart did a funny little dance in her chest. "But the princess wants ever so much to go. Would my chief deny me this?"

"Chief thinks he would rather keep her all to himself."

"Great chief is wise beyond measure." She matched the seriousness of her tone to his. "But princess thinks white woman who gives party would be more dangerous than the cavalry if we don't go." And then she laughed.

Brandon joined his laughter with hers as he lifted a hand and guided her down the remaining steps.

Lawrence, in the meantime, had risen from his chair, placed his hat over his white hair, and joined them near the doorway. "You look wonderful, my dear," he told Chelsea. "Our coach awaits. Shall we go?"

Chelsea nodded and linked her arm through his elbow.

Molly watched the threesome depart. A lump formed in her throat and her eyes misted.

Chelsea was so lovely. Molly could scarcely believe she was the same girl who'd left Hawklin Hall less than a fortnight ago. And when she

thought of the girl she'd been before the fire
. . . No, it was better Molly not think of Chelsea
as she'd been before the fire. Everything had
changed since Brandon Fitzgerald came to
England. It was better to let the past be, better
it was forgotten for good.

She turned and went back into Chelsea's
room. Mrs. O'Grady had set a fire in the fireplace, and Molly dropped into a chair nearby,
her thoughts still on Chelsea.

The glow in the girl's eyes. That smile of hers.
Who'd have thought things would turn out so
well? Certainly not Hayden Fitzgerald. My, how
that man had railed when he learned Molly had
thrown out the medication he'd insisted Chelsea take ever since she first awakened after the
fire.

"Are you crazy, old woman? Do you know
what that girl could do to us?"

Molly had stood up to him for the first time in
twenty years. "I don't care. She's happy now.
Leave her be, m'lord. Leave be."

Hayden had raised his hand to strike her, but
Molly had dared him with her eyes. He'd wa-
vered, then slowly lowered his arm.

"If aught goes wrong, woman, you'll regret
the day you were born. I'll see to it personally.
You remember that." He'd turned toward the
door. "Get your things together. You're going
to Teakwood to keep an eye on Chelsea."

Molly shook off the dark memory. She would
rather think of Chelsea's sparkling face when
she'd left here on his lordship's arm.

"Be happy, luv," she whispered as she stared into the fire. "Be happy."

Bellfort was ablaze with light, a yellow glow spilling out of every window onto the groomed lawn below. Before they'd even turned up the drive, the ducal coach had become part of a steady stream of conveyances headed for the ball.

Chelsea leaned forward and watched as the carriage drew closer to the mansion. Her heart beat a rapid rhythm; her palms were moist.

The duke reached over and patted her knee. "Nervous, my dear?"

"A little." She met his kind gaze.

"Needn't be. They're just a lot of people who think they're someone. A few are. Most aren't. You just go in there and enjoy yourself."

The carriage rolled to a stop. A bewigged, liveried footman opened the door and bowed before offering a hand to Chelsea. She glanced quickly over her shoulder at Brandon, then took the man's hand and stepped to the ground.

Chelsea stared up at the three-storied stone and brick building. White pillars lined the front. A large gathering of guests stood on the portico awaiting entrance.

"They can't be announcing the guests or it wouldn't be much of a masquerade," Brandon said as he stepped to her side. "Maitland must have invited all of England."

Lawrence joined them, and their carriage rolled away. Her escape vanished with it.

Chelsea lifted her chin and stiffened her spine. She had no need of escape. She had come to this ball to enjoy herself, just as Grandfather had said, and enjoy herself was what she was going to do. It might be the last ball she ever got to attend. She meant for it to be memorable.

"Will the fair Indian princess come with her chief?" Brandon held out an elbow toward her.

"I will obey, great one."

She caught the glimmer in his eyes and suddenly smiled.

Maitland was surrounded by several admirers. Walter Covington had been spouting compliments about her beauty all evening, as had Evan FitzHugh and Roger Worth. She paid them little mind. She *was* beautiful, and of course, she expected to be told so. It was simply that none of these whelps garnered much interest. Walter had no title. Evan was nearly as poor as a church mouse. Roger was handsome but an absolute bore.

She sensed the dimming of conversation before it actually died away. She saw heads turning in unison toward the sweeping marble staircase; it looked like a wave cresting before reaching the shore. Before she could look herself, she heard the whispers begin.

"Who are they?"

"Who is she?"

"Who is he?"

Brandon Fitzgerald's war paint didn't disguise his identity from her eyes. She felt her

153

vitals lurch. Now *there* was a man who could hold her interest, a man who would never be boring—in or out of bed. Too bad he had bound himself to that sickly thing on his arm. He would have made Maitland a fine husband. Short of that, she meant to make him into a fine lover.

"Excuse me, gentlemen," she said, never taking her eyes from Brandon. "I have guests to welcome. Roger, come with me."

Brandon felt Chelsea quiver. He glanced down at her. Her mask hid none of her beauty; it only added a mysterious quality. She would soon have every swain in the room buzzing around her, eager for an introduction and a promised dance.

"Courage," he whispered, squeezing her hand between his elbow and his side.

She tilted her head back. Sky blue eyes looked at him through the slits in the fitted doeskin mask. "Indian princess not afraid."

Brandon smiled. "They're all dying to know who you are, you know." His gaze swept across the sea of upturned faces.

"But *you* are known, great chief. See the face of the woman with blazing hair as she comes this way."

Brandon found Maitland just as Chelsea finished speaking. Their hostess had arrived at the bottom of the stairs. She was wearing a filmy white costume that exposed a shocking amount of her generous bosom. Bare toes peeked from beneath the Grecian gown, her feet clad in sandals. Her auburn hair, dressed high on her head, sported a spectacular diamond tiara. She was watching him with a frankly approving gaze.

"Well, I guess it can't be helped," he said, his reluctance clear in each word.

Chelsea's laughter was like chimes in the wind. It tugged tenderly at his heart. He hoped this night would be all she wanted it to be.

"Brandon, how utterly ingenious. An Indian chief." Maitland's arm hooked possessively through Brandon's free one. "One would have thought you stepped right out of Mr. Cody's Wild West show, you look so real." She glanced toward the duke who had followed Brandon and Chelsea down the stairs. "Your grace, you are simply stunning."

"And you, Lady Bellfort." Lawrence bowed at the waist.

Chelsea felt a knot forming in her stomach. Maitland was intentionally ignoring her, but she wasn't sure what she should do. She was like a fish out of water. Whatever had made her think she could fit in among the cream of society?

A man stepped up beside Maitland. "And who is the chief's charming companion, might I ask?" He was dressed as a pirate, a patch over one eye. A thin black mustache rode his upper lip, and when he grinned, he revealed an even row of white teeth.

"Roger Worth, may I present Viscount Coleford and his wife, Alanna. Oh, I nearly forgot.

She favors a nickname, don't you, dear? What is it? I can never seem to remember."

"It's Chelsea," came a familiar voice, "and I hope she'll do me the honor of dancing with an unworthy highwayman."

Chelsea recognized Roxley's smile beneath the black mask. In fact, he was clad in black from head to toe.

"You don't mind, do you, Brand?" he asked, his eyes never wavering from her face.

Chelsea looked up at her husband, uncertain what she should do. It suddenly occurred to her that she might not even know how to dance. The couples waltzing around the magnificent ballroom were so beautiful, every move breathtaking. What if she tripped? What if she stumbled? Perhaps she should refuse and stay with Brandon. Perhaps . . .

Brandon passed her hand to Roxley. "Go on, Chelsea. Enjoy yourself. That's why we came."

Roxley swept her away before she knew what was happening. His right hand on her back guided her effortlessly into the midst of the circling dancers. It was a moment more before she realized she was having no trouble at all following his lead.

"You're all the buzz, Chelsea. Everyone is wondering who you are."

"That's what Brandon said."

"It's true. There's not a more beautiful woman here tonight, with or without a mask."

"You'll turn my head with such talk, kind sir."

Roxley's grin faded. "It's not just talk. And

there'll be plenty of men determined to tell you how beautiful you are . . . and a few who'll hope you'll be so flattered you might slip away with them for a walk in the garden."

"But I'm married. I couldn't walk out with anyone," Chelsea responded.

"Ahhh, true innocence! How refreshing." His voice was kind, his words not cynical as they might have sounded from someone else.

The dance ended at that moment. Before Roxley could lead her back to Brandon, Roger Worth had asked for the next dance, and she was off again in a whirl of doeskin fringe.

Names filled her head until it nearly burst in confusion. She danced until her feet hurt. Glasses of punch appeared out of nowhere to quench her thirst. Even when she rested, she got no rest, for she was surrounded by people, all of them asking questions, trying to find out about Viscount Coleford and his wife.

She heard an occasional whispered, "I heard she . . ." "Did you know she . . ."

Several times throughout the evening, Chelsea's eyes sought Brandon in the crowd, hopeful he would come for her, wishing he would dance with her. Always she found him with Maitland close at his side.

Brandon clenched his jaw as Maitland leaned up against him. But it wasn't Maitland that was causing his tension. It was the way that fellow on the dance floor was holding Chelsea. Much too closely. Too close by far.

"Lord Fitzgerald, I don't believe you've heard a word I've said," Maitland chided.

"What? Oh, I'm sorry." He forced his gaze back toward his hostess.

Her almond-shaped eyes fluttered. "I said it's dreadfully hot in here and I asked if you would mind escorting me onto the terrace for some fresh air."

"Not at all," he lied as he offered his arm, even while his head turned again toward the dance floor. He couldn't find Chelsea before Maitland was tugging him away.

Roxley observed his sister drawing Brandon toward the terrace doors. He knew Chelsea had witnessed their leaving too. He saw her face pale.

There was no denying the look. Chelsea Fitzgerald was in love with her husband, and the fool was leaving her to these jackals while Maitland shamelessly threw herself at him. Roxley had thought Brandon had more sense than to be taken in by his sister.

"Roxley?" Chelsea's fingertips caught at his loose shirtsleeve. "Would you take me someplace quiet?"

He drew her up from the chair where she had sought refuge just moments before. Hooking her arm through his, he tossed the other gentlemen a dark look that warned them not to interfere, then led her out of the ballroom.

They walked in silence down a long hallway until they reached the alcove. Roxley extinguished the lamp, and then they sat together in the darkened recess. For a long time, neither of them spoke.

"You know, Roxley . . ." Chelsea's voice was

a mere whisper. "Sometimes I want to do the wildest things. I look out my window at night and I think how wonderful it would be to run outdoors in just my night rail, bare feet in the grass and my hair flying out behind me." She paused. "Do you ever hear the dogs baying at the moon and feel like baying too? Sometimes I do. Strange, isn't it?"

He held her hand, offering what little encouragement he could by his presence there.

"I detest needlework. My stitches are never dainty and pretty. Molly says it should relax me. I like to sing, though. Do you like to sing, Roxley?"

"Yes, Chelsea. I like to sing. But most folks prefer that I don't."

"He's afraid I'm mad. I see it in his eyes sometimes. It isn't that I just can't remember the past. He's afraid I'll do something crazy."

"Chelsea—"

"No. It's true. He doesn't want to admit it, even to himself. But it's true. Roxley?" She turned toward him. Her voice softened even more. "Do *you* think I'm mad?"

He touched her face even as she seemed to touch his heart. "No, Chelsea dearest. I don't think you're the least bit mad." He felt the tear trickle down her cheek and onto his finger.

"Thank you for saying so, Roxley. Even if it isn't true."

"It's true," he whispered as he swore to himself he would make her laugh again before this night was over.

* * *

Brandon gave Maitland little time on the terrace. He wasn't much in the mood to spend his time parrying her attempts to entrap him, verbally or physically. When he could bear her cloying hands upon his arm no longer, he escorted her back inside and left her with the first group of people he could find, excusing himself from their midst.

His dark eyes forbade anyone to approach him as he made his way through the throng of revelers. He sought a glimpse of blond braids on the dance floor, but Chelsea wasn't anywhere to be seen. The longer he tried unsuccessfully to find her, the more sour his mood became.

He was standing on the marble staircase, his gaze sweeping once more over the crowd, when he saw them emerge through an open doorway at the end of the ballroom. Roxley no longer wore his black mask, nor was Chelsea wearing hers. Her hand rested on his arm, and they were talking, their heads turned toward each other. They paused, and Brandon saw Roxley lean close to her, as if to whisper something in her ear. Even from across the enormous room, he heard her laughter.

Brandon felt something hot and ugly growing in the pit of his stomach. He clenched and unclenched a fist and fought the overwhelming urge to punch something—or someone. He descended the steps and unwaveringly made his way toward the couple, unaware of how those before him fell back out of his way when they saw the dark look on his face.

Chelsea saw him first. She stopped whatever she was saying in mid-sentence. The lingering mirth vanished.

Brandon didn't waste even a glance at the earl. He glared down at Chelsea. He hadn't the time now to analyze the anger that filled him, nor to question the unrealistic possessiveness he felt toward her, especially since it was he who had left her to her own devices throughout this evening. He only knew he couldn't bear to see her in someone else's arms for another moment. Without a word, he took her hand and led her onto the dance floor. Their eyes were still locked as they began to waltz.

Chelsea felt a strange excitement flowing through her as Brandon held her close to his body, his hand firm on the small of her back. She wasn't afraid of his glowering dark looks. For some reason, she felt a sudden rise of joy, better even than the way Roxley had made her feel with his ridiculous stories about when he and Maitland were children.

They were on their second waltz when Brandon abruptly asked, "Have you enjoyed yourself tonight?" His voice was brusque.

She certainly would never reveal to him how hurt she'd been by his desertion. "Immensely, my lord." She smiled her prettiest. "And you?"

He stared down at her in stormy silence, then pulled her even tighter against him as he swirled her in graceful time with the music.

CHAPTER
TWELVE

The carriage ride home was tense. The few attempts the duke made at conversation were met with terse replies or stony silence from Brandon. When Lawrence looked at Chelsea for answers, he found her staring at her hands, folded in her lap. It was apparent to him that these two had had some sort of falling out. As soon as they arrived at Teakwood Manor, he excused himself and retired to his room, leaving the youngsters to resolve their own quarrel.

The parlor was lit only by the red coals glowing in the fireplace. Brandon left Chelsea standing near the door and crossed the room with quick strides. He yanked off the war bonnet and tossed it aside, then hunkered down and began stoking the fire with logs.

"Brandon, what is wrong?"

She had crossed the parlor on silent feet. When he twisted around, he found her only a few feet away. The light flickered against her face as the wood caught fire, sparkling in misty eyes of blue.

He hadn't meant to say anything. He hadn't sorted it out yet himself. But as he looked at her, he saw her once again as she had been tonight, surrounded by all those fawning young men. But mostly he saw her in Roxley's arms, laughing as he bent close to her ear.

"You seemed to forget this evening that you have a husband," he replied as he stood.

Her eyes widened. "I forgot?"

"And you were entirely too friendly with Randolph-Smythe."

"Too friendly?" she echoed once more.

"I don't want you seeing him again, Chelsea. There'll be talk after the way you behaved tonight. I'd hoped we'd dispel some of the rumors, but I'm afraid they'll only be worse now."

She stared at him while her face registered several different feelings—surprise, disappointment, hurt, anger. Anger was the last. "*You're* afraid of talk? That's terribly funny." She untied her cape and threw it off. "You may think me mad, my *lord*, but at least I'm no fool. It is not I who forgot she has a husband." She swiveled on her heel and stalked toward the stairs. "Though it would be easy enough to forget—and I may choose to do just that."

He was across the room in a flash. He caught her midway up the stairs. His hand on her arm swirled her around. "You'll not forget," he growled, then pulled her to him as his mouth crushed against hers in a fierce kiss.

Chelsea struggled in his arms, her hands pressing against his chest, her mouth trying to break free. Brandon paid her struggles no heed. He knew only that he must make her unable to ever forget she was his wife and he was her husband.

His tongue forced its way between her teeth until he was plundering the sweetness of her mouth. With his right hand, he steadied the back of her head, his fingers tangled in the silken braids. His left hand in the small of her back drew her body close to his, close enough to feel the wild patter of her heart.

The kiss lengthened, deepened. And then she wasn't fighting him anymore. Her hands inched up from his chest until they were locked around his neck. Hesitantly, and then with more confidence, her tongue sparred with his. Her body melded willingly against him.

Brandon pulled his head back and looked down into her face. In the dim light, he saw the heat of his desire mirrored in her eyes.

"Chelsea," he whispered as he swept an arm beneath her knees and carried her up the stairs and into his room.

A lamp, turned low, threw its soft light across the white counterpane. The fireplace was cold and dark, the rest of the bedchamber lost in varying degrees of shadow.

Brandon carried her across the room with long, quick strides. Chelsea turned her cheek against his chest and cast a furtive glance at the approaching bed. It seemed enormous.

Beside the bed, Brandon gently lowered her feet to the floor. His hands slid up her sides and around to her back as he drew her to him once again. His mouth was tender this time as it savored her lips. An aching want welled within Chelsea. It started low and spread throughout her body, leaving her knees weak. She moaned as she pressed closer to the warmth of his body, as if that would assuage the need inside her.

Brandon's mouth broke free. His brown eyes searched her face. He was asking her something with his eyes, demanding an answer. Instinctively, although she didn't fully understand the question, she knew her answer must be yes. She hoped he could see her response. She willed it to be there for him.

Chelsea knew the instant Brandon understood.

A strange new look crossed his face. Perhaps it was only the war paint that still streaked his cheeks, but she thought not. The planes and angles of his face seemed harsher, sharper— and more handsome than ever. He was savage, yet she wasn't afraid.

Brandon eased his hold on her back, gliding his hands up her spine and then out to her shoulders. Slowly, he turned her around. She wasn't sure at first what he was doing. There was no sound, no touch. She might have been all alone in his room. Then she felt the gentle tug on her scalp. He was untying her long braids.

She shivered and closed her eyes, enjoying the strange sensations flowing through her veins. Her skin seemed especially sensitive to everything around her, to each soft movement of air, to the freed tresses as they fell in waves around her shoulders and against her back.

She sensed him moving away from her. Opening her eyes, she watched as he moved across the bedchamber to the wash basin against the wall. With deliberate, measured motions, he poured water into the bowl, then washed the paint from his face. But when he turned and came back to her, she thought none of the savage fierceness was gone. There was a feral gleam in his eye; he was the hunter and she his prey. The flesh prickled on her arms.

Brandon placed himself between her and the bed, and as she watched, he removed his leather jerkin, allowing her to feast on a new and very pleasurable sight. The skin on his chest was dark, his shoulders broad. She lifted a hand and curiously ran her fingers through the black furring on his chest. The hesitant action brought an instant response.

"My Chelsea."

Her name came out in a harsh whisper as he drew her into his arms, his kiss once more demanding. His hands played an intricate melody upon her skin as his fingers freed the loop at the back of her neck, then pushed the doeskin dress from her shoulders. It fell into a puddle around her feet. Her chemise quickly followed.

Her head fell back as his lips worked their way down the length of her throat, not stopping until he had gently captured a rosy teat between his teeth. She gasped as a thousand pleasurable shock waves shot through her. The ache in her loins became a white-hot fire. Her fingers threaded through his hair as she held his head between her hands, both drawing him closer and pushing him away.

"Brandon, please," she begged, not knowing even what she pleaded for.

With a sudden tug, he released the cambric drawers she'd worn beneath her Indian costume, then picked her up and laid her on the bed. She was aware of her nakedness, aware of the way his eyes hungrily perused her, yet she felt no shyness, no shame. She belonged here. She knew it with all her heart.

His gaze captured hers as he completed disrobing, then joined her on the bed. She longed to let her eyes wander across him, memorizing each muscular inch, just as he had done with her. Yet he wouldn't allow it. She could only look into his eyes and wait for him to touch her again. She longed for his touch.

When at last he moved toward her, her eyes fluttered closed. His lips toyed with hers in small, nibbling kisses. Her breasts brushed against his chest, and she sighed into his mouth. When his hands began to explore new places, she could only hold her breath and quiver with unfamiliar delight.

And when he rose above her, she looked at him and offered him her heart with her eyes. Then all else was forgotten as he took her to new places in an act as old as time, as joyous as sunrise, as exciting as thunder.

And finally, when their cries had faded in the night air and the lovers lay replete upon the twisted counterpane, Chelsea wondered if she might awaken and discover it had all been a dream, for surely nothing so wonderful could be real.

CHAPTER THIRTEEN

Chelsea awakened slowly. Languor held her in bondage; a sweet lethargy flowed through her. She opened her eyes and peered with blurry vision about the room.

She was alone in the bed, but she knew this morning that nothing about last night had been a dream. Twice more in the long nighttime hours he had reached for her. Twice more he had taught her what it meant to be a woman in his arms.

Chelsea raised herself on her elbows and surveyed her husband's room. Sunlight spilled in through the large windows lining one wall. Two leather-upholstered chairs framed the fireplace. Umber and russet-colored rugs were scattered about the gleaming hardwood floor.

An enormous oil painting of horses and riders and hounds at the hunt filled the wall behind the four-poster bed. It was a masculine room, smelling of leather and pipe tobacco, and Chelsea found it very appealing.

Dragging the sheet from the rumpled bed and wrapping it around her, she padded across the room. She could hear the chirping of birds from the branches of a large sycamore as she pushed opened a window. The air was crisp, sending gooseflesh up her arms and down her legs. She hugged herself and rubbed at the shivers but chose not to close out the cool air.

She heard the door open and turned toward it as Brandon stepped into the room. He paused with his back to the door and let his eyes wander from her tousled silver-blond hair, over the gently curved body wrapped in a wrinkled sheet, and down to the leg, exposed from thigh to ankle. She felt herself growing warm as his gaze made its unhurried return to her face.

"Good morning," he said, his voice as rich as the hot chocolate he'd brought with him on a silver tray.

Feeling suddenly shy, she dropped her gaze to the floor. "Good morning."

She heard him laugh. "Is this the same vixen I held in my arms last night?"

How did he mean that? "Vixen, my lord?"

Brandon set the tray on the window ledge, then lifted her chin with his fingers, forcing her to look at him. "A perfectly lovely vixen. Wild and breathless." His expression sobered. "I am your husband, Chelsea. Don't ever be ashamed of our lovemaking. It is meant to be beautiful, to bring us closer together."

A hesitant smile pulled at the corners of her mouth.

"Now . . ." He handed her a cup of hot chocolate. "I have a surprise for you."

"What is it? I love surprises."

"Grandfather has decided it's time he should return to Hawklin Hall. Before long, we must go too. Grandfather's counting on me to help him with his estates."

Her smile vanished. Crestfallen, she looked down at the fine china cup in her hand.

"But before we go, I thought we might visit London."

She quickly looked up again, meeting the twinkle in his brown eyes.

"You've never been to London. I think you might enjoy it. We could visit the races, go to the theatre. Perhaps we'll get you a few more new frocks. How does that sound?"

"I'd like it very much," she replied, holding her elation in check. Anything to delay returning to Hawklin. Anything to prolong this wonderful time with Brandon when he was hers and hers alone.

The well-sprung traveling coach rocked gently as the matched pair of black geldings galloped toward London, trying hard to reach their destination before the settling dusk became the darkness of night. Inside the closed carriage, Chelsea slept with her head against Brandon's shoulder. Across from them, Molly also dozed.

Brandon glanced down at his bride. A pale lock of hair had escaped her bonnet and curled upon her rosy cheek. Looking at her, he was filled with a sense of well-being. It was possible for him to believe all would go right from this moment on. Chelsea no longer had nightmares nor did she seem afraid her madness would return. She was happy and carefree. In the past few days, he had heard her laugh often. The sound was balm to his spirit.

His gaze shifted to the sleeping nanny. The woman was an enigma. She seemed devoted to Chelsea, yet there were moments when he thought she wished for the old Chelsea, the girl held captive in her rooms at Hawklin. Perhaps she feared she would be put out once Chelsea was entirely recovered. Brandon would have to see that she understood she would always have a home with the Fitzgeralds.

Brandon hoped Chelsea would enjoy their visit to London. He'd thought of the trip to serve dual purposes. First of all, the repairs to the nursery at Hawklin were not yet completed. He wanted no traces of the workmen when they returned, no reminders of the fire. Second, he'd been as reluctant as he'd known Chelsea was to end their idyllic time together.

He'd never imagined he could care so much for a woman, especially not such a woman as

Chelsea. He'd always preferred the more sophisticated, worldly women, women who knew exactly how to please a man. Instead, his wife seemed . . .

He looked at her once again. What was she like? Delicate, yes. And beautiful. She was wonderfully innocent, yet brave in the face of danger, imagined or otherwise. There was a strange elusiveness about her, an almost otherworldliness. She was like a will-o'-the-wisp, something not quite within his reach. There were times when he gazed into her eyes . . .

She stirred. A tiny frown knit her pale brows, and she pursed her lips in silent objection to something in her dreams. She looked so vulnerable, it caused his heart to tighten.

He reached up with his free hand and swept the recalcitrant hair from her cheek. She mumbled something unintelligible and nestled closer to him. Brandon smiled tenderly, then closed his own eyes and sought some much needed rest.

Chelsea didn't recall their arrival at the duke's new London townhouse. Nor did she remember Brandon carrying her in his arms up to their second-story bedroom. Exhaustion kept her in deep slumber throughout the night, and so it was with some disorientation that she awakened to a strange bedroom the next morning.

The walls were covered with lilac-flowered wallpaper. Bric-a-brac filled several small mahogany tables and the shelves along one wall. Oriental rugs, brightly colored and fringed, covered the floor. Heavy velvet curtains framed the windows, one on each outside wall of their corner bedroom. A huge gilded mirror hung over the white marble fireplace, giving the room an even larger, airier look. On either side of the hearth stood two ceramic greyhounds, so lifelike she fully expected them to wag their tails and bark.

In the bed beside her, Brandon slept on. A night's worth of beard darkened his cheeks and chin. An arm was thrown over his eyes, blocking out the persistent morning light. Above the sheet, his bare chest rose and fell in a steady rhythm.

She considered slipping from the bed and getting dressed, then discarded the idea as a poor one. Instead, she allowed her fingers to slide over the sheet until they reached Brandon's chest where they became entangled in the dark hair. Then she leaned forward, stopping her lips just a hairsbreadth away from his ear. Softly, she blew. He wrinkled his nose and shook his head.

A mischievous grin lighting her face, she let her lips touch his stubble-roughened jaw, then slowly, lightly nibbled her way to his mouth. There was no reaction.

She was contemplating her next move when suddenly his arms captured her like a vice. He pulled her above him as his mouth lay claim to hers. The kiss sent desire jolting through her, and she was left gasping for breath when at last he set her free.

"You tempt me, Chelsea," Brandon said with a low chuckle, "but I think we'd best be up. Judging by the sun, the hour is already late."

She was surprised by the sharp disappointment she felt. But perhaps it wasn't proper for a lady to want to make love so often. Perhaps a true lady waited for her husband to reach for her and didn't initiate such acts herself. She wished suddenly that she could be different. But how?

Brandon threw off the bed covers and dropped his feet to the floor. "There are sure to be callers today, as soon as word spreads that we're in residence."

"Callers?"

"Of course. You made quite an introduction of yourself to society at Maitland's ball. Now they'll want to look you over close up."

"Oh dear," she breathed, her heart hammering in her ears. "Brandon, I don't know anything about meeting people."

Brandon had donned his buckskin breeches as they spoke. He turned now, buttoning his white shirt, and gave her a reassuring smile. "Just be yourself, my dear. They can't help but love you."

"I'm not so sure. . . ."

"Well, I am." He pulled her up from the bed by her shoulders. "Have courage, my little vixen," he whispered, then kissed the tip of her nose. As he released her, he winked broadly. "I have a few calls of my own to make this morning, but I'll be home to have tea with you."

"Brandon, you're not leaving me alone, are you?" Panic returned.

His expression sober, he leveled a steady gaze upon her. "You can do this, Chelsea. You don't need me. You were fine at the ball."

"That was different. I . . ."

She didn't finish. She couldn't tell him she'd accepted Maitland's invitation simply because the woman's flirtation with Brandon had made her jealous. She didn't want to tell him she had been fine at the ball only because pride wouldn't allow her to let him know how hurt she was by the way he'd left her alone. She had only been all right because Roxley had shown her such care. Besides, most of her time had been spent on the dance floor in the company of men. She'd known she was safe with them because she was Brandon's wife. Her callers today would be women, and she wouldn't have Brandon to hide behind.

"Brandon?"

"Yes?"

"What do I tell them if they ask about my past?"

He gathered her into his arms once again. His voice bore a hard edge. "Tell them nothing. Let them guess and suppose. Make them curious. The only thing they need to know is who you are now." He turned her toward the mirror. "Look, Chelsea. Look at who you are."

She stared at her reflection. She saw nothing

more than a disheveled blond woman in a white nightgown.

"Remember how you told me you didn't want to be Alanna? You wanted to be Chelsea?"

"Yes."

"Well, now you can make Chelsea anyone you want her to be."

She felt tears burning the back of her eyes and swallowed hard. She would do this for him if it was what he wanted. It seemed so important to him. She would get through it somehow. He believed in her; how could she disappoint him? Besides, he could be wrong. Perhaps no one would even come to call.

Eleanor Randolph-Smythe, Countess of Roxley and the earl's mother, sat on the edge of the velvet settee, her back ramrod-straight. A striking, white-haired woman in her fifties, she carried herself with an air of royalty. In the chair next to her was Diana, Lady Chesterfield, wife of Sir Maxwell Chesterfield, the renowned physician.

"I was sorry to miss Maitland's ball," the countess said, her dark eyes inspecting Chelsea with unnerving intensity. "The viscount's and your costumes caused quite a stir, I understand."

Chelsea felt herself blushing to the roots of her hair. She reached forward and picked up the teapot. "More tea, Lady Roxley? Lady Chesterfield?"

Eleanor waved away the offer with an impatient hand. "Good heavens, put that thing down. You'll drown us, my dear girl."

Chelsea wished the floor would open up and swallow her whole.

"Indians, I believe. Your costumes?"

"Oh . . . yes."

"Whatever made you think of them?"

"Mr. Cody's Wild West show."

"Oh, you saw Buffalo Bill Cody when he was here for the Jubilee? What a grand event."

Lady Chesterfield said something next, but Chelsea wasn't listening. How had she known about Mr. Cody and his Indians? She hadn't seen his show. She *couldn't* have seen his show. She'd been at Hawklin. But . . . but *something* had made her think of those costumes. She'd been so specific in telling the dressmaker what she wanted.

"Lady Alanna!" Diana spoke her name sharply.

Startled, she blinked her eyes. "I'm so sorry, Lady Chesterfield. I—"

"I asked about your mother. How is she?"

Chelsea had trouble focusing on the question, the puzzle of Mr. Cody and the Indian costumes still gnawing at the back of her mind. "My mother?"

"Are you deaf, young lady, or simply addle-pated?"

"No, Lady Chesterfield. I'm most certainly not deaf." Angry now, Chelsea set down her teacup and leveled a piercing blue gaze upon her guest. Why must she be put through this inquiry in her own drawing room? Did this woman really care about Sara Fitzgerald? "My mother is most definitely well. If you are interested in her health, she and my father are living in London now. Perhaps you could call on *her*." She turned her eyes upon the countess. "But they may not have returned to London yet. They were staying at Bellfort."

Eleanor's expression had softened considerably. There was the hint of a smile at the corners of her mouth and a twinkle in her black eyes. "You know, my dear, I never cared much for your mother. But you . . . I like you. I see why my Wellington is so taken." She rose from the settee. "A shame my son didn't meet you before this American-born husband of yours did. Things might have been quite different for Wellington—and for you, too."

Chelsea rose too. "I consider Roxley a good friend. I hope we always shall be."

"Indeed. I'm sure you will. Come now, Diana. We have imposed long enough on this dear girl. She must be weary after so long a journey." Eleanor Randolph-Smythe swept regally across the room toward the entry hall. "Tell the viscount I'm looking forward to making his acquaintance."

"I shall."

"Good day, Lady Fitzgerald." She turned at the door and looked at Chelsea. "It's been a pleasure."

Brandon returned from the solicitor's to a quiet house. He found Chelsea alone in the drawing room, staring pensively into the fire. He wondered how many callers she'd had. Had he been right to leave her alone? Had something gone wrong?

He cleared his throat.

Chelsea started, turning her head in his direction.

"I'm later than I expected to be. Is everything all right?"

She nodded as a frown returned to crease her forehead.

Brandon removed his coat before walking across the room to stand near her chair. "Then what is it, Chelsea?"

"The most peculiar thing." Her gaze returned to the crackling fire. "Brandon, did you wonder about the costumes I selected for the ball? I mean, did they seem a strange choice to you?"

"I'm not sure I understand your question." He hunkered down beside her.

She turned her blue gaze upon him once again. "If I've never been away from Hawklin, how did I know about Mr. Cody's show? How did I know about the Indian costumes?"

"I don't know. Perhaps someone at Hawklin told you about it."

She shook her head slowly. Her voice dropped to a whisper. "I don't think so, Brandon. I think I was there."

There was a strange light in her eyes that sent a chill down Brandon's spine.

"Sometimes I can almost see it," Chelsea continued. "My past. It's as if I'm looking through a long tunnel and at the end there's a door. Sometimes I can almost get the door open."

Brandon's impulse was to pull her into his arms, to hold her there until she forgot she'd ever had a past before he arrived in England. If she should slip through that mysterious door in her mind, he thought he would be lost as well.

CHAPTER
FOURTEEN

Gray skies hovered over London. The air was bone-chilling, and only a few brave souls were out in it by choice that day. The Fitzgerald drawing room was one of only a few with visitors.

Hayden leaned against the mantel, his eyes brooding as they followed his daughter's movements.

The Earl of Roxley sat on the same velvet settee where his mother had been only a few days before. His eyes were also on Chelsea, but there was a twinkle in them and a smile to go with it on his lips.

Chelsea was flushed from so much laughter. Roxley had just finished an hilarious tale about Lady Chesterfield and his mother on their last journey to Bath. Even Brandon had seemed to enjoy it, much to Chelsea's relief. She didn't want her husband to be at odds with such a good friend as Roxley.

She turned her head, drying the tears from her eyes with her handkerchief. "Really, Roxley. You are entirely too much. The countess would no doubt be furious to know you're bandying that story around London."

"Are you jesting? Who do you think I heard it from? And in a drawing room full of a lot more people than this one, too." He looked at Brandon. "When will you and Chelsea return to Hawklin?"

"Probably within the week."

"Then I'll look to see you there. I'm leaving tomorrow for Rosemont."

Chelsea rose from the sofa. "Excuse me, gentlemen. If I don't see what's keeping that girl with our tea, we may all have gone to the country before it arrives."

She hurried out of the drawing room and down the narrow hall toward the kitchen at the back of the house. She pushed open the door just as Gertrude stepped toward it on the other side. Tea and scones and strawberries and cream went flying over the servant girl and the black-and-white tiled floor.

Gertrude's eyes widened and her mouth formed a horrified "O". "Oooh, mum. I'm terrible sorry, I am. I'm a clumsy ox. Cook'll box me ears for sure."

"Heavens, Gertrude. It's not so terrible as all that. Here. Let me help you clean it up."

Chelsea knelt down on the floor beside the quivering girl and began to pick up the large pieces of broken crockery.

Molly, having come through the door at the other end of the narrow kitchen, joined them, bending over to pick up the teapot, now missing its spout. As she leaned down, what looked like a small bundle of rags fell out of her pocket.

"What is this, Molly?" Chelsea asked as she picked them up, noting the charred fabric.

"Nothin', m'lady." Molly reached for it, but Chelsea pulled back, keeping it from the nanny's reach.

It suddenly seemed as if the kitchen were full of smoke. The heat smote her cheeks, and her eyes watered. She heard laughter—high-pitched laughter that made her feel cold in her bones. And then she saw the doll, lying in the middle of the room. It was on fire.

Chelsea screamed and jumped to her feet, staggering backwards until she hit the wall, the tiny bundle of charred fabric still in her hand.

The kitchen door burst open and the three men tumbled in, almost on top of each other. Gertrude was still kneeling on the floor, her hands frozen in mid-air as she stared at her mistress. Molly, too, was watching Chelsea, her face gone a ghastly shade of gray.

Brandon was the first to move toward her. "Chelsea?"

"It's her doll." She held it up for him to see. She stared at the object a little longer, then raised terror-filled eyes toward Brandon. "I saw it. Burning. She dropped it."

"*Who* dropped it?"

She felt like screaming again. "Alanna dropped it." Her voice rose. "It's Alanna's doll. She dropped it. It was on fire and—and—" The room was spinning around her. She flung the doll away, raising her fists to press against her temples. There was a terrible shrieking in her ears.

Brandon caught her as she swooned forward. "Dear God," he whispered under his breath.

Hayden stepped forward, glanced down at his daughter, then turned toward Molly. "Don't just stand there, you bloody idiot. Get Alanna's medicine."

"M'lord, she . . ."

"Don't argue with me, woman."

Brandon was only vaguely aware of his father-in-law's angry orders and the nanny's hurried steps carrying her from the room. His thoughts were all on Chelsea. Her terror still lingered in the air about them, like the cold fingers of death.

Roxley's hand gently touched his shoulder. "We'd best get her to her room, Brand."

He didn't move.

"Brandon?" Roxley knelt down and slipped his arms beneath Chelsea, trying to ease her away from Brandon.

His grip tightened. "I'll do it," he said gruffly as his glance shot up to Roxley, darkly warning him not to interfere.

The earl nodded and rose.

"I told you long ago you shouldn't be bringing her out from Hawklin." Hayden stared pointedly at Roxley. "We'll not be able to keep it quiet now."

"If you're worried about me, Lord Fitzgerald, you needn't be. Chelsea is my friend. I won't betray her."

Brandon held Chelsea close against his chest as he stood. As he walked past Roxley, he said, "Thanks."

Molly stared at the girl in the middle of the bed. Chelsea was lost in a deep, drug-induced sleep. She wouldn't wake for hours. It had taken some effort for Molly and Roxley to convince Brandon his wife would be all right while he took a moment from her bedside for some supper. He hadn't eaten since breakfast. Molly had promised she would call if he was needed.

The door eased open, drawing Molly's attention. It wasn't with pleasure that she saw Hayden entering the bedchamber.

"How is she?" he asked with a quick glance toward the bed.

"She's quiet, just as you knew she would be."

"It's for her own good."

"Is it, m'lord? She's been happy since the viscount came."

Hayden's face hardened as he swung around to face the nanny. "She can ruin a lot of other people's happiness if we don't take care. I'm not about to let that happen. Do I make myself clear, Molly?"

"And what is it you'd have me do?"

"Get her back to Hawklin. And make sure she stays on her medicine. We don't want anything like what happened downstairs to happen again."

Molly drew herself up straight. "I won't do it, m'lord."

He stepped closer. His face grew red. "What!"

Her heart was racing in her chest. "I said I won't do it. It's time someone helped her, and I mean to do it."

Hayden raised his hand.

"You may strike me once, m'lord, but not again. The viscount will see to that. I'm in the Duke of Foxworth's employ now. Not yours."

"You'll regret this day." Hayden spun on his heel and stalked from the room.

Exhausted by her display of courage—courage that quickly faltered—Molly sank into the closest chair. Faltering it might have been, but the courage she'd found to tell Hayden she would no longer be a party to Chelsea's captivity had made her feel good.

She glanced once more at the girl in the bed. "I'll do my best t'help you remember, m'lady. I'll do my best."

A small cottage nestled against a rock-strewn hillside. Below, the boggy bottomland swept out in a sea of green grasses and sedges. Heather bloomed in rosy pink clusters, the bell-shaped blossoms bobbing in the breeze.

She sat astride her dapple-gray pony and stared across the moor at the whitewashed cottage with its thatched roof. Her hair blew free around her shoulders. Her feet were bare beneath the simple brown skirt. The sun kissed her face, and she let her head fall back, mindless of the rays that caused the freckles to darken the bridge of her nose.

Tapping her heels against the pony's ribs, she set him galloping across the rolling green landscape. She could hear sounds of wood splitting from behind a shed.

It had to be Papa!

Joy rose in her heart, and she laughed aloud.

But as she neared, the cottage vanished. She was suddenly in a carriage, alone, afraid. The carriage stopped. The door opened. An elderly woman awaited her. The old woman was dressed all in black. Her wrinkled face was kind, but there was great sadness in her eyes. Behind the woman stood a small, many-gabled house, its red brick walls obscured beneath the creeping ivy.

She stepped from the carriage, looking down at the shoes she now wore, shoes so small they pinched her toes. When she glanced up, the woman and the house were gone.

She was in a room. She could hear laughter beyond the door. But it wasn't a joyful laughter. It was hollow, hopeless, haunted. She moved toward the sound, her heart racing. Her fingers touched the doorknob. She paused . . .

"Chelsea?"

She bolted upright, a startled cry strangled in her constricted throat. Panic-filled blue eyes flew open to a darkened room filled with ominous shadows. Red embers, like tiny, devilish sentinels, glowed in the fireplace.

"Chelsea!"

Brandon's voice was forceful as he bent forward, drawing her eyes to his. A tiny gasp of relief escaped her lips as she leaned into him. His arms embraced her; he pressed her head against his chest.

His voice softened. "It was only a nightmare, Chelsea. It's all right." Gentle fingers stroked her hair.

Only a nightmare, she repeated silently. *Only a nightmare*. But she knew it was more. So much more.

"Go back to sleep. We'll talk about it in the morning."

Her limbs felt leaden. Her head seemed to be stuffed with cotton. She couldn't fight him as he eased her back on the down pillow, but she didn't want to sleep. She wanted to understand.

Brandon placed a kiss on her forehead. "Sleep, Chelsea. I'll be here beside you."

He watched her until her chest rose and fell in a steady, slow rhythm. Finally, assured she slept, he rose from her bedside and walked to a window, pushing aside the heavy draperies. A dense fog shrouded the neighbor's house and all beyond from view. He could hear the clip-clop of hooves upon cobblestone as a hansom cab passed by on the street below.

Brandon hated the helpless feeling that kept him company. How could he fight the images Chelsea saw in her mind? He didn't want to lose her. She meant too much to him. How could he bear it if she were to slip away from him?

He closed his eyes and leaned his forehead against the glass, swearing to himself that he wouldn't lose her. He would fight it any way he could. He wouldn't let her return to madness.

CHAPTER
FIFTEEN

Dr. Haversham, an extremely tall and thin man in his early thirties, wrinkled his nose as he slid his glasses up toward his eyes. "I knew Dr. Weick only by reputation, but of course his notes on this case were quite copious. My advice to you, Lord Fitzgerald, would be to put your wife in an asylum before she harms herself or someone else."

Brandon felt the muscles in his neck growing tense. "You've not even *seen* my wife, doctor."

"No, my lord, I haven't. But I've been advised of her condition by her father. And as I've said, I have read Dr. Weick's notes. His treatment—"

"His *treatment*, from what I've seen, consisted of sedation and locked doors. You can't expect her to recover under those conditions."

"Mental illness is not easily explained to the layman, my lord," the doctor replied, his tone overly tolerant, as if he were dealing with an imbecile. He turned toward Hayden with a silent plea for help in his eyes.

"Brandon," Hayden began, "I assure you, we all want what's best for . . . for my daughter."

"Do you?"

Hayden's complexion reddened. He drew his paunchy figure to its full height. "You have no right—"

"I have *every* right." Brandon jumped to his feet. "I intend to see that Chelsea recovers, and it won't be in a place like St. Mary's of Bethlehem. Oh, yes. I've heard of the infamous Bedlam."

Dr. Haversham also stood. His face was pinched, and his voice was filled with indignation. "Lord Fitzgerald, I can almost assure you there is little hope for recovery. The young woman has suffered from these fits all her life. There is no cure. We can only try to make her life comfortable between her spells of delusion. Her confinement needn't be in Bedlam. There are other choices." He motioned toward the chairs. "Please. Let's sit down and discuss this matter calmly. I assure you, I'm only here to help."

Chelsea stared despondently at the wall beside her bed. A feeling of hopelessness held her captive beneath the embroidered counterpane. She heard the door open but closed her eyes and pretended to be asleep, unwilling to face anyone just yet.

"Chelsea." Molly's voice was stern. "Chelsea, *get up*."

"I can't," she answered in a whisper.

The counterpane was flung to the foot of the bed. "You can and you must. His lordship's brought in a doctor, and if he has his way, you'll be locked up somewhere for good. I cannot bear to see it happen to you, luv. Get up and fight for yourself."

Chelsea opened her eyes and turned her head to look at the nanny. Molly's cheeks were red and her eyes sparked in anger.

"Lock me away?" Would Brandon do that to her?

"It's what it sounds like to me, m'lady."

She swallowed back the lump in her throat. "Perhaps it would be best. Perhaps . . ."

"Don't you wallow in self-pity, luv. There's no time. What happened yesterday means nothin'. You're a sight healthier in the mind than that bloody idiot who calls himself your father." She leaned over, placing her fingers on Chelsea's cheek. Her green eyes misted. "There's naught wrong with you, girl, that time and love won't cure. You're not crazy. It's only pieces of memories that haunt you now. Trust me that it's true. Please, don't let them lock you away."

Chelsea's own eyes were teary. It was frightening to think they might send her back to her lonely rooms at Hawklin—or perhaps to some place even worse, to a life of seclusion, re-

stricted movement, oblivion. But worse—
much worse—was that Brandon seemed to
want it. If he didn't believe in her . . .

Wait. . . . What was it Molly had said? Only
pieces of memories. Could that be what she
saw, what she heard, what she dreamed? Was it
only her memory coming back? But if that
were true, wouldn't it bring the madness with
it?

"Why do you think I'm no longer crazy?" she
asked softly.

Molly's voice was strained as she answered,
"Perhaps because you're not my Alanna any
longer. Perhaps because you're Chelsea.
There's no other reason I can give you. I only
know it's true." Molly kissed her brow, then
straightened as she wiped away her tears.
"You've a right to the happiness you've found,
luv. Don't let them take it from you. Fight for it,
Chelsea."

Molly was right. She could lie there and just
let things happen to her, or she could fight
back.

"Bring me my yellow dress." She sat up and
dropped her feet over the side of the bed. "The
one with the big bow on the bustle."

"Yes, m'lady." Molly flashed her a triumphant grin. "We'll have you ready in no time."

A very short while later, cleansed and per-
fumed, Chelsea sat down at her dresser and
brushed her silken hair until it gleamed. She
left it free to cascade down her back; Brandon
liked it that way best. Its pale silver-gold color
seemed even lighter against the buttercup yel-

low of her gown. Her skin had a healthy glow with light touches of pink on her cheekbones. Her summer-sky eyes stared determinedly back at her reflection, ready now to challenge the world.

Hayden threw up his hands in frustration. "Why won't you listen to reason, Brandon? You saw her yesterday. There can't be any denying her illness."

Standing by the fireplace, Brandon turned slowly to look at his father-in-law. He had a bitter taste in his mouth, and he was sure it wouldn't go away until Hayden Fitzgerald did. And he was just as eager for the doctor to take his leave. Neither man had said anything to change Brandon's mind. He had no intention of putting Chelsea in an institution for the mentally insane. If nothing else could be done, if she worsened as these two predicted, then he would return her to Hawklin where he could surround her with people who would care for her with tenderness and concern.

Before he could speak, the drawing room doors opened and Chelsea stepped in. She looked nothing like the frightened young woman he'd found screaming in the kitchen the day before. Nor did she resemble the lost-eyed soul he'd comforted in bed last night. She looked completely well and entirely beautiful.

Her hair fell in soft waves over her shoulders, tiny wisps curling near her temples. The gay color of her gown seemed to mock the solemn mood of the men discussing her. She carried

195

her head high and proud and seemed unperturbed by the night of disquiet just past. Her eyes met briefly with Brandon's, then moved on to her father and then to the doctor.

"I trust, gentlemen, that I am the subject under discussion."

Dr. Haversham stood, disbelief written across his face. "Lady Fitzgerald?"

"Yes." She walked toward him and held out her hand. "And you must be the doctor Molly told me had come to call. Dr. Haversham, is it?"

The doctor continued to stare as he lifted her fingers to his lips. Chelsea smiled sweetly at him.

He cleared his throat and straightened. His Adam's apple bobbed as he swallowed. "Yes, my lady. Dr. Haversham."

"His lordship and I are happy to have you in our home. It's a shame you've come needlessly. As you can see, I'm quite well. I had a silly scare, but I'm over it now." She turned toward Hayden and seemed to force herself to lean close to him. She kissed the air near his cheek, then backed away. "I'm sure you've been worried, Father, but there's no cause for alarm. I'm quite all right."

Brandon felt as if a large weight had been removed from his shoulders. Surely now the doctor could see how mistaken he was. She belonged nowhere else. Only here. With him.

Chelsea looked at Brandon then. He was surprised to find a flash of anger in her eyes. Anger and something else. Disappointment perhaps. Then, as suddenly as he'd recognized it, the emotion vanished, and he could read nothing in the cool blue depths.

Chelsea sank onto the sofa and waved her hand in invitation for the men to be seated as well. "I suppose you would like to discuss this matter with me further, Dr. Haversham, but there is very little I can tell you. I have no memory before one month ago. There was an accident in my home. I suffered a blow to the head. Now I have—what is it called? Oh yes, amnesia. My parents and the servants tell me I've always been ill, and I can't very well deny it. But I am not insane. Perhaps my dreams and nightmares are caused only by my trying so hard to remember. Perhaps they could even be memories from my past. Could that be so, doctor?"

"Well . . . yes, it could be. . . ."

"Memories!"

Chelsea looked at her father. His usually ruddy complexion had paled, and he wore a horrified expression.

"Memories of what?" he continued, turning his gaze upon the doctor. "She's spent her life locked up at Hawklin with that nanny of hers. She doesn't know anyone but that fool woman, and she's never been anywhere else. The most notable thing she's ever done is set fire to the house. It's Molly who's filling her head with this nonsense. By heaven, I'll see that woman—"

Chelsea stood, her eyes still locked upon her father. "Why don't you want me to be well?"

Hayden turned toward her.

"Is there something in my marriage contract that says you must return his money should I ever be well?" She moved toward Hayden, her voice rising. "Tell me, Father. What is it?"

"That's enough!" he exclaimed, raising his hand to strike her into silence.

Brandon's hand closed around Hayden's wrist before the blow could fall. Chelsea stepped back, nearly tripping over an ottoman in her haste, frightened by the hateful look that appeared in her father's eyes.

"I think it's time you left," Brandon growled. "Before I lose *my* temper."

"You'll regret this, Brandon," Hayden responded. "You're married to a madwoman, and you'll not know a safe moment until she's put away. She ought to be in Bedlam this very moment. She's dangerous, I tell you."

Chelsea felt herself grow cold even as Brandon's face grew dark with rage.

Dr. Haversham reached out and grasped Hayden's free arm. "Come along, my lord. I believe we've overstayed our welcome." He snatched his hat up from an end table and placed it on his head. "Good day, Lord Fitzgerald, Lady Fitzgerald. Do call upon me if I can be of help."

Brandon made no response other than an angry nod of his head as he walked out of the drawing room behind the two men.

Chelsea felt frozen in place. She listened as the footsteps faded, then heard the closing of the front door. Suddenly, she was drained of all energy. She hadn't enough strength left to be angered or frightened or defiant. But she couldn't hide in her bedroom as she longed to do. She still had to face Brandon.

She looked up, knowing somehow that he'd returned and stood watching her from the doorway. His expression was solemn, his gaze inscrutable. She wished she knew what he was thinking as he looked at her.

He came toward her then, stopping a few feet away. "They're gone," he said.

"Brandon . . ." Her voice quivered.

"Yes?"

"Believe in me."

He didn't answer her. Instead, he pulled her into his arms, crushing her against his chest.

Chelsea knew he didn't speak because he couldn't give her the answer she wanted. His tenderness seemed a bittersweet substitute for the belief she sought.

Days later, Brandon watched Chelsea over the breakfast table. Every time she looked at him, he could see the hurt behind her eyes of blue. Her father's cruel rejection had wounded her spirit, and Brandon felt helpless not knowing how to repair it. He had treated her more gently the past few days, trying to be tender and thoughtful in all that he did and said. But there was no change. She remained withdrawn from him. She was meek and agreeable, as if afraid she might somehow offend or anger him.

The distance between them hurt Brandon more than he cared to admit. He'd had such hopes for her, for the two of them. He missed her smile. He missed her spontàneous laughter. He missed her sudden bursts of energy. He would have liked to see her running barefoot in a rainstorm. He wished he could take her back to Teakwood, to the carefree days they'd spent riding their horses across the fields, soaring over fences and walls.

But it wasn't to Teakwood they would go. "I've had a message from Grandfather. He'd like us to return to Hawklin."

Chelsea looked up. He saw the dread pass across her face before she quickly disguised it. And could he blame her? Why should she look forward to returning to Hawklin?

"I have a few loose ends to tie up with my solicitor in London before we leave. Why don't you take Molly and go shopping? You haven't been out of the house in nearly a week, and you haven't received a single caller."

"I have no wish to visit with strangers," she replied in a subdued voice, "and I don't need any more dresses."

Brandon's frustration caused his voice to grow harsh. He stood and tossed his napkin onto his plate. "Then, for pity's sake, go for a ride in the park. Just get out for some fresh air."

"If that's what you wish, Brandon."

"It's what I wish!" He spun on his heel and marched out of the dining room, more angry with himself than with Chelsea.

He grabbed his coat and hat and left the townhouse, choosing to walk to the solicitor's rather than wait for the carriage.

"Bloody hell!" he cursed, unconsciously mimicking his coachman's favorite phrase. *What am I to do?*

She had found her way into his heart, and there was no denying it. From the first moment he'd seen her at Hawklin, he'd begun losing his heart to her. And now he was afraid. Afraid of her dreams and nightmares. Afraid of her terrifying visions. Afraid of her retreat into silence.

Afraid of losing her.

He stopped dead still on the sidewalk, shaken to his soul.

He loved her.

He loved her and could not bear to lose her. If it were another man threatening to steal her away, he could fight that. But how could he fight a phantom? How could he fight the things she saw in her mind?

He had no answers. There didn't seem to be any.

CHAPTER
SIXTEEN

Chelsea was descending the steps of the townhouse when the hansom cab pulled to a halt in the street. The door opened and Roxley's familiar face appeared in the opening.

"Chelsea!"

"Good day, Roxley," she said with a note of surprise. "I didn't expect to see you in London. I thought you'd have returned to Rosemont by now."

"And not wait to see how you're feeling?" He hopped down from the cab. His smile vanished as he gave her a hard once-over with his eyes. "How *are* you feeling?"

"Much better," she answered softly, uncomfortable beneath his scrutiny, all too aware that he had witnessed her latest spell.

"Where are you off to?"

"Brandon thought I could use an outing."

"Ah, a wise suggestion. You're far too pale, I think. The two of you can join me."

"Brandon isn't here."

"All right, then. *You* can join me." Without waiting for a reply, he took her arm and assisted her into the black cab.

The front door of the townhouse slammed closed behind Molly as she quickly came down the steps. "Your lordship, what is it you're about?" the nanny demanded.

"You're welcome, too, Molly. Here you go." And he hoisted her up into the hansom as well.

"Roxley, I . . ." Chelsea began.

The earl shook his head. "No arguments, Chelsea. I'm making it my business to see that you have a wonderful morning."

Chelsea couldn't resist his friendly grin. For the first time in days, she smiled.

"That's better. Now, what do you say to a spin around the park before we find a place to take tea? I know a splendid little tea room. . . ."

A short time later, Roxley strolled with Chelsea along the bank of the lake, her hand resting in the crook of his arm. Two swans floated across the still water. Their long white necks were stretched in proud arcs above their white-feathered bodies. Gentle ripples left a trail on the lake's surface behind them.

He glanced surreptitiously at the woman at his side. She seemed more at ease now. The strained look had disappeared from around her eyes. He fancied there was even a little more color in her pale cheeks.

Ever since he'd heard her scream and then seen her faint in the kitchen of the Fitzgerald townhouse, he'd been worried about her. He'd longed to call before now but had hesitated. He wasn't sure Brandon would welcome his concern. He'd recognized Brandon's jealousy, probably even before Brandon recognized it himself. It wasn't difficult to understand. If Roxley were in his shoes, he would feel the same way.

Roxley drew a deep breath and looked away. It wasn't wise for him to look at her too long. It made him wish for things that couldn't be. He could be her friend, but nothing more. He would have to content himself with that.

"It's so peaceful here," Chelsea said, breaking the silence. "Thank you for bringing me."

"The pleasure was most surely mine."

She turned her face up to him. "You've always been so kind to me, Roxley."

"It's because I care." He squeezed her hand against his side. "We're friends, after all."

"Dear friends."

He nodded.

Chelsea's gaze moved back to the lake. The water glistened beneath the autumn sunshine. A crow mocked them from the limbs of a willow tree, then took flight.

"Something's happening to me, Roxley," she said suddenly, her voice barely more than a whisper.

He stopped and leaned closer.

"I don't understand what it is, but I can feel it. It isn't madness. It's something else. . . ."

He waited, not daring to speak.

"That doll. And the fire in the nursery . . ." She looked at him again. Her eyes were round, luminous. She looked as if she would say more, then shook her head.

Roxley's hand slid beneath her chin. "It doesn't matter, Chelsea. When it's time, you'll have your answers."

"I wish Brandon believed in me." Her voice was choked as tears filled her eyes.

"He does."

"No. He cares for me. As one cares for a sick child."

"You're much more to him than a child, Chelsea."

She turned from him and dashed away her tears. Her shoulders straightened; her chin lifted. When she turned back to him, she was wearing a determined smile. "That's enough of feeling sorry for myself for one day, Roxley. You've done so much to lift my spirits. I refuse to think gloomily any longer." She slipped her hand into his arm once again. "What did you tell me about a charming place to have tea?"

Roxley felt a strong urge to kiss her. He was wise enough to resist it.

Brandon was halfway home when a black coach, pulled by two, high-stepping bay geldings, stopped in the street. The door of the carriage was emblazoned with the Marquess of

Bellfort's coat-of-arms. The coachman hopped down and hurried to open the door, then looked expectantly toward Brandon.

He saw no polite way to avoid the encounter. "Good day, viscount," Maitland said as he stepped up to the coach. "I had no idea you were in London."

The shadows inside the coach were kind to Maitland, making her seem years younger and even more beautiful. Her auburn hair was worn in a high cluster of curls. Her almond eyes caught the glimmer of sunlight spilling through the doorway. She fluttered them provocatively in his direction. She was wearing an amber-colored gown of lush velvet that brought out the golden glow of her complexion. Her flawless breasts seemed daringly close to spilling over the low neckline as she leaned toward him.

"I wouldn't have known you were here, of course, but I saw Roxley with your wife in the park not more than a half hour ago." She laughed, a low husky sound deep in her throat. "They didn't notice me. They didn't seem to know anyone else existed."

A muscle twitched in Brandon's cheek, but nothing else gave away how he felt about Maitland's news. He forced a smile. "I'm glad to hear Chelsea obeyed my order. She's been spending too much time in the house since we came to London. I told her before I left this morning that she was to go out. And I can always count on Roxley to show her a good time. He's a good friend. To both of us."

"Isn't he though?" Maitland leaned back against the plush seat. "Why don't you get in, and I'll have my driver take us to them. Then the four of us can have a nice visit."

"They're still at the park?"

"Heavens no. They drove away together. But if I know Roxley, he'll have been reluctant to take her home so soon. My guess is he's taken her someplace for tea. My brother is a terribly predictable fellow, and I know all his favorite haunts. It won't take us long to find them."

Brandon was tempted to refuse, but there was a strange gnawing sensation in his belly that he couldn't deny. He wanted to find Chelsea and Roxley. He didn't want them too long alone together. And if Maitland could help him find them, then all the better.

"Thank you, Lady Bellfort," he said as he pulled himself up through the coach doorway. "I'd like that."

"If you don't mind, luv, I've an errand to run while you have tea with his lordship. I won't be long."

Chelsea watched as Molly hurried along the busy sidewalk toward Fortnum & Mason, then allowed Roxley to guide her into the shop. The small room already had several customers. Waitresses in prim black dresses with white aprons and caps hurried back and forth from the kitchen. The tables, set close together, were covered with pink tablecloths and surrounded by fragile white chairs. The air was alive with wonderful fragrances—fresh baked breads and pastries and spices. The delicious scents made her mouth water and her stomach growl.

Roxley chose a table near the window and pulled out her chair. "Wait until you taste their scones, Chelsea." He patted his flat stomach. "I confess a terrible weakness for them."

While Roxley ordered their tea, Chelsea turned to gaze out the window. The shop was on Piccadilly in a busy section of the city. Hansom cabs, pulled by trotting horses, hurried up and down the street. Businessmen in their suits and hats and starched collars walked briskly to their appointments. Ladies in beautiful clothes entered shops and came out after buying more beautiful clothes.

It crossed her mind briefly to wonder what errand Molly might have had to run, but by this time, their first course was being served, and the cress and mustard sandwiches demanded all her attention.

She was pouring cream into her teacup when she heard the woman's voice. "What did I tell you, Brandon?"

Chelsea felt a sinking sensation in the pit of her stomach. Her appetite was lost. She looked up as Maitland, her arm linked with Brandon's, came toward their table.

"I told Brandon we would find you here, Roxley," the marchioness said to her brother. A triumphant glint flashed in her brown eyes as she turned them on Chelsea. "Your husband and I have had a most delightful visit, Lady

Fitzgerald. You don't mind if we join you, I hope?"

"Not at all," Chelsea replied.

Brandon pulled out a chair. As she thanked him, Maitland reached up to touch his sleeve. The gesture seemed terribly familiar. Chelsea's head began to ache just behind her eyes.

"My mother tells me she's met you, Lady Fitzgerald. You seem to have captivated her as you have my brother."

"I found the countess quite pleasant company." Chelsea's reply sounded wooden in her ears.

Roxley grinned at Chelsea. "What Maitland failed to say is that Mother doesn't take to very many people. If she likes you, you can be sure there's something quite special about you."

She thanked him with her eyes.

"How true," Maitland bit off sharply. Her voice softened as she turned toward Brandon. "You haven't met the countess yet, Brandon, but I know she would like you." She leaned toward him, offering him a better glimpse of her full breasts. "My mother and I have always had the same taste in men."

Chelsea glanced at Brandon's profile. He seemed so distant, so removed from her, so charmed by all Maitland so obviously offered. Her headache intensified.

Roxley tossed Chelsea a mischievous wink. "You know, dear sister, I just realized why you're in London so unexpectedly. Next week is your birthday. What is it this year? Thirty-five or thirty-six?"

Maitland's head snapped around. Her eyes threw daggers in her brother's direction. "Neither."

"Oh, that's right. It's only thirty-four. Is there a party planned at Mother's?"

Chelsea spoke without forethought. "I never would have guessed you were as old as thirty-four, Lady Conover." She was satisfied to see the angry color rising in Maitland's cheeks. "I hope I shall look as well a decade and more from now." With feigned innocence, she turned her eyes back upon the sandwiches. Her appetite had returned, and she felt inexplicably giddy.

She heard Roxley choke back laughter as he picked up the tray. "Care for a sandwich, Maitland?"

Brandon suffered in silence through the sandwiches, through the scones with Devonshire cream and strawberry jam, and finally, through the petit-fours. He tasted little that he ate. He merely wanted to get through the damnable tea and get Chelsea out of there. Each time he saw Roxley look at her, he wanted to bound out of his chair and toss the fellow through the window.

At least Maitland's blatant overtures had ceased. He stifled a sudden grin as he raised the teacup to his lips, remembering Maitland's expression when Chelsea mentioned how well the marchioness looked for her age. He'd thought Maitland might suffer apoplexy on the spot.

It was that sort of unexpected action Brandon had come to love in his wife. Meek and fragile one moment, then full of pluck the next. She kept him slightly off balance whenever he was with her. Reluctantly, he confessed to himself that, if her afternoon with Roxley had brought back the color to her cheeks and zest in her eyes, it had been worth the miserable hour of jealousy he'd suffered.

"Look," Chelsea said above the silence. "I wonder what's happening."

Three sets of eyes turned out the window. Just down the street from the tea shop a crowd had gathered in the middle of the street.

"Looks as if there might have been an accident," Roxley offered. "A cab probably lost a wheel or something."

As they watched, a young lad broke through the crowd and came running down the street toward them, then passed the window. Brandon had just shifted his gaze toward Chelsea when the door of the shop burst open.

"Is there a Chelsea 'ere?"

Brandon rose from his chair and turned toward the entrance. "What is it you want?"

It was the boy who'd just run down the street. He had a smudged face and his clothes were tattered. A street urchin, no doubt, searching for pockets to pick.

"She's askin' fer Chelsea."

"Who is?"

"The lady wot was run down. She kept sayin' tea an' Chelsea an' tryin' t'point, an' they sent me 'ere t'see."

Brandon heard a chair crash to the floor. He turned to find Chelsea standing. Her eyes were wide as they met his. Her hand reached out to clutch at his arm.

"It's Molly. It has to be Molly. No one else knew we were here."

He took her hand and led her through the maze of tables toward the door. The young boy looked up at him expectantly as they reached him, his palm lifted toward them.

"Go on, Brand," Roxley's voice came from behind. "I'll give the lad something for his trouble."

With a nod, he hurried on out the door.

The crowd had grown since they'd first looked out the window. Brandon shouldered his way through, pulling Chelsea behind him, trying to protect her as best he could from the jostling onlookers. At last they reached the center, finding several policemen trying to hold back the crowd.

He peered over the tops of their heads, looking into the center of the circle. He couldn't see the woman's face, but there was no mistaking the curly red hair.

"Excuse me," he said, trying to break through.

"Stand back, sir," an officer demanded.

"The woman is my servant."

The officer hesitated, then motioned him on.

He wouldn't have brought Chelsea if he'd known what they would find. But it was too late.

A groan rose in Chelsea's throat as she

dropped to her knees beside Molly's bruised and broken body. A leg lay at an odd angle from beneath her torn gray-striped gown. Scrapes and cuts bled on her face and arms.

"Molly?"

She cradled the woman's head in her lap.

"I'm here, Molly. It's Chelsea."

Molly moaned but didn't open her eyes.

"What happened, officer?" she heard Brandon ask.

"Run down by a carriage. Driver never even stopped. Just kept on going. Cold-blooded bastard. We'll find him, sir." There was a pause. "Poor woman. We've sent for a doctor but . . ."

There was a lump in Chelsea's throat.

"Alanna . . ." Molly whispered hoarsely. Her eyes slowly opened. They were glazed with pain.

"Yes. Yes, Molly." Chelsea was crying. "It's your Alanna. I'm here. You're going to be all right. They've sent for a doctor. He'll be here soon."

"No . . ." Molly's voice could barely be heard. "Not . . . true . . . Alanna . . ."

Chelsea held the nanny's head against her chest, unmindful of the blood that stained her bodice. "Yes, it *is* true. You'll be all right. You will. You will."

With great effort, Molly raised her hands to Chelsea's shoulders. Her fingers gripped tightly as she pulled her head toward Chelsea. For a moment, her green eyes seemed to clear. They stared hard into Chelsea's misting blue eyes.

"Devon . . ." she whispered. Her fingernails

clawed at the fabric of Chelsea's gown as she slid back toward Chelsea's lap.

"Devon? Who is Devon, Molly?"

"Dev . . . on . . ."

Once again, Molly's eyes glazed over, but this time without pain. Tears scalded Chelsea's eyes as she heard the breath leave Molly's body one final time.

CHAPTER
SEVENTEEN

Chelsea stood in the doorway, staring at the
empty room, her mind flooded with images of
Molly. It seemed impossible that she was gone.
Chelsea couldn't remember a time without
Molly. It seemed she had always been there.

She stepped into the bedroom.

There, luv. Your Molly's here.

She tried to remember something before
Molly's voice. There was nothing.

My poor Alanna.

Her gaze drifted to the bed. For how many
weeks had she lain there, Molly laying a cool
cloth on her fevered brow, Molly with her
medicine, Molly holding her as she retched
into the washbowl?

Molly had been there when Chelsea had first

seen Brandon. Protective, yet hopeful. Always wishing her happiness.

I'm glad for you, Lady Alanna, since he seems to make you happy.

She walked over to the window and looked down upon the sculptured gardens. The first happiness she could remember was of her time there with Brandon. Molly had been so afraid to let her go. But later, much later, it had been Molly who had unlocked her door and allowed Chelsea to leave these rooms, allowed her the chance to get well. It had been Molly who encouraged her to fight everyone for the chance to be free.

You show them what you're made of, Chelsea girl. You show them all.

But now Molly was gone. Who was there left for Chelsea to trust?

"Chelsea?"

She turned to meet Brandon's concerned gaze.

"Grandfather would like to see you when you feel up to it."

She nodded and turned her back to him once again. She waited until she knew he was gone, then sank onto the window seat.

What would happen to her now that she was back at Hawklin, now that Molly was gone? Would these be her rooms again? Would Brandon lock her away and forget he ever had a wife? Perhaps he'd already forgotten. In her mind, she saw Maitland on Brandon's arm, leaning into him, laughing up into his face. Perhaps . . .

She shook her head, warding off the doubts that plagued her. She couldn't deal with them now. Not now while her heart was sore over Molly's death.

Chelsea rose from the window seat and left the bedroom. She walked slowly down the hallway, pausing at the top of the curved staircase as her eyes strayed toward the northeast wing.

The nursery . . .

The fire . . .

The doll . . .

Chelsea, come look. Come look.

The voice seemed to echo down the hall. She felt a sudden chill, followed by an urge to flee. It was an urge she quickly obeyed, her feet skimming over the marble steps as she descended toward the first floor.

Bowman was crossing the entry hall just as she reached the bottom step. His eyebrow rose almost imperceptibly. "Is there something amiss, my lady?"

She stopped and stared at him.

"My lady?"

"No, Bowman," she answered, forcing her voice not to quiver. Her hand came up to smooth her hair. "Where will I find his grace?"

"In the library."

"Thank you, Bowman." She nodded slightly in dismissal.

The butler returned the nod, then proceeded on his way.

The house seemed so silent. So empty.

217

Chelsea, come look.

She rushed on toward the library.

Brandon looked up as Chelsea swept into the room. Her face seemed even more pale than when he'd seen her upstairs. She looked breathless, and there was something in her eyes that made him think of a trapped fox as the hounds close in.

Lawrence rose from his chair. "Chelsea, my dear, I was so sorry to hear about Molly." He rounded the long table to embrace her.

Her eyes glittered with sudden tears. "Thank you, your grace."

"Here now. What's this 'your grace' nonsense?"

Chelsea offered him a ghost of a smile. "Grandfather."

Lawrence kissed her forehead. "That's better. Now, come sit and tell me of your stay in London."

"There isn't much to tell." Her gaze darted to Brandon.

And suddenly, he truly saw what was there. For the first time, he understood what had erected the wall of silence between them. She feared him. The fragile trust they had known at Teakwood was gone. What had he done wrong? He had protected her from her father's wish to send her away. He had given her his name. He had given her his heart. What more could he possibly do? Perhaps it was only a symptom of the madness that lurked always in the shadows, waiting to snatch her from him when he was least prepared. Perhaps there was nothing more he could do to win her trust, to win her love.

Lawrence led Chelsea to a comfortable leather chair near the fireplace, then sat beside her in its twin. "Surely you enjoyed yourself before Molly's tragedy. Did you take in the theater?"

"I . . . I was ill for a while. We didn't go out much."

"Oh. I see."

Chelsea stood suddenly. "Grandfather, please excuse me. I—I really must be alone for a while to . . . to think." She didn't wait for a reply.

Lawrence's gaze moved from the doorway through which Chelsea had just passed to Brandon. Concern darkened his faded brown eyes.

Brandon answered the silent question. "She had another spell in London. Something about a doll, the one Molly found up in the nursery."

"I think you should follow her, Brand."

Brandon felt as if a vice were tightening about his chest. He nodded, then hurried from the library.

Chelsea chose a lanky chestnut mare from among those stabled in the barn. She stepped into the stall, talking softly to the skittish horse. "Easy, girl. Easy, Lady," she crooned as she stroked the glossy coat.

The horse eyed her suspiciously.

"Easy now, Lady. You'd like to go for a run, wouldn't you?"

The mare quieted, as if she understood and agreed.

Chelsea buried her face in the mare's dark mane. "I wish we'd never left Teakwood," she whispered.

The horse snorted and bobbed her head up and down, then pawed at the straw on the stall floor.

"Let's go. I want out of here, too."

It took hardly any time at all to brush and bridle the animal. Chelsea decided against the saddle. She wanted to ride today just like the first time she'd ridden Duchess. She wanted to race the wind and feel the power of the horse beneath her.

Before the disapproving eyes of the groom who appeared just as she led Lady from her stall, Chelsea grabbed a handful of mane and swung up onto the mare's back, her skirts hiked up above her knees. In a last rebellious gesture, she tore the pins from her chignon and set her pale blond hair free. Then the pair thundered out of the barn and toward the woodlands beyond the sweeping lawns and gardens of Hawklin Hall.

More than an hour later, Chelsea dismounted by a quiet forest pool. The glen was cool and shadowed, the thick, tall trees blocking out most of the autumn sun's rays. Lady plunged her nose deep into the dark pool and drank noisily while Chelsea seated herself on a round rock, removed her shoes, and dangled her toes in the water. She shivered and drew her feet back, tucking them beneath her soiled blue skirt.

Bracing her chin on her knees, she asked, "What am I to do?"

She wasn't even sure to what she referred. What was she to do now that Molly was gone? What was she to do about Brandon? What was she to do about all the questions and doubts that plagued her?

Dear God, help me. Help me to find the answers.

Chelsea lay back on the rock and closed her eyes. Too much to think about. Too much to feel. Too much . . . too much . . .

"It's a pitiful job I've done raisin' you, my girl. Your mother, God rest her, would never forgive me. Her daughter runnin' wild all the time, as wild as that fox of yours. She was a lady, my Catherine. Born to the gentry. I should never have taken her away from it. It's my fault she's gone. This life was too hard for her."

He was a tall man with golden hair and beard, his eyes a piercing blue. His forehead was deeply lined, his hands calloused and gnarled.

"If your mother was here, it's a lady you'd be, too. A lady, I tell you. Well, it's still a lady you'll be. I've heard from your aunt."

"No!"

Chelsea sat up with a start. Her heart was pounding rapidly in her chest. She glanced about her, sure she would see the man who'd been speaking. Surely he was there. Surely he was real.

Dusk had fallen over the glen. Had she been sleeping? Had it only been a dream?

No, not a dream. It was too real. She could still see him if she closed her eyes. She could see him and the white cottage behind him. Whoever he was, he was real and so was that place. The image made her feel wistful, lonely. Who was he?

Slowly, she became aware of the sounds of night around her. Tree limbs swayed in the breeze. An owl hooted in the distance. The long grasses rustled as the field mice skittered toward their holes in the earth. A frog croaked from beyond the pond. Even as she sat there, the forest darkened. It was time to return to Hawklin.

"Lady . . ."

She realized then that she couldn't see the mare. Her horse had wandered off as Chelsea dozed.

"Lady?"

She stood and began walking, picking her way carefully, squinting to see the ground beneath her feet.

A child's laughter. Her laughter. It was dark and she was seated in the long grasses of the moor, tall shrubs shading her from the summer sun. A baby fox was crawling over her lap and up onto her shoulders. Then it was licking her ear, tickling her and making her giggle. And behind her, bathed in moonlight, was the tall blond man, a smile upon his face.

Chelsea froze in place and held her breath. She wasn't asleep this time. Her eyes were wide open. And once again the vision was all too real. *She* had been that child. But, of course, that couldn't be. It couldn't. Was it madness? No. No, it wasn't madness. What she saw left her feeling calm, comforted, almost happy. Madness wouldn't make her feel that way.

"Then what's happening?" she whispered. She jumped at the sound of her own voice in the still night. Her hand flew to her throat where she could feel her fluttering pulse.

The jingle of a bridle drew her attention elsewhere.

"Lady? Lady, where are you?"

An answering snort guided her into the dense woods. She found the mare, her reins snagged by the limbs of a fallen tree.

"Can you find your way home in the dark, girl?" she asked as she untangled the reins, then stepped up onto the tree and slipped onto the horse's back.

As the mare moved through the trees, Chelsea glanced back over her shoulder toward the glen and the forest pool. She almost hated to leave. She almost believed that if she'd stayed a little longer, everything would come clear to her.

Brandon rode through the woods for hours, tracking and backtracking, looking for some sign that she'd been there. But it was hopeless. He was no mountain man with an eye for the trail. All he could do was call out her name and hope she would hear and answer him. As darkness settled around him, he had to fight off the persistent thought that something tragic had befallen her. Or that she'd run off, never to be found again.

It was nearing midnight when his weary horse found its way to the barn. A bleary-eyed stable boy took the animal's reins from him.

"Have horses saddled and ready at first light. Tell Cooper I want several of the men to go out with me in the morning. We must resume the search for Chelsea in the morning."

"'Er ladyship, sir?"

"Yes. I couldn't find her anywhere."

"But she's 'ere, sir. She come in 'ours ago."

"She's here?"

But Brandon didn't wait for the boy's answer. He ran across the lawn toward the house. He took the back stairs up to the second floor, bursting into Chelsea's old room with a crash of the door against the wall. The room was dark . . . and empty.

He turned just as a maid, a lamp held above her head, stepped into the hallway to see what the ruckus was about.

"Where's Lady Fitzgerald?" he demanded.

The girl quaked before his dark glare.

"Where is she?"

"In—in your rooms, m'lord," she answered, pointing her finger. "It's where his grace said t'put her things."

Brandon's increasing fury didn't allow him to admit that was exactly where he'd wanted her things put when they'd arrived. She had come directly to her old rooms, and so he'd assumed that was where she'd be now.

He brushed passed the maid, his long legs carrying him quickly down the hall toward his own bedchamber.

Hours ago. She'd come home hours ago. And he'd spent that time in worry while she was curled up, all nice and warm and comfy in his bed. How dare she cause him so much concern! She'd been mournful and depressed for two days. How was he to know what she might do in that state?

Hours ago, blast her!

CHAPTER
<u>EIGHTEEN</u>

Chelsea rolled over onto her back, her eyes wide open. Sleep just wouldn't come. She wondered where Brandon was. She missed his arms around her. She missed . . .

She turned onto her side, squeezing her eyes closed. She didn't want to think about their lovemaking. Not once since her spell in London had he reached for her, drawn her into his arms, and made love to her. The brief desire he had known for her seemed to have been spent. Or perhaps she had destroyed it herself. If only she hadn't seen that doll. If only she didn't keep envisioning things.

Her thoughts moved back a few hours. If she cleared her mind of everything else, she could see the blond man once again. He had a friendly smile. Laughter warmed the blue of his eyes. Who was he? And the tiny fox. It was almost as if she could still feel it nibbling at her ear.

She had returned to Hawklin with a strange sense of excitement, as if she'd discovered something important. She'd wanted to share it with someone. She had sought for Brandon, but no one was able to tell her where he'd gone. The duke had already retired for the night, so she couldn't ask him where Brandon had gone or talk to him about the things she'd envisioned. Finally, she'd asked the maid to take her to her room. She'd been almost surprised to find her things were in Brandon's bedchamber. She'd half expected him to relegate her to a more secluded room. Maybe that was what he really wanted. Maybe he hadn't told anyone to bring her things there.

As she rolled onto her stomach, her thoughts changed direction once again. Now she could see Maitland in her mind. She wondered about Brandon's interest in her. It was obvious that Maitland had a great fascination for Brandon. If he were a free man . . . But he wasn't free. He was married to her.

She felt a spark of anger as she tossed onto her back again. Did Brandon really have business with his solicitor two days ago, or had he been with Maitland Conover the whole time? She would have asked him, too, if it hadn't been for Molly's accident.

Molly . . . Dear Molly. She had been Chelsea's only true friend. Except, of course, for

Roxley. He was her friend. But he would like to be more than just friends, and that made Chelsea uneasy. She was in love with Brandon. She knew that. Completely and without end. She loved him.

The bedroom door was flung wide. She could see Brandon's silhouette in the light from the hall. She sat up.

"Where were you?" he asked in a terse voice.

"Where was—? I've been right here for hours."

"I've searched half the countryside for you."

Long strides brought him to the bed. He grabbed her by the shoulders and pulled her up onto her knees. "Don't you ever leave here like that again."

"Don't leave?" She was inexplicably angry. "Why? Am I your prisoner?"

"If it will keep you out of trouble, yes."

She struggled free of him, sliding off the bed. She flung her loose hair over her shoulder, then grabbed hold of one of the bedposts as she glared at his shadowed form. "I *won't* be your prisoner, Brandon Fitzgerald! Is it a crime for me to take a horse for a ride? I needed time to myself. Time to think. It got dark faster than I expected. I wasn't in any danger."

"Not in any danger! Are you mad?" He stepped quickly around the edge of the bed and captured her in his grasp once again.

"No! No, I'm not mad. I'm not." She began to pummel his shoulders and chest with her fists. "I'm not mad!" She wasn't even aware that tears were streaming down her cheeks or that her voice was rising. "I'm not mad!"

Brandon's mouth silenced her protests.

She continued to fight him, sobbing now.

I'm not mad. The thought echoed in her mind. *I'm not mad.*

His hands loosened their hold on her shoulders, moving slowly around to her back. He pulled her closer to him as his kiss deepened, lengthened. His touch lit a fire somewhere in the most secret part of her heart. It spread like hot lava through her veins. Her protest stopped as she succumbed to his kisses and anger turned to passion.

Perhaps I am mad at that, she thought as her arms slid up from his chest to wrap around his neck. And then all conscious thought ceased. There was no room for it. There was only the desire to become a part of him. That was all she knew.

Brandon moaned deep in his throat, then bent low and swept her legs off the floor, never once breaking free of her lips. Together they fell onto the bed, their bodies straining to be closer. Legs tangled in the folds of her long nightgown and the tousled blankets.

Impatiently her hands moved to unbutton his shirt. In her haste, she tore two buttons from it. She was only vaguely aware of the sound as they bounced across the tiled floor of the bedroom. Pushing the shirt back from his shoulders, she ran her fingers through the black hair on his chest, her fingers pausing to feel the thunder of his heartbeat.

Brandon's hands were equally busy. They

moved deftly down the front of her nightgown, then pushed it downward as her fingers moved to the waistband of his breeches. In a short time, they lay beside each other, naked and on fire with desire.

Her mouth opened to his kisses just as her body opened to receive him. Their joining was almost violent, their hands roaming over heated flesh, their mouths drinking in the taste of the other.

In crashing waves, the wondrous feelings swept through her, over her, around her until she thought she might drown in them. She cried out, her arms tightening about his neck, as she reached for the pinnacle of passion. His own cry mingled with hers as the darkened room seemed to explode into a thousand flashes of light.

Exhausted, they clung to each other, dragging in deep gasps of breath as their bodies slowly returned to earth. And finally, they slept.

She lay in the crook of his arm, her head on his shoulder, her breast against his side. She sensed it was just before dawn, but she was unwilling to open her eyes to confirm the notion.

She drew in a long, deep breath, then let out a soft sigh. She replayed their lovemaking in her mind once again and felt a tiny thrill swell in the pit of her stomach. She wasn't even sure how it had happened. One moment they'd been exchanging angry words, the next they were locked in a fiery embrace.

I will not let you go, Brandon.

Whatever else was wrong with her life, whatever unsolved mysteries still remained, she knew she belonged with Brandon. She would rather die than lose him. It didn't matter that he thought her a madwoman. It didn't matter that one day he might decide to send her away to an asylum for the insane, as her father had wanted. It didn't even matter that he didn't love her as she loved him. Nothing mattered except that she be with him. He cared for her, desired her; that was enough for now.

And the woman—any woman—who tried to steal him from her would rue the day she was born.

"Are you awake?" Brandon asked softly.

"Mmmm."

"Promise me you won't go off like that again, Chelsea."

This morning she would have promised him anything. Anything at all. "I promise."

So if she weren't to go riding alone, just what was she to do with herself?

Chelsea stood at the window in the great drawing room. Even without her promise to Brandon, she couldn't have gone riding, she admitted to herself. The weather had taken a sharp turn from sunny late autumn to damp and dreary early winter. Outside, the rain fell in great sheets, rattling the windowpane, the wind whistling around the corners of the mansion. Though it was midday, it was nearly as dark as night. She shivered and turned from the window, her eyes sweeping over the vast, empty room to the cheery fire burning on the hearth.

Brandon and his grandfather had disappeared into the library hours ago. A letter from Justin had arrived from America that morning. She had caught enough of their conversation to know it concerned Foxworth Iron Works.

She tried again to interest herself in a piece of embroidery, but it was pointless. She just hadn't the desire nor the patience it required. Pent-up energy made her restless. She was tired of sitting and doing nothing.

She wandered out of the drawing room toward the entry hall. The house seemed dreadfully silent. Not even Bowman was in sight. She wondered where everyone had taken themselves to.

This is my home, and I don't even know where anything is.

The thought disturbed her. She *should* know. One day it would be hers and Brandon's. One day he would be the Duke of Foxworth and she would be his duchess. Perhaps it was time she took charge. Perhaps it was time she learned to administer their household. Surely Grandfather would welcome a woman's touch.

What do I know of running a household?

Nothing. But she could learn. She knew she could learn.

Resolutely, she turned up the stairs in search of the housekeeper. Of course, she wouldn't know the woman if she saw her. But she would find someone who could tell her.

Chelsea wandered the hallway, opening doors and peeking into bedchambers. She paused in one room and ran her finger over a chiffonier. Not even a trace of dust. Whoever the housekeeper was, she had her staff well ordered. Perhaps Chelsea wasn't needed after all.

She shook off the thought. Of course she was needed. She would be mistress of this house one day. She couldn't ignore her duty to that position. She pressed on with her search.

She found a maid in the southeast wing near her old suite of rooms.

"Excuse me."

The girl turned from her dusting with a gasp.

"I'm sorry. I didn't mean to startle you."

"'Tis all right, m'lady. You just come up so sudden-like. I wasn't expectin' nobody."

"I'm Lady Fitzgerald."

She curtsied. "Yes, mum. I know." She was a petite girl with strawberry curls tucked under a prim, white cap. Freckles dotted her tiny nose. Her fingers twirled the feather duster in front of her white apron.

"I was looking for the housekeeper."

"Mrs. 'ardwick? She'd be in the kitchen most likely. She likes to oversee the supper preparations 'erself."

"The kitchen." Chelsea smiled. "Thank you." She turned to go, then looked back over her shoulder. "What is your name?"

"Leigh, m'lady."

"How long have you worked here, Leigh?"

"Since summer."

"Well, it looks like you're doing a fine job, Leigh. I'll tell Mrs. Hardwick so."

The girl blushed to the roots of her hair. "Thank you, m'lady."

Chelsea hurried back toward the stairs. She felt a tiny thrill of excitement. The idea of running Hawklin Hall had taken hold. What a challenge it would be. And if she did it right, Brandon would be proud of her. She would like it very much if Brandon were proud of her, if he could see her succeed at something.

Once she'd reached the base of the stairs, she had no idea which way to turn. The center of the house was massive. Four wings spread out from each corner. The kitchen could be anywhere. She did know where the dining room was. Perhaps the kitchen was close by. She turned left and hurried in that direction.

Chelsea discovered two maids in the dining room. They were dressed just as Leigh had been, in simple black dresses with starched white aprons and caps. They were spreading a clean white tablecloth over the lengthy oak table.

"Hello," she said as they looked up. "I'm looking for Mrs. Hardwick. Do you know where she might be?"

"In the kitchen, m'lady," one of the young women answered.

Chelsea hid her embarrassment at having to ask. "And can you point me in the direction of the kitchen?"

One of them walked toward the door and pointed across the great hall. "Down that hallway there, m'lady, beyond the dressing room."

"You've been very helpful." She paused. "What is your name?"

"I'm Elsbeth, m'lady. That's Anna."

"Elsbeth. You used to bring food to my room, didn't you? When I was . . . when I was ill?"

The dark-haired woman nodded.

It made Chelsea a little self-conscious, knowing the servants knew about her illness. But she would have to overcome that. And she would. "Have you worked here a long time?"

"No, m'lady. The duchess—I mean, Lady Fitzgerald—gave me the position last summer. July, I think it was."

Anna set a silver candelabrum in the center of the table, then walked across the dining room toward Chelsea. "I'm on my way to the kitchen now, m'lady. I can take you to Mrs. Hardwick."

"Thank you, Anna."

As she followed Anna down the long corridor into the northwest wing, she craned her neck to see into the rooms they were passing. There was a large dressing room, probably a busy place when past dukes and duchesses had entertained. They passed an enclosed courtyard, a dreary place at the moment as the rain continued to fall, drowning the last of the fall flowers, scattering leaves across the stone floor and ironwork benches.

She stopped suddenly as her eyes glanced into an ornate bedchamber. "Anna, wait." She opened the door farther and stared in. "Whose room is this?"

"It's the state bedchamber, m'lady. For her royal highness, should she come to visit the duke."

"The queen? Has she ever been here before?"

"Not since I've been here, m'lady."

"How long is that, Anna?"

"I came at the same time as Elsbeth. We're from the same village, and when we heard the Duke of Foxworth was looking for domestics, we came here straight away." She pointed down the hall. "The kitchen's right this way, m'lady."

The queen at Hawklin Hall. Wouldn't that be something?

Reluctantly, she left the state bedroom and followed Anna toward the kitchen.

CHAPTER NINETEEN

Brandon looked across the supper table at Chelsea, feasting his tired eyes upon her. He didn't think she had ever looked lovelier than she did tonight. Her silver-gold hair was gathered high on her head; soft wisps curled at her nape and across her forehead. She was wearing a pink and cream-colored satin gown that brought out the rose tint of her cheeks and revealed the long stretch of white throat. There was still a touch of sadness in her eyes, yet he was encouraged by the spark of new interest he saw there too. He wondered what thoughts were churning behind those beautiful eyes of blue.

"Grandfather?" Chelsea looked up from her supper plate.

"Yes, my dear."

"I spoke with Mrs. Hardwick today."

"Mrs. Hardwick?"

"The housekeeper."

Lawrence placed his napkin on the table as he cleared his throat. "Oh, yes. Mrs. Hardwick. I've spoken with her a number of times. Industrious woman."

"Well . . ." Chelsea glanced nervously toward Brandon, then back toward the duke. "I thought . . . I was thinking, perhaps it would be good for me to—to take a hand in the running of Hawklin Hall. I don't really know anything about it, but I think I could learn."

"Chelsea, my dear, I think that's a splendid idea. Don't you, Brandon?"

Brandon was looking at his wife with undisguised surprise. It hadn't occurred to him that she might want to tackle something like running the ducal manse.

"Brandon?" Lawrence persisted. "Isn't that a splendid idea?"

Chelsea's eyes were such a beautiful shade of blue. There had always been something about them that made him want to hold her, protect her. But there were times, like last night, when they could flash with fire and strength. She had needed no protection then. And when she was strong, he still wanted to hold her.

Those blue eyes were turned on him now, watching him, waiting for his answer. Filled with hope, uncertainty, determination.

"Do you really want to take on such a large task, Chelsea?" he asked. "You"—he searched

238

for the right words—"you've just had a terrible shock from Molly's accident. Don't you think—?"

"I think it would be good for me." She met his gaze squarely. "I've too much time on my hands. You and Grandfather are busy, but I have little to do. And Grandfather needs a hostess. He should be entertaining. I could plan things for him, see that all runs smoothly."

"By heavens!" the duke exclaimed. "That's exactly what we need to be doing. It's time this place knew the sounds of laughter and filled rooms. A ball at Hawklin. It would be like when I was a young man. The parties we used to have here. . . ."

Brandon continued to look at his wife, hardly hearing his grandfather's words. He couldn't stop the terrible doubt that nagged at him. He remembered all too clearly the scene in London. That had been a gathering of only a few people, but look what had happened. How could they be sure something so innocent wouldn't trigger another episode? If the strain were too much . . .

"I can do this, Brandon." Chelsea's voice was low, her gaze direct.

Hoping he wasn't making a mistake, he nodded.

Chelsea's smile lit the room. "I met several of the staff today. Mrs. Hardwick was most helpful. I know she'll teach me what I need to know. She told me how much she liked Molly, even though she'd only known her a short time." A puzzled expression crossed her brow. "I just realized something. Every one of the servants I met today has been here only a month or two."

"I suppose your parents took those who'd been with them for years to London," the duke said as he lifted a glass of wine toward his lips.

Chelsea's frown deepened. Her glance shifted to somewhere on the white tablecloth. Her mouth looked strained. "It's just as well. Perhaps they won't . . . won't know much about me."

"What's to know, Chelsea?" Brandon asked, leaning slightly forward. "Do they need to know more than that you're warm and kind and gentle?"

Round, luminous eyes lifted to him. Slowly, the smile returned, this one just for him. "I'll begin tomorrow. Really begin," was all she said.

Chelsea was in the small office off the kitchen the following morning, going over Mrs. Hardwick's meticulous household records, when Bowman appeared in the doorway.

"Lady Fitzgerald, guests have arrived."

"Who is it, Bowman?" she asked, glancing up briefly before her eyes strayed back to the book before her.

"Lady Bellfort and Lord Roxley, my lady."

She couldn't contain the tiny groan. She glanced down at the simple white blouse and tan skirt she had chosen upon arising.

"I've shown them into the salon."

"Thank you, Bowman. I'll be right with them." Perhaps, if she hurried, she could slip up to her room and change into something more elegant.

"Lord Brandon is with them now."

She grimaced. Her choices were to leave Brandon alone with Maitland a little longer while she changed or to go directly to the salon. Neither was desirable. But somehow, it seemed much worse to give that woman any more time alone with Brandon than was unavoidable.

With a sigh, she rose from the cane-backed chair. She nervously touched the chignon at her nape, then ran her hands over her skirt to smooth out the imaginary wrinkles. Then she squared her shoulders and left the office.

The salon was a large, airy room on the east side of the house. One wall was made of glass windows and doors which opened onto the white-pillared portico. In good weather, the room was brightened by the morning sun, but today, a gray fog hovered over the porch and the salon seemed damp and chilled. Fires had been lit in all three fireplaces, but they did little to brighten Chelsea's spirit.

From the doorway, Chelsea's eyes fell instantly upon Maitland. The marchioness looked more exquisite than ever in an elegant French walking dress of plaid brown with tan suede drape and bustle. A perky hat graced her coiffured auburn locks. She was holding a dainty china cup in one hand while she leaned toward Brandon, obviously captured by his every word.

Chelsea glanced down at her simple skirt and cursed herself for not changing first. A few more minutes couldn't have made much difference. Perhaps it wasn't too late. No one had seen her. She could just back out of the doorway. . . .

"Chelsea!"

Roxley had seen her.

Caught, she pasted a welcoming smile onto her lips and walked into the room. "Hello, Roxley. Lady Bellfort. How kind of you to call. We weren't expecting visitors on so dreary a day."

"Terribly unfashionable to come so early, I know," Roxley said as he took Chelsea's arm and escorted her to a nearby chair. "We just arrived at Rosemont last night. We would have waited to call, but we were concerned about you. We know how much you cared for Molly. You left London so quickly, we hadn't time to express our condolences."

Maitland's glance flicked over Chelsea's attire, then returned to Brandon. "It isn't often one acquires such affection for one's nanny."

"Molly was more to me than a servant," Chelsea said stiffly. "She was my friend as well."

"Yes, of course." Maitland's smile was condescending.

Roxley sat down across from Chelsea. "You're looking well, Chelsea."

"I'm feeling much better, thank you." She looked toward Brandon and found him frowning at her. Was he ashamed of the way she looked? Had she said something amiss? Would he rather she hadn't come to the salon so he could have had time with Maitland without her?

"And what are your plans now, Brandon?" Roxley asked. "Are you going to stay at Hawklin for a while?"

"Yes. Through the fall and winter, I expect."

"Splendid. I'll see more of you then."

Maitland set her china cup on the low table before the settee. Her voice sounded husky, almost intimate. "I was rather hoping you would come to Teakwood again." Her almond-shaped eyes were turned upon Brandon with open admiration.

Chelsea felt as if she were intruding, just being there. Her cheeks felt flushed. Her hands were moist; she tucked them into the pockets of her skirt. She wasn't sure what she might have done next if Lawrence hadn't entered the salon.

The duke strolled across the long room toward the small group, his hand extended. "Roxley, my boy, whatever brought you out on a dismal morning such as this?"

"Maitland returns to Bellfort tomorrow. . . ." He cast a pointed glance in his sister's direction. "And she insisted she couldn't leave without paying her respects to Brandon and Chelsea. We both felt terrible over what happened in London."

Lawrence's wrinkled hand fell lightly on

Chelsea's shoulder. "It was a terrible tragedy. Molly was a part of this household for years, though I hadn't the chance to know her long. We'll miss her."

Chelsea felt a lump forming in her throat and swallowed back the hot tears. She wasn't going to cry in front of Maitland Conover. Not even if it killed her.

"How about you, Roxley? Are you staying on at Rosemont?"

"I am, your grace. There's no reason for me to return to London now."

"Good," the duke continued. "Then you'll be able to join us for the party we're planning. We've been much too secluded since arriving in England. It's time I renewed a few old friendships and made some new ones." He sighed as his gaze moved around the room. "It will be good to have some excitement around the old hall."

Maitland's eyes were lit with new interest as she looked at the duke. "What kind of party, your grace?"

"Well," he replied as he sat down. "I rather thought it might be fun to have a fox hunt, followed by a ball the next day. I remember when I was a young man—before I left for America—we used to have houseparties that would last for days on end." He sighed. "Of course, I was much younger then."

"Why, your grace, you're not the least bit old."

Lawrence's reply was to chuckle and shake his head.

Chelsea listened to the exchange with a growing sense of dread. She would never have chosen to include Maitland Conover in their plans if there were any way to avoid it. But what could she do now? The duke had already invited Roxley. Good manners wouldn't allow her to exclude his sister. She would have to extend an invitation now. It was unavoidable. She opened her mouth to speak but never had the chance.

Maitland had turned once more toward Brandon. "I wish I could be here for your party, Brandon, but pressing matters demand my return to Bellfort Castle. I suppose my steward could handle things, but . . ." She shrugged. "You understand the responsibility on my shoulders. It's difficult, being a woman alone with so much that must be done, but I owe it to my son Edgar to see that all remains well until he comes of age."

Chelsea couldn't restrain the relieved smile that brightened her face. "How very sorry we are that you can't join us, Lady Bellfort." It would have been difficult for anyone to believe she was sorry, judging by the lilt in her voice. She looked at Brandon. "My husband and I shall miss you."

That too was a lie, at least for her part. What about Brandon? Was she mistaken or did she see a twinkle of laughter hidden in his dark brown eyes? She looked back at Maitland. The widow's mouth was set in a grim line, and her eyes had narrowed. But Chelsea didn't care. The woman wasn't going to be here forever, after all. Chelsea only had to get through a short while longer in her company. Only as long as was polite.

Lawrence cleared his throat. "Yes, well—we all shall." He turned his head toward Roxley. "Why don't you two stay and dine with us this afternoon?"

Chelsea could have kicked the old man right in the shin, despite her affection for him.

"We would love to," Maitland answered quickly. "Wouldn't we, Roxley?"

To Brandon, Maitland Conover was a simple annoyance. Her blatant sexuality and conspicuous flirtation were mere irritations. He found Roxley's obvious infatuation with Chelsea much more disturbing.

Throughout the luncheon, Brandon observed the way Roxley's eyes seldom left Chelsea, the way he laughed warmly whenever she addressed him, the way his voice lowered when he spoke to her. To be fair, Roxley's behavior never went beyond the bounds of propriety, but still . . . He was relieved when it was time for the pair to go.

The rain had returned and was falling in great sheets from a roiling black sky. While the duke, his family, and his guests stood in the great hall, Bowman brought Maitland's wrap and Roxley's cloak from the dressing room.

Maitland slipped into the satin-lined cape the butler held up for her. "This has been a delightful afternoon, your grace," she said softly.

"You must return the favor and call upon me at Bellfort."

"I've enjoyed it, too, my dear. Perhaps I shall pop in if I'm up your way."

Maitland glanced around her. "Bowman, you seem to have forgotten my reticule from the dressing room."

"I am sorry, my lady. I'll get it at once."

As soon as the butler had disappeared, Maitland's eyebrows lifted. "How silly of me. I think I left it in the salon. I'll only be a moment, Roxley." Then she hurried off toward the salon in a rustle of silk petticoats.

Roxley raised an eyebrow before glancing at Brandon. "Maitland rarely goes after anything herself."

The words were scarcely out of his mouth when they all heard Maitland's cry.

"Good heavens!" Lawrence said in hushed surprise.

The three men, followed by Chelsea, hurried toward the salon. They found Maitland lying in the middle of the floor amidst a tangle of skirts.

"Maitland, what's wrong?" Roxley asked as he dropped to his knee beside her.

"I . . . I fell. There was something slippery on the floor." She moaned. "I'm afraid I've injured my ankle." Her gaze lifted to Brandon. "I don't think I can walk."

"Roxley," Lawrence said, taking control, "take your sister to one of the bedchambers. Chelsea, show him the way. Brandon, you'd best send someone to fetch the doctor."

CHAPTER
TWENTY

"The very least I can do, Chelsea, is help you with your plans for the houseparty."

Chelsea carefully lifted Maitland's foot and slipped another pillow beneath it. "That's most kind of you, but I assure you, it isn't necessary. We just want you to rest and get well." *So you can go home*, she finished silently.

Maitland had been there for three days now —and it already seemed an eternity. She showed no signs of improvement or of any plans to take her leave of Hawklin Hall.

The marchioness flipped her long auburn hair over her shoulder. "But I know you haven't had any experience in planning such a large gathering as the duke wishes. I'd be more than happy to lend a hand to assure its success."

Chelsea gritted her teeth and held her peace.

"Perhaps I shall take a short nap before tea time." Maitland yawned. "Tell the maid to wake me in time to freshen up before the footman comes to carry me downstairs."

"Of course."

Of all the gall! Chelsea seethed as she left the guest bedchamber. She even doubted Maitland's injury was real. If the physician hadn't said it appeared to be a bad sprain, Chelsea would have called the woman a liar to her face.

Chelsea hurried down the hallway. The door to another bedchamber was ajar, and as she passed, she heard voices. She paused.

"Rachel, the baker's daughter, she said you could see the fire for miles. Flames shootin' right out of the roof, they did. But it was 'er ladyship 'erself who was said to 'ave set it."

"Nooo. I don't believe you."

"'Tis true. I swear on me mother's grave, I do."

Chelsea stepped closer to the door.

"Bloomin' gives me the creeps to even go near those stairs. I don't care 'ow much fixin' they've done up there. Rachel says it's 'aunted." The voice fell to a whisper. "The girl, she was 'er ladyship's companion, she went in t'try t'save 'er and died in the tryin'. They say she comes back now an' again. She comes back lookin' for 'er ladyship."

"Go on, Leigh. You're frightenin' me. Besides, what would the baker's daughter know about what goes on here?"

Leigh sounded indignant. "She's been keepin' company right regular with John Booth."

"John?"

"You know. The skinny fellow wot works wi' the 'orses. 'E's been 'ere longer than most of us. 'E should know, shouldn't 'e?"

"But why would her ladyship set fire to the house? She seems so nice and all."

Leigh's voice fell even further. "There's rumors she's been mad since birth."

"Lady Coleford? Go on with you. She's the nicest lady I've ever worked for."

Chelsea stepped back from the bedchamber door. Her heart was hammering in her chest as if she'd just run a mile.

The fire in the nursery. She hadn't imagined it. There'd been a fire and someone had died in it.

She turned her eyes down the long corridor. A cold wind seemed to sweep toward her, enveloping her in icy tentacles. She felt as if fingers had closed around her forearms, fingers that tugged and pulled her toward that dreaded room.

Chelsea, come look.

Panic filled her breast, and she turned and fled to the safety of her room.

When Brandon stepped into their bedroom that evening, Chelsea was seated at her dressing table, staring at her reflection. A sixth sense warned him something was wrong. He walked slowly across the room, stopping behind her and placing his hands on her bare shoulders.

Chelsea's gaze came up to meet his in the mirror. Her face was pale, even in the golden light of her lamp. Her eyes seemed larger than usual.

"Good evening, Chelsea." He placed a kiss on the crown of her head.

She stared at him for a long time, but it was almost as if she were looking through him. Perhaps it was a trick of the mirror, yet a dark premonition made his blood run cold.

Finally, in a remote, toneless voice, she asked, "Did you know the nursery is said to be haunted?"

A terrible, sinking sensation tumbled in his belly. Unconsciously, his fingers tightened on her shoulders.

"The servants say she comes back now and again." Chelsea twisted on the stool, tipping back her head so she could look up at him. "The fire I set killed her. You knew about the fire, didn't you, Brandon?"

"A little." He sank to one knee beside her, his hands slipping from her shoulders to her arms. He didn't want to let go. It was as if he had to hold on to keep her there.

Chelsea's gaze shifted to somewhere beyond him, as if she were looking into another time, another place. "She was there because of me, you know. She was hired to be my companion. Ha!" She laughed sharply, but there was no humor in it.

The sound cut Brandon like a knife.

"A companion to a lunatic. How desperate

she must have been for a position."

"Don't say that." Cold dread was seeping up his spine.

"I want to know who she was, Brandon. I want to know if she had family or friends. I want to know what she was like. I want to know. I *need* to know."

"Then we'll find out. I'll help you. I promise."

Her glance returned to him. The haunted, faraway look in her eyes faded and cleared. "You'll help me?"

"Yes, Chelsea. I'll help you. Somehow I'll help you. I swear it."

Chelsea sat at the supper table, barely aware of those around her. When asked a question, she responded in monosyllables. Her food went untouched on her plate. A strange feeling enveloped her. She felt as if she were being pulled away from them, as if she watched from a distance. She wanted to cry out to Brandon, beg him to bring her back, but she kept silent. Fear was her companion now.

"Why don't we go to the drawing room for our brandy?" The duke rose from the table. "Chelsea, will you join me?"

"What? Oh. Of course."

Lawrence pulled out her chair. She stood and took his arm. Brandon followed, carrying the cloying Maitland in his arms. Their footsteps seemed to echo through the entry hall as they passed on their way to the drawing room. Silence cloaked the interior of the house as surely as the dark of night cloaked the stone walls.

The duke led Chelsea to a chair near the fireplace, but she didn't sit down. Instead she wandered to a window and gazed outside. A gusty wind bent the trees, the branches swinging and swaying, black silhouettes against a blacker night.

Drawn irresistibly from the window, she glided toward the piano and sat down. Her fingers trailed across the length of white keys. She stared at her hands, unaware that the other three people in the room were watching her, waiting.

She began to play, hesitantly at first, and then with more confidence. The strange melody whipped up brooding images and caused a poignant longing in her breast. Tears welled in her eyes, spilling over unheeded. On she played, the tempo increasing, the song one of passion and wild abandon. The music reached its crescendo, then faded away in a final, haunting melody. Her fingers lingered on the keys as the room fell into silence once again.

Chelsea sat for the longest time, unaware of her surroundings. But slowly, ever so slowly, she remembered she wasn't alone. She twisted on the piano stool and found the others watching her with surprised gazes.

"Good heavens, Chelsea." Maitland's voice was scarcely a whisper. "Wherever did you learn such music?"

"My aunt taught me to play, but it was Papa's song," she answered.

"Hayden? I've never seen the man go near a piano."

Chelsea blinked. Hayden? No, it wasn't Hayden. It was . . .

As swiftly as it had come to her, the music vanished, along with whatever images it had evoked.

Lawrence cleared his throat. "Brandon," he said gently, "perhaps you should see Chelsea to your room. She's looking a bit pale."

"No!" She held up her hand in a frantic gesture.

Brandon stared at her with undisguised concern.

More calmly, she continued, forcing a smile. "No, Brandon. Please don't spoil your evening because of me. Please stay and enjoy your brandy." She glanced at Lawrence, conveniently ignoring Maitland, although she knew the woman was watching her with keen eyes. "I am feeling a little tired. I think I shall go to bed."

Brandon watched her retreat with a growing sense of dread. Never had he heard such a strange, yet beautiful song. And Chelsea had played it with skill, never missing a note, her fingers dancing with certainty over ebony and ivory keys. He hadn't even known she could play.

"Do you suppose she's all right, Brandon?" Maitland asked breathlessly. "She seemed— well, she seemed a trifle strange, didn't she?"

Before he could answer, Lawrence rose from his chair. "I'd wager there're few who could play such a song the way our Chelsea did. You're very fortunate to have been here, Maitland. She doesn't play often for others."

Brandon silently thanked the old man. He couldn't seem to gather his wits about him. The melody continued to haunt him, as did the unanswered questions. Where had she learned to play like that? Why had she said it was her father's song? Even her voice when she spoke had sounded odd, distant.

A terrible foreboding washed over Brandon, warning of disasters to come.

CHAPTER
TWENTY-ONE

The small cottage was drenched in shadows. The fire had burned low on the hearth. She was lying on a small cot in the corner of the room, blankets piled over her. Outside, the wind whistled through the trees and shook the thin panes of glass in the lone window of the cottage.

The melody filled the room, a song as wild and strange as the land outside the cottage walls. The musician played the flute with the precision of a master.

He laid aside the flute, his gaze moving toward her. He smiled. "You're to be asleep, my girl."

"I wanted to listen to you play, Papa. It's so beautiful."

"Like the moor, child."

"Mother liked it too."

He sighed. "That she did."

"Play some more."

He smiled. "If you wish it, I'll play."

The melody began again, and she fell asleep to its haunting refrain. . . .

Nothing.

There was nothing.

The music was gone.

She was coughing, the air so thick and hot about her.

"Chelsea, come look. Come look."

The room was filled with smoke. Her eyes stung. Her chest hurt. She searched for the door. The knob burned her fingers as she found it.

Fire was everywhere, climbing the draperies, licking at the walls, consuming the furniture. On the ledge beyond the windows, she saw the girl in her white nightgown, twirling and twirling, her long golden hair billowing out against the blanket of night, her face alight in the fire's glow. She was laughing and twirling as she called to her. "Come look, Chelsea. Come look."

She reached out her hand, a scream rising in her throat . . . and then she was enveloped by fire.

Chelsea sat upright, choking on the silent scream. She gulped for breath; her throat felt parched. A cold sweat had broken out on her skin. She glanced about her, disoriented. Beside her, Brandon slept soundly, undisturbed by her sudden awakening.

It was a dream. That same dream.

The nursery . . . The fire . . .

And that girl.

She was afraid, but she had to know what happened. She had to know.

Chelsea slipped silently from beneath the covers, reaching for her robe. She flipped her loose hair over her shoulders as she tiptoed toward the door, her eyes peering into the darkness before her while she prayed she wouldn't stumble over anything.

A single lamp, burning low, sat on a table at the end of the hall. She hurried toward it. In the table drawer, she found a candle. She lifted the lantern cover and held the tip of the candlestick against the burning wick. The light was meager comfort as she turned and faced the long corridor.

Rachel says it's 'aunted. Chelsea shivered as she heard Leigh's voice in her head.

But she had to go on. She had to face it. She had to find out what frightened her about that room, what caused her time and again to dream that same dream.

And if there were ghosts in the nursery, she had to face them too. She squared her shoulders and headed for the northeast wing.

Wind buffeted the walls of Hawklin Hall and whistled around the corners and gables. Everything was silent except for the mournful sounds of wind and storm outside.

Chelsea, come look.

That voice. That damnable voice. It wouldn't let her go.

Who called to her? Who wanted her so badly? Was it her companion, the girl who had died in the fire? Was she calling to Chelsea, wanting her mistress to join her in death? Was it because she had set the fire and then survived?

She moved on, her fingers clasping the quivering candlestick, her eyes staring straight ahead. Her lips were pressed together in determination. Her heartbeat thundered in her own ears.

The narrow stairs leading to the nursery had a new bannister. Chelsea ran her hand over the smooth wood as she drew in a steadying breath. She wanted to flee but knew she couldn't. She must face whatever demons awaited her in that room.

Chelsea, come look.

She must face whoever—or whatever—called to her.

Resolutely, she mounted the stairs and reached quickly for the door. It opened easily.

One large, shadowy room greeted her. She could smell fresh paint. The hardwood floor, buffed to a high sheen, glowed in the flickering candlelight. There was no furniture, only a great empty expanse. Chelsea knew instantly that it wasn't the same, yet she couldn't for the life of her remember how it had once been.

She walked into the middle of the room . . . and waited.

* * *

*Alanna's doll. It lay in the middle of the room.
It was burning.*
And so was Alanna!
She screamed and hurried forward.
Pain. The pain.

Chelsea dropped the candle and raced toward the far window. She was out there. She was out there, laughing and dancing and burning. Chelsea beat on the window frame, trying to open the window. Again and again she hit it, unaware that she was screaming, sobbing.

She thrust again, this time missing the wood. The glass shattered, cutting her wrist. Blood spurted from the wound.

"No . . . no . . . no . . ."

She hit the glass again, breaking away more pieces.

"Chelsea!" a new voice called.

She whirled around, her eyes wide with fear.

He stood in the doorway, the lamp in his hand casting eerie shadows across the angles and planes of his face.

"She's out there," she said hoarsely. "She's going to die."

Scarlet stained the white of her nightgown. Blood dripped from her wrist, spattering the floor.

"Dear God," Brandon whispered.

Chelsea lifted a hand toward him. "She's going to die," she said again. There was a whimper in her voice. "I can't save her, Brandon."

He was afraid to move, afraid to speak. He was afraid.

"Brandon . . ."

He set the lamp on the floor and stepped cautiously forward.

"Brandon, I'm not Alanna. I can't be Alanna." Round, luminous eyes pleaded with him. "Don't you see? I can't be Alanna. Alanna's dead."

He had to calm her. There was no telling what she might do.

"Of course she is," he said soothingly. "But you're Chelsea. You're alive. Now come back from the window. Let me take you to our room."

"You don't understand. You don't understand."

She let him gather her up without resistance. Holding her against him, Brandon felt as if it were he who was about to die.

She watched as he gently bathed her arm, plucking tiny shards of glass from the delicate skin. His face was an impenetrable mask. She wished she knew what he was thinking.

He's thinking I'm mad.

With her left hand, she reached out and clasped his forearm. "Brandon."

Worried brown eyes met hers.

"I don't know how to explain what happened. I know what I did seemed . . ." She let the sentence die, unable to speak the word aloud. "Brandon, I don't belong here. Don't you see?"

"I see that you're tired and need some rest."

Softly, she asked, "How did you know I'd be in the nursery?"

He shrugged. "Just a guess."

"I dreamed of the fire."

"Forget it now, Chelsea. Get some sleep." He pulled the blanket up over her clean nightgown.

I'm not Alanna, she wanted to say again. But he wouldn't believe her. He would try to pacify her, and she would only convince him further of her madness. And maybe that's what it was. She certainly felt insane at this moment.

Yet she couldn't shake the growing feeling that this was not her home, that she was not Alanna.

Brandon leaned down and kissed her forehead, pushing away her tousled hair with gentle fingers. "Sleep, Chelsea. You'll feel better in the morning. No more nightmares."

"No more nightmares," she agreed despondently.

But how was she to escape a nightmare when she was living in it?

"Elsbeth, get me my diamond necklace from the case."

"Yes, m'lady."

Maitland held up the hand mirror and studied her face. She had artfully blended the face powder and rouge so no one could tell she had used them. She still looked young. She still looked beautiful. No one just meeting her would ever guess she had a son of nearly thirteen.

A tiny frown formed between her two arched eyebrows. There were plenty of men out there who were interested in removing widow from the adjectives used to describe Maitland Conover. But none of them interested her. None had interested her since she first laid eyes on Brandon Fitzgerald. And she had no intention of letting some mealymouthed chit like Chelsea keep her from him. There was a mystery about Chelsea Fitzgerald. Maitland meant to learn what it was and reveal it to the world. That would put an end to this silly infatuation Brandon seemed to have for his bride, once and for all.

Elsbeth returned to the bed with the requested jewelry. Maitland held out her hand, and the diamond necklace fell into it like water cascading over a waterfall.

"Elsbeth . . ."

"Yes, m'lady."

"Your mistress is such a strange creature. How terribly unhappy she must have been when she was growing up, never being allowed to meet anyone or have any friends. Why would anyone do that to their only child?"

The maid's eyes widened. "I'm sure I wouldn't know, m'lady. I wasn't workin' here then."

"But I'm sure she had friends among the servants. She seemed terribly close to that nanny of hers."

"Molly wasn't just a nanny. She raised her ladyship from birth, all right, but she was her nurse, too, when she needed one. And that's mostly why she's needed her in recent years."

"Her nurse?" Maitland smiled to herself. "How very interesting."

Elsbeth didn't reply.

"That will be all." She waved the maid away with a flick of her wrist.

Her nurse.

This became more interesting all the time. How many young women kept their nannies with them clear into marriage? None that Maitland had ever known. But then, how many young women did Maitland know who had grown up without ever being seen in society? Why had her parents kept her so closely guarded and shut away? And why had she needed a nurse so desperately, as Elsbeth had suggested?

Thoughtfully, she chewed on her lower lip. Sara and Hayden Fitzgerald were two of the most socially involved people she knew. They thrived on parties and balls and hunts. In fact, now that she thought of it, they had spent very little time at Hawklin Hall in the past. They'd moved from one estate to another constantly, but they'd never entertained at Hawklin. Why?

Maitland's gaze swept over the luxurious bedchamber. She needn't look into any of the other rooms to know they would all be as beautiful. She'd heard other rumors, of course. She'd heard that this past year they'd been nearly penniless until the sudden return of

Lawrence Fitzgerald from America. But surely the duke hadn't made that many changes in only a couple of months? Hayden and Sara had always seemed to have enough money to entertain lavishly in their other homes. Why hadn't they done so here?

And too, there was the matter of the fire this past summer. She'd overheard a maid at Rosemont gossiping with another, saying the fire had nearly spelled Alanna's demise and that some thought she might have set it herself. But that was the last Maitland had heard of it. No one else ever mentioned the fire. When she'd asked Brandon about it weeks ago, her meddlesome brother had interrupted before the viscount could answer. Another mystery for Maitland to solve.

She smiled. Her stay at Hawklin might prove very interesting. Very interesting, indeed.

She thought of Brandon. Her stay at Hawklin would also be entertaining, spent mostly in the viscount's company. She promised that much to herself.

Alone when she awakened, Chelsea dressed quickly in a long-sleeved gown to hide her bandaged right arm. She wondered nervously if anyone else had heard of her nighttime foray into the nursery and of the ensuing scene.

In the light of day, she considered how she must have appeared to Brandon. No, not just appeared. Her actions had been wild. What sane person would smash a window with her bare arm to reach an illusion?

Chelsea crossed the bedroom and looked out the window. The storm had passed, leaving behind a blanket of mist to hover above the lawn.

She tried to sort out the jumble of thoughts in her mind, but it seemed impossible to do so. Everything was in such confusion. How could she look at the things she'd done, the things she had seen and said, and still protest that she wasn't as mad as a March hare? Yet, despite it all, she couldn't shake the conviction that the things she saw, the things she dreamed, were real.

But how could they be real? She imagined Alanna Fitzgerald as dead, yet here she stood, staring out a window at Hawklin Hall. She shook her head slowly. What did it matter what she thought if Brandon believed her mad? What hope had she of making him love her now?

With a deep sigh, she turned from the window and left the room. She moved with unhurried steps, almost afraid to face Brandon again and see what might be hidden in his eyes. She stopped midway down the staircase, her pulse quickening. Perhaps she wasn't ready for this encounter quite yet. Perhaps she should return to their room and close the door. Perhaps . . .

"Is something wrong, my lady?"

She whirled about, her hand at her throat. "Bowman!" she said in a relieved whisper. "You startled me."

"I beg your pardon. I was just coming down from Lady Bellfort's room."

Chelsea's eyes widened; she had a sudden inspiration. Bowman could help her. "How long have you worked at Hawklin Hall?"

"Worked here? I've been at Hawklin nine years December next, my lady."

"Then you worked here when . . . when fire destroyed the nursery?"

Bowman's craggy face was devoid of expression. "Yes, my lady."

"Tell me about it."

"About the fire?" There was the briefest lift of an eyebrow.

"Yes. I want to know what happened that day." Her eyes pleaded with him for an honest answer. "Please, Bowman. I need to know."

He shifted uncomfortably. "There's not much I can tell you, my lady. I was in Bristol visiting my sister at the time."

"What about the girl?"

"The girl, miss?"

"The girl who died, Bowman. My companion. Who was she?"

"I never met her, my lady."

"Never met her? But Bowman, you know all the staff."

He didn't quite meet her gaze. "His lordship —your father—he hired her for your companion. So you wouldn't be alone when Molly was occupied elsewhere. Lord Fitzgerald thought it better if she didn't mix with the rest of the staff, considering . . ." His voice died away.

"I see." And she did see. It seemed all so very clear to her. Of course, considering the secrecy that had surrounded her mere existence, considering her history of madness, her father would have wanted to keep anyone who cared for Alanna from talking with others. Servants were known to gossip, and that gossip had a way of spreading from one estate to another. And then his friends and peers would have heard the news and then . . .

Chelsea turned her back toward Bowman. "Did she have a name, this companion of mine?"

"Miss Pendleton, I believe, my lady."

"Miss Pendleton. Thank you, Bowman."

He stepped around her and descended the stairs to the bottom.

"Bowman, wait!"

He turned.

"Are there any other servants at Hawklin Hall who were here at the time of the fire? Anyone I might ask about that night?"

"I'm sorry, Lady Fitzgerald. Your father thought it best, under the circumstances, to replace them all. Molly and I were the only ones he kept on in the house."

"Thank you," she said again, dropping her gaze.

She heard his receding footsteps in the entry hall.

Miss Pendleton. Chelsea tried to conjure up the girl's face but failed. How long had she worked here? Why didn't she escape the fire? Was it she who had danced on the ledge? Had she been driven mad by her care for Alanna? Were there kinfolk who had mourned the girl's passing? Had Chelsea liked her? Had they been friends? She wanted to know. She *had* to know.

If only she'd asked Molly more questions while she was alive. If only she'd insisted on being told more of her past, instead of letting Molly sweep it aside as unimportant. Now it was too late. Too late.

She felt tears of frustration threatening and swallowed them back. She would not give in to weeping and carrying on. There had been enough of that for a lifetime. There would be no more today. Straightening her shoulders, she went down the stairs and into the dining room.

As soon as she was through the doorway, Brandon was on his feet and rushing to her side. Deep concern was etched in his handsome features. "How are you this morning, Chelsea?"

She wouldn't let him see her doubts again. She would keep her questions to herself, seek her own answers. Brandon must see her as well, as normal. She must do all she could to allay his fears.

"I'm fine, Brandon," she answered, rising on tiptoe to lightly brush her lips against his cheek.

And saying so, she did feel better.

CHAPTER
<u>TWENTY-TWO</u>

Roxley removed his coat and handed it to Bowman.

"His grace and family have finished their tea, my lord, and have removed to the drawing room," the butler said in his usual superior tone.

"Thank you, Bowman. I'll show myself in."

"Very well, sir."

Roxley's boot heels clipped sharply on the tiled entry floor as he made his way around the grand staircase toward the drawing room. He was feeling more than a little irritable today. His sister's insistence that she couldn't bear to be moved to Rosemont was all an act; he was sure of it. He wasn't even convinced she'd injured her damned ankle at all. He thought there was a good chance Maitland had seduced the old sawbones into saying she had a bad sprain when there actually wasn't a thing wrong.

And she'd done it all so she could cause trouble between Brandon and Chelsea.

Well, his friends might not be able to politely suggest the marchioness leave Hawklin, but he could do something about it. Three days was enough time to let her do her dirty work. He promised himself that he would have her out of there this very day.

Brandon and Chelsea were seated at a table near the fireplace when he entered the drawing room. Maitland was reclining on a sofa not far from Brandon's left side. It was the duke who first looked up and saw him.

"I say, Roxley. This is a surprise."

"I hope I'm not intruding, your grace."

"Not at all, my boy. Come in. Come in. We're glad to have you."

Brandon had risen from the table. "You're just in time to rescue me, Roxley. I've been teaching Chelsea about chess, and she's about to beat me."

Roxley's eyes strayed to the other side of the table. "Beauty and brains too? How lucky you are, Brandon."

Chelsea smiled at him and inclined her head slightly in acknowledgment of the compliment.

"And good afternoon to you, too, brother." Maitland's voice was sharp, drawing his gaze away from Chelsea.

"Hello, Maitland. You're looking well."

"I wish it were true." She glared at him. "But I'm afraid just being brought down from my room causes my ankle to throb painfully. If it weren't for missing this delightful company, I would gladly stay upstairs."

Roxley clicked his tongue. "Such a shame, Maitland. I was hoping I could send the carriage for you tomorrow. You'll miss all the excitement at Rosemont."

"Excitement?" Maitland pushed herself up on the arm of the sofa. "Whatever are you talking about, Roxley?"

Trying to hide his grin, the earl's eyes moved from his sister to Chelsea, and finally to Brandon. "We've a guest arriving from London in the morning. You two should drop by tomorrow, Brandon. I should like you to meet the man."

"Roxley, to whom are you referring?" Maitland demanded in a vexed tone.

"Mr. Disraeli."

His sister sat up completely. "The prime minister? Whatever is he doing at Rosemont?"

"Oh, we're merely a convenient stopping-off place. But it would have been nice to have you at Rosemont as my hostess for the evening. Mother is in Bath for a week or two, and I did want to have in a few friends. Oh well, I'll just have to do the best I can without you or Mother." He sighed.

"Roxley," Maitland said sternly, "you'll do no such thing. You'll make a terrible botch of it. I'll just have to bear up under the pain. That's all there is to it. You'll have to take me home with you tonight. There's not a moment to lose."

"Well—if you think so. . . ."

"Of course I think so, you fool. You can't welcome the prime minister to Rosemont without my help. Do you realize what an opportunity this is?" She tossed aside the blanket that had been lying over her legs. He wondered if she would forget herself completely and stand up. "Have someone get my things together. Tell Bowman to bring me my wrap. We haven't a moment to lose."

Roxley knew he would pay for his lies later. Mr. Disraeli was nowhere near Rosemont as far as he knew. But it would be worth Maitland's vile temper to help out Chelsea and Brandon now.

He dared a glance at Chelsea. A tiny smile was curving the corners of her mouth, but he wasn't sure she knew what he was up to until she met his gaze—and winked.

Brandon returned to the drawing room after having seen off their guests. Chelsea was still seated at the table. She was bent forward, intently studying the chessboard. He paused in the doorway long enough to feast his eyes upon her.

She was wearing a particularly pretty gown of lavender silk. Her fine blond hair was tied at the nape with a matching ribbon. She looked scarcely older than a schoolgirl, yet her beauty was unmistakably that of a woman.

He let out a long breath, suddenly aware of the tension leaving his body. All afternoon he had been half-expecting something to go awry, waiting for Chelsea to say or do something that would draw Maitland's curiosity—or even worse. Now that the woman was gone from Hawklin, he could relax.

Chelsea glanced up at that moment, her gaze meeting his. A hesitant smile curved her mouth. He returned it as he headed across the room.

"I think I'm beginning to understand this game," she said as he sat down. "Check."

Brandon looked down at the table with disbelief. His king was definitely in trouble. Why hadn't he seen it coming?

The duke chuckled as he rose from his chair and came to stand behind Chelsea. "Good show, my dear."

"She hasn't won yet." Brandon frowned down at the chessboard.

He studied all his choices and all the moves she might make following him, then reached out and moved his knight, enjoying her look of consternation as she realized what he'd done. Her pale brows drew together.

Again Lawrence laughed. "Well, I can see you two are in for a lengthy game of wits. I think I shall find a good book to read from the library." He kissed Chelsea's head and whispered loudly, "Give him a run for his money, my girl."

The frown disappeared as she looked up at the old man, her hand moving to cover his where it rested on her shoulder. "Don't worry, Grandfather. I shall."

Brandon caught a glimpse of the bandage from beneath her sleeve, bringing up a vivid memory of last night, of the way she'd looked, spattered with blood. Could this possibly be the same woman?

Throughout the day, Chelsea had been as lovely, as poised, as delightful as he'd ever known her to be. There had not been so much as a hint of the hysteria he had witnessed in the nursery. If it hadn't been he himself who had found her there, he would have said it was an outrageous lie.

A band seemed to tighten about his chest. There was a stinging pain in his heart. How he wished *this* were how things would always be for them—he and Chelsea sharing a quiet evening of enjoyment, a sense of peace and fulfillment warming them as surely as the fire in the fireplace. This was how it should be for them, always. What could he do to keep it this way? What?

Chelsea's hand reached across the board and lightly touched her queen. She was frowning in concentration again. Then, suddenly, her face broke into a triumphant smile. The queen slid across the board before she looked up at him.

"Checkmate!" she proclaimed.

"What? It can't be." He perused the board. She had outfoxed him with a brilliant move.

"Do you concede defeat, sir?"

His eyes rose to meet a twinkling blue gaze. Splashes of pink colored her cheeks, and she was very obviously enjoying her victory.

"I concede, miss," he grumbled, "but I protest I've been played the fool."

Her smile faded a fraction.

"You've lied to me, Chelsea Fitzgerald. You *have* played this game before, haven't you?"

"I . . . I'm not sure."

He had meant it as a joke but failed miserably. He could see clearly Chelsea's effort to remember, an effort that drained the humor of moments ago from her face.

"I do seem to recall . . . Perhaps it was Miss Pendleton who taught me to play."

"Who is Miss Pendleton?"

"She was my companion. The girl who died in the fire."

Damn! It could have been anyone but her. He didn't want Chelsea reminded of the fire in the nursery or of people dying.

"No. No, it wasn't her. The woman who taught me was older—much older." The color was gone from her cheeks now. "Who could she have been?" she wondered aloud, but it was apparent the question was only for herself.

"Well," he said hurriedly, "you won't beat me a second time." He began moving the chess pieces back to their starting places. "What do you think, Lady Coleford?" He threw out the gauntlet. "Can you be that lucky again?"

There was a brief moment when he thought he'd failed, that she hadn't even heard him. Then her eyes cleared and she met his gaze with a challenging one of her own.

"Luck had nothing to do with my victory, Lord Coleford. I not only *can* beat you a second time, I *will*. Even if it takes me all night to do so."

Chelsea awoke late the next morning. The place in the bed beside her was empty. She no more had begun to wonder where Brandon was than she heard a knock upon her door.

"Come in."

Leigh entered with a breakfast tray. "'Is lordship said I should bring up your tray, m'lady, as you were most likely too tired after last night."

Chelsea laughed aloud. She could tell by the maid's expression that she suspected something far different than a lengthy game of chess had left her mistress too tired to rise for breakfast. The game had gone on into the evening, resuming immediately after supper, and hadn't ended until far past midnight. Brandon had been the victor, but Chelsea had given him plenty of competition before her defeat.

"Where is his lordship now?" she asked.

"'E said 'e was goin' t'the stables. Said 'e 'as some things t'do an' if you want t'join 'im for a ride, 'e'll wait for you."

Chelsea tossed the blankets aside. "Go tell him I'll be dressed and ready in a few minutes, Leigh."

"But your breakfast, m'lady."

"Don't be silly. I couldn't eat a thing."

Chelsea hurried to wash and dress. Her heart was singing. He wanted her to join him. She had been so afraid, after what happened in the nursery, that things would grow only more strained between them. But there had been the chess game yesterday and now this. Perhaps it really could be put behind them.

By the time she was outside, Brandon had their horses saddled and waiting. He grinned at her as she approached him, then placed his hands about her waist and lifted her effortlessly onto the sidesaddle.

"You look lovely," he said, kissing the knuckles of her left hand.

"So do you."

She meant it. He did look lovely—or rather, dashingly handsome. Sometimes she wanted to pinch herself, but was afraid she might wake up and he too would vanish from her memory.

"Where are we going?" she asked as he stepped up into his saddle.

"Just for a look around the countryside. I haven't checked the Hawklin lands for Grandfather since we first arrived. Does that sound satisfactory?"

She nodded. "Of course." She didn't really care what they did as long as they were together.

"Besides, with the hunting party Grandfather is planning, it wouldn't hurt to take a few hurdles. Do you feel up to it?"

"More than to chess."

Brandon laughed. "Don't think you'll beat me at this, either, my lady."

"We'll see," Chelsea cried over her shoulder as her bay gelding burst into a gallop.

An hour later, they reined in. Their cheeks

were red with cold; their eyes flashed with exhilaration. Brandon helped her down from the saddle, then they walked side by side along the country road.

"Everything is so beautiful this time of year," Chelsea said as her eyes swept the autumn-painted trees. "I think this is my favorite season."

"Mine, too. Justin and I used to spend a lot of time together in the fall, hunting for deer."

She glanced sideways at Brandon. "Do you miss your brother a great deal?"

"Yes. I wish sometimes we'd brought him with us."

"Do you ever think of returning to America?" Funny how she'd never considered that this wasn't Brandon's first home, that there might be somewhere else he'd rather be. The thought disturbed her.

Brandon stopped walking and turned to face her. "When I first decided to bring Grandfather back to Hawklin to regain his title, I meant only to stay until . . . well, until he died. Then I was going home."

"And now?" she asked in a small voice.

"Now I don't know. I hope Grandfather will live a long, long time."

He dropped the reins to the ground and reached for her, gathering her close against him while his mouth brushed lightly against hers. Chelsea leaned into him, her arms circling his broad chest. She held on tightly, losing herself to his passionate charm. She felt winded by the time he released her, felt even more so beneath the studious gaze that captured hers.

"The title doesn't mean much to me. If Grandfather were to die, there wouldn't be much to keep me here."

She felt a tiny stabbing pain in her chest. Nothing to keep him there.

"Would you like to see America, Chelsea?"

The idea had come to him suddenly. It would be ideal. They could leave England, go to America where no one knew her, no one suspected her mysterious past. They could start again. Perhaps then her dreams, her nightmares would be forgotten.

"I think I would love to see America . . . with you."

"Good." He took her hand, and they began to walk once again.

His intentions this morning had been to begin searching for Miss Pendleton's family. It had seemed so important to Chelsea that she know more about the woman who was her companion and who died in the nursery fire. But now he wanted nothing more than to enjoy Chelsea's company. Perhaps her request was already forgotten.

He glanced at her, noting the bounce in her step, the twinkle in her blue eyes, the contented smile on her pretty, bow-shaped mouth. She looked so beautiful, so—so normal. Perhaps . . .

"Brandon, look." Chelsea pointed through the trees. "There's a house over there. Do you suppose we could stop there for a drink of water? I'm terribly thirsty."

"I don't see what it would hurt to ask," he replied.

His hands spanned her waist. Before lifting her onto the bay gelding, he kissed her one more time, then swung up onto his mount. He grinned in her direction as he rode past her, leading the way toward the house.

CHAPTER
TWENTY-THREE

"Brandon . . ."

He heard the strange note in her voice and twisted in his saddle to look at her. She had stopped her horse. The reins had slipped from her fingers and were trailing on the ground. Before he could move, she slid from the saddle and walked toward the brick home with ivy-covered walls. The windows and doors were shuttered, the house seemingly deserted.

"Brandon, I know this place."

What was it about her words, her voice, that sent chills up his spine? Was it so strange that she would have seen a neighbor's home before today?

"I lived here once."

He jumped to the ground and followed her.

He wanted to deny her words, tell her she had never lived outside of Hawklin.

"I've seen it. I've seen it in my dreams. Just like this. Except the shutters were open." She pointed. "That's the drawing room. There's a piano near the fireplace." Chelsea glanced at him quickly. "That's where I learned to play." Her voice was just above a whisper, yet laced with excitement.

"Chelsea . . ." he began, reaching for her.

She shook off his hand. "That's the library, and behind it is the dining room and the kitchen." She pointed toward the second floor. "That was my bedroom." Her hand was shaking.

Fear clenched his belly, twisting it hard. He was so helpless against this unseen foe! How could he protect her from the things she imagined?

Chelsea started forward, unmindful, uncaring whether or not he followed. She pushed through the overgrowth toward what she claimed was the drawing room window. Her fingers closed around the edge of the wooden shutters, and she began to pull.

"Chelsea, we shouldn't—"

"I must. I must see it."

What else could he do but step up beside her and pull the shutters loose? She was determined to see the inside. Perhaps once she had seen it, she would find she was wrong.

With a sudden jerk, the shutter pulled free of its anchors. Brandon and Chelsea stumbled backward, nearly tumbling into a rose bush.

Chelsea was the first to recover her balance. Pressing her hands against the window glass, she leaned forward and peered inside.

"The piano," she said breathlessly. "There's the piano."

Brandon moved to her side. A strange sensation swept over him as he looked first at the piano, then at Chelsea. Could it possibly be? No. No, it wasn't possible. There must be several, perhaps even dozens of explanations for her knowing this was the drawing room and that there would be a piano near the fireplace. There had to be a logical explanation. She had visited there as a child, before her illness was known. Her parents had arranged for the people who lived there to give their daughter piano lessons. It could be anything.

"Where is she now?"

He was almost afraid to ask. "Who?"

"The woman with the gray hair." Her eyes widened. "My aunt."

"She couldn't be your aunt, Chelsea. Neither Hayden nor Sara had sister."

Chelsea's fingers closed around his wrist, silencing him. "Brandon, please believe me."

He could hear the agitation in her voice. "I know it's what *you* believe, Chelsea."

Her hand fell away and she turned her back toward him. "That's not good enough," she said softly as she walked away from him. She paused at the corner of the house, looking over her shoulder. "Could it be I never was Alanna? It could, you know. Alanna's dead." And then she disappeared from view.

Blood was pounding in his temples. He reached up and rubbed the sides of his head, wishing away the headache. He had a helpless, hopeless feeling in the pit of his stomach. She was slipping away from him, and there was nothing he could do about it.

She shouldn't have said that to him. It was, indeed, an insane thought. She was surrounded by people who knew of Alanna Fitzgerald, knew she'd been locked away since birth, that she was mad, that she had set fire to the house. She had no memory save what people had told her. She was plagued by strange dreams and visions. What more proof did she need that her mind was unbalanced?

But despite all that, she couldn't shake the feeling that this house had been special to her. Mad it might be, but she was certain she'd lived there.

And I was loved here, too, she thought as she tugged at the rear door. Surprisingly enough, the door came open with ease.

A thick layer of dust lay over everything in the kitchen. The house had a sad aura of rejection about it. She felt tears stinging her throat but swallowed them back. She moved toward another doorway, knowing it would lead to the dining room.

A sliver of light filtered through the shutters, faintly illuminating the room. She glanced quickly at the marks left on the wallpaper where portraits had been removed. She noted the scuff marks on the floor where a large piece of furniture had been dragged across the wood.

285

She had a niggling feeling she should know what was missing. Or maybe it was only her imagination.

She left the dining room and passed through the library, not stopping until she reached the narrow staircase leading to the second floor. She stood still, listening, waiting, expecting another glimmer of recognition, wanting it terribly. But nothing came.

With a sigh, she began to climb. The stairs creaked beneath her feet, a bleak sound in the dark and empty house. To the left of the stairs was the room she'd pointed out as hers. To the right was another door. She went to the right first.

She drew a deep breath, half expecting some ghost to come flying at her when she opened the door. But it was just a bedroom. Dust lay as thickly here as it did elsewhere. The once-white counterpane was a dismal gray. But even with the musty smell of disuse, Chelsea had a strong sensation of sickness. Someone had been terribly ill. Perhaps they had died in this room.

Chelsea turned quickly and left the bedroom, closing the door behind her. Her heart was beating rapidly, and she felt somewhat sick herself. But she couldn't stop her quest. She must see. She must see it all.

Later, Brandon found her sitting on the floor, her cheeks smudged with dust and tears. As he stepped through the doorway, she looked up at him with wide, sorrowful eyes.

"I thought I would remember," she said. "I

really thought I would remember something. I was so sure. . . ."

"I know." He came toward her, reaching out his hands to draw her to her feet. With his handkerchief, he wiped at the dirt on her face. "We should go home, Chelsea."

She nodded miserably and allowed him to lead her from the house.

Lawrence was watching from the salon window when the pair walked toward the house from the stables. Even with his tired old eyes he could see the tension in Brandon's shoulders. And Chelsea looked like a lost child.

He opened the French doors and waved to them. Brandon's hand slipped beneath Chelsea's elbow as he guided her toward the duke. She came obediently, her eyes downcast. Lawrence opened his mouth to say something, but she moved past him without even a glance. Brandon stopped at his grandfather's side.

"What's happened?" Lawrence asked softly.

Brandon shook his head. "She saw something she thought she recognized."

"It must have been something more than just that." The duke closed the door. "You'd better tell me."

Brandon sagged into a nearby chair. His head dropped into his hands and he raked his fingers through his shaggy hair.

Lawrence sat down beside him. "What is it, my boy?"

"I think we'd be wise to cancel the hunt. I

287

don't think Chelsea can handle the—the strain of so many people. She—"

"I *can* handle it, Brandon."

The two men's heads turned sharply. Chelsea had returned to the salon unnoticed. Except for a few stubborn smudges of dirt, her face was still pale. But now she stood with a ramrod-straight back, her chin held high.

Brandon rose slowly from the chair. "Chelsea, I—"

"You needn't explain. I know what you think, Brandon, but I *can* do this. Your grandfather's party has nothing to do with what happened today. I promise I won't embarrass either of you. I shall behave perfectly. I shall fool them all."

That said, she spun on her heel and was gone.

Lawrence looked at his grandson. "I think you'd better tell me everything that happened today."

Back in her room, Chelsea tugged off her boot and threw it with all her might across the room. She was nearly blinded by frustration and anger.

Why must it be like this? Why? Why? Why?

But she couldn't escape what was within her.

"I'm not crazy. I lived in that house," she whispered.

Brandon didn't believe her. He thought her as mad as everyone else did. And she would never convince him otherwise as long as she told him the things she saw and felt. There would never be any hope for them until the dreams and visions went away. Perhaps there was no hope anyway.

Brandon dismounted before a small, squat cottage. He could hear a baby crying lustily inside. He paused a moment, letting his weariness wash over him, tempted to remount and ride away. It was a harebrained scheme anyway. What good was it going to do to learn who had owned that deserted old house? It might even make matters worse.

He might have left if the door hadn't opened at that moment and a young lad come running out, bucket in hand. Carrot-red hair drooped across a freckled forehead. The boy stopped short. Surprised green eyes stared up at Brandon; the bucket fell from a small, grubby hand.

"Mama, there's someone 'ere!"

A bedraggled woman appeared in the doorway, the crying infant in her arms. She eyed him fearfully.

"Excuse me, madam. I am Viscount Coleford from Hawklin Hall. May I trouble you to answer a few questions?"

"I don't want no trouble, m'lord."

"And I won't give you any. I give you my word."

She let her eyes trail the length of him, then return to meet his gaze. As if concluding that he meant her no harm, she nodded. "Harry, take the baby in to your sister. Now."

The boy returned to his mother who placed

the baby in his arms, then disappeared into the dismal cottage. The woman closed the door behind him.

"What is it you want, m'lord?" she asked as she ran a hand over her hair, smoothing it back from her face.

"The brick house beyond the fork in the road. Can you tell me whose house it is?"

"Aye, I can tell you."

He waited.

"My Willy used t'work as a gardener there, now an' again. But the work's gone an' 'e's 'ad t'go t'London t'find work, leavin' me t'care for the young'ns as best I can."

"Who owned the house?" Brandon asked again.

"'Twas a Mistress St. Clair. I only seen 'er once. An old woman. Always dressed in black, my Willy said."

"And where is Miss St. Clair now?"

The woman shook her head slowly. "I don't know, m'lord. I 'eard 'er niece died an' the old woman took ill. One mornin' my Willy went t'do some gardenin' an' was told 'e wouldn't be needed no more. Then they closed up the 'ouse. I guess Mistress St. Clair died too."

"You say her niece died," Brandon said thoughtfully. "Was that this past summer?"

"It was."

He felt a tremor of excitement. "Could that niece have been a Miss Pendleton?"

"Sorry, m'lord. I don't know."

"Thank you, madam, for your help." He couldn't keep from smiling as he tipped his hat.

"I won't forget it." When he returned to Hawklin, he meant to see that Mrs. Hardwick sent over a large basket of food and maybe even a nanny goat for the infant.

He swung into the saddle and turned his mount down the road once again. His weariness of minutes before had disappeared.

It all made sense to him now. The "aunt" Chelsea remembered had actually been Miss Pendleton's aunt. She had probably told Chelsea all about this house, about her gray-haired aunt, about the piano. Perhaps she'd even taken Chelsea there for a visit. That would explain the things Chelsea remembered. When he got home, he would . . .

No. No, he wouldn't tell her yet. He would keep asking questions about Miss St. Clair and Miss Pendleton. He would learn all he could before talking to Chelsea about it. Once he could prove to her that she hadn't lived there, that the things she saw were only products of her imagination, once she understood how logical it all was, they could put the unfortunate incidents of the past few days, even the past weeks, behind them. Perhaps then they could find the measure of happiness that seemed almost within their grasp but was never quite attainable.

Brandon's sense of well-being was short-lived. There was still the troublesome matter of the duke's hunt and ball to contend with. What if Chelsea didn't accept his explanation of Miss Pendleton and her aunt's house? What if Chelsea imagined something during the ball? What if she told someone she was actually dead?

Could it be I never was Alanna? It could, you know. Alanna's dead.

That terrible sinking feeling returned to twist his innards. He didn't know how he would make it through the coming weeks.

CHAPTER
<u>TWENTY-FOUR</u>

A clear blue sky greeted the October morn. Trees were ablaze in orange and red and gold. The crisp air bespoke excitement and adventure. It was perfect weather for a hunt.

Chelsea stood at the second-story windows, directly above the great entry hall. Her eyes were trained on the long drive leading up to the manse. Nervously, she twisted an embroidered handkerchief. The guests could begin arriving at any time.

Perhaps Brandon had been right about this. Perhaps she shouldn't have done it. Perhaps she wasn't able. What did she know about playing hostess to the cream of English society? She would make a fool of herself. Worse yet, she might make a fool of the duke or Brandon.

"Ah, my dear. There you are." Lawrence stepped up beside her. His kind brown eyes viewed the tortured fabric in her hands. "Natural to be nervous, you know. I am."

"You?"

"Of course. You'll not be the only one being scrutinized, child. I'm the man who disappeared to America for half a century, then suddenly came back to claim title and lands. Not everyone views my return with delight. And the old hall hasn't been on display for a generation. People will be eager to see if it still has its splendor. I'll be to blame for anything that's not right."

Chelsea smiled fondly at the old man. She knew he was saying these things just to bolster her spirit, and she loved him for it. "Thank you, Grandfather."

At least her involvement in preparations for the big hunt and ball had served one purpose. It had taken her mind off old brick houses and burning nurseries. It had kept her from dwelling on dead companions and strange dreams and visions of other people and places. And it had taken her mind off her husband's many and long absences.

"Where is Brandon?" the duke asked, as if reading her thoughts. "Is he ready to greet our guests?"

"He was up and about early this morning, Grandfather," Chelsea responded. She tried to keep the tension from her voice. "I'm not sure where he is at the moment."

Lawrence frowned as he shook his head. "The boy hasn't been much like himself lately. And he doesn't seem to want to talk about what's troubling him."

She nodded but remained silent. She'd noticed it too. Brandon was gone for hours each day, and when he was at home, he seemed preoccupied, scarcely aware of the people around him. Even when they were alone in their room together, he treated her with kid gloves. They hadn't made love in over two weeks. Sometimes she could read a flash of desire in his eyes, but then it would disappear, as if he suddenly remembered who she was. Perhaps the pain of his no longer wanting her hurt more than anything else.

It was her turn to shake her head, this time to remove the doubts and concerns. She hadn't the time to deal with it now. There were sixty or more guests to be worried about, and soon they would begin arriving.

As if in response to her thoughts, an elegant black carriage with burgundy trimming burst through the curtain of trees and made its way up the long drive.

Lawrence turned his head and looked at her once more. He grinned and offered her his arm. "Shall we greet the first of our guests, my dear Chelsea?"

She drew a deep breath. Whatever else happened during the next two days, she meant to make Lawrence and Brandon proud of her. Furthermore, she meant to prove to her husband that she was a desirable, intelligent woman. This she promised to herself.

"With pleasure, your grace." She slipped her hand through his elbow, then moved with him toward the stairs, butterflies in an uproar in her stomach.

Penelope Cumberland fluttered her pretty brown eyelashes and giggled. Roxley bowed slightly at the waist, then excused himself. If he had to be introduced to one more simpering female, he thought he would drown himself in the first bottle of brandy he could find.

"That's the price you pay for refusing to find your own bride, Wellington."

He turned to look into the countess's sharp gaze. "Thank you for the advice, Mother," he replied, then leaned forward to kiss her cheek affectionately.

"You mustn't spend too much time wishing for what cannot be," she added wisely.

"We're friends, Mother. That's all."

"Is it, Roxley? I hope so. I rather like this brash American viscount of ours, and I like to think your friendship with him means something too."

"It does," he answered in a gruff tone.

The countess patted his cheek as she had when he was a boy. "Here. Let's not have you snarling at your fragile old mother."

"*Fragile*, Mother?"

"Terribly so, my boy."

They grinned at each other, enjoying their little joke. Eleanor Randolph-Smythe had more strength and stamina than many *men* half her age. Attractive she had been in her youth, but never fragile.

"Speaking of our host, have you seen Brandon?" Roxley's eyes scanned the great drawing room.

"Not since we first arrived."

"Well, I think I'll try to find him. Excuse me, Mother."

Roxley worked his way through the crowd, stopping to exchange words of greeting now and again. As he neared the doorway, Chelsea appeared.

She had changed from the dress she'd worn to greet her guests as they arrived. For the supper party, she had chosen a gown of the palest yellow, the fabric a shimmering silk and satin mixture. She wore a choker of golden amethysts around her throat. Her pale blond hair was clustered high on her head, its lustrous sheen reflecting the candlelight flickering from dozens of candelabra. She smiled when she saw him. Her blue eyes held a glimmer of excitement as well as a trace of anxiety.

"You look positively wonderful," Roxley said when he reached her. "The most beautiful woman in the room."

"Thank you, Roxley. You're obviously suffering from poor eyesight, but I love you for it." Her gaze moved beyond him. "It seems to be going well, doesn't it?"

"Perfect," he answered in a low voice. But anyone overhearing him would wonder if he meant the house party or his hostess, judging by the way he was looking at her.

"Have you seen Brandon?" Chelsea asked, unknowingly repeating the question Roxley had asked only moments before.

"No. I was looking for him myself. Shall we look together?" He held out his arm to her.

She nodded but didn't take hold of his arm. Instead, she turned and began walking. Roxley quickly fell into step beside her. They glanced into a number of other rooms without any luck and had just reached the entry hall when the door opened and admitted a laughing couple —Maitland and Brandon.

Chelsea felt a great, cold emptiness washing through her. It instantly occurred to her how right her dashing husband and the sophisticated marchioness looked together.

The moment Brandon saw Chelsea, the laughter died. His eyes flicked from Chelsea to Roxley, then back again. His expression hardened.

Chelsea forced a cheerfulness she no longer felt into her voice. "Lady Bellfort, how well you look. We didn't expect you to be able to join us."

"I couldn't possibly allow a sore ankle to keep me away," Maitland replied, her gaze lingering suggestively on Brandon. "Not after Lord Coleford's charming personal invitation last week. Besides, my ankle scarcely bothers me at all anymore." She glanced at her brother. "I would have come with you and Mother, but I just couldn't decide what to bring with me."

"Did Mother know you were coming?"

"No. I wanted to surprise everyone."

Brandon stepped away from Maitland's side, coming to stand before Chelsea. Dark eyes stared down at her. "I was returning from the stables when Maitland's coach arrived."

Was he trying to explain why he was with her?

Chelsea heard Maitland's throaty laugh and looked at her.

"And I thought you'd come out especially to greet me." Maitland's smile hinted at a special secret, shared just between two. "How disappointing, Brandon dear. You could at least let me believe you cared enough to be watching for me."

Had he issued a personal invitation, as Maitland suggested? Had he gone to visit her? Had he known Maitland planned to come?

"I thought," the marchioness continued, "after your visit last week, you truly didn't want me to miss the festivities."

Chelsea returned her eyes to Brandon. His face was closed to her. She hurt—and it suddenly made her angry. How dare he leave her alone for days on end, when she needed him most—to spend his time with the likes of Maitland Conover! Was that why he no longer made love to her? Not only because he thought her mad but because he found another woman more desirable?

Bowman stepped into the hall just as she opened her mouth to speak.

"Supper is ready, my lady. Shall we seat the guests?"

"Please, Bowman." Chelsea was relieved her

voice sounded normal. She turned and slipped her hand into Roxley's arm. "Brandon, why don't you escort the marchioness to supper?"

She felt his eyes on her back and knew some satisfaction at having surprised him.

Roxley leaned close to her ear as they walked into the dining room. "Are you sure you know what you're doing, Chelsea?"

"Not at all," she admitted with a nervous laugh. "But I suppose I'll find out."

The guests began filing into the dining room, filling it with a cheerful din. Roxley brought Chelsea to the foot of the long oak table and pulled out the chair for her. She slipped into it, then watched as he seated himself to her left.

Her glance moved on as others began to be seated around the table. Lawrence was at the head. Lady Roxley was on his right and Diana Chesterfield was on his left. Midway down the table, Brandon was pulling out a chair for Maitland.

She was stricken again with a terrible sinking feeling as she looked at the couple. Maitland was so elegant, so polished. Her auburn hair was lush, her face beautiful, her body perfection. She had been a part of these people all her life. They were her friends, her companions. She belonged among them.

Chelsea didn't. She was a mere curiosity. No one there was her friend, except Roxley. And, of course, the duke. Even now, she could feel Lawrence watching her, wondering what was going on between his grandson and Chelsea. But what could she tell him? That Brandon preferred another woman's company to that of his own wife?

Roxley leaned toward her. "My sister is out to cause trouble, Chelsea. Don't let her get away with it."

"Nothing she does bothers me." She turned her gaze upon Roxley. "I am not so sheltered that I don't know these little liaisons happen now and then. He is still my husband."

"There's nothing between them," Roxley said in a low voice, thick with sincerity. "I'd lay my life on it."

Chelsea laughed, but it was a hollow sound. "However gallant of you, Roxley, but you needn't be so concerned. I'm not made of glass. I won't break. It matters little to me."

"Chelsea . . ."

"It was an arranged marriage, after all. No one could possibly have expected it to be a love match." She tried to believe what she was saying. She wanted very much to believe it. "Now, tell me about the hunt tomorrow. It will be my first, and I don't want to make a fool of myself."

Supper was a long, drawn-out affair. Course followed course, appealing to both the gourmet and the gourmand among them. There were tureens of turtle, a variety of shellfish, barons of beef, boiled turkeys and oysters, pheasants, hams, jellies, ice creams, and tarts. Along with the enticing spread went champagne, claret, burgundy, madeira, port, and sherry. And as they ate, the guests chatted noisily while music played softly in the background.

Throughout supper, Brandon watched as his wife held court at the end of the table. Opposite Roxley was Andre Guerard, the Marquis de Lyon, who was visiting his sister from Paris. Andre's black eyes had scarcely left Chelsea from the moment he was seated next to her. He vied with Roxley for her favors. It was enough to make Brandon grind his teeth.

It certainly wasn't the evening he had planned. He had hoped to have some news for her by tonight, at the latest, regarding the late Miss Pendleton and her aunt, Miss St. Clair. For the past two weeks, he had been combing the countryside, asking questions, following every clue, every lead. They had all ended in disappointing dead ends. He had managed to find a clerk in a village store who believed Miss Pendleton was the niece's name, but she couldn't be certain.

"Yes, I think that was her name, but I cannot be sure. She was a shy one. Never much to say. Mistress St. Clair usually sent that old butler of hers to do the errands that needed done."

"And where is he? The butler?"

"Like as not, he's as dead as she is by this time. Why else would they close up the house and go away?"

"Brandon, you haven't heard a word I've said." Maitland's honeyed voice cut through his distracted thoughts.

"What?"

"I was merely commenting that your wife has captured an enthusiastic admirer in the marquis. Does she speak French?"

"No." At least, he didn't think so. But she did seem to be hanging on Andre's every word.

Brandon saw red.

Chelsea wearily bade the last of their guests good night, then turned toward her own bedroom. Brandon's hand was firm upon her elbow. Tension sparked between them, so palpable it was as if there were a third person walking with them down the hall.

He was angry. And he'd had too much to drink. She knew it, but she didn't care at the moment.

She was aware, of course, that her behavior at supper had drawn a lot of attention. The men around her had flattered her outrageously. She had countered with flirtations of her own. They had all laughed often and noisily, especially as the champagne and sherry and madeira were consumed, and not once—not one single time —had she let her gaze meet her husband's. But she had noticed the number of times his goblet was filled and then drained and knew how angry he was with her. There couldn't have been a soul in that dining room tonight who didn't know that things were less than blissful between Viscount Coleford and his bride.

Brandon opened the door for her, then offered a mock bow and waved her through. She pretended not to see him as she swept by.

"Chelsea . . ." He closed the door.

She went to her dresser and unfastened the clasp of her amethyst choker. She laid it carefully in her jewel case, then turned around.

"I thought we'd settled the matter of you and Roxley after Maitland's ball." Brandon moved toward the center of the room.

"What matter is that?"

"You made a spectacle of yourself again."

"A spectacle?" She felt the heat rising in her cheeks. "What did I do?"

"You know perfectly well what you did. Our guests are probably making wagers on who it is you're having an affair with—the Earl of Roxley or the Marquis de Lyon."

Without a word, she moved toward him. Her head tilted slightly backward, she looked up at him for a long, breathless moment. Then, without warning, her hand flew up and slapped him with surprising force. It seemed as if the sound of her hand cracking against his cheek echoed in the room forever. Her palm stung as she turned her back on him.

She had taken only one step before his hands spun her around to face him. Dark eyes blazed with fury. But she wouldn't cower before him. He was in the wrong. He was—

He pulled her against him as his mouth attacked hers, his fingers bruising the tender flesh of her arms. She struck his shoulder blades with the heels of her hands and tried to protest, but his tongue silenced her as it invaded her parted lips. Her traitorous body swayed closer to him even while her mind screamed for him to free her at once.

"You're my wife," he whispered a fraction of an inch from her mouth, "and you'll not forget it."

Together they tumbled to the carpet in front of the fireplace. With a sudden movement, his fingers gripped the front of her gown and rent the fabric. She cried out in surprise but was silenced once again by his demanding lips. His hand cupped a breast, shielding it from the cool air of the room.

But she didn't notice the cold. She was aware only of the fire in her veins. She couldn't remember her anger. She could only think of the wanting, the need to be a part of him. She could think only of how very much she loved this man and how very much she wanted to be loved by him.

"Love me," she whispered.

Suddenly, he pulled away from her. Firelight played across his face as he rose above her, giving him a sinister look. "Who is it you're asking for?" he asked, his voice still filled with anger.

It was like a dousing in cold water. She scrambled away from him, pulling her torn dress over her exposed breasts. "Get out, Brandon. Get out of my sight. Leave me alone." She turned her face away from him, hiding the tears that suddenly coursed down her face.

"Gladly."

She heard his boot heels clicking across the floor, then heard the door open and close.

She had what she'd asked for.

She was alone.

CHAPTER
TWENTY-FIVE

The smell of warm leather and horseflesh. The sight of breath hanging in frosty clouds. The sound of dogs whining. The hunt was about to begin.

The orange autumn sun had barely capped the treetops, but horses and riders were already milling about the lawn. Chelsea moved among them in a daze. She hadn't slept a wink all night long. Her mood had shifted a dozen times from anger to indignation to sorrow and tears to anger once again. One moment she was glad she'd slapped him, wished only she could have slapped him even harder. The next she wanted nothing more than to find him and apologize, to tell him how very much she loved him and that she would never even speak to

Roxley or any other man again if that was what he wanted.

She was almost upon the groom and horse before her eyes focused and she realized they were waiting for her.

"Stewart!" she exclaimed. "You've brought Duchess down from Teakwood."

"We couldn't have you sittin' on less than the Duchess for this grand affair, now could we, mum? And who else would be mindin' all the horses for his lordship?"

"Of course. How stupid of me."

"Your Duchess is feeling mighty spry this mornin', mum. You'd best keep a tight rein on her."

Chelsea looked at the sleek sorrel mare. Her fine head was held high, her nostrils flared, her ears darting forward and back. A sliver of white showed in the corners of her wide-set eyes as she surveyed the turmoil around her, caught the scent of excitement in the air. Her flaxen mane was ruffled by the crisp morning breeze, and her arched tail billowed behind her like a flag.

"Allow me to give you a leg up, mum," Stewart said softly. "Your guests are waiting for you and his lordship."

She was suddenly aware of the sly glances and outright stares of the people around her. She felt a flush of embarrassment coloring her cheeks. She wished for one friendly face amongst them but saw none. Roxley hadn't been in the dining room for the light breakfast fare, nor had she seen Grandfather yet this morning. For that matter, she hadn't seen Maitland either. Could Brandon be with her? Is that where he'd gone after she'd ordered him from their room last night?

"Yes. Please help me up, Stewart." She tried to shake off the depressing thought. "You know I haven't much use for riding habits and saddles."

The groom chuckled. "No, you haven't at that, mum."

As if on cue, the master of the hounds rounded the corner of the stables just as Chelsea settled into the saddle. Aided by his two assistants, known as whips, he brought the pack of white-and-black foxhounds to the edge of the lawn.

"Just follow the hounds, mum," Stewart advised. "Get out quick and stay ahead of the others as much as you can. There'll be some spills, and I'd just as soon not have you behind them when they happen. The Duchess won't have any trouble with the fences. She's one of the finest mounts in England. She'll do you proud."

"I know she will, Stewart."

The groom frowned as he looked up at her. "Have you ever been in on the kill, mum?"

She shook her head.

"I'd advise you to pull back then. There's some ladies who enjoy it as much as the men, but you'd not be one of them, I'm thinkin'."

Suddenly, the milling of horses and riders intensified. The air was electric with anticipation. Gooseflesh rose on Chelsea's arms.

"Move to the front," Stewart said above the confusion. "And good luck, mum."

"Thank you, Stewart."

Chelsea concentrated on weaving Duchess through the crowd, working her way toward the pack of hounds. The huntsman was wearing a bright red coat, black cap, and white riding breeches tucked into shiny black boots. He sat calmly in the midst of the anxious hounds, watching as the last of the riders scrambled into their saddles.

She had almost reached the huntsman and his dogs when he lifted his horn to his lips. The horn's blast was followed by the cry of "They're off!"

The hounds, loose of their leashes, dashed madly across the open field that sloped toward the wooded area beyond Hawklin. Their harsh cries filled the air. More than fifty horses and riders thundered after the baying dogs.

Duchess leapt into the front of the fray, nearly unseating Chelsea with her sudden burst of speed. Chelsea groped for control and knew a moment of fear as she thought of the galloping horses all around her. If she were to fall . . .

But her fear was forgotten as Duchess's long strides carried them across the field. She forgot the hated saddle, paid little heed to the shouts of other horsemen. She was lost to anything save the feel of the horse beneath her, to the wind tugging at her hat, to the racing of her heart.

She saw the hedge nearing, felt Duchess gathering for the jump. And then they were soaring, easily clearing the green brambles. She felt an exhilarated laugh rise in her chest.

On they flew, the baying hounds leading the way into the woods. Chelsea gave the mare her head, trusting in her to find the best way through trees and across streams. The earth shook and the air thundered with the pounding of galloping hooves as Chelsea leaned low to avoid the branches that reached out to scratch at her jacket sleeves.

She lost all track of time. She was in her element now. Nothing else existed.

Brandon caught glimpses of Chelsea's silk hat and Duchess's golden mane. With his heels, he asked Warrior for more speed and was gratified as the black stallion gave what he wanted. They thundered past several riders before sailing over a low stone wall.

He wasn't sure why it was so important that he catch up with her before the kill. He only knew he wanted to be there. Not that he wasn't still angry with her. Or maybe he wasn't. He didn't know. He wasn't sure of anything anymore.

Brandon had spent a miserable night in a small servant's bedroom on the third floor. He hadn't slept much until nearly dawn, but once he slept, he'd slept hard. By the time he awoke, he was almost too late. He'd barely found his mount before he heard the huntsman's horn.

The sun climbed as the hounds pursued the frightened fox. Warrior didn't catch Duchess as quickly as Brandon had hoped, but little by little, they were gaining ground. He knew by the sound of the dogs that the end was near.

Chelsea reined in. The pack of hounds was circling a hollow log. Now and again, one of them would dart forward, poking his head into one darkened end. The fox was cornered.

The sense of *deja vu* almost stopped her breath. Suddenly, time seemed to stand still.

She wasn't on horseback. She was running, running until she thought her lungs would burst. She could hear the difference in the cries of the dogs. They were closing in for the kill. Her bare feet flew over the leaves and pine needles that covered the woodland floor. She had to reach them in time.

The small red fox was cornered against an outcropping of rocks. Gamely, it bared its teeth as the foxhounds charged time and again. Beyond the dogs, she saw the riders. They had stopped their sweating mounts and were watching with smiles on their faces.

The fox. Her fox. She'd raised it from a cub, and now . . .

"No!"

Chelsea dug her heels into Duchess's side and rode into the skirmish. With her crop, she beat at the dogs, trying to drive them back. They yelped in confusion but paid her little heed. They had the scent of the kill in their nostrils and would not be swayed.

Chelsea slipped down from the saddle. "Get back! Get back!"

Tears streaking her cheeks, she fought her way through them, trying to reach the log before one of them succeeded in dragging the terrified fox from its hiding place. Her silk hat was knocked from her head. The dark skirt of her riding habit became muddied.

She wasn't aware that the huntsman had joined her amongst the dogs until he yelled at her, "What is it you're doing, m'lady?"

"Get them back! Get them out of here!"

The hounds swarmed in upon the fox. Snarling teeth tore at the lush red coat. She heard its yelp of pain.

"Flame!"

The tiny fox hadn't had a chance. Its blood stained the earth.

"Please! Please get them back."

She had almost reached the log when hands fell upon her shoulders. "What in the name of heaven are you doing?" Brandon demanded as he spun her around.

The faces of the hunters were alight with macabre pleasure. They laughed at her as she tried to reach her dying pet. One man rode forward to threaten her with his raised riding crop.

"Please. Please don't let them kill it."

"There's nothing I can do," he answered. "It's too late."

And it was.

Chelsea pulled away from Brandon. "You didn't try," she sobbed. "You didn't even try." Turning, she fled for her horse.

"Chelsea!"

She was heedless of the stunned expressions of those who had witnessed her futile attempt to rescue the fox. She scrambled into the saddle and yanked Duchess's head around, then kicked her into a gallop.

The exhausted mare did what she could, but it wasn't long before Chelsea knew she was driving the animal too hard. She eased in on the reins, slowing Duchess to a walk and finally stopping beside a gurgling brook. As she dismounted, she realized that her own breathing was nearly as labored as her horse's.

She dropped to the ground in a puddle of skirts and drew her legs up against her chest. She pressed her face against her knees and let the ache wash in crashing waves over her.

Roxley grabbed Brandon's arm. "Let me go. I think she'll listen to me."

Brandon started to say no. He didn't want it to be Roxley who comforted her. He wanted to be the one to hold her, to tell her he was sorry. But he couldn't help recalling her accusations. She'd thought it was his fault the fox was killed. She'd blamed him for it. What could he say to her to make things right? Especially after the way he'd treated her last night? He'd been a fool. An angry, jealous fool.

"All right, Roxley. Follow her. She shouldn't be alone."

Roxley found Chelsea in the shade of a giant oak. She was huddled in a ball, her horse standing nearby. He dismounted and walked slowly toward her. When she lifted her face from her knees, he felt as if someone had thrust a dagger through his heart. He'd never seen the face of misery before.

He sat on the ground beside her, then reached out and took hold of her hand. They sat in silence for a long time, both of them staring off into space.

"Roxley . . ." Chelsea's voice was hoarse.

"Yes?"

"I had a pet fox. Its name was Flame. The hunters . . . killed it."

"This wasn't your pet, Chelsea."

Her eyes came round to meet his. "I know. But the memory . . . Roxley, I didn't live at Hawklin as a child." Her blue eyes were so round, so troubled.

His throat felt tight. He tried to swallow.

"I don't know what the truth is anymore."

He didn't know what to say, or how to answer her.

"I'm not mad." Her words were whispered; he could scarcely hear her. "Roxley, I don't understand what's happening to me. I don't know—I don't know why I'm here, but I don't belong. I'm not—I'm not who they think I am."

He squeezed her hand. "Chelsea, you—"

"I can't go back. Will you take me away from here? Please."

Roxley was helpless against her plea. He loved her; he wanted her for himself. Brandon was his friend, but Chelsea meant even more to him. He would do anything she wanted. Anything.

"I'll take you away, Chelsea." He paused, then asked, "But what about Brandon?"

"I don't know. I . . ." Tears welled up and

spilled over. "I love him, but I can't stay."

She loved Brandon. She wasn't running because she didn't love him. Roxley drew a steadying breath. It didn't change what he would do for her. It only made things harder. But perhaps, with time . . .

"He would be better off without me," she said, choking on her tears. "You saw how they looked at me. Brandon belongs with someone like—someone different."

He knew whom she meant. He should have told her how wrong she was. Brandon didn't want Maitland. Any fool could see how the man felt about Chelsea, except maybe Brandon himself. In which case, Brandon *was* a fool, the biggest fool he'd ever known.

"Come with me." Roxley stood, pulling on her hand. "I'll take you to Rosemont. You can stay there until you feel better."

He crushed the hope that her stay would be a very long one.

Brandon met each gaze with a frigid glare that turned all eyes aside. He could hear the murmured whispers as the hunters followed him back to Hawklin.

"Brandon . . ."

Heaven help him, not now.

Maitland drew her horse up beside his. "Good lord, Brandon. What are we going to do about this?"

"*We* are going to do nothing. The party is over."

"My dear, I only want to help you."

In answer, he spurred Warrior into a gallop, leaving an indignant marchioness in his dust.

Brandon secluded himself in the salon throughout the afternoon. The house was in an uproar as the guests took their abrupt leave. He didn't care what they were saying about him or about Chelsea. To the devil with the lot of them. He only cared about getting Chelsea safely home. He only cared about Chelsea.

He kept watching out the French doors, waiting to see Roxley and Chelsea riding up to the stables. But they didn't come, and as the hours slipped from afternoon into evening, he knew they weren't coming. He knew it even before he received the note from Rosemont informing him that Lady Coleford would be a guest of the countess for a few days.

Chelsea had refused to come home.

Brandon stepped out onto the portico and stared unseeing across the back lawn as he leaned against a white pillar. The night air was crisp, the dark sky dusted with stars. The house, at last, was silent, the guests long since departed. The house servants were moving about on tiptoe, afraid of disturbing the scowling viscount.

"My boy . . ." Lawrence stepped out from the salon and came to stand beside his grandson. He placed a comforting arm around Brandon's shoulder.

"I should have gone after her. I shouldn't have let Roxley go."

"She was upset with you, Brandon. You did

what you thought right at the time."

He rubbed his temples with the heels of his hands. "If you'd seen her . . ."

"I heard," Lawrence answered gently.

"Grandfather." He turned tortured brown eyes upon the older man. "I don't know what to do."

"About what, Brandon?"

"I kept thinking things would—would be all right between us, and then she does something like—" He shrugged helplessly, letting his words die away.

Lawrence squeezed his grandson's shoulder, then turned and walked to a chair and sat down. His wizened eyes studied Brandon for a long time before he spoke. "Like what, my boy? Like trying to save a small animal from being torn limb from limb by a pack of dogs? Seen through her eyes, I must agree it isn't much of a sport."

Brandon glanced at his grandfather, grudgingly admitting the old man was right. Then he turned his eyes once more upon the sculptured gardens. "They won't let her forget what happened here today. Maitland will be certain of that. We won't be able to keep her madness a secret any longer. Not after today."

"Brandon." Silence followed.

When Lawrence didn't continue, Brandon turned once again.

"Not once in all these weeks since we came to England have I seen madness in that girl's eyes. I've seen confusion and fear. I've seen her struggle to remember people and places and things, trying to piece together a past that doesn't seem to exist. She has a right to be afraid. Wouldn't you be if you awoke with no memory? But I've not seen madness. Lately what I've seen in her eyes is love." Lawrence rose from his chair. "It's not madness you're afraid of, my boy. It's losing her. It's losing her to Roxley—or someone like him. Stop thinking of her as a fragile object that might shatter into pieces at the drop of a hat. Start treating her like the woman you love, Brandon."

The duke turned and walked toward the salon door. Once there, he looked back over his shoulder and said, "Perhaps *you* are the one who is mad, my boy. For letting her get away."

CHAPTER
TWENTY-SIX

Maitland swept into Chelsea's bedroom unannounced.

"Do you know what you've done, Chelsea Fitzgerald?" the marchioness demanded haughtily.

Chelsea looked at her with red-rimmed eyes.

"You've made him the subject of gossip from here to London. Soon enough it will be all over England." Maitland approached the chair near the window where Chelsea was seated. "Brandon has great prospects here. He's the heir to the Duke of Foxworth. One day he could sit in the House of Lords. He has untold wealth. And he is saddled with a woman who will surely destroy him."

"I have no wish to destroy Brandon," Chelsea whispered, dropping her gaze to her lap.

"Then do the right thing. Grant him a divorce. If it's done properly, the scandal will soon be forgotten. It was an arranged marriage, not a love match. He'd never set eyes upon you until he arrived at Hawklin. With a good solicitor—"

Chelsea's voice broke as she asked, "Does he want a divorce?"

Maitland threw up her hands. "Of course he wants a divorce, you little fool. What man wouldn't?"

"I see." She squeezed her eyes closed, fighting back the tears.

"No wonder your parents kept you shut away from society. You haven't the least idea how to behave. Brandon should marry me. You and I both know it."

Chelsea held her breath and fought for control. She felt as if she'd been struck, but she didn't want to break down in front of Maitland. She didn't care what people thought about her. Nothing mattered now that she'd lost Brandon. But she didn't want to cry in front of this woman.

"Maitland," a male voice demanded, "what are you doing here?"

Both women looked toward the open doorway. Roxley stood just inside the room, his gaze moving between them.

Chelsea pushed herself up by the arms of the chair. "I think I should like to be alone, Maitland," she said hoarsely.

The marchioness cast her a meaningful glance, then nodded and left the room.

"Chelsea—" Roxley began, taking a step toward her.

She put out an arm, palm toward him, stopping him in his place. "Don't!" she cried. She swallowed, then spoke again, this time more softly. "I *really* should like to be alone."

"But—"

"Roxley, I'm forever grateful for your friendship, but I cannot stay here at Rosemont. It can only cause more trouble."

"I'll have the carriage readied. We can have you back to Hawklin by nightfall."

There was a terrible pain behind her eyes. She squeezed them shut. "You don't understand. I can't go back to Hawklin. Not ever." There was no holding back the tears this time. When she opened her eyes again, she viewed Roxley through a watery mist. "I don't ever want to see Brandon again."

Ignoring her request to stay away, Roxley closed the door and then crossed the room. He closed his fingers around her arms, offering support through the strength of his hands. "Where would you go if you left Rosemont?"

"Perhaps to my—my parents in London."

But even as she said it, she knew she couldn't bear to live with them. Her father would rather see her put away. Her mother seemed totally indifferent to anything concerning Chelsea. No, she wouldn't be welcome at the Fitzgerald townhouse. And if not there, where else had she to go?

"You can't go there," Roxley said, echoing her thoughts. "Chelsea, are you sure you don't want to go back to—"

"I'm sure."

The earl stared thoughtfully at her for a long time. "All right then," he said at last. "If you're sure this is what you want, I have a small cottage near Lynton in Devonshire. I'll take you there."

"Roxley, you . . ."

He placed his lips gently against her forehead, then stepped back from her. "You needn't say it, Chelsea. I ask nothing more than that you let me take care of you. I won't—I won't ask for anything more than friendship. I give you my pledge."

He turned on his heel and left the bedroom. The empty silence of the room reminded Chelsea of her future without Brandon. Turning, she threw herself across the bed and wept.

Brandon's horse galloped up to the front of Rosemont. He catapulted to the ground before the animal had slid to a halt. He took the steps three at a time, then pounded forcefully on the door.

It was opened by a startled-looking butler. "My lord? It's early for—"

Brandon pushed his way past the servant. "I've come to see my wife. Please tell Lady Coleford that I've come for her."

"But, your lordship—"

"Tell her," Brandon snapped as he tugged

the gloves from his fingers.

Shaking his head, the butler scurried from the entry hall.

Brandon paced impatiently, stopping occasionally to cast a glance toward the stairs. Finally, he sat on a chair and leaned his arms against his thighs as he stared at the floor.

Once again he cursed himself for letting Roxley go after Chelsea. If he hadn't let his jealousy get the better of him the night before . . . if he'd only tried to beat back the dogs . . . if only . . .

"My dear viscount, what an unexpected pleasure."

Brandon rose quickly as the countess swept into the hall. "Lady Roxley." He offered a curt bow.

"Please, let's go into the salon." She cast a glance over her shoulder. "Morton, bring us some coffee."

As soon as they were seated, Brandon said, "I've come for my wife, Lady Roxley."

"Please. Call me Eleanor." She held up a quizzing glass and perused him. "Young man, your wife is not here," she said after a lengthy silence.

"But, Roxley's note said—"

"She *was* here, but she's left."

He got to his feet. "I must have missed her on the road. I'm sorry for disturbing you so early."

"Sit down, Brandon," Eleanor said in her most authoritarian tone. When he'd done so, she continued. "She has not gone to Hawklin."

Brandon raked his fingers through already tousled brown hair. "I'm afraid I don't understand, Lady—Eleanor."

"What Mother is trying to tell you is that Chelsea has left you." Maitland strolled into the salon and stood behind her mother's chair. "She has gone away with Roxley."

"Do be quiet, Maitland," the countess snapped. "It is not as bad as it sounds, Brandon. Chelsea felt the need to be alone after—after yesterday's little trouble."

"Trouble!" Maitland exclaimed with a sharp laugh. "The girl was positively insane. She's made herself an object of gossip for every servant and lord from here to Ireland."

Brandon managed to ignore her. "Where have they gone, Eleanor?"

The older woman met his gaze. "I cannot tell you. I gave her my word."

He stood once again. "I'll find them." He turned toward the doorway.

"Brandon?"

He glanced back at the countess.

"I won't deny that my son cares a bit too much for your wife. And I can't say that I blame him. I'm rather enchanted with her myself, despite her—eccentricities." She rose regally from the chair. "But Roxley is your friend as well as hers. He will not dishonor her nor will he shame his family's name."

"You'd better pray to God you're right, good lady. I'd hate to have to kill him."

With that, Brandon left Rosemont.

* * *

It was dark before the Earl of Roxley's coach reached his private cottage near the north coast of Devonshire. It had been a silent journey for the inhabitants of the carriage. And a weary one.

Chelsea scarcely gave her surroundings a glance as Roxley helped her to the ground and walked her toward the gray stone house with its pitched roof and narrow windows. He unlocked the door and opened it before her.

"Stay here. I'll get a light."

She waited, her eyelids drooping. Emotionally and physically exhausted, all Chelsea wanted was to find a bed and collapse into it.

It wasn't long before Roxley was coming toward her, lamp in hand. "I'll show you to your room."

She nodded.

"I've sent the driver for Claire. She's the girl who cooks and does the cleaning here. She'll come and stay with you."

"You're not staying?"

"I've thought about it all day. I think it would be better if I went on to Lynton and stayed at an inn. I'll come see you tomorrow."

Again she nodded. It would be better that way. For everyone concerned.

"Come on," Roxley said, taking her arm. "You're about ready to fall asleep on your feet. Things will look better in the morning."

She allowed him to lead her up the steep, narrow steps. He opened a door and ushered her into a sparsely furnished bedroom, but she paid little note to the room or its lack of furniture. She moved stiffly toward the bed and sat on the edge, staring at her hands folded in her lap.

Roxley leaned down and lightly brushed her forehead with his lips. "I'll return in the morning."

Just as he reached the doorway, Chelsea looked up. "Brandon wants a divorce."

He turned around and stared at her as if she had truly lost her mind this time.

"It's true," she whispered.

"You're mistaken, Chelsea. Brandon would never seek a divorce from you. He—"

"Good night, Roxley," Chelsea said quickly. She couldn't bear it if he told her Brandon loved her, just to bring comfort. And she'd been certain that's what he was about to tell her. "Good night," she said again, more gently this time.

The look in his dark eyes was heart-wrenching. It seemed an eternity before he turned away and closed the door, leaving Chelsea to face a long and lonely night.

CHAPTER
TWENTY-SEVEN

Fog shrouded the upland moor. Chelsea stood
at the window of her small bedroom, staring
out at the eerie sight. Night was past, but
morning was yet to arrive. She felt strangely
peaceful after the turmoil of the previous two
days. It had something to do with this place.

It wasn't at all what she'd expected. When
Roxley had said he had a cottage, she hadn't
really expected it to *be* a cottage. The gentry
were usually quite adept at understatement
when it came to their homes and estates. But
this was just what Roxley had said it would be.
Only a few rooms, all of them with plain floors
and rough wooden furnishings. Thankfully,
there was a fireplace in the bedroom, for the
nights were already cold this close to the sea.

Soon the sun would rise above the treetops and begin to disperse the low-lying fog. In a few hours, it would be gone. Chelsea reached for her wrap and headed for the door.

Exmoor spread out before her. A wild section of land, some forested, some seemingly desolate. The moor was cut by deep glens and high ridges, and hidden beneath the scenic beauty of this place roamed great stags—fit for a king's hunt—and the rare red deer and wild ponies of the moor.

Chelsea walked away from the cottage and, before long, was embraced by the fog. It was comforting somehow. Familiar. Hands deep in the pockets of her cape, she walked for nearly an hour, not stopping until she reached a craggy ridge. She looked up the rocky slope, its peak just now kissed by the morning sun. Pursing her lips, she found a foothold and began to climb.

It took her only a few minutes to reach the top. Once there, she drew an exhilarating breath of crisp air. A cool wind whipped her hair back from her face and flared her cape out behind her like wings. She hugged her arms to her chest as she stared out at the bleak landscape.

Brandon.

She remembered him now as she'd first seen him, in her locked apartments at Hawklin. How terrified she had been of this husband she'd never seen, and how surprised she had been by his tenderness, his kindness. She visualized him on horseback, riding through the fields near Teakwood, laughter on his lips. She recalled how he'd looked in his chieftain's costume, war paint streaking his handsome face and something much more savage in his eyes when he reached for her.

How she loved him.

She remembered the first time he'd kissed her, the first time they'd made love. She remembered the times she'd awakened in bed beside him and watched him sleep. She remembered the comfort of his arms when she'd been frightened by a bad dream and the twinkle in his eyes when she amused him.

How she loved him.

And, too, she remembered the horrified look in his eyes when he found her, spattered with her own blood, in the nursery at Hawklin. She remembered his disbelief when she tried to tell him the things she recalled, things contrary to everything they'd been told but things she somehow knew to be true. And she remembered the cold disdain in his voice when he left her in their bedroom the night of the supper party.

And *still* she loved him.

If only things could have been different for them. If only they had met in a different place, in a different time. If only he had fallen in love with her as she had with him.

"I tried to make him love me," she whispered to the silent moor.

Did you? the land seemed to ask back.

She sank to the ground, wrapping her cape around her legs as she tucked them up near her breasts.

Had she? Had she done all she could? If she were well, would he still choose to divorce her? Would she so willingly back away and let Maitland have him? If she truly loved him, wouldn't she fight to keep him as she'd promised herself time and again that she would?

"If I were well . . ."

The sun was beginning to burn off the fog, leaving pockets of white mist in the deepest glens and valleys. Across the valley floor, a great stag stepped from a wooded hillside into the meadowland, picking its way through the sedge, nibbling at the grasses. Chelsea held her breath, mesmerized by the animal's sleek beauty.

Its head came up. Great antlers formed a royal crown as it swung around. Deep brown eyes stared at Chelsea across the sweep of land that separated them. She tried not to move, not even to blink, caught in the majesty of the moment.

It knew she could mean danger, yet it faced her with quiet dignity, waiting to see what she might do. Then, slowly, it turned and walked back into the shelter of the forest.

If I were well . . . The words returned to her as if there had never been a break in her thoughts.

"There's naught wrong with you, girl, that time and love won't cure. You're not crazy."

She could almost hear Molly speaking those

words to her, scolding her, telling her to get up and fight back. And what was she doing now? Hiding, retreating into self-pity. Was that what Molly would have wanted her to do?

No. Molly would want her to face it as the stag had faced her. With dignity. Head on. Without a show of fear.

"But what do I fight with? I can't remember my past. I don't know who or what I am." She shouted the words this time, her voice breaking the solitude of the morning. "Something always comes between us. Something I don't understand." She choked back a sob and buried her face against her knees.

What was she to do?

Find out what's true, my girl. That's what Molly would say to her. *Demand to know. Fight back, child.*

Chelsea drew back her head and dashed away her tears. She would. She would fight back. If she wanted to *be* well, she had to *act* well. And to do so, she must find out what her dreams meant. And they did mean something. They weren't just the imaginings of a crazed mind. She was positive of that. She would find the missing pieces to her jigsaw memories.

There seemed to be only two people who could help her now. Hayden and Sara Fitzgerald. They were all that remained of those who had known her before this summer. Everyone else was gone. Molly—her nanny, her nurse, the woman who had raised her—was dead. Miss Pendleton, the companion she couldn't remember, was dead. Even the servants who had cared for the house in the years she was growing up, imprisoned in the nursery, were no longer at Hawklin.

She stood and absently brushed the dirt from her cape. It was settled then. She would go to London. She would confront her parents. She would know the truth, no matter what it was.

Roxley leaned back, swaying with the carriage as it jostled and bounced its way along the road back to Gloucestershire. He hoped Chelsea would understand why he hadn't gone to the cottage. He barely understood himself.

No, that wasn't true. He understood more than a little too well why he hadn't gone. If he'd gone to see her, he never would have been able to keep his promise to her and to himself to keep things on the level of friendship. He would have pressed for more. He would have demanded more. He would have thrown honor and reputation to the devil. And then he would have ruined what they did share.

It was best this way. He had sent her a note, telling her that business had called him back to Rosemont and saying she would be well cared for while in Devon. His hunting cottage was remote, and the people who tended his property could be trusted to care for her.

Divorce.

Strange how a word could bring him both sorrow and hope. Chelsea loved Brandon. Roxley knew it. She had told him so, not just with words but with the way her eyes followed Brandon when they were in a room together, by the soft inflection in her voice when she spoke Brandon's name. Yes, Chelsea loved her husband, and his rejection of her was breaking her heart. She might never recover from it.

But still, if Roxley could be there to comfort her . . . She cared for him, considered him a dear friend. If he were there to help her through these dark hours and days, might she not turn to him for more than friendship in the future? Might she not even be willing to marry him and come to live at Rosemont as his countess? If he were careful not to rush her, wasn't it possible she might consent to marriage after time had begun to heal her wounds?

Maitland would rage against it, and even his mother would most likely oppose him marrying a divorced woman. But what cared he for scandal if it meant living with Chelsea for the rest of his life? What cared he for anything save bringing her happiness?

It was nearly noon by the time Chelsea returned to the cottage. A young woman was dusting the parlor. She turned with a start when the door opened and Chelsea entered.

"Hello," Chelsea said, a question in her eyes.

The raven-haired girl, perhaps a few years older than Chelsea, bobbed a curtsy. "M'lady."

"You must be Claire," Chelsea said as she hung her wrap on a peg near the door.

"I am, indeed. His lordship asked me to come see to you while you're here."

Chelsea nodded silently.

"I was gettin' a might worried, m'lady, not

findin' you here when I come this mornin'. There's a message come from his lordship while you were out." Claire held out a scrap of paper.

Chelsea breathed a sigh of relief as she read it. She would have a little more time to sort things out in her mind before she had to explain them to Roxley—or to anyone else, for that matter.

"Would you care for a bite to eat, m'lady? I've brought some cheese and bread from home."

"Thank you, Claire. I would like that very much. I'm terribly hungry."

As Chelsea ate, Claire took a brush and bucket of water and began to scrub the floor on her hands and knees. Whenever she thought Chelsea wasn't looking, she would eye her critically.

Chelsea was aware of the girl's perusal. At first it amused her, but after a while, it began to irritate her. Had Roxley told Claire about Chelsea's strange behavior? Was she waiting for Chelsea to suddenly go into some sort of fit? Finally, she set down the chunk of bread in her hand and twisted in her chair.

"What is it you're wondering about, Claire?"

The woman sat back on her heels. "Wonderin', m'lady?"

"Come now, Claire. You've been staring at me the whole while I've been eating. You must be curious about something. What is it?"

Claire looked a little frightened. She swallowed hard, then said softly, "I was wonderin' if you're his lordship's—well, you see, he's never brought a woman here before. . . ."

"Oh." Chelsea shook her head. "I am *not* the earl's mistress, if that's what you're asking. We are merely friends. His estate borders on my husband's property."

"You're a *married* woman?"

"Yes, Claire. I'm married."

And I'm going to do all in my power to stay that way, she thought as she turned once more toward her meal of bread and cheese.

"Your lordship?"

Brandon turned toward the butler.

"I've just learned the Earl of Roxley has returned to Rosemont, sir."

His fingers tightened around his brandy glass. "Thank you, Bowman."

"What are you going to do, Brandon?" Lawrence asked as the butler departed.

"I'm going to pay a visit to our neighbor, first thing in the morning. And then I'm going to bring my wife home where she belongs."

The duke shook his head as his light brown eyes studied his grandson. "Don't do anything foolish, my boy," he advised.

Brandon laughed sharply. "Foolish! Aren't you speaking to the wrong man about foolish?"

"Perhaps. Perhaps not. Just don't jump to conclusions about Roxley and Chelsea. I don't believe it's as bad as it looks at the moment."

"I wish I could believe you, Grandfather."

Brandon set down his glass and excused

himself, then strode from the drawing room. He swiftly ascended the stairs to the second floor. His destination was his bedroom but he found himself instead traversing the hallway of the southeast wing, not stopping until he reached Chelsea's old rooms. He paused, resting his hand on the doorknob, then opened the door.

Nothing had changed there since the day he'd first entered the room. The same white counterpane covered the narrow bed. The same chair sat to one side. The same draperies framed the window overlooking the gardens.

Brandon stepped inside, remembering with sharp poignancy the moment he'd first laid eyes on his bride. He'd been so struck by her beauty—her silver-blond hair, haunting blue eyes, exquisite cheekbones, flawless skin. Except, she was Alanna then. Alanna Fitzgerald. A girl who'd been shut away from society, even from servants, most all of her life. A girl with a dark past, now secret from her.

But Alanna had existed for him only for a very short time. The woman he loved was Chelsea Fitzgerald. A girl filled with a sparkle for life, a quicksilver temper, and lilting laughter. Confused and frightened by the amnesia that blacked out her past, she faced her future with courage and determination.

What could he have done differently to have helped her? How could he have avoided this crisis in their lives?

Brandon's fingers traced the lacing on the

counterpane, then paused on the pillow.

Perhaps there was nothing he could have done to avoid it, but he could do something now. Nothing and no one was going to keep him from bringing Chelsea home. Where she belonged.

CHAPTER
TWENTY-EIGHT

Dawn was hardly more than a promise on the horizon when Brandon paused midway in his descent of the stairs leading to the entry hall. The butler was just crossing the hall, headed toward the kitchen, when Brandon's voice stopped him.

"Bowman, have my horse saddled and brought round."

The butler turned. His usual remote and proper facade faltered. "You're going after her, sir?" There was hope in his question.

"I'll be bringing her ladyship home," Brandon answered with great finality.

Bowman's face broke into a grin. "I'll have your horse readied at once, my lord."

Brandon couldn't help a small smile himself.

He didn't think he'd ever seen Bowman lose his imperious air before. Trust Chelsea to be the cause of it.

He continued down the stairs, then crossed the hall to the massive doors. He pushed aside the draperies at the window, noting the frost on the lawn and trees. The house seemed deathly silent; nothing stirred outdoors. It seemed only he and Bowman were up and about this early.

The scent of hot coffee wafted down the hallway. He turned, sniffing the air. But then his stomach knotted, and he knew he would be better off with nothing. If this morning's confrontation with Roxley led to more than words . . .

He let that thought die unfinished. He preferred to think they could settle this in a calm and gentlemanly fashion. He'd liked Roxley from their first meeting. He wanted to think their friendship could ride out the problems this morning would bring.

Brandon heard the clip of horse's hooves against the stone drive. At the same time, Bowman reappeared, carrying his coat and hat. The butler held up the coat to Brandon, and Brandon slipped his arms through the sleeves.

As Brandon turned to take his hat from the butler, Bowman said, "Good luck, sir. We'll be watching for you and her ladyship." His expression was inscrutable; he had regained control. But Brandon could still hear the wistful tone in the servant's voice.

339

"Don't worry, Bowman. We shouldn't be long."

It was Stewart himself who brought round Warrior. He was standing with his hand on the stallion's muzzle, stroking and talking softly, when Brandon came out of the manse. The groom raised troubled eyes, then ran his free hand through his graying hair. The deep wrinkles around his eyes and across his forehead became even deeper when he frowned.

"M'lord," he said as he passed the reins to Brandon, "tell her ladyship for me that I'm sorry for not warnin' her better about the hunt. I'd no idea she would—well, I feel it was my fault for not sayin' more."

"Don't worry, Stewart." Brandon laid a comforting hand on the groom's shoulder. "I'm sure Lady Coleford knows you weren't at fault for what happened. When we get back, she'll tell you that herself."

"Thank you, m'lord."

Brandon swung up into the saddle. He tugged at the brim of his hat to secure it, then nudged Warrior's ribs with his heels.

As the ground fell away beneath his mount's hooves, Brandon found himself grinning once again. Was there no one Chelsea hadn't charmed as soon as they met her? Certainly no one at Hawklin.

"Come on, boy," he said, urging more speed from Warrior. "Let's bring her ladyship home where she belongs."

* * *

Dressed in the simple cotton blouse and wool skirt she'd borrowed from Claire, Chelsea boarded the London coach in Lynton. She returned the looks of the other passengers with a nod, then turned her eyes out of the coach window, not wanting to be drawn into conversation if it could be avoided.

She wished now that she had had the foresight to send for some of her clothes from Hawklin before leaving Rosemont, but at the time, it only seemed important to be away. Luckily for her, Claire was about her size. Thinking of all the fine gowns she had hanging in her wardrobe—some she'd never even worn yet—she decided then and there she would send Claire a gift of one of them as soon as she could. Something far different from the rough wool skirt Chelsea now wore.

Chelsea tugged her cape a little closer about her shoulders, trying to keep out the chill air.

"Allow me, miss," the gentleman across from her said as he leaned forward and closed the flap over the window. "It will help keep some of the cold out."

"Thank you."

The man smiled and looked as if he might say more. There was a light in his eyes that indicated interest, an interest Chelsea would just as soon not encourage. Unable to think of anything else she might do to dissuade him, she closed her eyes and feigned sleep.

It wasn't long before the rocking of the coach took away the pretense of her actions.

The blond man stood outside the coach. His blue eyes were misty, but he stubbornly refused to let the tears fall.

"You mind your mother's aunt, girl. You make me proud. She's a fine lady, your aunt. She'll teach you what I can't. She's got a good heart, takin' you in now when she's got troubles of her own."

"I don't want to go, Papa. Please let me stay."

"Look at you. It's near a woman you are. The moor's not the place for you."

"But, Papa . . ." She was crying, big tears streaking her cheeks unchecked. But it was no use arguing with him. "You'll take care of Flame's pups?"

"I will, girl. Don't worry about them. And your pony too."

The coach jerked forward as the door closed.

Brandon stopped his horse at the end of the long drive and stared at Rosemont. He was glad Roxley and Chelsea had decided to return. He only hoped he wouldn't have to call Roxley out to get this matter settled. He nudged Warrior forward, this time at a walk.

He dismounted before the front entrance. The door opened immediately and a footman appeared to take his horse's reins. Brandon nodded to him silently, then stepped toward the doorway.

Rosemont's butler—a slightly younger but even more hubristic version of Bowman—took Brandon's hat and coat, then ushered him into the salon. Brandon was left there to cool his heels alone. Impatiently, he paced the length of the room, waiting for the butler to bring the earl to him.

"Brand."

He turned quickly. Roxley was framed in the salon entrance. His expression was somber, his black eyes wary.

"I didn't expect you."

Brandon took two steps toward him, then stopped. "You didn't?"

"I was coming to Hawklin later this morning."

"Well, that isn't necessary now, is it? If you'll have your butler tell Chelsea to get ready, I'll see her home."

Roxley's eyebrows rose a fraction before he turned his head away and motioned toward a grouping of chairs. "Why don't we sit down?"

Brandon's anger began to surface. "I didn't come here for a pleasant chat with you, Roxley. I came for Chelsea. My *wife*. Remember?"

"Yes," the earl responded, a trace of anger in his voice as well. "I remember perfectly well. I'm surprised you have."

Brandon's hands clenched into tight fists. He headed across the room toward Roxley. "See here—"

"No!" Roxley's index finger poked him in the chest. "*You* see here. What do you think Chelsea is? Some sort of toy to be battered back and forth between players? You've thrown her aside. Must you torture her as well?"

"Thrown her aside? Good heavens, man! What are you babbling about?"

Roxley's face was only inches away as he shouted, "The divorce! I'm talking about the divorce."

Brandon stepped backward as if he'd been struck. He felt the blood draining from his face. Then, just as suddenly, it came back boiling. The veins at his temples felt ready to burst. "What divorce?" he asked softly, controlling his fury by a thread. "If you think I'm going to divorce Chelsea so you can have her, you're crazy. I have no intention of ever getting a divorce."

It was Roxley's turn to step back. His expression would have been funny at any other time. He turned and sat down on the nearest divan. "Chelsea said *you* wanted a divorce."

"I what?"

"She said you wanted a divorce," Roxley repeated.

"Why would she say a fool thing like that?" Brandon's anger had begun to cool. He took a seat across from Roxley. "I love her," he finished, his voice breaking as he admitted his feelings.

"I thought . . ." The earl's eyes widened; he groaned. "Maitland."

Roxley didn't have to explain any further. Brandon understood only too well what he meant. Maitland had been up to her dirty tricks. His fists balled again. If she were in this room this minute, he would . . .

Brandon forced control upon himself. "Why don't you just tell Chelsea I'm here."

"Because she didn't come back with me."

"Didn't come—? Then where is she?" He rose swiftly to his feet.

"Don't worry, Brand. I left her at my hunting cottage in Devonshire. She's being well taken care of by my servant girl."

Brandon headed for the door. "You don't know her as I do, Roxley. If she takes it into her head to leave, she'll do it. She could go anywhere. If she thinks I want a divorce, I might never find—" He stopped himself before he could speak the words aloud.

Before Brandon reached the salon door, Roxley caught up with him. His hand fell on Brandon's shoulder and spun him around. "Wait. I've got something to say to you. Maitland may have put the idea of divorce into her head, and I may have been at fault for giving her a place to run to. But, by the heavens, Brand, this is your own damn fault, and if you think you're just going to—"

Almost as a reflex action, Brandon took a swing at Roxley. The earl ducked and came up with a sudden jab under the chin, knocking Brandon back a step. Brandon countered with a vicious hook that split Roxley's lip. The earl's return swing caught Brandon in the stomach.

"Now we can continue this outside," Roxley growled through clenched teeth as Brandon advanced toward him, "or you can listen to some sense. Have you ever *told* Chelsea you love her?" He glared at Brandon. "No, I didn't think you had. Well, would she have believed Maitland if she'd known how you felt?"

Roxley's voice echoed around the salon, fading until all that could be heard was hard breathing as the two men stared at each other.

"Brand, I won't lie to you." Roxley drew himself up, his fists relaxing. "I care a great deal for Chelsea. If she weren't your wife . . . But she is, and she loves you. She's hurting right now more than I care to think about. She's certain your only feelings for her are what anyone would feel for a sick child."

"She's not sick. She's—"

"No, she's not sick. And she's not mad. She's been telling me that ever since the night of Maitland's ball. And I believe her. Whatever caused Hayden to lock her up as a child doesn't exist anymore. She's just a young woman with no memory beyond you." Roxley's voice softened as he wiped the blood from his mouth with his handkerchief. "And isn't that what every man dreams of? To have a woman love him so much that she has no thought, no memory of anything or anyone before he entered her life? I know it's what I would want."

Brandon swallowed hard. He nodded. "Where do I find her?"

"I'll take you there myself, if you'll let me." Roxley stepped toward Brandon, holding a hand out toward him. "Truce?"

Brandon took the hand and squeezed. "Friends," he replied. "And thanks."

Roxley's eyes showed the sincerity of his feelings. "Wait here. I'll have my horse saddled and be ready to leave in a moment."

As soon as the earl had left the salon, Brandon walked over to the fireplace and leaned against the mantel, suddenly fatigued. Everything Roxley had said was true. He was at fault. He was at fault for the whole blasted mess. If he'd told Chelsea he loved her when he first realized it . . . If he hadn't always been watching and waiting for her next nightmare, her next fainting spell, her next anything . . . Why had he allowed himself to get so caught up in worrying he would lose her to madness one day that he hadn't noticed how normal she was? So she had amnesia. Was that so unusual after being struck on the head by a falling beam? He was lucky she was alive.

"Brandon, my dear. It is you. I didn't believe my maid when she told me you'd come calling so early."

He turned slowly around until his gaze fell upon Maitland. She was wearing some frilly morning concoction of apple green with a low neckline trimmed with lace and long sleeves. Her thick auburn hair waved down her back and spread over her enticing white shoulders. As he watched, she yawned daintily, hiding her mouth behind her hand.

He walked toward her, the hot fury he'd felt earlier now turned to an icy rage. It must have shown on his face, for the closer he came, the more worried she looked.

"Lady Bellfort," he said when he stopped, his voice deep and threatening, "I don't want to be in the same room with you. I don't want to be in the same house you're in. You are unwelcome at Hawklin Hall or Teakwood Manor or any other Fitzgerald estate, no matter what the occasion. If you ever so much as speak to me again, I may be forced to wring that pretty white neck of yours. Do I make myself clear?"

Her almond eyes stared at him; her hand moved to her throat.

"Good. I think you do understand. See that you don't forget it." He stepped around her. "Good-bye, Lady Conover. Go back to your spider web and weave a trap for some other fool."

He heard her gasp. It gave him a small measure of satisfaction. Very small.

As he headed for the front entrance, he saw the butler watching him from a far corner. "Tell the earl I'll be waiting for him outside. The salon suddenly became too crowded for my taste."

CHAPTER
<u>TWENTY-NINE</u>

The coach stopped for the night at an inn that had apparently seen better days. The cramped, gloomy common room was filled with travelers partaking of their evening meal. Chelsea was hungry, but there was little change left in her pocket from the money Roxley had given Claire to buy food and other supplies. Most of it had gone for her coach fare.

She wanted a bath almost as much as she wanted food, but she knew that too would cost extra. With a room to herself, she could sponge off the day's travel in the basin. Tomorrow she would arrive in London and could relax in a hot bath at the townhouse.

As Chelsea followed the obese proprietress up a rickety flight of stairs, she glanced back at the common room. Several pairs of male eyes were fastened on her. The motley group of men were swilling ale at a table near the far wall. She shivered and quickened her steps.

"It's not fancy, but it's clean," the woman said as she opened a door, revealing a tiny room with a bed near an outside wall.

Chelsea glanced behind her, feeling vulnerable. "Is there a lock for the door?"

"Lor', miss, there's a lock all right. An' if the men downstairs get t'prowlin' as they've been known t'do, it'll be glad to 'ave it you'll be." The woman flashed an almost toothless grin as she passed the lamp into Chelsea's hand. "Pretty, you are, too. Sleep well, miss."

Chelsea tried to smile in return but failed. She stepped into the room and quickly closed the door, drawing the bolt at once. Still, it didn't seem much of a door, and the laughter from downstairs sounded threatening in her ears. She grabbed the nearby chair, the only piece of furniture in the room besides the bed and night table, and shoved it up against the doorknob.

Her sponge bath forgotten, Chelsea crossed to the bed and set the lamp on the nightstand. Then she dropped her cape on the floor, removed her shoes, and crawled beneath the covers. Huddled with her back against the wall, she stared at the door, certain she would get no sleep that night.

It was well after nightfall when Brandon's and Roxley's weary horses cantered into the yard of the hunting cottage in Exmoor. All was still; the house was dark.

"She must already be in bed," Roxley said, pointing toward a second-story window.

They dismounted and tethered their horses to a hitching post. Roxley led the way into the stone cottage. Brandon waited near the doorway while the earl went to light a lamp. Even in the dark silence of the house, Brandon's eyes managed to find the stairway. As soon as the match was struck, shedding a weak light across the small parlor, Brandon was headed for the stairs. He didn't need the lamp. He would find his own way.

"I'll wait here," Roxley said unnecessarily.

Brandon paused outside the bedroom door. During the arduous ride from Rosemont to Devonshire, he'd tried to practice what he might say. He knew in his heart all the things he wanted to tell her, if only he could find the words. And when he did find the words, he prayed she would listen and forgive him.

His hand slowly lifted the latch. He pushed the door open.

"Chelsea?" he whispered, moving more by instinct than by sight toward the bed. "Chelsea?"

The bed was empty. He swirled around and bolted from the room.

"She's not here," he bellowed at Roxley. If he'd been led on a wild goose chase, he would—

One glance at Roxley's face dispelled his

momentary doubts. Roxley had expected her to be there.

"Neither is Claire. She was to stay here with Chelsea until I returned. Maybe they went to her home for the night." It was obvious from the tone of Roxley's voice he didn't believe it, yet hoped it was true.

"Let's go." Brandon turned on his heel.

"Wait, Brand. We can't go barging in on Claire and her father in the middle of the night."

"Maybe you can't, but I can. Just show me the way."

The two-story house was small by most standards, but to her it seemed a mansion. The white cottage with its thatched roof and two rooms would fit into the parlor of this place.

The woman standing before the red brick house was elderly with thin graying hair and sad eyes. But a smile brightened the woman's wrinkled face as she looked at the girl stepping down from the pony cart.

"So, you're Catherine's daughter. Let me look at you. Yes, you've got her eyes. Come inside, and we'll get acquainted."

Chelsea woke with a start. For a moment she was disoriented. She was sitting up in bed, the thin blankets tucked up around her neck. She blinked, trying to shake off the fatigue that pulled at her eyes.

She'd been having another one of those

dreams. The ones that haunted her long after she was awake. The ones that seemed to speak to her from times past. The ones so real she felt she could step into them and live there.

This time it was the ivy-covered brick house. When she'd slept in the coach earlier in the day, she'd dreamt of the man and the small cottage. That man. Papa? This woman. Aunt? Who were they really? Their faces were so clear in her mind. Why did she dream of them? Why always of them?

She heard the rattle of the latch and looked toward the door. Her heart seemed to stop as she saw the handle moving, heard the slight squeak of the wood as someone moved against it. She held her breath, waiting for the door to give beneath the pressure.

"It's locked," a slurred voice whispered.

Chelsea scrambled out of bed and backed against the far wall.

"Ge' out o' me way. I'll ge' it open." This voice was louder, deeper.

This time she could see the door bulging inward as she imagined the muscular shoulder pressing against it from the other side. A silent scream seemed strangled in her throat.

She glanced about her, panic rising. What was she to do? She couldn't just stand there and wait for them to have their fun with her. There had to be some way to protect herself.

Her hand fell against the nightstand at her side. The pitcher! She picked it up and dumped the water into the bowl. Quickly, she blew out the lamp, then tiptoed over to the door. She pressed her back against the wall. She lifted the pitcher above her head. Her heart was hammering in her ears.

"'Ere goes, mate."

Just as she heard his voice, the wood around the bolt splintered and gave way. The chair slid away as the door burst open.

"All righ', me pretty. Ol' Shelby's 'ere t'see you."

The brawny form stepped into the room. There was only a moment's hesitation before Chelsea brought the pitcher crashing down upon his head. The man spun around, the light from the hall revealing the stunned expression on his grizzled face before he toppled to the floor.

His partner started forward. This time Chelsea's scream was not suppressed. The man stopped, looked down at his friend, then made a run for it out of there. It was only seconds more before people were spilling into the hall from rooms on either side of hers. The gentleman from the coach was the first to reach her.

"What the—" Holding his lamp high, he glanced at the man at his feet, then back at Chelsea. "Are you all right, miss?"

She nodded her head but couldn't answer. She was suddenly shaking uncontrollably.

His frown began to fade. "Yes, I can see you are." He turned toward the hall. "Get this refuse out of the lady's room."

"Th-thank you, sir," she stuttered, watching

as some men dragged the intruder from her room by his boots.

The man picked up the toppled chair. "You'd best sit down."

She decided he was right.

"My name's Preston Ward."

"How do you do, Mr. Ward."

He grinned. "Very well, thank you. And might I ask your name?"

"Chelsea. Chelsea Fitzgerald."

Preston offered a sweeping bow. "Pleased to make your acquaintance, Miss Fitzgerald. Are you on your way to London?"

She nodded.

"Miss Fitzgerald, allow me to offer you my room. It has a proper lock. I'll sleep in here the rest of the night."

"Oh, I couldn't—"

"But I insist."

"Well, I—"

"Please, Miss Fitzgerald."

This had to stop. "Mr. Ward, it's *Mrs*. Fitzgerald."

There was only a slight pause before Preston said softly, "How very fortunate for *Mr*. Fitzgerald." Then he held out his arm to her. "Your room awaits you."

Brandon's fist pounded on the door. "Wake up in there!" he shouted.

A moment later, a thin light appeared beneath the bottom of the door.

"Who is it?"

"Brandon Fitzgerald."

The door opened a crack. A bewhiskered face stared out at him. "What is it you want this time o' night? Decent people are asleep."

Roxley stepped up to Brandon's side. "Mr. Wheeler, it's me. Please open the door."

"Your lordship?" The door opened a little further. "What do you want 'ere in the middle of the night?"

"We're looking for Lady Coleford. We thought she might be staying here with Claire." Roxley glanced at Brandon, then back toward Olin Wheeler. "Claire is here, isn't she?"

"Aye, she's 'ere all right." Claire's father turned his back toward his nighttime visitors and bellowed, "Claire! Get in 'ere!"

Clad in a white nightgown with long sleeves and a high neck, Claire hesitantly entered the small parlor on bare feet. Seeing who was there, she blanched. "Lord Roxley," she whispered.

"His lordship wants t'know where the lady went you were t'be tendin' to. What 'ave you done, girl?"

Roxley laid a hand on Olin's arm as he stepped into the house. "Claire, where is Chelsea? She's not at my cottage."

"No, sir," she answered with a shake of her head. "She took the coach this mornin' for London."

"Why?" Brandon asked.

"Are you her husband, sir?"

"Yes."

Claire's eyes flicked quickly over him, taking in his tall, muscular frame, the rugged handsomeness of his face. "Fancy that," she mumbled, still staring.

"Why did she go to London?" Brandon repeated.

"She didn't tell me, your lordship. Just said it was something she had to do. Said there was something she had to find out."

Roxley and Brandon exchanged glances.

"I gave her the money you left, Lord Roxley, and she borrowed some clothes of mine since all she had to wear was that fancy riding habit of hers. I—there wasn't really anything I could do to stop her, sir."

"We know that," Roxley replied in a reassuring voice. "And we thank you for helping her." He turned around. "Come on, Brand. We'd better get some sleep. We've got a long day ahead of us tomorrow."

Despite the night's excitement, Chelsea did manage to fall asleep. When she awoke, she freshened herself as much as possible, then joined the other travelers in the common room for a quick repast before boarding the coach.

Preston Ward sat across from her once again. He seemed unfazed by her announcement that she was a married woman. His eyes still gleamed with a light of interest; his mouth still curled in a slightly insolent smile. He had been kind to her, but still she didn't feel entirely comfortable with him. The vulnerability she'd felt last evening hadn't dispelled with morning. In fact, it seemed to intensify the closer they came to London.

Preston leaned forward. "Will Mr. Fitzgerald be meeting you at St. Martins-le-Grand when we arrive?"

"Where?"

"At the General Post Office. Where the stagecoach stops."

"Oh. No, he won't be. He—he's in the country at present."

"Then please allow me to see you home in a hansom cab."

A cab. She hadn't thought of how she would reach the Fitzgerald townhouse. She hadn't any idea how to find it. She was unfamiliar with the streets of London. If she were to get lost . . . And there were only a few coins left in her pocket.

"I don't think—" she began.

"I insist. I won't take no for an answer."

"Mr. Preston—" She saw the stubbornness in his face. She was too tired to fight it. "Very well, sir. You may see me to my home." She hoped her decision would not prove a mistake.

Maitland sat stiffly in her carriage as it rolled away from Rosemont. Fury still strained her face. How dare that man speak to her as he had yesterday? He would pay for his rudeness. Didn't he know what she had offered him? Had he any idea how easily he could have been free of that blathering idiot he was married to?

Yes, he would pay. And so would Chelsea.

Maitland Conover would see that everyone in London knew about that girl. She suspected there was some dark secret that had forced Hayden and Sara Fitzgerald to lock up their only child. Maitland had gleaned enough from servants to suspect Chelsea hadn't been quite right as a child. And her behavior at the hunt proved she still wasn't quite right. But eccentricities among the gentry weren't all that unusual. She needed to know more, and she meant to learn more today. Then she would expose it to all society. Chelsea and Brandon would be barred from every gathering of note. Oh, she might have to spice things up a bit. But who would bother to separate truth from falsehood once the rumors began?

Maitland struck the point of her parasol against the front of the carriage. "More speed, driver!" she shouted.

She wanted to see Hayden Fitzgerald before nightfall.

The cab driver reined his swaybacked horse to a halt before the townhouse. Preston opened the door and looked out. His eyes widened as he turned them on Chelsea.

"Do you work here?" he asked.

"No, Mr. Ward. This is my home."

"But I thought . . ." His gaze drifted over her simple attire.

"My husband's grandfather is Lawrence Fitzgerald, the Duke of Foxworth. My husband is Viscount Coleford."

She couldn't help it. She was enjoying his

discomfiture. She'd been right in surmising his intentions. He'd thought he would ingratiate himself with her, then presume upon her for favors.

"The Duke of Foxworth." Preston swallowed hard. "Is the duke in London?"

"No. He is in the country with my husband." She knew the moment she'd spoken that it was a mistake. She didn't want to reveal to him that she was alone in London, so she quickly added, "They will be joining me here later tonight." She moved as if to leave the cab.

Preston quickly jumped to the ground and offered her his hand.

"Thank you, sir," she said as she stepped out, her gaze moving beyond him to the tall house. She felt a great relief in being there. Then, recalling her manners, she turned to face him again. "Mr. Ward, I do thank you for your assistance last night and again today. You have been most kind to me and have behaved entirely like a gentleman."

"It's not difficult when one is with someone like you, Lady Coleford."

"You're very kind. You know, I never once asked you what brings you to London."

"My work. I've come from Lynton to clerk in my uncle's bank."

"May I repay you for what you've done?"

Preston raised her hand to his lips. "You've done enough just sharing your company with me during this journey." He kissed her knuckles lightly. "Good day, Lady Coleford."

"Good-bye, Mr. Ward." She turned and climbed the steps toward the front door.

It must have been fate that caused her to order the driver down this particular street on her way to Hayden and Sara's home. Maitland glanced out the window of her carriage just in time to see the tall young man kissing Chelsea Fitzgerald's hand as they stood by a hansom cab.

So this was where her brother had brought her. And this was how she spent her time. In the company of other men.

Maitland hadn't had a very long look at the fellow, but she didn't think she knew him. A common clerk, judging by the cut of his suit. How scandalous! This might be even better than anything Hayden could tell her.

She opened the small window at the front of the carriage. "Driver, go round and down that same street once again."

She meant to find out just exactly who had been kissing Chelsea's hand.

Chelsea sank down into the tub of steaming water and closed her eyes. She felt bruised in every muscle in her body from the jostling of the public coach—not to mention feeling covered with dust from head to toe. A hot bath and a good night's sleep were all she needed now.

Tomorrow would be soon enough to visit her parents.

CHAPTER
THIRTY

Chelsea executed a languid stretch with her eyes still closed. She knew by instinct that the sun was already well up in the October sky. Her sore muscles screamed for more rest, but she ignored them. Throwing the covers aside, Chelsea sat up and slid her feet to the floor. She groaned, then forced open her eyes.

When she left Devonshire, her mission to London had seemed urgent. However, at this particular moment, it didn't seem quite so important as getting another hour or two of sleep.

"Get up, lout," she scolded herself.

At least her bedroom was warm. One of the servants had already been in and fed the fire.

Heat radiated toward her from the brick fireplace.

She stood and stretched once again, then availed herself of the pitcher and basin on the washstand. Quickly, she bathed away the traces of sleep from her face before turning to her wardrobe and pulling out the first dress her hand came upon. Now that she was fully awake, she was eager to get on with the task at hand.

Just as she was buttoning the last button on the bodice of the musk rose gown, the bedroom door opened and Gertrude, the young servant girl, appeared with a tray.

"I've brung you some tea an' honey bread, m'lady."

"Thank you, Gertrude, but I couldn't eat a thing this morning."

It was true. Her stomach seemed full of butterflies, all of them frantically flapping their wings in search of a way out.

"Please have a carriage brought round for me."

"Yes, m'lady." Gertrude bobbed a curtsy before backing out of the room.

The butler gazed at her balefully. "Yes?"

"I should like to see Lord and Lady Fitzgerald. Tell them their daughter is here."

"Daughter?" The door widened.

Chelsea walked past him, her eyes already sweeping the spacious entry. Exquisite tapestries lined the walls. A massive chandelier hung overhead, glittering with crystal teardrops; tiny rainbows sparkled on the floor as the morning sun was reflected in the glass. Heavy velvet draperies framed the windows at the end of the hall. Two long mahogany tables stood against the side walls, both of them cluttered with statues and sculptures, some of which were layered with gold.

If what she'd learned was true, her parents had been nearly bankrupt before the duke returned from America. That was obviously no longer the case. They had profited well by the marriage of their daughter.

Hayden was the first to descend the stairs. "Chelsea? What brings you to London?"

"Hello . . ."—It was always difficult for her to say the word—". . . Father." She met his gaze. She was reminded of their last encounter and stifled a shudder. What if he had succeeded in having her put away?

"Come into the drawing room. Sara will be down in a moment. It's a little early for callers. We—" He stopped in mid-sentence and stared at her again. "Is something wrong?"

"No, I—I just needed to speak with you and—and Mother." Chelsea sat on the edge of a velvet-and-satin settee. She folded her hands primly in her lap and waited.

Hayden sat down across from her. "Milton," he said to the butler, "bring us some coffee."

"Yes, my lord."

Her father's eyes stayed on her while silence filled the room. Chelsea fidgeted but remained silent. She wanted both of them present when she explained why she'd come.

It seemed an eternity before Sara finally came through the drawing room doorway. She was wearing a bright yellow morning gown that revealed a generous amount of cleavage and accentuated her still small waist. The wary look in her eyes mirrored her husband's.

"My dear, what a surprise," she said as she kissed the air several inches from Chelsea's cheek. She turned, the train of her gown sweeping over the tips of Chelsea's shoes, and seated herself beside Hayden.

Milton came in behind Sara with the coffee tray. He set it on a side table near Sara's right arm, then left the room as silently as he'd come.

Hayden cleared his throat. "Well, Chelsea. We're both here now. Tell us why you've come."

She wondered why there was never any warmth in her parents' voices. Did they hate her so? Had she been such a despicable child?

"I've come because of Brandon. He wants a divorce."

"A divorce?" Sara paled.

"What have you done?" her father demanded.

"Please. Let me explain." She waited until they seemed to be listening. "We haven't spoken of it. I was told by—by someone else."

"Well, you shan't give him a divorce," Hayden sputtered.

"I don't *want* to give him a divorce. I love him."

Sara's eyes widened in surprise. Her hand closed around Hayden's, as if to keep him from speaking again.

Chelsea rushed on. "I need your help if I'm to save my marriage. Will you help me?"

"Of course. We will do whatever we can, my dear," Sara said gently.

Chelsea glanced away from the two people across from her. It was hard enough to speak these things aloud, even more so when she felt no true affection from them. Or for them. They seemed more like hostile strangers than the loving parents she wished them to be.

She found a loose thread in one of the carpets and held her gaze there as she began to speak. "I believe Brandon cares for me, at least a little. I think if I could prove to him that I'm not—that I won't—" She glanced up at the ceiling, then back at the floor. "—that I won't suddenly go mad, he might truly learn to love me as I love him. But I can't prove it because—because I don't know who I am."

"What a perfectly ridiculous thing to say!" Hayden exclaimed. "You are Alanna Fitzgerald, though you insist on calling yourself something else. You are our daughter and Brandon's wife. What more do you need to know?"

She lifted her gaze to meet her father's. "That isn't what I mean. I—I feel so lost, so confused. But I don't feel ill. I don't feel mad. But how can I know? I can't remember anything beyond a few months ago. I want to know about my childhood. I want to know why Miss Pendleton died in the fire and I escaped. I want to understand these dreams that keep coming back time and again."

Something flickered in Hayden's eyes. His voice was low as he asked, "What dreams are those, Chelsea?"

"Sometimes I dream about the fire at Hawklin. I know I'm supposed to have set the fire, yet . . . yet I don't *feel* as though I did. And there's someone else there in my dream. Miss Pendleton I suppose, but I'm not sure."

"You *remember* Miss Pendleton?" Hayden asked. He glanced at Sara who sat with a wooden expression on her face.

"No, but . . . It's strange the way I seem to see things."

The memory tried to assert itself, but she pushed it back. She didn't want to discuss her confusion over that dream, that she saw Alanna as someone other than herself. That sometimes she was convinced she was not Alanna. Such a confession would only confirm to Hayden that she was mad. He might even spirit her away to Bedlam before she could stop him.

"But it isn't *that* dream that troubles me," she said, not exactly a lie, but a half-truth. "It's the man I keep seeing. The blond man in front of a small white cottage. And there's the little red fox and a pony. I keep seeing them too. I feel as if they meant the world to me. And then there's the woman with the gray hair and the sad smile. Who are these people? How do I know them?"

"They're just dreams," Sara said firmly.

Chelsea shook her head. "No. They're more

than dreams. I'm sure of it."

It was Hayden's turn to silence Sara as she opened her mouth to contradict Chelsea.

"Daughter, your illness didn't always keep you shut away. When you were very young, you used to play with the children of some of the servants. You even visited their homes with your nanny. One of them probably had a red puppy. Perhaps that explains the things you see. Perhaps the man you see was one of our servants. I seem to recall the smithy had blond hair."

But the man in her dreams had never been a servant at Hawklin. She knew it deep in her soul. And somehow she knew her father was lying to her; Hayden knew who the man in her dreams was but refused to say.

"When you first started acting . . . strangely, we hoped it was only temporary. But you were inclined to"—He glanced at Sara—"to try to harm yourself."

He wasn't going to tell her anything she hadn't heard before. She wanted to know what she had done every day in the years she was locked up at Hawklin; she wanted to know who she had talked with, how she learned to ride horses, how she learned to write and to read. She wanted to know about the woman in the brick house and the piano and the haunting melody. *Papa's song*, she had called it. Why?

But he wasn't going to tell her those things. She knew it instinctively. Her visit here had been pointless. She had been wrong to even try.

Chelsea pulled at the shoulders of her cloak as she prepared to rise.

"Come in, young woman." It was Hayden she saw, seated in the drawing room at Hawklin. *"So, you want to work here."*

Chelsea blinked, then looked at Hayden. He was seated, but they were in the London house, not Hawklin. Still, there was something . . .

"You know about our daughter, of course."

She felt as if she were choking, her throat closed, unable to draw a breath.

"She's quite mad and needs constant supervision."

Hayden's eyes narrowed, and she felt a rush of cold fear spreading through her.

"Your lordship," Milton said, returning to the drawing room. "Lady Bellfort is here."

Chelsea jumped to her feet. "Maitland?" Was Brandon with her?

"Hayden. Sara." Maitland swept into the room, stopping abruptly when she saw Chelsea. "Why, if it isn't Chelsea. What a surprise."

"I really must be going," Chelsea said through a tight throat.

"Don't be silly. Why cut a pleasant visit short? If I'm not mistaken, you haven't the chance to see your parents very often." She smiled slyly. "But perhaps you'll see more of them if you decide to move to London."

Maitland had a way of bringing out the fury in Chelsea with just a few words.

Robin Lee Hatcher

Chelsea's chin jutted out and, putting all her pent-up feelings into her eyes, she turned a cold glare upon her nemesis. "What makes you think I'll be living in London, Lady Bellfort? Brandon would never consider leaving Hawklin permanently, and my place is with my husband." Chelsea turned toward Hayden and Sara. Her voice was still icy as she said, "Good day Mother, Father. Perhaps I'll see you again before I return to Hawklin."

And then it was her turn to sweep regally out of the room.

"How very strange," Maitland said as the door slammed.

Behind her, she heard Sara's tense whisper, "What are we going to do? She knows something is—"

"Shut up, Sara," was Hayden's harsh return.

Maitland turned slowly, her sharp eyes taking in the strained expressions of her host and hostess. Something was very much amiss here. Could it be more grist for the rumor mill?

She smiled as she settled onto the settee. She certainly meant to find out whatever she could.

Chelsea just couldn't bear to return to the townhouse yet. She felt like a coiled spring. Any moment now, she was going to fly loose, totally out of control.

She told her driver to take her to the park, hoping that a breath of crisp fall air and enough time would settle her anger with Maitland and her frustration with her parents.

Once in the park, she descended from the

carriage and walked alone along the shore of the pond. Two swans, oblivious to the gray clouds overhead and the chill wind stirring the surface of the water, glided gracefully toward the far shore. Chelsea paused in her walking and watched them, silently wishing she could find the peace they seemed to live in.

"Peace," she whispered. What a unique emotion that would be.

Bedraggled and wearing a two days' growth of beard, Brandon dismounted in front of Hayden's townhouse. The door opened almost immediately after he knocked. Brandon didn't wait for an invitation from the butler to enter; he pushed his way past the startled man.

"Chelsea!"

He glanced from side to side, guessing which room might serve as a drawing room, then headed in its direction. Three faces, mirroring the startled look of the butler, turned toward him as he marched into the room.

Hayden rose. "Good lord, man, what's happened to you?"

"Where's Chelsea?"

"She's not here."

"The servants at the house said she was coming to see her parents."

"She *was* here," Hayden replied, "but she left. She was acting quite strangely, Brandon. I'm concerned about her. Is there . . ." He glanced at Sara. "Is there some problem between the two of you?"

Maitland stared down at her tea cup. "Perhaps she's with that nice looking young man she was with last night. She hasn't left you for another man, has she, Brandon? My, wouldn't that set all London on its ear."

Brandon ignored her. He'd already made it perfectly clear what he felt about anything she had to say. He knew that if he gave her comments a moment's thought, he would turn and strike her. Hard.

"You don't think she'll do anything foolish, do you?" Sara asked, taking hold of her husband's arm as she, too, rose from the sofa.

"I'm returning to the house," Brandon said, choosing to ignore Sara's question as well. "If you see her, tell her I'm there."

"We'll do that, my boy," Hayden replied as he followed Brandon into the entry.

Brandon was back on his horse before he allowed the fatigue to sap the last of his strength. Wearily, he turned his mount toward his own townhouse. After riding nearly straight through the night, following two full days in the saddle, he could hardly think straight. He had no idea where else to look for her. He would have to wait for her now.

"Perhaps she's with that nice looking young man. . . ."

He grimaced as Maitland's words attacked him. He knew she had been trying to provoke him, but could there be some truth in what she said? Could he already be too late in telling Chelsea what he should have told her long before?

"She was acting quite strangely. . . ."

"You don't think she'd do anything foolish. . . ?"

Hayden's and Sara's voices smote him. Could it be that Chelsea wasn't all right? Could it be that she might disappear forever? Might she . . .

Feeling despair clawing at his heart, he rode on toward home.

CHAPTER
THIRTY-ONE

It was late in the afternoon before Chelsea ordered the driver to take her home. A light drizzle was falling from the low gray ceiling of clouds. And she felt just as gloomy as the bleak autumn day.

As the carriage stopped in front of the house, Chelsea glanced up at the flickering light showing in the bedroom window. She smiled sadly, remembering how lovely their first days in London had been. Days when Chelsea had thought . . .

Oh, if only she hadn't seen Molly's doll! That had started the whole unraveling of the delicate tapestry of their lives. If she and Brandon had had a little more time together . . . If he could have learned to trust her, believe in her . . . If he weren't so afraid she would . . .

But it was too late for that. She *had* seen the doll. She *had* imagined the fire again. She *had* fainted and been sedated. Those were things she couldn't change now.

Holding her skirts out of the way, she stepped down from the carriage, then climbed the steps to the front door. Just as her fingers reached for the knob, the skies opened and dropped their watery burden in great sheets. She pushed open the door before her, but it was already too late. She was soaked.

As she closed the door, she leaned her forehead against it. A pathetic laugh rose in her throat. Somehow, it seemed a fitting finish to the disastrous day.

She heard footsteps behind her. "Gertrude . . ." she said, turning around.

He stood in the entry, clad in gray and black striped trousers and a loose white shirt, open at the collar. His chestnut hair was combed back from his handsome face. He appeared freshly shaven, but she sensed a weariness there to match her own. His dark brown eyes, a strange brooding hidden in their liquid depths, held her captive. She had nearly forgotten how just being near him could take her breath away.

As the clock on the mantel of the drawing room fireplace chimed the hour, she raised a nervous hand to push back the wet tendrils of hair clinging to her forehead and the sides of her face. The silence seemed to stretch out interminably. He continued to watch her with a disturbing intensity.

"I—I didn't expect you," she said at last in a breathless voice. "How did you find me?"

Brandon took a step toward her. "Roxley took me to his cottage in Devonshire. Claire told us you'd come to London."

"Oh." She watched wide-eyed as he came a little closer. Her heart was racing.

"We have to talk, Chelsea."

She wanted to die. How could she bear hearing him tell her he wanted a divorce? She'd been prepared to fight, but what was it she could do? She had nothing to fight with except her love, and he didn't seem to want it.

Two more strides brought him within inches of her. His gaze still held hers in a timeless spell; her head dropped back, turning her face up to his. Her heartbeat raced.

"I've made a muddle of things," he began, "but that stops as of now."

She still hadn't made sense of his words before his mouth was lowering toward hers. His hands gripped her shoulders, pulling her up and against him. Braced on tiptoes, her eyes wide open, she surrendered to him, still disbelieving.

And when she was most thoroughly, most tenderly kissed, he gently released her and stepped back.

"I love you, Chelsea Fitzgerald. Nothing you have ever done, nothing you will ever do can change that fact. I care nothing for your past as long as your future is with me. I've known it for a long time, but I was too big a fool to put it into words."

A lump formed in her throat as tears stung her eyes. She wished she could reply, but words seemed impossible.

His hands moved up to her throat. He unfastened the frog of her cloak and slipped it from her shoulders, letting it drop to the floor amidst the puddle of rainwater already around her feet.

"You are my wife," he whispered, "and there'll be no divorce in this family. Understood?"

Mesmerized by the new light in his eyes, she nodded as he drew her close once again. His hands framed her face, but he didn't kiss her. He seemed to be waiting.

And she responded. "I've loved you from the first moment I saw you, Brandon. I always shall." Tears of joy spilled over.

Roxley paused in the doorway. The lovers' words were bittersweet in his ears. He was happy for them but felt a great loss for himself. The last of his secret hopes were dashed, hopes which never should have surfaced.

He turned and silently returned to the library whence he'd come. He would most definitely be unwelcome company this night.

Brandon slipped his arm beneath her knees, damp skirts and all, and carried her up the stairs, her head against his chest. He knew a burning passion such as he'd never known before, yet it was tempered with a tenderness he hadn't known could exist.

He pushed the half-open door with his foot and carried Chelsea inside the bedroom. Pausing near the blazing fire, he lowered her feet to the floor. She watched him with wide, trusting eyes. Something new, something wonderful swelled within his heart. Though they had made love before, he knew it would be different tonight. Tonight their love had been declared. Tonight they were truly loved as well as lovers.

Nimbly, the fingers of his right hand moved down the front of her bodice, loosening each button from its hole. Finished, he used both hands to push the fabric of the gown from her shoulders. With equal patience, he pushed away her chemise.

Her breasts were perfectly formed, alabaster skin tipped by rose. He bent and suckled, first one breast, then the other. He heard her draw in a sudden breath through parted lips. Her fingers tangled in his hair.

He returned to her mouth, tasting anew the sweet nectar that was uniquely Chelsea. Warm and sweet. Drawing her against him, he could feel the mad patter of her heart through the thin fabric of his shirt.

His hands resumed the delightful chore of disrobing her while his mouth lingered upon hers. He was unhurried. They had the night. They had a lifetime.

An almost painful wanting was set afire within Chelsea. Emotions warred within her. She wanted him to continue at the same leisurely pace he'd established, yet she wanted him to join with her now. The confusion of her own desires only added fuel to the stormy passion taking hold.

Each place his hands touched seemed to burn, leaving her branded with desire. His mouth trailed once more from her lips, moving down her throat and across one shoulder. Every once in a while, his tongue would dart out, as if to taste her flesh. She shivered. Her head dropped back. She moaned through parted lips.

Her dress and petticoats were freed from her waist and fell in a heap around her feet. She was left with only her cambric drawers. Then she felt the drawstring give way, and she was standing nude before him.

Brandon's dark eyes reflected the firelight— or was it the fire from within that she saw? He caressed her with his gaze, making her knees turn to jelly just by his look. There was a white-hot fire burning in her loins, and only Brandon could quench it.

As if he understood, he picked her up again, cradling her tight against his chest as he walked with measured steps to the large bed. He laid her in the middle of it, then stepped back and began to undress.

Mesmerized, she watched him, reveling in the ripple of muscles as he moved. He was so strong, so beautifully made. Black hair covered his broad chest, narrowing as it swept toward his waist. His skin was dark, as if tanned by the sun.

He was perfection. He was marvelously male. He was hers.

Even after he had joined her on the bed, he was slow to take her. His mouth continued to explore, softly teasing her flesh until she could bear it no more. She cried out his name.

He came to her then. With her name upon his lips, they joined in an act of love such as neither of them had experienced before.

Brandon was the first to stir. He reached to pull a sheet over their damp bodies as the cool night air became noticeable once again. Chelsea moaned, objecting to his slight movement away from her, unwilling to give him up. If she had her way, they might never leave this room again.

"I love you, Chelsea."

"Now and always, Brandon."

Exhaustion claimed them, and they slept.

"Lady Coleford."

"Mmmm?"

"I'm hungry. Wake up."

Chelsea opened one eye. She was lying on her side, her head nestled upon Brandon's shoulder, her naked body curving against the length of him as he lay on his back. This she knew by touch, not by sight. The room was cloaked in utter darkness. Only a few fading coals lingered in the fireplace.

"It's the middle of the night," she objected.

"I haven't had a full meal in days. I'm starved."

She laughed and nibbled on his neck. "I'm starved, too," she answered in a husky voice.

"No, you don't." His own laughter mingled with hers as he rolled over her, taking her and the blankets with him as he tumbled to the floor. "I need food. Real food."

"All right. We'll see what cook has hiding in the kitchen."

Donning robes, Brandon carrying a candle, they tiptoed down the stairs like mischievous children. Before long, they were dining on cold chicken, hard cheese, bread, and wine, the candlestick flickering between them on the table. Chelsea was surprised to learn she was as hungry as Brandon.

Their appetites sated, their eyes met above the candle.

"Grandfather will be anxious to know what's happened. We'll go home to Hawklin tomorrow," Brandon said softly.

"So soon?"

"You don't want to return?"

Chelsea shook her head slowly. "There's so much I still need to—to sort out. So much I don't understand." She reached across the table and laid her hand over his. "I have so much to tell you, Brandon. I need you to listen to everything. All the things I've imagined, all the things I've dreamed. Brandon, if ever I was mad, I'm not anymore. I need you to believe that. Do you?"

She stared into his dark brown eyes and felt a warm strength transferring from him to her. He did believe her. Perhaps only because he loved her. But he did believe her.

"I need your help to find out what it all

means. But I don't think I can do it at Hawklin."

He nodded. "Would you rather return to Teakwood?"

Teakwood. There were so many happy memories there. But there was also Maitland, who lived close by. And where Maitland was, so was there trouble.

"No. Not Teakwood. Let's go someplace where no one knows me. Where no one knows you."

Was there such a place?

Brandon frowned thoughtfully. Then, suddenly, his face broke into a grin. "Devonshire," he said. "We'll go back to Roxley's hunting cottage on the moor."

"Do you think he'd let us?"

"Why don't we ask him in the morning? He's sleeping in one of the guest rooms right now."

Chelsea felt her face flush. "He's here? Now?" She was recalling the way she had cried out at the peak of their lovemaking.

Brandon chuckled, seeming to read her thoughts. "Yes, my love, he's here. But you needn't worry. Only I was listening."

She was afraid this was one time he must surely be lying to her.

CHAPTER
THIRTY-TWO

"I think it's a splendid idea," Roxley said when asked if they could use his cottage on Exmoor.

Brandon laid a hand on his shoulder. "Thanks."

"Don't mention it. I'm happy for the two of you. You need some time away."

"I've sent for the ducal coach to take us there. Will you stay on in London?"

Roxley shook his head as he glanced across the table at Chelsea. "No. It's time I returned home. I think I can trust you to take care of the lady now."

"Yes," Brandon answered in a husky voice as his gaze settled on his wife. "You can trust me to do just that."

Chelsea felt heat rising in her cheeks. She smiled almost shyly and dropped her eyes to her breakfast plate. She wanted to add her thanks to Roxley for all he'd done, but remembering her embarrassment over what he might have heard, she just couldn't voice her thoughts.

"M'lady . . ." Gertrude stepped hesitantly into the room. "You've a gentleman caller."

Chelsea looked up in surprise. "Who is it, Gertrude?"

"He says his name is Ward, m'lady. Preston Ward."

Brandon's gaze was curious. "Who is this Ward fellow, Chelsea?"

"I met him on the coach from Lynton. He gave me aid when we ran into a little trouble."

"Trouble?"

She knew she should have told him sooner, but when had there been time? It seemed such a minor incident now that she was safely home with Brandon. "I'll tell you about it later," she replied, rising from her chair. "Please come with me so I can introduce you."

Brandon offered his arm and they left the dining room together. She sensed the tension in him and wished again that she had said something sooner. He was obviously displeased that Preston had felt familiar enough to call upon her.

Preston turned with a beaming smile when he heard the footsteps. Then his expression turned to one of surprise and consternation when he saw she wasn't alone.

"Mr. Ward, how nice of you to call. May I present my husband, Brandon Fitzgerald."

Brandon held out his hand. "Good morning, Mr. Ward. Chelsea tells me you were of some assistance to her on her journey to London. You have my sincere thanks."

"It—it was nothing really. I was glad to help."

"Would you care to join us in the drawing room?" Chelsea asked. "I could have Gertrude bring us some tea or coffee."

Preston twirled his hat nervously with one hand. "No, thank you really. I just dropped by to see how you were. But I see you are fine, now that your husband is with you."

Chelsea didn't know what else to say, and Preston was at an obvious loss for words. She laid a gentle hand on Brandon's arm, then stepped away from him, moving toward the door. Preston followed after a quick glance at Brandon.

"I'm sorry if I've caused any—problems, Lady Coleford," Preston said in a secretive tone. "You see, I understood that . . . Well, I didn't expect your husband to be here."

"But I told you he would be."

"Yes, I know, but I thought that . . ." He looked almost pained.

"What was it you thought?" Chelsea pressed.

"Well, I thought—I believed you were leaving your husband."

She gasped.

"I can see I was wrong." Preston reached for the door handle, but not before Brandon had drawn to Chelsea's side, having heard her startled breath.

"Yes, you were wrong, Mr. Ward," Chelsea said in a firm voice. "And I gave you no reason to believe any such thing."

"I'm sorry." He glanced nervously at Brandon once again. "I've made a terrible error, my lord. I beg your pardon. I really must be on my way." He turned to leave.

"Wait!" Chelsea cried, suddenly suspicious.

Both men looked at her.

"Someone sent you here, Mr. Ward, didn't she?"

His coloring darkened.

"Someone meant for you to cause trouble between my husband and me, whether or not you were aware of it. Who was it?"

"I . . ." His expression looked as if he meant to deny her charge, but then he shook his head guiltily. "I'm afraid I don't know, Lady Fitzgerald. The woman appeared at my door after I brought you here from the General Post. She suggested I call upon you. She said she was a friend of yours and it had come to her attention that I was"—His eyes darted toward Brandon, then back—"interested in your welfare. She said you were in need of comfort over the dissolution of your marriage."

Chelsea's hands clenched at her sides. "And the woman had auburn hair and golden brown eyes and was extremely beautiful."

Preston nodded.

Brandon and Chelsea turned toward each

other, their faces mirroring the same restrained anger. "Maitland," they said in unison.

Preston edged closer to the door as he placed his silk hat on his head. He mumbled a parting farewell and escaped, barely noticed by his hosts.

Chelsea drew a deep breath. "Before you imagine anything more, I mean to tell you exactly what happened. How I met Mr. Ward."

"You may if you want," he replied, his gaze softening, "but I know his interest was not encouraged by anything you did."

She was warmed by his trust, but she told her tale anyway. She told him of the trip from Lynton, of the men breaking into her room, of Preston Ward's generous help in offering her his room for the night and then providing the cab ride home.

And when she had finished, he gathered her close to him, pressing her cheek against his chest as he whispered into her hair, "I'll never put you in such a position of danger again. Never."

Lawrence sat in the library at Hawklin, a warm fire burning on the hearth. A good book was open in his lap, but the words on the pages were blurred. He couldn't get his mind off of Brandon and Chelsea. What was happening between those two at that very moment? He wanted to believe all would go well once Brandon caught up with her. They deserved to be truly happy.

Ah, such a delightful child, that girl. Just like Brandon, he'd been smitten with her from the start. Whatever had she done to warrant a sentence of madness? He wished he understood more. He wished he'd asked Hayden and Sara more questions when he'd had the opportunity.

But it didn't matter now. That was behind her. It was behind them all. She and Brandon were in love and had a bright future together. Wasn't that what he'd wanted for his grandson? To be married to the woman he loved, to a woman who loved him equally? If coming to England had accomplished nothing else, it had accomplished that. All in all, not a bad benefit.

He closed his eyes and sighed. *Old man*, he thought. *I'm a very old man*.

And Brandon didn't want to be the duke when he was gone.

It had taken Lawrence some time to face that fact, but face it he must. His eldest grandson had no interest in living in England, in ruling the vast ducal properties, of ever sitting in the House of Lords. He was only here out of devotion for an old man.

"Perhaps I made a mistake in coming," he whispered as he closed the book.

He'd had a good enough life in America, he admitted to himself now. Along with all the hard times, the harsh times, there had been happiness. He had learned to survive as he never would have learned here. He had learned what it meant to struggle and to achieve. Yes, his life in America had been good. He had been a fool to want this so very much that it nearly killed him. They could easily have stayed in America.

But if they hadn't come, Chelsea would still be locked in that room upstairs.

"And I'd be dead this very moment."

If they hadn't come, he wouldn't have learned how very little this all really meant. It was the family that was most important. It was Brandon and Chelsea and Justin. Position and money only made things more pleasant, but they couldn't replace the love. Nothing could replace that.

He rose from his chair and walked to the window, moving aside the drapes. The night was as black as pitch. A harsh wind swayed the treetops with its cold breath.

He hoped Brandon had found Chelsea and all would be well.

Roxley stepped into the entry hall of Maitland's London home. Ignoring the butler, he walked toward the salon. He could hear voices and laughter, but he felt no amusement himself.

He stopped in the doorway and glanced around the room. It was only a small party of five or six couples, all of them elegantly clad and chatting in animated voices. His eyes found Maitland and he waited for her to look his way.

"Good heaven, look who's here," she said when she looked up at last. "Roxley, my dear, how nice of you to call." She hurried toward him, grasping his elbow. "Come in. You know everyone."

"I must speak to you alone, Maitland."

"But I could not possibly leave my—"

"Now." His voice was low and harsh.

A dark eyebrow arched over one gold-flecked brown eye. "Really, Roxley," she said with a hiss in her voice. "You are being most impolite."

Roxley quickly reversed positions with her, his fingers closing over her upper arm as he propelled her from the salon. "I don't give a damn about being impolite, dear sister." He slammed the study door behind him.

Maitland stared at him as if he'd lost his mind. She backed away from him until the bustle of her gown met with the back of the desk.

"You have pulled your last stunt, Maitland. It's time you learned to behave yourself."

"Whatever are you talking about?"

"You know what I'm talking about, and you'd bloody well better listen to me. You are going to pack your things tonight and be ready to leave first thing in the morning. You're returning immediately to Bellfort Castle where you will remain through the winter. If you so much as set your big toe outside the doors without a good reason, I'll know about it and you will regret your actions."

"Just a moment, Roxley. Who do you think you are to order me about this way?"

"I am the executor for Edgar's inheritance."
His voice was low, almost inaudible.

But Maitland heard him well enough. She
gasped; her eyes widened.

"The marquess left your son and his inheritance in my care. I have let you have your way
in the past, but no more. You have behaved like
a common streetwalker, Maitland. I'm not
proud to be your brother, but I had no choice
in that. I do, however, control your purse
strings. Those strings have been pulled tight.
Do you understand me?"

"Roxley—"

"Don't meddle in Brandon and Chelsea's
lives again. Do you hear me, Maitland?"

"Chelsea!" Maitland's face grew red. "What
has that simpering wench to do with us?"

Roxley rested his hand on the doorknob.
"Preston Ward. Does that name ring a bell
inside that empty head of yours? Yes, I can see
that it does. It didn't work, Maitland. Chelsea
and Brandon have gone away together. There'll
be no divorce. Ever."

"And what of you, Roxley, you stupid fool?
You could have had her for yourself. You've
wanted her badly enough. But apparently you
weren't man enough to take her."

Shaking his head, he pulled open the door.
He felt a great sadness replacing his anger.
"You haven't the slightest idea what love is
about, have you? I pity you, Maitland. I pity
you."

His sister grabbed a porcelain vase and threw

it wildly in his direction. It hit the wall and shattered into a hundred tiny pieces. "Get out of here!" she screamed.

"Gladly." He turned. "And don't forget about packing tonight. I'll be here for you early tomorrow morning."

CHAPTER
THIRTY-THREE

She was a fey creature, as wild as the moor, as beautiful as the heather.

Brandon watched Chelsea as she knelt in the dirt, coaxing the scrawny kitten from beneath a corner of the barn. He grinned as the frightened animal slowly crept toward her. She had charmed the wild kitten, just as she charmed everyone she met.

The past few days had been an enchanted time for them. During the day, they strolled through the moor, hand in hand, or rode across the countryside for hours, jumping their horses over shrubs and sedge, then letting the animals graze while they sat in the cool autumn sunshine. Nights were spent wrapped in each other's arms beneath warm blankets, the room aglow from the blazing fire on the hearth as well as the fire of love that burned between them.

He had wondered often when Chelsea would feel ready to talk about the things that had brought them to Devonshire. But, in truth, he was in no hurry. He would enjoy this interlude and treasure each happy moment. When Chelsea was ready to talk, he would be ready to listen.

"Look, Brandon," she called to him.

She cradled the orange-striped kitten against her chest. It looked up at her with trusting eyes as she gently scratched it behind one ear.

"She's near starved to death." Chelsea walked toward him, her brown skirt swaying gently around her legs. "Let's go inside and get her some milk."

Brandon reached out and placed his arm around Chelsea's shoulders. "If I'm not mistaken, we have ourselves a pet."

"You wouldn't mind, would you?"

"Not if you wish it."

Once in the kitchen, Chelsea poured some fresh milk from a pitcher into a small bowl and placed it on the floor. The kitten sniffed it warily, then quickly began to lap it up.

Chelsea sat back on her haunches with a self-satisfied grin on her face. "Look at her. Have you ever seen anything eat so fast?"

"Yes," Brandon answered. "My brother Justin."

Chelsea's gaze rose to meet his, and they broke into laughter.

Brandon reached down, pulling her to her feet and into his embrace. "Ah, Chelsea, I love you."

"And I, you." She kissed the tip of his nose. "What would you like to do today?"

"May we ride over to the bay? Claire says it's quite lovely near Barnstaple, and the day is so wonderfully warm for autumn."

Brandon brushed his lips across hers, enjoying the feel of her in his arms. "If that's what you wish, it's what we'll do."

"You're spoiling me terribly, you know."

"I know."

He was planning to kiss her again, but he felt a sharp prick on his ankle and looked down to discover the kitten climbing up his trouser leg.

"What's this?" he said gently, reaching down to free the sharp claws from the fabric. The kitten immediately began to purr loudly.

"She likes you, sir." Chelsea stroked the dull orange coat.

"Hmmm." Brandon wasn't sure if he liked the little cat or not. Not when he'd been planning to hold his wife instead of a motley orphaned kitten.

Chelsea stepped back from him, grinning widely. "Why don't you get the horses ready? I'll make a bed for the little tigress and be right out." Her hands reached out, and he passed the kitten into them.

"Little tigress, eh?" he asked, an eyebrow raised.

"She attacked you, didn't she?"

Brandon turned, chuckling once again as he

thought, *She could probably tame a real tigress, at that.*

To Chelsea, this had been the most perfect week of her life. Granted, her memory was short, but even their time at Teakwood couldn't compare with this. For now she knew Brandon loved her, and he knew she loved him. This day had been no different.

They had spent a lovely day, walking down the narrow streets of Barnstaple, peeking into shops, checking the wares of the different stalls. Chelsea had even pulled off her shoes to wade in the frigid waters of the bay, much to Brandon's disapproval. But she was heedless of his dire warnings of pneumonia, and she knew he was truly enjoying it as much as she.

But finally it was time to head for home. For a change of scenery, they followed a road south before turning east across the moor toward Roxley's cottage. The air was cooling and the sun was casting long shadows before them as, laughing, they pulled their horses back to a walk.

"I told you I would reach here first," Chelsea cried triumphantly.

Her hair had pulled free from its pins as they jumped the last hedge, and now it tumbled down the back of her black jacket. Her cheeks were as crimson as her red blouse, and her blue eyes twinkled merrily as she turned them upon Brandon.

"You cheated," he protested. "You had a head start."

In unison, they leaned to the side and stole a kiss as their horses continued to walk.

Suddenly, Chelsea's horse shied as a fox, in a flash of dark red fur, darted across the road just a few feet in front of them. She tightened the reins before the animal could break into a gallop, calming her with a soothing voice. When the horse was quieted, she glanced across the rolling countryside, the land dotted with grazing sheep.

"Keep a steady hand on the reins, girl, but never be pullin' on his mouth all the time. You'll have no control by bullyin' the horse. Just let him know you're in command. If you win the pony's trust, you'll have no trouble with him. And hold on with your knees, not your heels."

Her bare feet hung below the pony's belly, her skirt riding up above her knees. She laughed and trotted away from the cottage, the small red fox tagging along behind.

Chelsea gasped and looked around her. "It's here. It's around here somewhere."

"What is?" Brandon asked as he rode closer to her.

"The cottage. The white cottage."

"What white cottage?"

"The one I keep seeing in my head." She looked at him now. The familiar frown was returning to his brow, the one he always wore when she talked like this. "I want to find it," she said evenly, meeting his troubled gaze.

"It's late, Chelsea. We'll come back tomorrow."

She continued to look into his eyes. He was

promising to bring her back, promising to trust her, to believe in her. But he didn't understand, and it worried him.

It was time they talked.

She lay nestled in the safety of his arms, her cheek resting on his shoulder, his lips pressed against her hair. He didn't speak. Only the occasional tightening of his fingers told her he listened.

"I know it seems impossible, Brandon. Everyone tells me I never was away from Hawklin until you came. But I know I've lived somewhere on the moor. I can feel it. I've seen the cottage time and time again, just as I've seen the brick house with the ivy."

"I learned something about the owner of that house," he interrupted gently. "The woman's name was St. Clair. Does that mean anything to you, Chelsea?"

"St. Clair," she repeated in a whisper. Her eyes narrowed as she concentrated, trying to bring up an image with the name. "No. No, it doesn't mean anything."

"A woman told me Miss St. Clair's niece used to live with her. When the niece died, the old woman fell ill and then moved away." His arms tightened. "Chelsea, I think the niece was probably Miss Pendleton. I think she probably took you there to visit the aunt, and that's what you remember."

She heard the hopeful note in his voice. Oh, how she wished she could agree with him. It was possible, of course. In fact, it sounded very probable. Yet, she didn't believe it in her heart. Something told her it wasn't true. She hadn't just visited the St. Clair house any more than she'd just visited this moor as a child. But how did she convince anyone of it? How did she even convince herself?

She sighed deeply. "It's so awful not to really remember anything," she said. "Just snatches of dreams here and there. I see this man in front of the cottage. In my dreams, he's my father. He's blond and tall and blue-eyed and terribly handsome and kind. He loves me very much. My mother . . . my mother is dead. Her name was Catherine."

Brandon's arm tightened once again. "Chelsea, your mother is alive. Her name is Sara."

"I know," she answered softly. "I know, but . . ." Her voice drifted away. She felt the sting of tears. How she hated the incessant crying. It would be better if she could forget the dreams, forget the confusion of a past she couldn't remember. Why not just accept things as they were? Perhaps if she did, the dreams would stop and she could forget them.

Brandon's hand stroked her hair. "Let's not talk about it anymore tonight, my love. You're tired. Get some sleep. Tomorrow, we'll go back and look for the cottage."

"Thank you, Brandon," she whispered.

"No thanks needed."

She turned her face toward his and kissed him.

* * *

Brandon awoke to the smell and sizzle of bacon frying on the stove. His hand stole out, but Chelsea's side of the bed was already empty. He opened his eyes to find sunlight pouring in the window. He couldn't believe he'd slept so late.

He dressed quickly and went downstairs and into the kitchen. Claire was busy fixing breakfast while Chelsea sat on the floor, coaxing the kitten to eat just a little more solid food.

"You keep feedin' her like that, my lady, an' she'll be too fat to walk." Claire glanced toward the pair, both of the women unaware of Brandon's entrance.

"The same goes for me." Brandon walked over to the stove and sniffed the delicious odors wafting above the fry pans. "Mmmm. You're a good cook, Claire Wheeler. You're going to make some man a wonderful wife. And a pretty one, too."

Claire blushed. "Go on with you, your lordship."

"Does that blush mean you've a gentleman in mind?"

"Oooh, sir." Her head ducked forward, embarrassed by his teasing.

With a low chuckle, he turned from the stove and moved toward Chelsea. He hunkered down beside her, reaching out to pet the kitten. "She looks better today. Did just a little food do that?"

"I gave Tigress a bath this morning."

"A bath, was it?" he asked as he lifted the fluffy orange cat into the air. She meowed in protest, and he set her back down. "I don't think she likes me after all."

Chelsea kissed his cheek. "How could anyone not like you? It's just because her stomach is full."

"Ah, a full stomach. Now that sounds like a good idea." He glanced toward Claire as he rose. "How about it, Claire? Is breakfast about ready?"

"It is, m'lord," she answered as she turned from the stove, a platter in hand.

Brandon made the food vanish in short order and was just pushing back his chair from the table when a knock sounded at the door. He cast a questioning glance toward Chelsea, wondering who might be calling this early in the day, while Claire went to answer the knock.

"Lord Brandon, there's a message for you." Claire brought an envelope toward the table.

Brandon opened the envelope and quickly scanned the missive.

"What is it, Brandon?" Chelsea asked.

"It's from Grandfather. It says he needs my help with something to do with Foxworth Iron. He's had a letter from Justin."

Chelsea sighed. "Well, I suppose our holiday is over. I'll get our things ready to leave."

"No. He says it will only take a day or two. He suggests you wait here for me, and he'll send me back to you as quickly as possible." He glanced up at Chelsea. "I think he wants us to have lots of time alone."

She turned a very becoming shade of pink. "He must know how wonderful it's been for me to have you all to myself."

"And you to myself," he answered in a suggestively low voice.

"If I went with you, we wouldn't have to be apart, even for one day."

Brandon nodded. "Yes, but it might be too easy not to return. If you wait here, I have to come back."

"You'll hurry?"

"I won't waste a single minute."

"Then I'll wait for you."

Chelsea waved to Brandon as he rode away from the stone cottage. She had a terrible empty feeling in her heart. The place seemed so lonely all of a sudden. She glanced toward the barn. Well, there was no point in her staying there and moping. They had planned to ride out on the moor and look for the white cottage today. There was no reason she shouldn't go on her own.

A half an hour later, Chelsea cantered away from Roxley's hunting cottage, going in the opposite direction from the one Brandon had taken. She rode astride, something she hadn't done in ages, and she felt wonderfully at ease. The day wasn't nearly as warm as the day before, but the sky was clear except for a few fluffy white clouds dotting the western horizon. Fall colors splashed the moor with oranges and yellows and browns.

Chelsea smiled and coaxed a little more speed from her horse. She wasn't sure what it was about today, but she felt, despite missing

Brandon, that a great weight had been lifted from her shoulders. Perhaps it was simply the knowledge of how much Brandon loved her, loved her despite all the unanswered questions, despite her odd behavior and confusing dreams. Whatever the cause, she meant to enjoy the feeling.

Brandon loped his horse along the deserted stretch of road. He wondered what Justin could have written Grandfather that would require Brandon's attention. No one knew more about Foxworth Iron Works than Lawrence. Although he'd turned over the company to Brandon and Justin a number of years before, he certainly didn't need his grandsons to make decisions. The more Brandon thought about it, the more peculiar it seemed.

Perhaps something else was wrong, and it was Grandfather's way of keeping Chelsea in Exmoor, so she wouldn't be concerned. Perhaps he was ill. Could that be it?

Brandon quickly rejected that thought. If the duke were ill, he would want to see Chelsea. She meant the world to the old man. He loved her as much as he loved his own grandsons. No, if he were ill, Lawrence probably would have demanded her return rather than discouraged it.

Could it be something was wrong with Justin? Could his brother be in some sort of trouble? He smiled wryly. If that were it, the trouble would most likely include a young woman. He hoped she wasn't one who had a husband somewhere. That would be a difficult problem to handle with an ocean between them.

He shook his head. There was no point in mulling over all the possibilities. He would know soon enough. It wouldn't take him but a few hours more to reach Hawklin Hall.

She rode the moor for hours, seeking the familiar white cottage. She found other cottages, of course, but none were the small, thatched-roof house in her dreams. At last, with storm clouds gathering in the west, she conceded defeat for that day and turned for home.

But, she promised herself, tomorrow she would search again. Her determination hadn't waned, nor had her belief that the cottage existed.

CHAPTER
THIRTY-FOUR

The day that began with clear skies had suddenly turned dark with heavy black storm clouds. Brandon cast a wary eye skyward and prayed he would reach Hawklin before the rain began. He didn't much care for the thought of an icy drenching.

As he neared a fork in the road, he saw the coach turned on its side. A man lay in the road, his leg trapped beneath the roof of the coach. A second man was bent over him. Brandon nudged his horse, hastening toward the accident scene.

Hearing Brandon's approach, the second man looked up. "Thank God," he called. "I was afraid no one would come. Please help me lift this blasted thing so I can free my cousin's leg."

Brandon vaulted from the saddle and hurried forward. He glanced down as the injured man groaned. "How badly is he hurt?" he asked.

"I think his leg is broken. If you can lift it for just a moment, I think I can drag him free."

Brandon nodded as he grasped the top of the solid wood coach. Grimacing, he lifted, throwing all his weight into it.

"A little higher. I can't budge him."

Brandon nodded again but couldn't answer. He needed all his strength to lift and had none left for talking.

"There! It's moving," the man shouted. "A little higher. I've nearly got him."

Brandon held his breath and strained to lift the coach further. Sweat beaded on his forehead and upper lip.

"Hold it. I've nearly got him. There. There. He's out!"

With a thud, the coach dropped back to the ground. Brandon wiped away the sweat from his forehead with his coat sleeve, then leaned his head against the gilded edge of the coach roof. He drew in a deep breath.

"Can't tell you how much we appreciate your help, sir," the voice said behind him.

"Not at all." Brandon turned. "Glad I could help." He glanced at the man on the ground. "How is he?"

"Lucky. I don't think his leg is broken after all, but I know he could use a doctor." The man held out his hand toward Brandon. "I'm Elton Simpson."

"Brandon Fitzgerald."

Simpson shook Brandon's hand firmly. "Might we impose on you further, Lord Coleford? I think I should stay here with my cousin. If you could send a carriage for us. Our home is just a little way farther up the road."

"Of course. I'll go for help at once." Brandon turned toward his horse. "I'll be back in no time at all."

His hand had just gathered the reins, his fingers clasping the pommel, when the terrible pain burst at the back of his head. Light exploded in his brain, blinding him. Then he was falling into a black and bottomless pit, spiraling, spinning madly into darkness.

Brandon stood on a far ridge, his hand outstretched as if beckoning to her. Fog wrapped the upper moorland in a gray shroud. The cold crept into her bones. Even her heart felt chilled.

She called to him, but he couldn't seem to hear her. Slowly, the fog rose until the thick mist hid him from view.

He was gone. Gone forever.

"Brandon!" Her own cry drew her out of the nightmare's grasp.

Chelsea lay quietly on her bed, listening to the rapid beat of her heart. She was more frightened by this dream than any she had dreamt before. This one had cost her Brandon. She would rather die.

She got out of bed, drawing a blanket around her shoulders. She walked over to the window and peered outside. A storm buffeted the stone walls of the cottage, whistling around the corners and beneath the eaves. Dried leaves rolled across the yard before the gusty winds. The barn door banged open and closed, and she heard the shrill whinny of the horses. Lightning flashed a jagged streak across the sky, dancing from cloud to cloud.

It was an appropriate night for such a dream as hers.

She let the curtains fall back into place and, after tossing another log upon the fire, returned to the safety and warmth of her bed.

It was just the storm, she chided herself. *The dream means nothing*.

Of course, it didn't. It was just because she missed him. That and the storm outside. Nothing more.

Yet, she couldn't find the solace of sleep again.

Brandon returned to reality by inches. The pain in his head was ferocious, and there was a ceaseless ringing in his ears. It would have been much easier to sink back into the realm of unconsciousness, yet he fought against the temptation.

What happened? he asked silently, forcing himself to concentrate.

He remembered helping the men with the overturned coach. He had turned to go for help and then nothing—nothing except pain.

His eyes still closed, he tried to raise his hand to touch the back of his head but discovered his wrists were bound behind his back. Next, he attempted to move his legs but they too were tied together. When he moved, the hard cot beneath him creaked. The rope around his ankles was anchored to something, most likely the bed frame itself. He opened his eyes, but it served him no purpose. The room was as black as pitch. And cold and dank, as well. Brandon shivered.

"You're a pair of fools."

He heard the voice, distant and muffled, coming from somewhere above him. He must be in a cellar.

"Why did you bring him here?"

Brandon felt the shock of recognition. That was Hayden's voice.

"We had little choice, sir. We couldn't very well leave him beside the road. He might have been found. And it was your coach, after all, that was lying on its side for all to see."

Footsteps paced across a squeaking floor.

"Well, you take care of him in the morning. Make sure you get rid of the body where no one will ever find it."

Brandon heard a door slam.

"Who does the bloody fool think he's talking to?"

"Ah, forget him, Chadwick. I'm hungry. Let's get something to eat."

The voices and sounds of footsteps faded away, leaving Brandon in silence. Awareness spread through him with a chilling certainty. They meant to kill him. And if Hayden were in on it, that meant Chelsea was in danger too. He didn't know why, but why wasn't important.

He jerked on the rope around his ankles. He was rewarded only with the creak of the bed frame. He held his breath, waiting to see if the two men upstairs had heard and would come to check on him. When nothing happened, he began exploring with his fingertips the rope around his wrists.

There! There was the knot. If he could just work it loose . . .

Chelsea paced the length of the bedroom for perhaps the fiftieth time. Waiting for dawn had become a test of will. She had tried to go back to sleep but couldn't. And try as she might, she wasn't able to rid her mind of the dreadful nightmare either. The sense of danger had become almost another presence in the room.

The rain came then. She heard it striking like needles against the window glass. She shivered and drew the blanket more closely about her. She prayed it would be morning soon.

The rough fibers of the rope were burning into his flesh. He could feel the warm trickle of blood in the palms of his hands. Ignoring the pain, he continued his efforts to pry the rope free.

He hadn't heard any sounds from upstairs in hours. He could only assume it was the middle of the night and his abductors were asleep in their beds. Whatever fate they had planned for him would arrive with the dawn.

His head dropped back against the wall as a wave of dizziness assailed him. He drew a deep breath, steadying himself. A little longer. Just a little longer. He couldn't give in. There was so little time.

He felt the knot give a little and increased his struggles. Then, suddenly, the rope loosened. With a jerk, he was free. Brandon pulled his aching arms around in front of him and took a moment to rub life back into the limbs before tenderly reaching up to touch the back of his head. His hair was matted and sticky with dried blood. But at least the wound didn't seem to be bleeding any longer.

He bent forward and untied his ankles, then carefully eased his legs toward the side of the bed and lowered his feet to the floor. He cursed the solid darkness as he rose unsteadily. It seemed as if he were swaying in a high wind. He felt the pain in his head and wrists well enough, yet his legs were almost numb. He reached out to the side, touching the wall to steady himself.

Time. He hadn't much time.

Brandon worked his way around the small cellar, feeling carefully before him to avoid a trip in the dark. Finally, he found the door. His fingers were just closing around the latch when he heard the voice.

"You get the horses ready while I bring him up. We'll be done with this bloody job in a few hours and can get back to London."

Brandon pressed himself back against the wall. A sliver of light shown beneath the door. Just enough light for him to see the shovel leaning against the coal box. He reached for it, pulling it to him just as the door opened.

"All right, Fitzgerald. Time to—"

As the man stepped into the room, Brandon swung the shovel. The iron blade struck the side of the man's head with a sickening "thump." He pitched head first onto the packed dirt floor of the cellar.

Brandon stared down at the body, breathing hard and trying to listen. He heard no telltale footsteps. This man's accomplice must already be awaiting them with the horses. He crouched down and rolled the man onto his back. It was Simpson's "cousin," the one who'd supposedly been trapped under the coach yesterday. Brandon felt the man's neck for a pulse. There wasn't any.

Well, he couldn't ask a corpse any questions about Hayden, and there wasn't time for conjecture. He had to get out of there.

"Lady Coleford, you can't mean to go out. It's barely dawn and it's bitter cold. There looks to be more rain coming, too."

Chelsea glanced at Claire as she fastened her cloak. "I'm not afraid of a little cold and rain."

"If you catch your death, it'll be me who has to answer to his lordship when he gets back."

Chelsea just shook her head as she opened the door and went out.

Claire was right, of course. It was miserably cold, and it did look as if it would be raining again soon. But she just couldn't stay closed up in the house a minute longer. She couldn't shake the feeling of impending disaster, the feeling of loss and loneliness.

Was it only yesterday, she wondered, when she'd felt aglow with a sense of well-being?

She quickly saddled the quiet gelding, then rode away from Roxley's cottage and into the mist-covered moor.

The sky was a steel gray, dark clouds hovering just above the earth. An icy breeze rustled trees and shook free the dead leaves still clinging stubbornly to the branches.

Brandon pressed his back against the wall, then leaned slowly forward to look outside. He spied a large shed and thought he saw some movement inside, but he couldn't be certain. There just wasn't enough light.

Cautiously, he slipped out the door and sprinted toward the grove of trees near the side of the house. In only a moment, his clothes were damp from the rainwater clinging to the bushes and trees. Shivering once again, he hunkered down and waited.

He wasn't surprised that it was Simpson who led three horses from the shed. In fact, he'd rather expected that was who it would be. Hayden had hired these men to waylay him, to get rid of him. But why?

Simpson tethered the three horses and stepped up to the door. "Hurry along! It's cold out here."

Brandon waited, scarcely daring to breathe.

"What the bloody hell is keeping you, Chadwick?"

Finally, it happened. Simpson went inside,

presumably to see why Chadwick wasn't answering. Brandon didn't waste a single moment. He raced from his hiding spot toward the horses. He thrust a hasty prayer skyward that he was choosing the fastest of the three horses as he grabbed a pair of reins and vaulted into the saddle.

The horse had barely hit its stride when a bullet whizzed past Brandon's ear.

The small, whitewashed cottage with its thatched roof was just as she had dreamed it, nestled against a rocky hillside, its front door opening to the sweeping moorland, a small pony shed standing behind it. Only now the front door was missing, the thatched roof leaked, and the shed had tumbled into a pile of firewood.

Chelsea stood in the doorway of the cottage. A poignant wave of familiarity clutched her heart. The memories were there. She could feel them taunting her. Damn it, they were there, but she couldn't grasp them.

She leaned the side of her head against the doorjamb and closed her eyes. "Please let me remember," she whispered. "I want so very much to remember."

But no matter how long she stood there, the memories remained hidden from her. It was no use. She had found this cottage just as she had found the brick house, and neither of them had brought her the answers she'd hoped for.

"It's time to forget it, just as Brandon says," she said aloud, turning her back on the desolate cottage. "It should be enough that we have now."

She mounted the patient gelding and turned him toward home.

Brandon shinnied along the broad branch of the mighty oak tree which stretched above the narrow trail. He knew his pursuer wasn't far behind. He had only to wait a little longer.

A light drizzle was falling. Raindrops beaded his forehead and rolled down his cheeks. He was cold and sore, and the wound on his head had begun to bleed again. He had this chance, just this one chance to beat Simpson. There hadn't been much hope of outrunning him, and the muddy tracks left by his horse made him easy to follow. He was weaponless, and Simpson had a gun. If he didn't catch him by surprise, Brandon would probably be dead in a matter of minutes.

And then, what of Chelsea?

He heard the swish of undergrowth against horse and saddle, heard the slap of hooves against damp earth. Simpson was coming. Only a moment more. If he just didn't look up . . .

Brandon threw himself at Simpson's back, sending the two of them crashing to the ground with bone-jarring force. Brandon knew he had only a moment to wrest the gun from Simpson. While he had the element of surprise, Simpson had the greater strength. Brandon's had been sapped by his head wound and a long night in the damp cellar.

They rolled across the muddy trail, Brandon's hands clenched around Simpson's wrist as they fought for control of the weapon. With all the strength he could muster, Brandon slammed Simpson's arm against the trunk of a tree. The gun flew loose as the two men rolled in the opposite direction, locked in a deadly battle.

"You killed my cousin, you bloody bastard," Simpson ground out as they struggled to their feet. "You'll pay for that."

Brandon's fist caught Simpson beneath the chin, sending him rolling away. Brandon struggled to his feet. He barely had time to brace himself before Simpson dove for him, his meaty fists driving into Brandon's belly.

They fell back together, landing at the feet of the frightened horse Simpson had been riding. The animal reared, striking the air as its eyes rolled and it whinnied in terror. They tumbled beneath the dancing hooves, heedless as the horse shied away, then galloped with trailing reins away from them.

Simpson caught Brandon alongside the eye with a sharp left. Brandon's head reeled back as an explosion of light flashed in his head. He gasped for air as Simpson's hands closed around his throat.

"You're a dead man, Fitzgerald." The fingers tightened.

Brandon's right hand pushed at Simpson's face, gouging at his eyes. With his left hand, he clawed at the earth as he bucked, trying to throw Simpson from him.

Chelsea! his mind screamed as he choked, gasping for air.

His hand touched the cold metal of the gun. His brain almost didn't register what it was. Then his fingers closed around the barrel, and he drove the butt of the weapon against the side of Simpson's head. Simpson was knocked away and dropped in a still heap on the ground.

Dragging in great gulps of air, Brandon staggered to his feet. Jagged streaks of pain racked his head. His throat felt raw. He leaned against the giant oak, the gun hanging from limp fingers in his left hand.

He barely turned in time to see Simpson's approach. Instinctively, the gun came up and he fired. Simpson's face registered surprise as a dark stain spread out from the hole in his coat. Then, slowly it seemed, he crumpled to the ground.

Almost in unison, Brandon's back slid down the length of the tree trunk, exhaustion and pain sapping the last of his strength. His last conscious thought was of Chelsea.

Chelsea recognized her father's coach as she rode into the yard. She suppressed the groan and hurried to dismount and unsaddle her horse.

"There's a gentleman in the parlor," Claire told her as she entered through the back door. "He says he's your father."

Chelsea shrugged out of her damp cloak. "I know. I saw the carriage." She removed her sodden hat and handed the wet articles to

Claire as she left the kitchen.

Hayden rose from his chair when she entered the small sitting area. "Good lord, Chelsea. I can't believe you were out riding in this miserable weather."

"Hello, Father." She didn't bother to pretend any affection. She sat on the edge of a ladderback chair, her hand tucking the wet tendrils of hair back behind her ear. "What's brought you to Devonshire?"

"I was visiting Lawrence at Hawklin Hall when he received some sort of message from his other grandson in America. I knew that he sent for Brandon, so I decided to come visit until his return. So you wouldn't be all by yourself in this dismal little place."

"I don't find it at all dismal," she replied. She rose from the chair. "If you'll excuse me, I'll tell Claire to prepare the other room for you. Then I think I'll change into something dry."

"Of course. Please do before you catch your death."

She didn't want him there. The last person in the world she wanted to spend time with was Hayden Fitzgerald. Still, she couldn't very well send her own father away, especially now that evening was so quickly approaching. She supposed she could stand his company for one evening. Brandon would probably be back tomorrow.

Please hurry, darling, she thought as she left the parlor. *Please hurry.*

CHAPTER
THIRTY-FIVE

"Are you feeling all right, Chelsea? You've hardly eaten a bite of this delicious meal."

She looked at her father across the table. "I'm fine. I'm just not hungry."

"That's a shame." Hayden speared another slice of roast. "That girl is a good cook. Do you suppose she'd care to take a position with me in London? That cook of ours is getting old, and all her meals are beginning to taste the same."

"I haven't any idea if Claire would want to move to London." Chelsea placed her cloth napkin on the table beside her untouched plate. "You might ask her in the morning."

Hayden cocked an eyebrow. "She isn't here now?"

"No. She was only staying here because

419

Brandon is gone, so I wouldn't be alone. Since you're here, she's returned home for the night to see to her own family." Chelsea's stomach knotted. She wished Claire hadn't chosen to leave, but there hadn't been anything she could say to keep her there. She couldn't very well have said she didn't want to be alone with her own father.

"She's married then?"

Chelsea shook her head. "No. It's just her father and a much younger brother."

"Well, well. It seems I may have solved a domestic problem by my little journey to Devonshire. Sara will be pleased. What time will she return in the morning? In time for breakfast?"

Chelsea's head was throbbing. Perhaps she had taken a chill from her ride today. "No," she replied, rubbing her temples. "I told her she needn't come until noon."

"Noon, is it?" Hayden was staring at her with an odd expression on his face.

"Father, please excuse me. I'm truly not feeling well. I know you came to visit, but I'm afraid I must take to my bed." She shoved back the chair and rose quickly.

"Of course, dear."

"Just leave the table as it is. Claire can see to it tomorrow."

"Yes. Yes. You just get on to bed, and don't give me another thought."

She fled the room as if pursued, hurrying up the narrow stairs to her second-floor bedroom.

420

Once inside, she leaned her back against the door. Then, with unreasonable panic rising in her chest, she turned and bolted the lock.

Why was she feeling this way? It was merely a friendly visit. But when had her father ever been friendly toward her? He thought her mad. Thought she should be placed in an asylum for the insane. Did it seem reasonable to believe he was suddenly awash with fatherly concern?

Chelsea moved to sit on her bed. The bedroom felt cold despite the fire on the hearth. Chelsea shivered and hugged herself as she prayed once more for Brandon's swift return.

It took all of Brandon's concentration to remain in the saddle. The horse had slowed to a walk. The animal was in need of rest nearly as much as Brandon was. Yet he couldn't stop. Even now Chelsea might be in grave danger. He had to keep going. It would be morning before he arrived at the hunting cottage as it was.

His body ached from head to toe, and he was hungry, not having eaten in more than a day. It was sheer willpower that kept him going. He had to reach Chelsea before Hayden did.

Chelsea awoke just before dawn. The house seemed deathly still. She sat up slowly and gazed at the dying embers in the fireplace.

It came to her, perhaps as suddenly as her memory had been taken from her, just as the doctors had said it might. Or perhaps she had known for a long time but hadn't dared to believe it because she thought herself to be mad. She'd thought herself mad because she'd been told it was so.

Whether she'd known it a long time or only just remembered, she knew the truth now.

Hayden wasn't her father.

She wasn't Alanna Fitzgerald.

In great crashing waves, the memories flooded her. All of them. Without gaps, without questions, she remembered it all.

Her father was Carson Pendleton, a poor but honest Devonshire shepherd. He'd married Catherine St. Clair, a woman of gentle birth but little money, who died when Chelsea was a small child. Exmoor had been Chelsea's home throughout her childhood. She had lived as wild and free as the fox she kept for a pet and the pony she often rode from dawn until dusk.

Aunt Regina. At sixteen, she'd gone to live with her mother's aunt so she could become a lady. It was what Catherine would have wanted, her father had told her. Regina St. Clair had taught her to play the piano. She'd taught her how to speak properly and how to walk and dance. Though loved by her aunt, Chelsea had been unhappy there, longing for the freedom she had known as a child. She had kept to herself, making no friends, spending long hours wandering alone through the woodlands nearby. But when her father was killed in an accident, her last hopes of returning home had died with him.

Tears fell unnoticed down Chelsea's cheeks. This past spring, Aunt Regina had heard from her solicitor. The little money her squandering father, the Baron St. Clair, had left to her was gone. Except for the house, she had nothing left. They were penniless. Chelsea had immediately begun searching for work. She'd found it at Hawklin Hall.

Chelsea rose from her bed and went to sit near the fire, stirring the embers with a poker to bring the fire to life. She placed a log amidst the coals and watched as it burst into flames.

Alanna. Poor, poor Alanna. Chelsea recalled the girl with heartbreaking clarity. She had, indeed, been mad. Driven by demons no one else could see. A beautiful girl with yellow-gold hair and dark blue eyes. A child in a woman's body. Chelsea had been hired as Alanna's companion, an assistant to Molly. She had been as closed away from everyone as Alanna herself, forbidden to mingle with the other staff.

She remembered the night of the fire. She had heard Alanna's cry of "Chelsea, come look!" When she entered the main nursery room, she'd found it in flames. Alanna had been standing on the window ledge, laughing and dancing hysterically, her nightgown already ablaze. Chelsea had tried to reach her, and nearly died in the trying.

So that much was true. She had been struck on the head, but what had come after that was all a blur. What had made them substitute Chelsea for Alanna?

The money, of course. She remembered Molly's horror when she repeated that Alanna had been married by proxy to a distant cousin in America, a man who was coming to England with his grandfather, the man who would one day be the Duke of Foxworth. With Alanna dead, Hayden and Sara could not hope to bargain with Brandon or his grandfather.

A new chill crept into Chelsea's bones. What had they planned to do with Chelsea if she were to regain her memory? She rose stiffly from the chair and turned to look at the closed bedroom door.

That was why he'd come. To make sure she didn't remember.

She hurried to the wardrobe and pulled out a warm woolen dress. Her fingers shook as she shed her nightclothes. She must get out of there. She must leave at once.

Hayden had wanted to see her shut away in an asylum. That was what he'd planned. He'd tried to make certain her husband thought her mad, and he'd nearly succeeded. Perhaps he'd come here to spirit her away. Who would believe her once she was placed in a madhouse such as Bedlam in London. And Brandon would never know what had happened to her.

Chelsea picked up her cloak and quickly fastened it, then grabbed a shawl for her head and tiptoed toward the door. If she moved quietly, she could reach the barn and saddle her horse and be gone before Hayden awoke. The stairs creaked beneath her feet. She grimaced and held her breath but heard no other sounds. She should have been comforted by the quiet but wasn't. She was too frightened to be comforted by anything.

She lifted the latch and slowly pushed the door open before her. A dense fog hid the barn from view. It blanketed the moor in a silent, silver mist. Her heart thumping noisily in her breast, she stepped outside.

"Chelsea, where are you going?"

She whirled to see Hayden standing midway down the stairs. A tiny cry escaped her throat, and she turned to run, dropping her shawl by the door. She raced away from the house, away from the barn, disappearing into the swirling gray veil.

"Chelsea!"

She glanced back over her shoulder. He was following her. She could hear his running footsteps. She turned and stumbled over a clump of grass. She scrambled to her feet, fearing the touch of his hand on her shoulder at any moment. Now she couldn't hear anything except the blood pounding in her ears.

On she ran.

Brandon saw the Fitzgerald carriage standing near the barn. Alarm spread through him.

He rode up to the front of the house and slipped out of the saddle. He wobbled slightly as his feet hit the ground, then steadied himself. His eyes registered the open door, a piece of cloth lying across the threshold. He stepped forward and picked up the shawl. It was Chelsea's. He recognized it.

Was he already too late?

Then he heard movement inside. "Chelsea?" he called.

Claire stepped from the kitchen into the parlor. "It's me, your lordship. There's no one about."

"Where are they?"

"I don't know, sir. I just come from home and found the door wide open an' the house empty."

Brandon turned and faced the yard, his gaze transfixed on the thick fog as it crept across the earth in eerie silence. "You didn't stay here last night?"

"No, m'lord. I went to see to my father."

"I'll kill him if he harms her," he whispered, unaware that Claire had come to stand nearby.

"Lord Coleford, what's happened to you?" She reached up and tenderly touched the blood-matted hair on the back of his head.

Brandon winced. "Nothing."

"You'd best let me see to it," she persisted.

Brandon shook her off. "Not now, Claire. I've got to find Chelsea." *Before it's too late*, he added silently.

"Chelsea, you're being foolish. Come back here. Stop. I only want to talk to you."

It was difficult to tell where he was. The fog seemed to mix up sound as well as sight. Was he behind her or off to the side?

Chelsea continued to push herself, trying to move stealthily through the moor. Tall shrubs seemed to reach out to grab and hold her, snagging her cloak, scratching her legs. She wondered how long she'd been running from him. How far had they gone from the cottage?

Should she try to circle back, try to get a horse to make her escape that way? Did she even know which way was back?

Suddenly, the ground seemed to fall out beneath her. She cried out as she tumbled forward, then rolled and slid her way down an embankment. She hit the bottom of the hill with a resounding thud. The air whooshed out of her, and she lay panting, trying to drag a deep breath into her burning lungs.

She could hear him crashing through the undergrowth somewhere nearby. Close. He was so close. Stifling a fearful whimper, she got to her feet and began running once again. She kept glancing behind her, certain she would see him at any moment.

And she was right. When she turned her head, there he was, standing in front of her. Before she could whirl away, Hayden's hands were gripping her arms.

"That's enough."

"Let go of me!" she cried, but his fingers only dug into her flesh.

She fought him, struggled to pull away. His right hand released her, only to rise in the air and come down again, striking her across the cheek. Her head reeled to the side.

"You're coming with me, you little fool."

"I won't. I won't."

He struck her again. "Be quiet, or I'll break your bloody neck." Hayden's threat was spoken in a low, spine-chilling voice.

Chelsea instantly stilled. She looked at him. Really looked at him. His eyes had a half-crazed look about them. He meant it. If she didn't stop, he would kill her right there.

"Now," he said with finality. "We're going back to the house, and then you're leaving with me in my carriage."

"Where are you taking me?"

His reply was simply to push her out in front of him, shoving her forward.

She tried to think what to do, but sheer terror clouded all other thoughts. Locking her away wouldn't satisfy him now. He was going to kill her. She didn't doubt it for a moment. She must get away from him before they reached the cottage.

They climbed their way back up the hill she had tumbled down not long before, then walked along the ridge, still surrounded by the swirling fog.

"Which way?" Hayden suddenly asked her.

She felt a glimmer of hope. He was as lost as she was. "I don't know. I'm not sure."

"If you're lying to me . . ." His fingers bruised her arm once again in their vice-like grip.

"Why did you do it?"

"Do what?"

"You know what. Why did you substitute me for Alanna after she died? How could you think you could get away with it?" She turned to look at him.

"So . . . you *have* remembered."

"Why?" she persisted.

"It wasn't planned. When Alanna died, we thought all was lost, but when you awakened without any memory, it seemed the perfect solution."

"But surely someone would have recognized me."

"That was the beauty of it, my girl. You were as unknown to everyone as Alanna herself. We got rid of all the house servants who might have seen you. And your coloring was enough like Alanna's that we thought no one would guess. We took every precaution." He shrugged his shoulders. "Of course, you were supposed to be kept heavily sedated until you were safely put away somewhere, but that nanny of yours was a fool. She threw away the laudanum."

She took a small step back from him. Suddenly, she was remembering so many things Molly had said to her. And then she remembered the woman as she lay dying on that London street. "Devon . . ." Molly had said. She'd been trying to say Devonshire. She'd been trying to tell Chelsea where she was from.

"Mother of God," she whispered, her eyes widening. "You killed Molly so she couldn't tell me the truth."

Again Hayden shrugged. "I didn't kill her personally, but it had to be done. She had become a threat. If Brandon had let us put you in an asylum, she wouldn't have had to die. She would still be alive today. So, you see, it's really his fault."

He was mad. All this time he'd been trying to make her believe she was mad, but he was the one who was truly insane. And now he would kill her and no one would ever know the truth.

"Get going," Hayden said gruffly, giving her another little push.

She stumbled forward, then caught herself. She felt the sting of tears in her throat. How could she ever hope to escape him? Even if she found a chance to run away, she didn't know where to run to. The fog was as thick as ever. She could barely see three feet in front of her, and Hayden still held tightly to her arm.

Brandon heard the voices. A sixth sense seemed to guide him through the fog. His fingers tightened around the butt of Simpson's pistol. With his other hand, he reached up to touch the back of his head. The blood had congealed in a sticky mass with his hair. Shards of pain penetrated his skull around the wound. He could feel the weakness spreading through him.

If he didn't find them soon . . .

Chelsea didn't even know what was happening. One moment she'd paused on the craggy ledge above what seemed to be a deep but narrow glen, trying to get her bearings. The next moment, Hayden had jerked her back against his chest. His forearm pressed tightly against her throat.

Then she saw him, a shadow in the fog. She knew it was Brandon.

"Let her go," his deep, threatening voice said from within the mist.

"Do anything foolish, and I'll kill her, Brandon. Now come out where I can see you."

430

As if the fates were in league with Hayden, a breeze blew up from the glen, parting the fog. She could see him clearly for only a moment; then her eyes misted. Her throat felt too tight to even try to swallow back the tears.

He took a step toward them. She didn't notice his gun at first. All she could see was his face, pale and haggard. There was blood on his coat.

"Brandon," she whispered.

"It's all right, Chelsea. I'm here."

Hayden's arm tightened around her throat. She choked as the air was cut off from her lungs.

"Drop the gun," Hayden ordered. He jerked his arm again. "Drop it."

Chelsea clawed at the arm over her throat, and finally, it loosened.

Brandon hesitated only a moment before dropping the gun to the ground. Chelsea groaned. Hayden would kill them both now.

"Now, kick it over to me."

Brandon did as he was told. The gun slid across the rocky ground, stopping a foot or two in front of Chelsea.

Hayden chuckled. "You weren't supposed to live through the night, Brandon. How did you get away?"

"It's a long story," Brandon replied.

"She wasn't worth dying for, you know. By gad, she isn't even your wife. Your wife is dead."

Brandon's eyes were on her now. Questioning eyes.

"I'm not Alanna," she replied softly. "I'm Chelsea Pendleton, the companion who supposedly died. Brandon, he killed Molly so she couldn't tell us the truth."

"You won't get away with this," Brandon said as his gaze shifted to Hayden.

Chelsea saw Brandon stagger slightly. She could almost see the last of his strength draining from him.

Hayden saw it too. Again he chortled. "I already have." He moved Chelsea forward and bent to retrieve the gun.

It was a reflex action. When his grip loosened, she flung herself around and pushed him with all of her might. He stumbled backward, stopping on the edge of the precipice. He teetered there a moment, his arms flailing the air, striving for balance. Then, with a startled cry, he disappeared over the edge. The thump of body meeting earth was a long time in coming. It was a sickening sound.

In the next instant, Brandon was holding her, cradling her fiercely against him.

"Chelsea. Thank God. Chelsea," he murmured into her hair.

Yes, she was Chelsea.

And she was in Brandon's arms.

That was all she needed to know.

CHAPTER
THIRTY-SIX

Chelsea rose from the breakfast table and walked to the front window, pushing aside the drapes to stare pensively at the blustery November morning. Filmy gray clouds raced before the winds, allowing only an occasional glimpse of a weak autumn sun.

As happened so often of late, she was thinking about the past months, replaying each and every detail, wondering, had she done anything differently, if Alanna or Molly or even Hayden might still be alive. But no matter how often she thought it through, she didn't see how anything could have been different. Even now, it didn't seem real to her. From the first moment she'd awakened after the fire to the day Hayden had fallen to his death on the moors in

Devonshire, it all seemed just another one of her dreams.

"He'll be here, my dear," Lawrence said behind her. "You don't think that boy would miss his wedding day."

"I wasn't thinking of Brandon," she answered honestly.

"Well, he's all you should be thinking about today."

She let the drapes fall back into place as she turned around. Grandfather was right, of course. And, to be honest, she had been thinking of him, too. She'd been thinking of him a lot—and missing him. "I wish he'd told me where he was going. He left so suddenly. And he's been gone for two days now."

Lawrence offered a tolerant smile. "You should be resting. A wedding this afternoon, an ocean crossing at the end of the week."

A wedding this afternoon. Her wedding. At last, she would truly be Brandon's bride. It was only to be a small affair. Just the couple and Lawrence and Roxley. No other guests. But she would belong to Brandon forever after.

She returned the duke's smile. "I'm fine, Grandfather. How could I not be?" She crossed the room to stand beside his chair. "You're not terribly disappointed that Brandon isn't marrying a proper noblewoman, are you? I mean, he might have married someone like the marchioness if it hadn't been for—"

Lawrence took hold of her hand. "What a question! I never wanted my grandson to marry any woman except the one he loves. That's you, my dear. Don't you ever doubt it."

She nodded as she sank into the chair next to his.

"I only wish Justin could be here for your wedding. But, if we're lucky, he'll arrive before you leave England. He'll like you a great deal, you know. My grandsons have both always been great judges of beautiful women, not just beauty in looks but in their hearts. You, Chelsea, have a truly beautiful heart."

Chelsea leaned forward to kiss the old man's cheek. "You're a dear," she whispered.

She knew it was hard for Lawrence to see Brandon and Chelsea leaving England. He had wanted his title and lands as much for his eldest grandson as for himself. But Brandon had no real interest in it, and everyone recognized how much better it would be for the couple in America, where no one knew the story of Chelsea and Alanna.

Without telling anyone, Lawrence had sent for Justin weeks before when he thought Brandon might need his brother's moral support. Now he would be arriving just as Brandon left England.

She heard a commotion in the entrance hall and jumped quickly to her feet. It had to be Brandon.

"They're in the dining room, my lord," she heard Bowman saying.

She hadn't time to wonder again what mysterious errand had taken him away for so long. She had only enough time to rejoice at his return.

Her heart did a tiny somersault as he stepped through the doorway, smiling broadly. "Chelsea, I have a surprise for you." He stepped to one side.

A moment later, a small gray-haired woman entered the room.

"Aunt Regina!" Chelsea raced toward the woman and embraced her. "I thought—"

"I know what you thought," her aunt said brusquely, "but as you can see, you were greatly mistaken. I've been living in Liverpool with old friends. But you weren't nearly so mistaken about me as that evil Hayden Fitzgerald was about you." She held Chelsea at arm's length. "Now, let me have a look at you. Yes. Yes, your young man was right. You are happy."

"Oh, I am." Chelsea turned her eyes upon Brandon. "Happier than I've ever been in my life."

Regina patted her cheek, then glanced around her.

Chelsea turned to face the duke. "Aunt Regina, let me introduce—"

"There's no need for an introduction, my dear." The elderly woman stepped away from her niece and walked slowly toward Lawrence. "Larry and I are old friends."

The duke wore a puzzled expression. "I'm sorry, madam. You seem to have the advantage over—"

"The years have not been kind to me, Larry. But that's not true of you. You're as handsome as ever."

Lawrence stared at the woman, his white brows drawn together in concentration. Then, registering disbelief, his brows rose on his forehead. "Reggie? Little Reggie. Is it you?"

"It is I, Larry." Regina smiled.

The duke turned toward Chelsea. "Your aunt is Regina St. Clair?"

Chelsea nodded but had no chance to speak.

"You should have told me you were going to America, Larry. I would have gone with you. All these years I've lived with a broken heart. All these years I thought you were dead."

"There seems to have been a lot of that going around," Brandon commented as he placed an arm around Chelsea's shoulders.

"You never married." Lawrence tenderly touched the woman's cheek.

Regina shook her head. "I loved you too much."

"You were only a child."

"I was old enough to know I couldn't love anyone but you."

Lawrence cupped her head between his hands, then leaned low to kiss her on the mouth. "I loved you, too, Reggie. When I came back, I sent inquiries, trying to find you. But I was told . . ."

Tears glittered in Regina's eyes. "Brandon is right. There was far too much of that going around. I'm very much alive, as are you and Chelsea."

The two older people turned in unison to face the young couple. "And now," Lawrence said with pride, "your niece and my grandson are going to be married. It seems rather fitting, doesn't it?"

Regina nodded as she smiled at Chelsea.

"And perhaps, my dear," the duke added, "it isn't even too late for us."

The wind whipped Chelsea's hair as she leaned into the rail at the bow of the ship, enjoying the feel of salt spray on her cheeks.

"I thought I'd find you here." Brandon's arm slipped around her waist. "There goes England," he said as he gazed to the right. "We'll be out of the Channel before long."

Chelsea watched in silence.

She wasn't sad to be leaving England. She would gladly go anywhere with Brandon. But it hadn't been easy to leave behind the ones she loved. She remembered the way everyone had looked on the docks as they waved good-bye.

Grandfather with his arm firmly around Aunt Regina. And her aunt hadn't been clad in black. She'd been wearing a pretty blue frock that made her look like a girl again. At least that's what Lawrence had said of her. Chelsea imagined the two would marry before long. And about time.

Justin had been there, dashing in his black frock-coat. He'd drawn the eye of many a young lady as passengers boarded the ship. In just a few days, she had come to love him as if he were her own brother.

And Roxley. He had been there too. She knew he loved her a great deal. She knew it because he so selflessly wished her all the happiness in the world, even when it meant he could never have her. She prayed he would find someone new to love soon. Someone who would bring him the joy she knew in Brandon's arms.

People she loved. People who loved her. It was difficult to bid them each farewell, and she would miss them. But she could never be happy anywhere unless she was with Brandon.

"I'm glad you got to meet Justin before we left," Brandon said, interrupting her musings. "Now that he's seen you, I think he's sorry he wasn't the one who came with Grandfather last summer."

"I love your brother. He's rather like you." She smiled as she turned toward him, nestling against his chest. "But he's *not* you. I couldn't be happy with anyone else."

"You are happy." It was a statement, not a question.

"You know I am." Her arms tightened possessively about him. "Brandon, there's something I've wondered but never asked."

"What is it?"

"If things had been different, if you'd met me as Chelsea Pendleton, lady's companion, instead of Alanna Fitzgerald, would you still have chosen me? I mean, you could have had anyone. You're rich and handsome and titled. You could have had Maitland Conover or someone like her. You could have married a real lady."

"I never wanted a Maitland Conover, Chelsea. I wanted you. I've been looking for you all of my life. I just didn't know it." He slipped a hand beneath her chin and tipped her head back. "You captured my heart the first moment I laid eyes on you. And I thank God He led me to you."

Chelsea felt as if she might burst from happiness. It seemed impossible for one heart to hold so much joy. "All those weeks I spent searching for the truth . . . but the only thing I really wanted to know was that you loved me."

"I do love you, Chelsea. I always will." He kissed her, then pressed her cheek against his chest as they turned to gaze one last time upon the shores of England.

"Brandon?"

"Hmmm?"

"This is the best dream I've ever had."

"It's no dream, my love. This time, it's not a dream."

Dear Reader:

I was pleased when my editor, Alicia Condon, called to tell me she liked the proposal for *Dream Tide* and Leisure wanted to publish it. Because of its Gothic overtones, *Dream Tide* was a departure from the Westerns and adventure romances I've written in the past, and I looked forward to the new challenge. Alicia's enthusiasm for this book and her expert guidance, along with the excitement of my friend April Romero (who was the first to hear the concept when it was a mere wisp of an idea and who has waited *very* impatiently for its completion), made the writing extra special. I hope the reading was equally enjoyable.

I would like to thank all the readers who sent so many wonderful letters and cards with their best wishes and congratulations on my marriage to Jerry in May 1989. While reading (and writing) romances is certainly great fun, romance is never so wonderful as when it's your own.

All my romantic best,
Robin Lee Hatcher

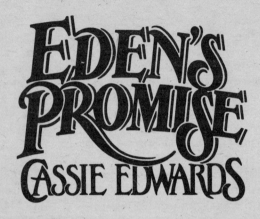